To Ruth Anne
I hope you

Sarah

A Forgotten Patriot

Bravery & Patriotism know no gender

Mark A. Reardon

Sarah

A Forgotten Patriot

The Story of an American Camp Follower

First in the *Camp Follower* Series

Mark A. Reardon

inkwell book co.

For information regarding permission, write to
Inkwell Book Co., 604 South Nansemond Steet, Richmond, VA 23221
www.InkwellBookCompany.com,
or email info@inkwellbookcompany.com

ISBN 978-0-9907170-0-3
Library of Congress Number 2014948987

 Published by
Inkwell Book Co.

Printed in the U.S.A.
First Edition

Dedication

To Sarah Osborne Benjamin,
for being the inspiration for this book.

AND

To my beautiful and remarkable wife, Cindi,
a dedicated camp follower and true patriot.
Your love, understanding, humor, and selfless sacrifices
have made life a wonderful adventure.

Introduction

While working as a docent at the Yorktown Victory Center in Yorktown, Virginia, I came across a story about one Sarah Osborn Benjamin. Sarah was the wife of a soldier who fought in the Revolutionary War, and she followed him through his experiences. More importantly she put down in her own words, in a request for a pension, the things that happened to her during this time. To the best of my knowledge, hers is the only firsthand account we have of a woman who served as a camp follower in the American Army during the Revolutionary War.

Since the beginning of war there have been women who have followed the Army. These women were given the name "Camp Followers." Unfortunately, that title has come to mean something derogatory in its common usage today. But most of these women were good, hardworking people who were following their husbands or other family members to wherever fate was leading them. All the while they did the cooking, the mending, the nursing, the cleaning and all the other tasks that needed doing throughout the camps. Yes, some even had and raised children while doing it. Many of them were often close—perhaps too close at times—to the action, as well. Some even took part in battles, and others risked their lives as spies.

The American Revolutionary War was no exception. Unfortunately, the history of that period was written mostly by men. So, aside from Sarah's pension request and a few references to women being with the army in official reports, we do not have many actual accounts of the experiences of these women.

There are any number of stories replete with the struggles and deprivations the men went through throughout the war. Tales of the disease, sickness, and agonies they suffered in camps like Valley Forge, Pennsylvania and Morristown, New Jersey, or on battlefields throughout the war are easy to find. Lost in those stories and tales is the fact that there were always women there. Their suffering was at least as great, and probably greater. Few, if any, accommodations were made for these women. They served the men, and the army, daily, and if they were lucky they were able to draw half rations. Although there was a price set for the work they did, collecting it from soldiers who themselves were not getting paid for months on end meant that there was precious little coming in to buy anything extra.

These women created a camaraderie among themselves that exists in the military to this day. Often left to their own devices, they managed not only to survive, but to instill a bit of humanity into an otherwise brutal existence.

General Washington often wished he could rid himself of the camp followers. To him they were a drain on his meager resources, and they got in the way of the army being completely military. He was not against senior officers' wives, including Martha, joining them during the winter months when no fighting was going on, but he could not understand these women who were with the army all the time. They were not the gentile women he was used to. Instead they were tough, hard-working women for which there was no job too big or too hard for them to accomplish. They often worked alongside the men, and were covered in sweat and dirt just like them. They could be gruff in their manners and language, but that was part of who they had to be in order to survive in a world completely dominated by men.

Even George Washington had to back down from them. For if he had sent them away he knew they would take their men with them. He also had to admit that many of the men were not going to perform duties they thought were women's work. They would allow themselves to wear filthy rags rather than do laundry or sew up tears. He knew these women were necessary to his army, regardless of what he might have thought of them.

This novel is not an attempt to rewrite history. Rather, it is an attempt to add an unheard voice to that rich history of our nation's beginning. Women during the Revolutionary War, like women throughout every war, served in many capacities. They stayed at home tending to farms, they ran stores, they led boycotts from their homes, they made clothes for the army, and they performed many other duties that were not traditionally theirs.

A very special group of them chose to serve by joining their men in the field. To be sure, many, if not most, were poor and had no other choice but to follow their men. But that misses the point of what they contributed to the army's success.

This novel is an effort to present a picture of what life might have been like for these women. How did they exist? What was daily life like? What were the challenges? And maybe most of all, how might they have felt about their situation?

This is a novel. Sarah and the main characters of this novel are figments of my imagination. Generals like Arnold, Gates, Morgan or Burgoyne or other historical figures are, of course, real. I have placed Sarah in proximity to them to enable the telling of the story.

Additionally, I have tried to be historically correct about where actions have taken place. Any mistakes in that regard are wholly my own.

We celebrate Mary Hays, from the battle of Monmouth Court House, as "Molly Pitcher." But, in truth, there were many Molly Pitchers.

This is their story.

MAPS LISTED IN THIS BOOK

Page 21.............Fort Ticonderoga
Page 273...........The Northern Theater
Page 363...........First Battle of Saratoga
Page 387...........Second Battle of Saratoga

Acknowledgements

I wish to thank Sarah Lapallo of Inkwell Book Co., my publisher, for guiding me through this daunting maze called publishing. She has made what I feared would be a nightmare a pleasure. And Jacki Vanderbloemem and Christina Cox, my editors, for their tedious efforts in helping to bring this book to its completion. Their attention to details and insightful corrections and suggestions added greatly to the finished product.

Although this is a novel and no bibliography is required I would be remiss if I did not point out several references which I found to be invaluable.

Sarah Osborne Benjamin's pension request is a wonderful firsthand account of the life of a camp follower during and after the war and was the genesis of this novel.

A Narrative of a Revolutionary Soldier: Some of the Adventures, Dangers and Sufferings of Joseph Plumb Martin, by Joseph Plumb Martin, provides an excellent firsthand account of a private's life during the Revolutionary War.

For the history of the Northern Campaign and the Battles of Saratoga there is no better book than Richard M. Ketchum's, *Saratoga, Turning Point of America's Revolutionary War.*

For information on women of this period several books were especially helpful: Linda K. Kerber's, *Women of the Republic,* Carol Berkin's, *Revolutionary Mothers, Women in the struggle for America's Independence*, and Holly A. Mayer's, *Belonging to the Army, Camp Followers and Community during the American Revolution.*

Additionally, the essays of John U. Rees on the Camp Followers of both armies during the Revolutionary War were very helpful.

The history of the New York 1st Regiment can be found on its Web Page and at www.myrevolutionarywar.com .

I would also like to thank the Jamestown-Yorktown Foundation and especially the Yorktown Victory Center for giving me the opportunity to be a docent there and for introducing me to the real Sarah.

Finally, I am most grateful to my wife, Cindi, for her love and encouragement in helping to make this dream of mine a reality. She read and reread every page, probably more than she cared to, and her imagination of how Sarah and her cohorts would have felt and reacted to this strange world they found themselves in added the female touch that I, a mere male, could have never divined.

One

Sarah had been dreading this day for weeks. Ever since word had come in April of the fighting that took place between the local militias and the British Regulars in two little towns in Massachusetts, John had been talking about his militia company heading off to lend a hand. Now word had reached them that the Americans had fortified a hill outside of Boston, and in June the British had attacked them. As best that could be made out from the reports, the British had won the battle, but at an awful price, and had gone back into the city. The Americans were at this minute laying siege to the city. There would be no holding John or the men back from going over there now.

John and Sarah had been squabbling for days about it. She could not see how this fighting in Massachusetts had anything to do with them in Albany, New York. In fact, she could not even understand what all the turmoil was really about. People argued in town meetings and in the Public Houses and at home about freedoms and rights being trampled by the British Parliament. But what were these freedoms and rights they were ready to kill each other over? As far as she could see they were just words, words that stirred men's souls to be sure. But what difference did it make who taxed you? In the end you were going to be taxed by someone. Maybe, as John and her father said, she was just a woman, and these political things were over her head, but she could not for the life of her understand what good could come of all that was happening.

These days Sarah's world seemed to be a constant string of changes. Momentarily she longed for that time only two years before, when she was still Sarah Howe and all of life's problems could be solved by her physically strong and strong-willed father, or her gentle but equally strong-willed mother. But then she quickly remembered that even then her world was changing and she could do nothing to stop it. She thought about all that she had seen in the past two years.

Back then she lived on a small farm near Newburgh, where her father also had a blacksmith's shop. She had two older brothers, Robert and James, a younger sister, Jane, and a baby brother, Henry. The two older boys worked in the shop with her father, and she, Jane, and Henry did all the chores with her mother on the farm. Life seemed so easy then. But she knew there were troubles going on in the country. Her father would talk about them every night at the supper table. He would rail on about the Tories and question how they could sit idly by as Parliament and the King robbed them of their rights as citizens. He and her two older brothers had joined the militia and called themselves Sons of Liberty. And hadn't she and her mother joined the Daughters of Liberty with other women of the area to help in the boycott of British goods in protest over taxes? It turned out that people they had once been friends with were some of those Tories her father spoke so disparagingly about, and the family was no longer allowed to have anything to do with them or anyone who claimed to be in favor of the Crown.

In the late summer of 1773, John Hardy showed up looking for work. He said he was a blacksmith's apprentice. Her father seemed to like him from the start, so John started work. He slept in a room behind the shop. As part of his pay he took meals with the family.

John was a large, broad chested man, perhaps six feet tall. His eyes were black. His strength showed in the noticeable muscles beneath his shirt. His darkened skin belied a man used to working out in the sun. He wore a rumpled brown hat that, when removed, revealed shiny black hair that always looked as if he had recently woken up.

Sarah was a pretty girl of eighteen. She was slender, and just blossoming into womanhood. Her eyes were emerald green. Her face, too, had a healthy tan from working in the fields. She had long auburn hair that she kept tied up under her cap.

It wasn't long before John and Sarah took interest in one another. After a short courtship John asked her father for her hand, and they were married. Sarah thought back on it. It wasn't a fairy tale love, but they liked each other. He was twenty-two, she was going to be nineteen, and they both needed to get on with life. So they married on her birthday, the first of June. At first, life seemed to go on as before, only now they had a room of their own and she shared a bed with John instead of her sisters. Sarah smiled remembering those first nights together. Married life was going to be wonderful, she thought.

A few months later, John said they needed to go off on their own and start their life alone. Sarah could see no reason for it. To her, everything was wonderful as it was. She argued, "Why should they leave? Where would they go? How would they live?"

His plan was to go up to Albany and get work. After he had saved enough he would start a blacksmith business of his own.

She thought that her parents would intercede on her behalf, and convince John that it would be better to stay in Newburgh. It was then that her mother taught her one of the hard lessons about marriage. She told Sarah that marriage was a partnership, but that the man in that partnership was the only one whose decisions counted. And it was her responsibility to go with her husband, and do as he told her. Sarah was heartbroken. The thought of leaving her family scared her. She could not imagine how they were to survive.

But survive they did. After the long trek up to Albany they both soon found work, he as a blacksmith's assistant and she as a house maid for a well-to-do family in Albany. They rented a one room place outside of the city, where she planted a small garden and set up their first home. Life once again seemed to be back on a good track. Maybe John had made a good decision. He soon joined the militia, and quickly got involved in a group that called itself the Committee of Safety. It was the Committee's job to keep in contact with the committees in other colonies to share information. Additionally, they set themselves up to protect the folks who now called themselves Patriots from the Tories.

At first these activities of John's didn't affect her too much. But that soon changed. He was elected to be a Sergeant of his militia company, and that started to take up a great deal of time as they now rendezvoused every weekend. As a sergeant he had responsibilities that caused him to be there earlier and stay later than the rest of the men. At this time he would also be gone a night or two each week on Committee business.

One day as she was shopping at the mercantile she overheard two women talking about how the Committee had burnt out the home of one of the Tory families the night before. John had been out that night and had come home after she had gone to bed. She could not believe that he could have been part of burning a family's home down and driving them out, no matter what they were.

When he got home she told him what she had heard and asked if it was true and whether he had any part in it. John explained that those people were Tories and, worse, the man was a spy for the Johnsons. It was not safe for anyone if they were allowed to stay. He told her not to get upset or worry about it. The family would be taken care of by the Johnson people, and probably go up to Canada with the rest of the Tories that were leaving. After that, the homes of families on both sides were destroyed sporadically, each one in retribution for the last. Sarah prayed that theirs would not be next. These were neighbors, not enemies, she thought. Someone had to find a solution to all this madness.

But the house burning was only the beginning. One day John came home from work and told her to come with him. The Committee was going to hold a trial of a Tory who was accused of treason against the Patriot cause. He said the Committee had decided everyone needed to see it. The trial was held on the steps of a Public House, and all the town's Patriots were in the street watching to see what would happen. No known Tories were to be seen.

The head of the Committee appointed himself Judge, and six Committee members, including John, were seated as a jury. The accused was seated on a chair with his hands tied behind his back. His wife and two children were made to stand to one side on the steps as the trial went on. Several witnesses stepped up and gave testimony of various acts that the accused had participated in that proved he was a traitor. The acts were mostly him saying things against the patriots and declaring the Parliament and the King were the only responsible government and that their laws should be obeyed. The accused was given a chance to speak on his own behalf, but his words were drowned out by the crowd. It took only moments for the jury to pronounce the man guilty.

What happened next, even now, made Sarah recoil in horror at how people could be so vicious, especially to someone they knew, and whose only crime was to speak his mind.

The Committee members dragged the man from the chair and stripped him naked in front of the crowd and his family. Then a large bucket of tar, which had apparently been simmering behind the pub, was brought out, and they poured it over the man. He screamed in pain as the steaming black goo slid over his body and burned into his skin. He begged for them to stop, and recanted all he had said. At last the tub was empty. They then dumped a bag of feathers over the man. He was hoisted up on a long wooden rail and carried round the square as the people cheered and shouted huzzahs. Finally, the man and his family were led to the edge of the city and told to leave and never come back. The Judge then announced, "Let that be a lesson to any Tory who dares to speak treason in this city."

Sarah walked home alone, shaken by what she had seen. What was going on that she could not understand? How were the issues going to get resolved if everyone was obsessed with this madness? How were these people ever going to be able to live with each other again?

Sarah started as her thoughts returned to the present. It was at that moment that she realized the people over in Massachusetts had answered her questions. For the first time it became clear to her that whatever the issues were, they were going to be resolved by war. The Tories and Patriots were never going to be able to live together again. The winners would have control of the colonies, and the losers would have to find somewhere else to live. Nothing was ever going to be the same again. She realized, finally, that regardless of what she did not understand, she had to take a side in that war, and the only side she could choose was that of her husband. The time for arguing was over. The first shots of this war had been fired. The first blood had been let. Now all that was left for her to do was to find her place in this war and fight to its end.

When John came home he had more news from the Committee. The Congress over in Philadelphia had appointed a man by the name of Washington, from Virginia, to be general in charge of all the American armies. They had appointed two New Yorkers as generals also. From right there in Albany, Philip Schuyler had been named a major general, and Richard Montgomery had been appointed a brigadier general, and as Schuyler's assistant. Sarah and John, of course, did not know either of these men personally, but had certainly heard of them. They were from the finest families in the city. And, at least in John's mind, the fact that Congress had appointed two New York men as generals could only mean that New York would soon be getting into the fight. That was fine with John; the sooner the better.

At last John brought up the subject that they both had been avoiding: going off with the army. He explained that New York had been required by Congress to raise four regiments for the new Continental Army. Colonel Ten Broeck, the commander of the Albany County Militia, had urged the men to join up in the 1st New York Regiment. He and Jeremiah Quinlin, the militia company's captain, and most of the unit had signed up to make a company. John then explained that they would be forming up and moving out in a week's time. He was ready to fend off Sarah's arguments against it, and besides, the act had already been done and there was no going back now. But he was surprised when Sarah did not raise one argument. Instead she said, "John, I have resigned myself to something like this happening, and the time for disagreement is over. I still don't fully understand what's going on, but I am going to support you in whatever you do. So what can I do to help?"

John was elated that Sarah had finally come to her senses and could see the importance of this coming fight and why he had to go and be in it. "Thank you, Sarah. You have set my mind at ease knowing that I can go off now without having to worry about you being against it."

But she startled him with what came out of her mouth next. "You say we have to leave in a week's time? What do we need to prepare to be ready for the trip? And where are we going?"

"We? What do you mean, we? You can't go. You must stay here. There is no place for a woman with the army on the march. No, you are staying here. I thought you would go back to Newburgh and live with your parents while I was gone."

This was one argument that Sarah was not going to lose. She had also thought about going to live with her parents. But she was a married woman now, and her place was with her husband, wherever that might take her. And she was not staying alone in Albany.

She explained, "John, my parents have their own problems. I hear the Tories are even more active down there, and they don't need me to add to their problems. Besides, my father and brother are probably arguing with my mother right now about this very same issue. So I'll not be going home. And there is no way I could afford to live here alone on only the pittance I earn, and with you gone that would be all the money that would be coming in. Army pay, if it comes at all, would not be enough to get me by. Finally, you may have made the decision to join this war, but since you have, you have made it my war too. I am not going to sit waiting day and night wondering where you are or whether you are injured, or dead, or alive. So whatever you have to do to ensure that I can go, you had better do immediately, because no matter what, I'm going."

John tried to argue with her that she had no idea what she was getting herself into. The army would be marching ten or more miles a day at times. And they would be living under the most primitive of conditions. There was no way a woman could hold up under those conditions. And if she was unable to keep up, there would be nothing he could do to help her. He couldn't leave the army to take her home, or even stop to help her.

But there was no convincing her or changing her mind. She had set her Irish mind to this, and she was going to carry it out. At last he relented, and told her he would go ask Jeremiah and the Colonel about it.

They walked the few miles over to Jeremiah and Martha Quinlin's place to ask Jeremiah what he thought he should do. When he explained his dilemma to Jeremiah, he was surprised to find that Martha too had insisted upon going. And Jeremiah thought it a good idea. Jeremiah explained that since he was a captain, and John a sergeant, it would be alright if their wives tagged along. They could be of some help along the way, cooking and washing clothes and such. And they would not need to be worrying about the women all the time if they were with the army. Anyway, they would not be gone for long. Once the British saw that the Americans meant business and were willing to fight for their rights, they would come to their senses and pull their army out and put things right again. Besides, they had only signed up till the end of the year. So no matter what happened, they all would be home by then.

John still wasn't sure, but he and Jeremiah went to ask the Colonel. When they returned John said, "You win, Sarah. The Colonel said that there would be several women accompanying the force and that as long as you followed regulations and did not interfere with army activities you and Martha could come along." So it was settled.

The regiment would be moving out in one week's time. They would not be going to Massachusetts as everyone had thought, however. General Washington had ordered General Schuyler to put together a force to invade Canada in an effort to solidify the American continent against the British and bring the Canadians into the fold as a fourteenth colony.

The men all thought this would be an easy task, as they were sure the Canadians were just waiting to join in the fight, and together they would easily overpower the small British force that was left in Canada. They should be able to take Montreal, and then Quebec, easily, and be home before the hard winter set in and the enlistments ran out at the end of December.

Two

Sarah and Martha had only met once before the meeting at Martha and Jeremiah's house. That was on a rendezvous day when the men had taken the women with them to let them see that they really were doing military training, and not just taking a day off from farming to go drinking with the boys.

Martha was a year or two older than Sarah. She was taller than Sarah, and had brown eyes that matched the color of her hair. She seemed to Sarah to have a calm quietness about her that set people at ease instantly. There wasn't much for the women to do, so Sarah and Martha found some shade under a large chestnut tree and talked away the afternoon, and a friendship was born.

Neither of them could realize how deep that friendship would grow in the coming years, but for the moment, at least, they were friendly allies in unknown circumstances. They each had someone to share their misgivings and ignorance of army life with. They would not only have to get their men ready to go, but themselves as well. The first question that Sarah and Martha had to answer was what they needed to take with them. The men had specific orders as to what they were to carry. Each man had to have: an effective fire arm, bayonet, cartridge pouch, knapsack, 30 rounds of cartridges and balls, and a blanket. As women were not considered soldiers, there was no list of what they might need. Not that there was much to choose from. The only stipulation was that whatever they brought, they had to be able to carry, as no army wagons were to be used for transport of the women or their belongings.

In the end Sarah put together her few things, amounting to a clean set of clothes, a cloak against the weather, a blanket, eating utensils, and soap, into a roll they devised from a sheet of canvas. Additionally, she had a canteen John had gotten for her from the quartermaster and a few biscuits and dried meat for the trip.

On the morning they were to depart, John and Sarah rose early and walked the few miles to the rendezvous point at the edge of the city. In addition to John and Jeremiah's company several other units from the area were there. They would pick up more units on the way north as they traveled to Fort Ticonderoga, which was to be their first destination. In addition to Sarah and Martha, Mary Caldwell, the young wife of a private from the company, was going with them. There were also several women from other companies there, two with young children. Sarah wondered how these children were going to be able to keep up, and how they would be taken care of.

The Colonel called all the women together to give them

their instructions. He very officiously told them, "Ladies, you are not soldiers, but you are expected to follow all regulations and orders given you by the officers. Failure to do so will result in punishment under the army's regulation and/or expulsion from the camp. Additionally, you will march at the rear of the column with the rest of the baggage, and are not to march among the men, nor are you allowed to ride in any of the wagons. You will be given rations equal to one half that of the men, but without spirits. Further, you are expected to be an asset to the regiment by performing such duties as might be required throughout your time with the army. In case of action with the enemy, you are to remain in the rear and assist the surgeon as nurses as he directs. At no time are you to interfere with the execution of the army's mission or cause your husband to be unable to tend to his duties. There is to be absolutely no fraternization with any member of the force other than your husband. And any violations of these rules will mean expulsion from the unit. If any of you women think you cannot abide by these instructions, you should leave the formation now." No one left.

The day was warm and sunny, and after several hours of organizing, reorganizing, and waiting, they finally began to move just before noon. Fort Ticonderoga was about 100 miles north, and it was thought it should take the formation about a week to get there.

The first leg of the trip should have taken only a short time, as they were only going to the Hudson's River's edge, just a few miles away. But, Sarah soon realized that moving an army was no small feat. It seemed forever before the women actually got moving at all. As they marched, the dust from all the men, horses, and wagons in front of them created a cloud which engulfed the women and isolated them from all else. Sarah could hardly see the wagons in front of them, let alone the men up at the head of the column.

As they walked along, at what Sarah thought was a snail's pace, Mary, a pretty girl of just seventeen with blonde hair and beautiful blue eyes, attached herself to Sarah and Martha like a young sister. She was obviously confused and frightened with what was happening. At first, she spoke nervously about herself. She had been married just two months, and her husband never told her about joining the army or that she would have to go with him on this trip. He was just eighteen, and she had married him to get away from a very strict household and a life she thought too confining. But she had never dreamed that anything like this would happen.

Sarah wanted to tell her that she too had fears and doubts about what they were doing. Instead she found herself speaking as though she was an experienced campaigner. "Mary," she said, "The men-folk aren't going to let anything happen to you. This is going to be an exciting adventure. You'll remember it all your life and tell your children stories about it." To her own surprise she then began to spout the men's lines, "This war will be over by Christmas. Once our men take Canada the British will realize they can't beat us, and everything will get back to normal. Don't you worry, Mary. You just stay close by Martha and me, and everything will be alright."

Martha looked at Sarah rather quizzically as if to ask, "What are you saying? We don't have any more of an idea of what's happening than this girl."

Sarah gave Martha a knowing look and a little smile, then she started talking about sewing, just to change the subject.

When they finally arrived at the river, everything seemed to be in confusion. Finally, someone decided that it was too late in the day to begin the water movement up river. Everyone was to make camp and they would start out at first light the next day. Sarah and Martha found their husbands, and asked them where they were to sleep. John said, "Well, ladies, welcome to the army. We are all going to be sleeping under God's roof tonight. Since we are leaving early in the morning, no tents are to be set up tonight. We'll be setting up camp over there under those trees. So follow us, and we will introduce you to your first taste of army life."

Mary's husband soon came up and introduced himself. He was not a handsome boy. His face still had the remnants of a bad case of acne that had not completely cleared up. Although he did not say much, Sarah thought he seemed nice enough.

John began to explain how the camp was arranged in regimental formation, with the privates in the front, sergeants behind them, and officers behind the sergeants. The privates were put together in groups of six, and would cook and eat as a group. The sergeants would be together in groups of four and the junior officers, like Jeremiah, would be paired up.

Sarah asked, "Yes John, but where are the women to sleep?"

John replied without another thought, "Why, with their husbands of course."

Sarah and Martha looked at each other, stunned at what they had just heard. Martha looked at Jeremiah and said, "You mean that there have been no provisions made for accommodating the women on this trip?"

Jeremiah smiled and said, "Not a one, my dear. The army has no intention of treating you any different than any other soldier. You will have to live like the rest of us."

Off they went to their respective sleeping areas, where Sarah was introduced to John's three mess mates.

Thomas Kent was a small, slender, studious looking man of about thirty, Sarah thought. William Johnson was probably a little older and looked, to her, as though he was not at all happy about having a woman sharing this man's world.

Finally, a very large man, with blond hair and blue eyes that sparkled as though he had just gotten away with something, came at her. "Ben Gruber! Well, technically it's Benjamin, but I ask ya to call me Ben. It's what I answer best to, unless you plan on being my mother," he laughed. Where the other men politely said hello, Ben grabbed her hand and shook it vigorously and said, "Sure am glad to see you here, Sarah. I was afraid I would have to eat our own cooking. Now that you're here, I'm feeling better about this war already."

Sarah was startled by Ben and could hardly think what to say. But she managed to get out, "I'm very pleased to meet all of you. It's kind of you to share your, ah, accommodations with me."

The men looked at each other, and then Ben laughed, a hardy man's laugh. "Sarah, my dear, you are most welcome to our humble accommodations. But are ya willin' to do the cooking? That's what I wanna to know. We've already built ya a fine fire for the purpose."

Sarah was overwhelmed by this great man's gregarious nature. She looked at John for support, but he just shrugged his shoulders and put his hands out as though there was nothing he could do about Ben. Sarah then said, "Well, Ben, since you've built such a fine fire I guess the least I could do is use it to cook something up. However, you men will have to provide the food since I have none on me."

John had drawn his rations as well as Sarah's from the Quartermaster in the morning before they left the rendezvous point. The rations he drew were to last four days, after which, if they had not reached Ticonderoga, he would draw some more. Rations consisted of one pound of salted beef and one pound of flour for each man per day. Women received one half that amount. Each mess also had one large pot and a large frying pan for cooking. The men turned over their rations to Sarah without explanation, knowing that she would know what to do with them. Sarah was simply amazed. Here she was, surrounded by hundreds of men, with no place to sleep, holding four and a half pounds of beef and flour and expected to prepare a meal for five people. She could only smile at the thought, and then began doing what she could about the meal she was to prepare.

As Sarah busied herself with the cooking, the men prepared a crude lean-to out of small trees and branches under which they would all sleep.

Sarah went and fetched water in the pot and set it to boiling for the beef. But she had no idea what to do with the raw flour. She saw an older woman and walked over to her and introduced herself and asked if she had any idea of what to make out of this flour. The woman laughed and said, "Dearie, these men don't care what you do with it as long as it looks something like bread. Now did you bring any salt with you?" Sarah answered sheepishly that she had not. "Well, here, you can borrow some from me tonight, but when you get a chance you get some for yourself and guard it religiously." The woman then showed Sarah how to mix the flour up in water and salt and then fry it in the frying pan with suet from the beef.

Sarah went back and prepared the food for the men's dinner. As the beef was boiling and the suet was melting in the frying pan, she suddenly realized that she had not eaten since breakfast and she was famished. For her first meal out in the open, the food was not too bad. At least the men all seemed to enjoy it.

Fort Ticonderoga

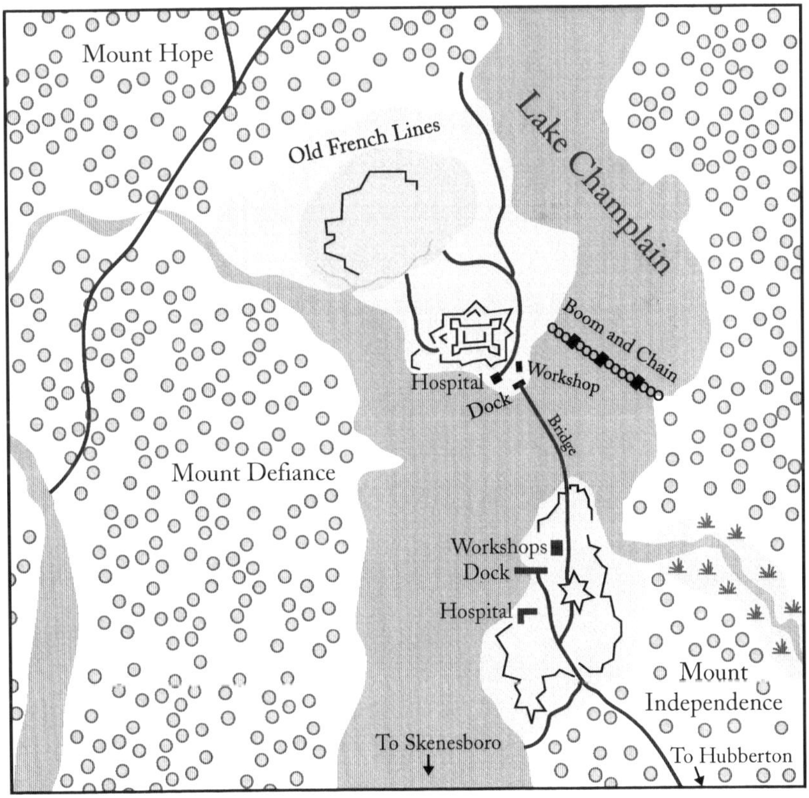

But then, they had not eaten since breakfast either. They washed it down with water along with a swig of rum each. The men had drawn four gills of rum each for the first four days of the trip and consolidated it into one canteen, which John carried. It was supposed to be used to purify the water in the canteens, but as Ben said, "That seems like such a waste of good rum." Women were not supplied with any rum, nor did the men offer her any.

Shortly after dinner, darkness began to set in, and it was time to get some sleep. But there was one other thing that Sarah had not done since breakfast. That was to relieve herself. And now she had to. But as she look around she again realized that she was a woman amongst hundreds of men. Where could she possibly get privacy? She asked John, who laughed and said he would take her into the woods and stand guard as she performed the necessary. It was then that she realized that no one had made any provision for anyone to relieve themselves in this camp, and that men were going anywhere they felt like it. Many days of this and everyone would be sick, she thought.

The night was pleasant and sleep came easily and soundly. As she was cuddled up next to John along with three other men in the lean-to, Sarah was satisfied with herself on her first day with the army. This army life was not as scary as she thought it would be and she thought that she would do just fine. After all, it would only be for a few months.

Three

As morning dawned fresh and beautiful, the camp came alive with activity. Someone from each mess got the fires started. Breakfast consisted of beef and bread once again. They cooked only half of the rations this time, as they would need the other half at dinner that evening. Once breakfast was over everything was packed up, and the men marched to the river for boarding onto the bateaux which would carry them to Half Moon.

John was not sure what the day would be like, or when he and Sarah would come together again that day, so he split their rations and gave half to Sarah and kept the other half for himself. Sarah was a little confused. She knew that Half Moon was only a little way up the river, and surely they should have no problem getting there today. But she took the food, and kissed John goodbye. The women would be the last to board the bateaux, and that would not be until sometime in the afternoon. Sarah, Martha, and Mary spent the morning comparing notes on how their evenings went and what they thought of their first day with the army.

Additionally, the older woman who Sarah had met the night before joined them. Her name was Elizabeth Hubbard. She was married to a sergeant from the artillery unit of the same regiment as John and Jeremiah. Older, in this case, meant that she was about forty. In addition to her husband, she had a son in the regiment. She also had a daughter who lived on their farm in Connecticut and had two children of her own. The daughter's husband had not joined this new Continental Army, staying home instead to take care of the farm. Sarah asked her how she came to be there. Elizabeth laughed and said, "I'm not originally from New York but from Connecticut. When the British fired on the Massachusetts Militia at Lexington and Concord my husband and I both enlisted in the local militia and had marched over to Boston to be with the Massachusetts people. Women could join the militia there, although our work was much the same as we will be doing with this regiment. We spent three months there and were at the battle of Bunker Hill. The battle only lasted one day, and a few days later our enlistments were up, so we went home. My husband was at Albany on some business when he heard about this regiment being formed under the new Continental Army. He joined up and as he had experience in Massachusetts, they made him a sergeant. They gave him time to come back over to Connecticut to get me. My son, Robert, came along and joined up as a private. Of course, women can't join this army, so here I am with you ladies, and glad of it too."

Sarah and the other women were amazed at this tale and wanted to hear more. But the time had come for them to move down to the wharf and get ready to leave. It was now about mid-day, and getting very hot. As they arrived at the wharf, men were fiercely trying to load some cannon onto the bateaux. The women could see that this was taking a very long time, and that there were still many wagons and the horses to load. Once again they were left with time on their hands before it would be their turn to board one of the boats. At that moment a sergeant came up to them and said, "Ah, ladies, I'm glad you are here. We are going to need your assistance in helping to load these bateaux. Nothing too strenuous, I just need you to relieve my men from tending the horses and moving some boxes so that the men can be better utilized loading these cannon and wagons."

The women followed the sergeant a little way off, where they found a makeshift corral with the horses enclosed inside of it. Additionally, there were many large boxes stacked up near the corral. The men had devised a sled to which a couple of the horses had been harnessed. The boxes were loaded onto the sled and then the horses would pull the sled down to the wharf for unloading and then loading onto the boat.

The sergeant then told them, "One of you ladies keep watch over the corral and make sure the horses do not break away, and you other three will just have to put these boxes onto the sled. Can any of you women handle a team?"

They all nodded that they could.

"Fine. Then once you've got the wagon loaded just guide the horses down to the wharf."

He then told one of the men to stay with the women and

supervise the process while the rest of the men went with him to load the boats.

Sarah, Martha, and Mary were speechless. They did not imagine that they would be put to work in this manner. Elizabeth, however, laughed, and they once again heard the refrain, "Welcome to the army, ladies."

Elizabeth immediately took charge and appointed Mary to guard the horses. Then she turned to the private and said, 'Okay soldier, what do we do? And don't take that supervisor idea too seriously, you are going to work right alongside us. If there is any supervising to be done, I'll be doing it."

He seemed intimidated enough to realize that he was not going to tangle with her and said, "Yes ma'am. Well, all we have to do is move these boxes from here to yonder wharf like the sergeant said. But I warn you they are heavy. I don't know how he expects women to do such work."

Elizabeth retorted, "Never mind what you don't know. Let's get to work."

The soldier timidly responded, "Yes, Ma'am."

The ladies left their belongings with Mary at the corral, then took off as much outer clothing as was acceptable and began to work right next to the private.

At first the work went slowly as the women learned how to maneuver the heavy boxes onto the sled. But once they got the hang of it, things moved along more quickly. The boxes were full of gunpowder for the cannon and, as the soldier said, they were indeed heavy. But they figured out the easiest way to load them by the second trip. They not only had to load them and take them down to the water's edge, they also had to unload the sled there. The day was very hot and the work was very hard, but the women handled it well. By the end of the afternoon they had moved all the boxes. During that time they had only taken a few minutes to eat some dried beef and biscuits.

In the early evening the officer in charge of the movement declared that no more boats could leave that day, as it would be getting too dark for them to go up river.

Sarah asked, "Will we be getting on one of these last boats?"

The officer said, "No, ma'am, you will be going with the boats tomorrow if we get them all loaded."

Sarah asked in disbelief, "You mean there is a chance we may not even get out of here tomorrow?"

To which the officer indignantly responded, "Madam, when we get everything else loaded and moving, you ladies will board with the rest of the baggage, and not until then. Now I suggest you all find yourself somewhere to set up camp and get some food and rest. Tomorrow will be another busy day. And if you want to get out of here I suggest you come early and lend a hand in getting this material loaded. Good day, madam. Ladies."

The women walked back to the encampment they had left that morning. The lean-to that John and his mess mates had built was still there, so they took it over as their shelter for the night. They were exhausted, but they scavenged up some wood and made a fire and cooked some of the rations that their husbands had left them. They immediately curled up under their blankets and went to sleep. During the night a summer thunder storm rolled up the river. The first crash of lightning woke all of them at the same time. The rain came down in a torrent, as it often does along the Hudson River. In minutes they were all soaked to the bone, along with all of their belongings. They tried to cover themselves with the canvas that their packs were rolled up in, but to no avail. The embers of the fire were quickly extinguished, and there was no way of starting a new fire this night. After about an hour of constant rain the storm moved on, and the rain stopped as suddenly as it had started. The wind that came behind the storm made the night seem like winter to the drenched women. Although they tried to find some way to get comfortable and get back to sleep, it was impossible. Daylight could not come soon enough.

As the sun came up the women, cold and shivering, attempted to find some wood to use to start a fire, but it was useless. Everything was soaked. They packed up their belongings and trekked down to the shore to begin the day. When they arrived they saw the men had fared no better than they had during the night. They all looked like wet rats, and they too had been unable to get fires started to cook breakfast. The women, at that moment, took the first real look at each other. They all laughed in unison at the sight they beheld. They were tired, hungry, completely disheveled, and their clothes and all their belongings were still wet. Elizabeth captured the moment by saying, "Perhaps it's best the men-folk are gone ahead of us. They sure wouldn't be enticed by the looks of us this morning." Once again the women laughed, and headed off to find the officer in charge.

The sun was fully up now and the day promised to be another hot one. They found the officer who greeted them almost cheerfully, "Good morning, ladies. I trust you had a comfortable night." As an officer, he had spent the night in the house of a local resident, so he was not seriously affected by the storm.

Upon looking at the women, he realized his mistake and corrected himself. "Er, I am sorry ladies. I can see that that remark was out of place. I was not thinking. Please forgive me. But I do have good news. Because of all the work we put in yesterday it looks like we will be able to get you off this morning and on your way to Half Moon. If you will just take a seat over there under that tree we will board you in a little while."

Sarah and the others were starting to understand what 'in a little while' meant in military language. That is, they could be waiting anywhere from ten minutes to ten hours. They all hoped it would be the former.

But the break was welcomed. The sun was not yet overly hot and their clothes were beginning to dry. They still had not eaten. As they reached the tree, Martha said, "Look over there. Someone has a fire started. Let's go over and ask if we might share it to cook some breakfast and maybe dry some of these things out."

They walked over to where a group of soldiers had gotten a very good fire going. They were cooking their breakfast as the women approached. Elizabeth, who had somehow become the leader of the women, asked if it would be alright if they used the fire to cook some breakfast. One of the men, a sergeant, said that it would be alright. So they took out some of the rations they had left and began to cook them up.

The sergeant inquired, "What are you ladies doing here?"

Elizabeth responded, "Our husbands are with the New York 1st Regiment and we are on our way to join them at Fort Ticonderoga."

The sergeant looked at them in amazement and said, "Ladies, I don't know exactly why you are doing what you are doing, but there is a couple of things you might outta know. First off, your men-folk won't be spending much time at Ticonderoga. Generals Montgomery and Arnold is waitin' on 'em now. As soon as they get there they'll be heading up Canada way. So I hope you get to see them before they leave. And second, are you going with that group of bateaux over yonder?"

Sarah, now very pensive upon hearing that John would be heading for Canada so soon, quietly answered, "Yes, why?"

The sergeant replied, "Well, maybe you already know this, but them boats ain't goin to take you all the way to Ticonderoga straight away. You ladies will have a bunch of hiking to do after you get to Half Moon, and there will be a lot of portaging to the next water ways along the way. So I hope you have enough supplies to get you there. By the way, if I was you I would cook all them rations here before you leave so's they don't spoil on the way. Here, I'll show you how to make what we call hard tack with that flour. Let me have some of that flour. Looks like the rain has already spoilt some of your vittles."

They all surrounded him as he took some of the flour, added some salt and water, and mixed it into a very thick paste. He then cut it up into small biscuit-like objects and set it on stones next to the fire to bake.

He said, "They are going to be hard as rocks, and they don't taste like much, but you'll get used to them, and if you can soften 'em up with a little sauce they can be mighty filling. And when you are on the march, break off a piece and put it in your mouth. It'll keep your mouth from drying out and keep the hunger down a little too. Well, it looks like my unit is moving out so I'll be leaving you ladies. Enjoy the fire, and good luck on your journey."

He and his men were quickly gone. The women found themselves alone. They looked towards where the bateaux were being loaded and the men were still busy getting everything on board. Sarah and Martha took over the job of cooking the rations and making the hard tack while Elizabeth and Mary used the time to get everyone's things dried out as best as they could. Once the food was ready they all sat down on stumps the soldiers had been using for seats and ate.

Soon a soldier came up to them and said, "Ladies, Captain says if you want to go up river with us you better get down to the boats now or he'll leave without you." They hurriedly put their things back together and nearly ran down to the boats.

The Captain met them and directed them to board one of the bateaux, which was loaded with a couple of wagons and stores. They found a seat in the rear of the boat and sat down. The boat was pushed off, and they were soon heading towards their destination. It had been a couple of hours since they had been told they would leave "in a little while." The sun was fully high in the sky and it was getting to be a very hot day. But they had accomplished the personal things that needed doing that morning, and they were feeling pretty good about the rest of the day. Soon they would be at Half Moon, and if they were lucky the men would be there too.

Four

It was about a fifteen mile trip from Albany to Half Moon, and the movement of the bateaux against the current was very slow with the heavy cargo aboard. But the day was beautiful, sunny and warm. Sarah was dazzled by the beauty that surrounded them. The rhythm of the river's gentle flow seemed to sway the bateaux just enough to put her in a kind of trance. The sun reflected off the water and made it a mirror, spoiled only by the ripples of the boat as it cut through it. The forests covering the hills and mountains on either side looked impenetrable. The trees were every possible shade of green and their reflection in the water seemed to make them look as if they would swallow up the bateaux and all that were in it. The stillness was only broken by the sound of the oars beating in their own rhythm against the current. For a while no one spoke; each one seeming to meditate deep in her own thoughts amidst the magnificence of the beauty that surrounded them.

Martha finally broke the silence. "Right after we got married, Jeremiah and I came down this river from the Mohawk Valley. I was awestruck then with the beauty of this country, and seeing it again I have that same feeling of my own insignificance in its vastness. You know, ladies, I don't know too much about what this war is all about. But when I see all this and know that it is ours, I can't help but feel that those people in England, who have never seen anything like this, have no idea what it means to us. Someday Jeremiah and I will own some of this land and no government thousands of miles away will have anything to say about it or be able to take it from us. They send their armies here to enforce laws that make no sense when you see all of this. They can only conceive of places like Boston and New York where they make money. But they know nothing about beautiful places like this only a few miles from what they call civilization."

Sarah then added, "I know what you mean about not knowing much about what this war is about. I guess maybe my father and John may be right that women don't understand the economics and politics of it. All I know is that once I lived what I thought was a pretty good life. John and I were just getting started and were saving so that he could open his own blacksmith shop and we too could have a small place of our own. But now we have nothing, and when this war is over, no matter who wins, we will still have nothing, and will have to start over again."

She thought a moment and then said, "And I don't understand who we want to be. Are we British, or are we this new name people having started calling us, Americans? When we are done what will we be? And what will happen to those who fight for the losing side? After watching friends and neighbors having their homes burnt down, and men being tarred and feathered for disagreeing with each other, I just don't know what to think. Whenever this war is done the British and Hessian Armies will go back to Europe or someplace else to fight another war. They're soldiers after all, and that's what they do. But what will happen to those of us left here? I'm here because my husband is here, and this is where I belong. But I wish I had some idea of what these rights are the men keep talking about, and how we are all going to be better off after this war is over. Are we going to still be part of England? If not, what will we be?"

Elizabeth nodded thoughtfully, "You ladies been doing some thinkin' on this subject, ain't ya? Well, I have too. You see I already got those things you two are dreaming about. Edward and me got a farm in Connecticut and children and even a couple of grandchildren. And you're right, Sarah, it sure was a pretty good life. And I sure hated to leave it. But I think this war was inevitable. Ya see, back a hundred and fifty years ago the folks here could call themselves British citizens. They still was. But we have all changed now. This continent has as many languages as Europe has. And even our own language ain't exactly like the King's English anymore. No, this war is about the fact that we are not British anymore. What we are gonna be will be determined by the results of the war. But whatever it turns out to be, nothing will ever be the same again. I'm fighting 'long side of Edward, yes, because he's my husband and that's where I belong.

But more importantly, to me, I'm risking everything we have on a belief that we can make things better for ourselves without the King and Parliament. I ain't smart enough to know what kind of government we'll end up with. I don't think most of the men do either. But there's something in all this patriotic talk that strikes me. I think we can rule ourselves better than they can from England."

She smiled and her eyes brightened as she said, "And you know what ladies? I think we women might just get to make a few changes to this world ourselves if we win. At least I'm planning on it."

She then turned to Mary and said, "What about you, young lady? What's your say on all this?"

Mary looked at the three women, and her voice broke as she said meekly, "I don't know why I'm here. I don't know what's gonna happen next. I don't know what will happen to us. And I'm scared. I was orphaned when I was very young, and went to live with my mother's sister and her husband. They were very hard and strict on me and I was miserable living with them. So I thought getting married would free me from them and life would get better. They didn't object. In fact they almost pushed me out the door."

She went on, "At first married life was nice. Richard was nice. But it didn't take long before he became as hard and mean as my aunt and uncle. I just traded one set of tyrants for another. I ain't allowed to have no friends and ain't allowed a thought of my own. I didn't get no say in being here, and I don't want to be here. But I got no place to else to go. My aunt and uncle won't take me back and I can't live alone. To tell you the truth, I don't care who wins this war. It means nothing to me. I don't see it changing my life none." She put her head down, seemingly lost in misery.

The other three were silent for a moment. Then Elizabeth went to Mary and put an arm around her. "You got friends now, dearie. You see, no matter what, we women here have to stick together. If you need anything you just call on one of us. You gotta hard row to hoe, Mary, that's true. But it won't get no easier if you try doin' it alone. We have to lean on each other and we're here for you to lean on if you need us."

She looked at Sarah and Martha with a sly smile, winked, and said, "Besides he don't know it yet, but your husband won't be getting a whole lot of say about how things are done out here. He'll be too busy soldiering to have time to run your life entirely. Now you cheer up, dearie. Pretty young thing like you shouldn't be so sad."

The women took out some biscuits they had brought with them and ate them with some water. As they sailed through the beautiful Hudson Valley, Sarah wondered what war would be like. "How could there be a war amidst all this beauty?" she sighed.

They navigated North past the mouth of the Mohawk River as it flowed into the Hudson and through a group of small islands that Martha said were called "The Sprouts." Finally, they arrived at Half Moon in the early evening. The place was a bustle of activity. There were units everywhere. Boats were being unloaded, but theirs would not be until the next day, at the earliest. The women went looking for their husbands, but were told that they had left earlier in the day and were probably already at Stillwater. They knew then that the men would be days ahead of them in arriving at Fort Ticonderoga. Since there was nothing for them to do, as the boats would not be unloaded and the wagons prepared for the land journey until morning, they found an inn where they could rent a room for the four of them. The price was dear, but it was good to at least sleep under a roof and be able to clean up after these last few days. They ate at the inn and then went off to their room for a good night's sleep.

The women woke early, ate some breakfast at the inn, and went down to where the boats were anchored. The men were already hard at work unloading the wagons, animals, and supplies from the boats. Elizabeth asked the captain what they could do to help out. He directed them to a sergeant who was with several teamsters organizing the wagon train for movement. This was the same sergeant who they had worked for in loading the boats. He greeted them and then told them that their job would be to assist the men in loading supplies onto the wagons. Elizabeth asked, "Do you think we will be leaving today?"

"Nah," said the sergeant, "we'll be lucky to get everything off the boats and loaded today. If we are lucky we will get moving tomorrow."

Rather dejected by this bit of information, the women worked alongside of the men, loading material onto the wagons as it was brought up from the boats. It was hot, sweaty work that went on until midday when they took a break for a meal that consisted of hardtack and cooked beef. Once they were done eating it was back to work, which went on until near dark. The women went back to the inn again that night, ate, and went to their room. Sarah said to the others, "We can't afford to stay too many nights in this inn. I don't know what the rest of this trip is going to be like, but if we have to pay for lodgings at each place I will quickly be out of the money John gave me. Tomorrow night we will have to find another way of getting shelter for the night." The others agreed.

Martha was a little bitter as she said, "The prices these people are charging for food and lodging is outrageous. Don't they know that this army is fighting for them?"

Elizabeth responded, "It's like that in all wars, ladies. There is always someone getting rich off the war and those who fight it. Let's be grateful we have a roof over our heads tonight and some food in our bellies. Like Sarah says, tomorrow we may be hunting for shelter." With that they all fell asleep.

The next day once again broke bright and sunny. When the women got down to the wagons they found that everything was in place for them to start out that morning. After a couple of hours more of 'army organizing,' the wagon train finally began to move. The women's place in the march was again at the rear.

Stillwater was the next stop on the trip. It was about ten miles from Half Moon, and as the river was impassable at this point it would have to be done over land. The going was very slow as the path they were traveling on was barely wide enough for the wagons to fit through. In addition, there were deep ruts, boulders and tree stumps left by the men who had tried to widen what had originally been nothing more than an Indian trail. The train dragged on with the women following behind until, in mid-afternoon, a summer thunder storm overtook them. Everyone and everything got drenched. There was no place to take shelter, so they kept marching on through the rain. As they went further along the road turned into a quagmire of mud. The horses were having a tough time pulling the wagons through the mud, slowing everything down. The women soon found themselves up to their ankles in mud. Their shoes were no longer of any use, so they took them off and carried them.

Within an hour the rain had stopped, but its effects were still to be felt. The afternoon seemed to get hotter, and steam came up from the ground as they marched on. At one point the entire train came to a halt. The women thought that it was to take a break, but a sergeant came back to them and said, "Ladies, we are in need of your assistance up front. Please follow me."

They went about halfway to the front of the train where one of the wagons was sunk to its rear axle in mud. There were several men already working on unloading the wagon, and the sergeant said, "If you ladies would be so kind as to assist in getting this wagon unloaded it will be most appreciated. The sooner we get it done the sooner we can get this wagon unstuck, reloaded, and we can get moving again." It took a half hour to get the wagon unloaded. Then Mary, who was the smallest one, was put in the driver's seat to control the reins as everyone, including the women, put their backs to the wagon to get it moving again. Once it had escaped from the mud everything had to be reloaded into the wagon. This happened two more times during the afternoon and early evening. As they marched on, their packs seemed to be picking up weight, and got heavier with each step.

They did not stop to eat as darkness set in, but kept on until they finally reached Stillwater. When they arrived they were still wet from the afternoon's rain, as well as from the sweat created by the march. They were covered from head to toe with mud. There would be no inn on this night. Instead they would sleep under the wagons. The first thing Sarah did was go through her belongings to find the soap she had brought with her. She and the other women went down to the river and stood guard for each other as first two, then the other two went into the river to bathe. When they were finished with their baths they each put on the change of clothes they had brought with them. They were not much drier than the ones they had taken off, but at least they were clean. Then they washed the clothes they had marched in that day and set them out to dry by the fire they had built earlier. Supper that evening consisted of hard tack and some of the beef they had cooked two days earlier. They were getting smarter about the weather now, and took care before they bedded down to keep the canvas cover close at hand and over their belongings.

The next day at Stillwater was spent unloading the wagons and loading everything back onto the bateaux. They were getting into a system now, and things went pretty quickly throughout the day. But at the end of the day they had still not left for Saratoga Falls, which would be their next stop. They would leave in the morning. To Sarah it seemed as if this army, at least this part of it, was not very interested in getting to Fort Ticonderoga in too much of a hurry.

The next few days went on as before. They reached Saratoga Falls, unloaded the bateaux into wagons, then took a short portage before they loaded the bateaux back up and sailed for Fort Edward. At Fort Edward they repeated the process of unloading and loading and made the trek to Fort George by land. From

Fort George at the South end of Lake George they sailed until they reached the North end of the lake and the La Chute River, where once again they moved the supplies from the bateaux to the wagons for the final leg of the trip to Fort Ticonderoga.

It was Sunday when they finally arrived. The trip had taken them fourteen hard days. When they walked into the fort, John, Jeremiah, and the rest of the men were waiting for them. Sarah rushed to John and hugged him as never before. As they embraced Sarah said, "Oh, John what a trip. I don't think I have ever worked as hard as these past two weeks or have ever been so tired. Is there a place to go and rest?"

John took her by the hand and headed out of the fort towards a city of tents. From the outside, the tent looked like it might be large enough for the two of them if they did not have to live in it for too long. As John opened the flap they were greeted by two of his mates, who were writing letters. John said, "Sarah, you know our tent mates, William and Ben. Where is Thomas?" he asked Ben.

"Oh, he went off to try and find some food. You know him, he is always hungry. He should be back shortly."

"I'm very pleased to see you gentlemen again. I hope you have been taking good care of my husband."

Everyone laughed, and the men said that they had indeed been taking good care of John.

There was an awkward moment at that point, then William said, "Ben, I'm getting pretty hungry myself. Why don't we go and find Thomas?" Ben and William got up and left. Sarah and John were finally alone.

Sarah asked, "How long will we have to share this tent with

your friends, John?"

John replied, "Oh, only a couple of nights dear."

"Why only a couple of nights? What's going to happen then?"

John took her hands in his and said, "General Montgomery has just been waiting for the arrival of the wagons and supplies for this regiment. I'm told he has been mad as hell at the delay. The army will be heading out for Canada in two days. General Arnold has already taken off with his force through New England. He is headed directly to Quebec. We will be going to Montreal."

Sarah could tell by the tone of his voice that there was something that John was not telling her. She said, "I guess after a day's rest I'll be up for another trek."

At that John dropped the other shoe. "Sarah, you can't make this trip. You and the other women are to stay here at Fort Ti. When we get to Canada we will be going into battle. It will be no place for women, and besides, the general does not want any women on the trip to slow us down or get in the way."

Sarah responded with the hurt she felt in her tired body, "Slow you down! Get in the way! I'll have you and your general know that it was not the women who slowed down this trip. We worked just as hard as any of the men, and in some cases even harder. It certainly was not us who made this trip take two weeks."

John looked at her, and could say nothing. She knew that he could not change what was about to happen and was suddenly filled with anxiety. The questions began to pour from her. "How long will you be gone? Am I supposed to stay here or go back to

Albany? How will I live with no money? What am I to do here? Am I expected to live in this tent all winter? How will I eat? What soldiers are not going, and why do you have to go if they do not? You have a wife. What am I to do if something should happen to you?"

John had no answers that would satisfy her at this moment. He took her in his arms, and as she began to cry she said, "Oh, John, I'm scared. I never dreamed it would be like this."

When she calmed down John began to explain, "First of all, this jaunt should not take very long. Only a few weeks at most. When we get to Canada the Canadians are all set to join in with us, and we will be able take care of the Redcoats in short order. We should be back before December. At any rate, like I told you in Albany, I only enlisted until the end of the year, so no matter what I will be back here in December."

"Now as for living arrangements, we will take care of all that tomorrow. There are some huts down the road that will be vacated by the soldiers as we leave, and you and Martha and a couple of other women should be able to get one of them. The most important thing is to make sure that you have a job with the army that entitles you to stay at the fort and be given rations. I know someone who can get you a decent job. We'll go talk to him tomorrow also."

"Now," he smiled, "Why don't we take advantage of this solitude? We can't keep our tent mates looking for food all day."

Sarah blushed and said, "We can't now. It's the middle of the afternoon. Someone will hear us. What if the men come back?"

"Trust me, the men will not be back for a while."

Having put up what objections she thought proper, Sarah

submitted. She found herself excited at the prospect of making love in the middle of an army camp. Their lovemaking was more passionate and filled with more desire than Sarah could ever remember. She never wanted to let go of him. As they made love, neither of them could have realized that their worlds were about to change them so much that when they would meet again they both would be almost unrecognizable to each other.

Five

When the men returned Thomas was with them. Sarah and John were sitting on a log in front of the fire talking.

Nothing was said but Sarah was sure that they knew what she and John had been doing. She blushed and wondered, "What must these men think of me?" And then her mind wandered. A month ago she would never have dreamed of making love so unashamedly in the middle of the day with the world only feet from their tent. What was coming over her? In only two short weeks she could feel herself changing. She was beginning to feel like a part of something she had never before experienced. She couldn't put her finger on it, but something was changing in her.

She was brought back to the present when Ben asked, "Sarah, what made you come along with this rag-tag army? Are you filled with this Liberty Fever, too?"

"Well, Ben, I'm not exactly sure what all this talk of liberty and independence is all about. I thought we were just trying to set right a few of the things that the King and Parliament have done wrong since George the Third became king. As for me, I don't know what this independence will give us. What does independence mean, anyway? What will we be independent of? Won't there just have to be another government, another king? Why will it be better than what we have now?"

She caught herself at that point, realizing that she had overstepped her place by getting involved in a political discussion. That was the men's realm, and she had no place in it. She quickly finished, "But I don't know much about these political things. I am here because my husband is here and I belong with him. I hope you men are able to end this war quickly so we can go back home and maybe start a farm and raise a family."

Ben chuckled, "You don't have to worry about that, Sarah. This war should be over by Christmas. What with the Yankees having 'em bottled up over in Boston, and after we whoop the Redcoats up in Canada they will realize that there's no way they can beat us, and they will come to see things our way. Besides, no one yet has seriously mentioned total independence from the crown. We just need to set that Parliament straight about who makes the laws over here and who can tax us. Once they understand that, why everything can return to normal. Don't you agree gentlemen?"

The men nodded, and conversation turned to eating. John asked Sarah if she would mind doing the cooking for them all, and she agreed.

Cooking was done at a communal kitchen. The kitchen was a large circular pit with a great mound built in the center.

Small ovens were built into the mound. Each tent sent one person to prepare the meals for its members. Sarah took the food and cooking utensils and went to the kitchen to prepare supper. When she got there she saw Martha, Elizabeth, and Mary. They had not seen each other since their arrival earlier in the day, so they had to compare notes on what they had learned. The other women were as concerned as Sarah to find that the men would be leaving so soon, and that they would not be going with them.

Sarah asked, "What are we going to do while the men are gone?"

Elizabeth came to the rescue. "We are going to take care of each other. We must stick together. Tomorrow we need to find a place where all of us can live together. We all need to get jobs of some kind attached to this fort. Without that we will be left out in the cold. Even then we can't plan on the army supplying us with everything. They already think of us as a drag on their precious supplies. So don't plan on them giving 'em up too willingly or overly generously."

Martha pouted, "But the Colonel told us back in Albany that we were authorized half rations. Isn't that true?"

"That Colonel will be leaving day after tomorrow with the regiment. We will then be part of this fort. General Schuyler is commander here, and he sets the rules. The only way we can guarantee anything is by making sure we all have jobs that the officers left behind here think are meaningful to the army. That is to say, meaningful to them."

"But what can we do?" asked Sarah.

"Oh, there are plenty of things that'll need doing around here after the majority of the army leaves. At a minimum there is laundry and sewing and cooking that will need doing. The menfolk just ain't equipped to handle such things. You know what I mean?" They laughed and nodded in agreement.

"And other things will turn up too. We just need to be smart enough to see them first and pick out the best ones for us. All the women in this camp are going to need to stick together if we are to survive. Some of them won't see it, and will try to handle it on their own. They won't make it. Some will quit and go back where they came from. A few will nestle up with some officers while their husbands are off fighting. Sorry Martha, I know your husband's an officer, no offense meant. It's just the way of things. They will be discarded like old baggage when the time comes. And others will find other ways to be driven from the camp. But we four have to take care of each other first and foremost. If we do that, we'll be fine."

Sarah said, "You're right, Elizabeth. We need to make a pledge to watch out for each other." It was at that moment they became a formidable team.

After they had promised to take care of each other, Mary blithely injected, "Besides, Richard says the men will all be back by Christmas. That's not too long. We can do that." Martha and Sarah agreed that their husbands had also said the same thing.

Elizabeth quickly put a damper on their beliefs. "Listen ladies, I hope the men are back by Christmas as much as anyone. But don't put too much store in these men's bragging. First they've got to get to Canada. And when they do they are going to find the British Army ain't going to roll over and play dead for them. There will be a fight, and when there's a fight the winner ain't decided 'till it's all over. So our men may have won the battle already in their minds, but they still gotta fight it. Then they can come back. I ain't sayin' they won't be back by Christmas. I'm just telling you not to be too disappointed if we end up spending Christmas with ourselves."

Sarah then said, "Well, John only enlisted till the end of December. So at the latest he will be home in early January."

Elizabeth looked at Sarah, nodded knowingly, and said, "Ehah. Well, it will all work itself out. We best be getting these vittles back to the menfolk before they starve to death. We'll probably all see each other here again tomorrow morning, so until then, have a pleasant night ladies."

On her way back to the tent Sarah worried about how Elizabeth had reacted when she told them that John's enlistment would be up in December and he would be returning then. It was as if Elizabeth didn't believe it.

Sarah served up the food to the men, then sat down next to John and began eating. She casually mentioned that the women were talking down at the kitchen and the topic of how long the men would be gone came up. She said that Elizabeth did not believe that they would be back by Christmas. Could that be true?

John interrupted, "Sarah, I don't want you to get involved in all this woman gossip about who thinks what about this operation. You women have been soldiering for what, two weeks now? And all of a sudden one of you knows all about military actions? The officers of this regiment have assured us that this battle will take little time. With the Canadians, we will have the Redcoats outnumbered at least two to one. Once we have beaten them, there is nothing that should keep us up in Canada, and we will definitely be home by Christmas—maybe even sooner. Now stop worrying about what women in the kitchen are saying. The army knows what it's doing."

The men all nodded in agreement, and the conversation drifted off to how the march would be and other military things that Sarah was not interested in. She took the plates and cooking utensils to a communal boiling pot of water and washed them, then returned to the tent. The men had taken out a bottle of spirits and had lit their pipes. This was a sure sign to Sarah that she was no longer needed or, indeed, even wanted in the discussion. She said good night, crawled to the rear of the tent, and placed herself sideways as John had told her to. She was just glad that John would be next to her.

The next morning Sarah was awakened by a sound she would grow to know all too well. It was dawn and drums were beating all over the fort, announcing reveille. The men started grousing about getting ready for their first formation of the day. It was at that point that she realized that she was the only one who had gone to bed fully clothed the night before. The men were in various states of undress, trying to get their clothes on. Sarah rolled over and turned her back until she was sure they were all dressed. Then she too crawled out of the tent.

Although it was still the last days of August, the morning was cool, and a heavy dew had settled on the ground overnight. But it was a beautiful morning, and as she looked out on the lake, shining like a mirror in the rising sun, she could not but think that Elizabeth had to be wrong about things.

As the men went off to formation Sarah got the food and cooking utensils together and headed for the kitchen. Martha was already there, but Elizabeth and Mary had not gotten there yet.

"Good morning, Sarah. Isn't it a beautiful sunrise? How did you sleep?"

"Good morning, Martha. I was just looking out over the lake and thinking the same thing. I haven't had much time to think about God these past couple of weeks, but looking at this beautiful sight makes one appreciate His marvels. Doesn't it?"

Martha nodded in agreement.

Sarah then said, "I slept very well. Guess I was pretty tired from the trip and all. But waking up with three other men besides John in the tent was quite an experience. I had to lay there pretending I was still asleep while they all got dressed," she giggled. "How 'bout you? How was your night?"

"Well, I guess being an officer's wife does have one thing going for it. Jeremiah and I only had to share our tent with one other officer. It was still kind of awkward, but I guess we will get used to it someday. But, like you, I slept very well." Martha then asked, "What do you think about what Elizabeth had to say last night about how long the men will be gone? I have been thinking about it a lot since then."

Sarah then told her about her conversation with John and the other men on the subject. "I think about the only thing we can rely on is what she said about everything working itself out in the end. I want to believe the men know what they are talking about, but really they don't have much more experience with this stuff than we do. So it's anybody's guess. I just pray that Elizabeth is wrong and the men are right."

"So do I, dearie," Elizabeth chimed in from behind.

"Oh, Good morning, Elizabeth. I'm sorry. I didn't mean..." Sarah stammered.

Elizabeth said, "Don't think a thing about it. And don't go apologizing. That's not a good way to start off a beautiful morning like this. First of all, you're right. I don't know any more about how things will work out than you do. Secondly, whether I'm right or wrong doesn't matter. What matters is that we can speak our minds out to each other. We got a long row to hoe ahead of us and we need to be able to say what's on our minds, 'cause ain't nobody else gonna listen. Now ladies, how was your first night being the only hen in a chicken coop full of roosters?"

They all laughed and settled into cooking breakfast and sharing small talk. Once the food was ready they all headed back to their tents to serve their men.

As they were eating, Sarah asked John what they would be doing during the day. He told her that first thing he had to go drill for an hour. Then he had meetings about the march. He should be done about noon. He then asked her if she would do the laundry for him and the other men so they could have clean clothes to start out with, at least. He said the men would pay her for theirs.

Sarah agreed. Then asked, "We are going to take care of getting me settled in this afternoon then, aren't we, John?"

He yelled over his shoulder as he walked off, "Of course dear. Don't worry."

She gathered up the clothes the men had left her and some soap she had brought along and went down to the lake to wash them. When she got there she found Elizabeth already at work doing the same thing.

"Can't send the menfolk off to war in dirty clothes, can we, Sarah?"

"No, I guess not," Sarah replied. After thinking a minute she asked, "Elizabeth, the men are leaving tomorrow morning, do you think they are going to have time to help us get settled today?"

Elizabeth's response was, "Dearie, once we get this laundry to drying, you and me are going to find Martha and Mary and we are going to find our own place and get ourselves settled. We've got a lot to do. We have to find shelter that will hold up in the winter, find jobs, and figure out the lay of the land around here. I don't figure the men are going to be of much use to us today. Remember, Martha's husband is an officer and ours are non-commissioned officers. They will be too busy taking care that their men are ready for the march tomorrow to be spending much time with us. Mary's husband is a private and will be busiest of all, probably. No, I think we are on our own for the foreseeable future, Sarah."

Sarah looked at Elizabeth in wonder. John had promised he would help her this afternoon. He wouldn't break his promise. Not on the last day before he was going off for God only knew how long. Was this army stuff really more important than taking care of his wife?

Elizabeth could tell by the look in Sarah's eye that she was hurt and disappointed. She said, "Look Sarah. It ain't that our husbands don't love us or don't want to help. It's just that there is no time. The general insists on leaving tomorrow, and the men can't do nothing 'bout that. In order for the move to happen they have a great deal to prepare. It will take them all day and probably part of the night to get it done. The best thing we can do is to relieve them of the burden of taking care of us. Remember what that Colonel said back in

Albany, the army will not tolerate our getting in the way of military operations. This is what he was talking about. Now let's get this laundry done and then show our husbands what independence really is. Let's show them that we will be fine, and that they will have no need to worry about us while they are gone."

Sarah could only say, "If this is what independence is all about, I don't think I want to fight a war to get it."

Elizabeth was right. Sarah did not see John the rest of the day. Instead, she, Martha, Elizabeth, and Mary went about the fort and the surrounding camp locating where everything was. They found some huts in the camp outside the fort that had been constructed by soldiers who had been there most of the summer and were leaving in the morning. They identified the best one they could find and made up their minds to claim it that evening when the men got back.

Next on the agenda was for them all to find jobs that would keep them at the fort and allow them to draw rations, and maybe even get paid. Mary and Martha found work with the baker. The bakery was tasked with making hundreds of loaves of bread each day, and they would be a part of the process. Their days would start before dawn and go until about noon each day. Elizabeth found work with one of the sutlers selling things to the soldiers and helping to keep the books.

Sarah set herself up as a laundress and seamstress for the officers' mess. The camp had a set price for each piece of laundry to be done, so she would get paid as she worked.

Each of them would be able to draw half rations from the commissary because their jobs were considered to be important to the running of the fort.

Their missions accomplished, they congratulated themselves and went off to their tents to greet their husbands feeling very proud of themselves.

It was about mid-afternoon when Sarah got back to the tent. Her laundry was dry, and she folded it and put each man's with his pack. She stopped and went to her things and got a piece of paper from a pack she had brought with her for letter writing. The paper had gotten wet at least twice, and was in pretty sad shape, but it could still be used. She sat down and wrote a note to John. The note read, "Washed and mended by the hands of your loving wife. Please don't get any bullet holes in these clothes. Bring them and yourself back safely to me soon. I love you, Sarah." She smiled and tucked the note away in the pocket of his shirt.

Then she began preparing the last supper they would share for she did not know how long. While they were out looking for jobs she was able to purchase some onions and potatoes from the sutler. The price was dear, and she had very little money, but she wanted this meal to have some taste, and be remembered by John as he traveled so far away from her. With the rations and vegetables she made a rich stew.

The men returned around dusk and John was full of apologies for not helping her during the day, but he just could not leave the men with all that had to be gotten ready for the morning. Sarah told him she understood, and then told him all about her day and all she and the other women had accomplished.

John looked at her in amazement, then at the other men. He joked, "Well, boys, I guess we're not needed around here. These women have got everything under control." He smiled and took her in his arms and hugged her and kissed her on the forehead. Then he said, "I'm proud of you. I'm a little jealous you could do it without my help, but it makes me feel a little easier about leaving that you were able to."

Sarah beamed with pride, then said, "Now you all sit down. As you men are leaving tomorrow and will be on your own for cooking, I have prepared something special for you." After the men had eaten and complimented her profusely, she told them she had a special treat for them. While they were out wandering around the camp, the women had found some apple trees that had the season's first fruit on them. Sarah and the other women picked all they could carry. Sarah had also bought some sugar and cinnamon from the sutler and had made an apple cobbler. The men were ecstatic. They dove into the cobbler like they had never eaten before. They joked with John as they ate that he had better keep a close watch on Sarah or they would steal her away. They all thanked her very much. Sarah could see the pride on John's face. As she went to clean up the dishes her heart was light, and she was happier than she had been in days.

When she got back to the tent, the other men were gone and John was sitting there alone. She asked where they had gone. John told her they had some things that needed finishing up before they took off in the morning. They would be gone for an hour or so. She smiled a knowing smile, and as John took her into his arms she melted away in his embrace. Sarah was beginning to like making love in the tent. She didn't care if the entire world was outside the flap. She savored the moment. Finally, John broke the mood and said that the men would be returning soon. He left her in the tent and went out to greet the men.

She could vaguely hear them talking outside as she drifted off to sleep.

The next morning when reveille sounded, the men were excitedly getting themselves ready to move out. Sarah prepared a quick breakfast at the fire in front of the tent, and the men wolfed it down. John lingered after the others had left, and kissed Sarah goodbye. They looked into each other's eyes. Sarah's showed the sadness she felt at their parting. John's, on the other hand, were filled with excitement for the coming adventure. She could hold him back no longer, and he was off to join the regiment.

Sarah wandered down to the shore where she met the other women. They stood in silence as they watched the men load into the bateaux. Each one keeping their thoughts to themselves. Each one wondering what was about to happen over the next few months. Some of the women could be seen holding back tears. Others were crying outright. As they stared out over the water, the four of them clasped hands. They did not say anything. There was nothing to say.

Finally, their regiment shoved off. The women watched for as long as it took the boats to disappear, each secretly hoping that they all would just turn around and come back and that this dream would come to an end. But once the boats were out of sight there was nothing to do but get moving to their new quarters. Some soldiers were already breaking down the tents and getting them ready to transport up the lake to Canada.

Six

It was the twenty-fifth of August, but the evenings were starting to get chilly, and fall could not be far off. One of the first tasks that needed to be accomplished was to get some fire wood stored up against the winter. But they had no tools. They spread out through the camp, going through the vacated huts looking for any tools that may have been left behind by the soldiers. They found the huts to be a treasure trove. They came up with one large axe, two tomahawks, and various pots, pans, and kettles for cooking that the men did not want to carry with them. Additionally, they found sundry other tools and gadgets the men had either accidently or purposefully left behind. The women weren't certain what all these things would be used for, but they collected them anyway. One never knew what might be needed.

Next, Elizabeth went to the commissary to see if she could

draw their rations. While she was doing that, Sarah and Martha went into the woods and started collecting wood. The days were still warm and the work was hot, but once they got into it they soon found they had built up quite a store.

Mary was sent out, with a basket they had found, looking for anything edible, such as nuts, berries, field onions or wild herbs. Additionally, she was to go to the apple trees they had found the day before and pick as many as she could carry. She came back with quite a load.

Elizabeth came back rather disappointed. She could only draw rations for herself. The other women would have to go over and get their own individually. That was no great problem, so they went off to get their rations.

When all was gathered, they sorted out what they had garnered and, all in all, they thought they would be in pretty good shape for a few days.

The day was coming to an end and Martha started a fire in the fire place. They all quickly realized that there would have to be a sorting out of duties as well as of food. First off, Martha and Mary had to be at work in the bakery too early for them to take on any morning chores. So as they ate they decided that Sarah and Elizabeth would start each morning collecting wood and edibles from the woods for as long as they lasted. There was also wood in the fort that the soldiers had chopped, and they could draw some of that each day also. The only meal that needed cooking was in the evening, and they could pass that around equitably.

After they cleaned up the dishes it was time for bed. Elizabeth and Martha got the lower bunks and Sarah and Mary the two in the middle. The higher ones were used to store their belongings and the community food. They all had failed to check out the mattresses that the soldiers had left behind. When they got ready for bed they realized that the straw they had been stuffed with had probably never been changed from the day the soldiers got them. Additionally, they were filthy. They would be sure to clean them and repack them the next day. They pulled the bed ropes as tight as they could, but since the mattresses were so flimsy they were not going to be very comfortable on this night.

As she lay there, Sarah wondered where John was and what he was doing. For the first, but certainly not the last time, she said a prayer for his safe return. Then she wondered what the next day would bring. She only knew that she had agreed to work at the officers' quarters in the fort to do their laundry and sewing. But that didn't seem like it would be too much. She drifted off to sleep wondering if there mightn't be more she could do, and what it might be.

The next morning, long before reveille, Sarah heard Martha wake Mary. It was still dark, and finally, as they were trying to feel their way around, Sarah whispered, "Light a candle; you can't see anything in this darkness." Martha apologized for waking her, but thanked her for understanding. By this time they all were awake. Sarah and Elizabeth got out of bed too. Elizabeth stoked the fire, put a small log on, and asked them all if they would like some tea.

As she said "tea" the other three stopped and stared at Elizabeth. Sarah asked enviously, "You have tea? Where did you get tea? I haven't had tea since my mother started boycotting all

British products last year." Martha and Mary were in the same position. All of them started whispering as though they were part of some conspiracy.

Elizabeth could see the questions in their eyes. She said, "Easy ladies. This ain't British tea. This is genuine contraband tea from the islands. No British have touched it or taxed it neither. It comes straight to us on ships working for our side. Now granted there ain't much of it, but seeing as this is a special occasion of us starting out our working lives, so to speak, I figure it might be nice to have a cup. Now would any of you care for one?"

They all greedily said yes. Elizabeth put some tea leaves into a ball. Each of them held out their cup for water to be poured in. Then Elizabeth passed the ball around so that each of them could steep the tea in their cup.

Sarah thought that it might have been the best cup of tea she had ever drunk. She savored every drop.

Elizabeth put the ball away with the tea still in it, saving it for another occasion.

Then Martha and Mary went off to the bakery for their first day of making bread for the army.

Sarah and Elizabeth still had a couple of hours before they would have to go over to the fort and start work. They busied themselves talking and trying to spruce up the hut as best they could. The first thing they did was take the bed mattresses apart and set them outside to be washed. Sarah put a large kettle of water on the fire and they sat down to wait for it to boil. While they waited Elizabeth poured them each another cup of tea using the same ball. It wasn't quite as strong but it still tasted awfully good.

Sarah asked, "What did you say your husband did in the army? By the way, what is his name again? We can't keep calling them your husband can we? Mine's name is John, John Hardy."

"Well, since you asked, his name is Edward, Edward Hubbard. He is a sergeant in the Artillery. Guess he thinks it's safer than being in the infantry. At least he isn't standing in a line shooting across a field. How 'bout yours?"

"John is in the infantry. He joined the local militia with Martha's husband, Jeremiah. Jeremiah was elected as a lieutenant and John as a sergeant. They both came home one day and said that they had enlisted in a regiment in the new Continental Army and were going to be regulars. At least until the end of the year. Then their enlistments are up and we should be able to go home."

"Well, Edward signed up for a full year. He don't figure this thing will be over until at least next summer sometime and he don't like leaving things half done. That's nothing against your menfolk. It's just his way. Personally, I hope you're right. I sure do want to get back to the farm."

Sarah asked, "What's your opinion on all this talk of independence? I'm not sure I understand what it's all about. Won't we just have to choose a new king if we get out from under George? I don't understand what the Continental Congress is all about either. Who's telling them what to do? It sure ain't John or me. The men seem to think they have some idea of what they are fighting for. But I sure can't figure it out."

Elizabeth thought for a minute and then said, "Sarah, you pretty much put into words the very things I been saying since the beginning. We live on a farm in Connecticut. These taxes everybody's so up in arms about don't affect me much. Besides, every time they pass one and we boycott it they end up changing it. Don't they? So it seems to me that our voices are being heard pretty good across that big ocean. But those Adams' and Hancock over in Massachusetts and the men from down South seem to have a whole different view of things. They think we need to be our own country. And I guess they will figure out how we're going to run it after we win this independence. Those men from down South bother me some too. They are all plantation owners and own slaves. How can you talk about liberty and then own slaves yourself? Yeah, there are some rich folks up here who own slaves too, and I don't think much of them neither. But we are just women, Sarah. And right now our view of things don't hold much water. So this war is going to go on, and if our side loses we'll have hell to pay. We'll probably lose our farm and some Tory will get it for next to nothing. So we have to win so the Tories lose their farms and people like you can take them over for next to nothing instead."

She continued, "There's another thing, Tories. I guess we are supposed to hate them for being loyal to the King. But a lot of these folks were my neighbors, and some were my friends before this all started. I just don't know how we Americans ended up on two sides of this thing so that now we are greater enemies with them than we are with the British Army."

Sarah said, "I know what you mean. I was really shaken when I heard that the Committee had burned out some of our neighbors. John was part of that too, I am sure. But it was really horrible when the Committee turned everyone out to witness the tarring and feathering of one of the Tories because he wouldn't sign an oath of allegiance. It made me physically sick to watch and I was upset for weeks afterward. What are we building if that is the kind of justice we will be dispensing?"

"Well, dearie," Elizabeth said, "we are not going to solve it this morning, and if we don't get on over to that fort we will be without work before we get started. And if that happens we won't be sitting around here worrying about what the war is all about. We'll be on our own worrying about where we will find our next meal."

They walked together over to the fort. When they got there they split up. Sarah went to the officers' quarters and Elizabeth went to the sutler's wagons.

When she arrived at the room she thought she was to report to Sarah was met by a very official looking major. He greeted her, "Good morning, Mrs. uh—Hardy?"

Sarah said quizzically, "Yes, good morning."

He then continued, "I'm Major Cardin. I am the general's aide. He asked me to meet you this morning and brief you on your duties here."

Sarah was stunned. "General?" she asked. "Excuse me, Major, but I believe there must be some mistake here. I was told I was to come here and do the officers' laundry and sewing. No one said anything about the general. Are we talking about General Schuyler, Major? What have I to do with him?"

"I'm sorry for the confusion, Ma'am. Let me explain. General Schuyler is in need of a woman who will attend to his housekeeping needs. Your name came up as a woman who was working in the officers' mess and might be willing to take on the task. I thought someone had already asked you if you would care to take on these duties. They would entail cleaning his rooms and doing his laundry and sewing and such other household tasks as he may require from time to time. For this you would receive a monthly salary of three dollars. Of course, you could still attend to the other officers' needs on your own time if you so choose. They would of course pay you directly and separately for anything you do for them. So then, let me ask you. Are you willing to attend to the general? I assure you that, although the hours might sometimes be long, in the end it would be to your benefit to take this job."

Sarah, a little overwhelmed, said, "Of course, Major. I would be happy to work for the general and do whatever he needs. I didn't mean to imply anything to the contrary. I am just a bit surprised is all. Where do I start, and what do I need to do?"

Major Cardin said, "Very well, then. As of now you work directly for General Schuyler. You will take your directions from me or him and no one else. Anything you might do on your own time should not interfere with your duties here. Understood?"

"Yes, of course," she replied.

He then took her on a tour of the general's quarters, which consisted of two rooms. The outer room was a large office with a desk, a large table, and a few chairs. On the walls were several large maps. Sarah had never seen such maps, and looked at them in amazement.

She asked, "Major, what are all these maps about?"

He looked at her as though he thought she should certainly know what they were. But he said, "General Schuyler is the commander of the Northern Department of the Continental Army, Mrs. Hardy. These maps are of the area that he is responsible for. This one is of New York. You are presently right here." He pointed to Fort Ticonderoga on the map. "This second one is of New England, and the third is of the Southeastern portion of Canada. What regiment is your husband a part of?"

She told him the 1st New York.

He said, "Ah, yes. Well, they are on their way to Montreal at the moment, so they are probably somewhere about here." He pointed to a position close to the border between New York and Canada.

As she looked at the map she felt a kind of comfort in seeing where John might be. It somehow made her feel closer to him having that knowledge. She asked, "Major, does the general get reports of where the men are and what's happening to them?"

"Of course, Ma'am. There are couriers who come and go to and from the army regularly. Or at least as regularly as one can expect, given the denseness of this country. The general is kept informed of all actions as soon as is humanly possible."

She then asked, "Is it ever possible to send a letter by one of these couriers?"

He looked at her, smiled, and said, "Why yes, Ma'am, the couriers do carry mail as long as there is not too much. Now getting it to your husband is another matter. The couriers are going to deliver orders and directions to General Montgomery and Colonel Arnold, so they will not go directly to the regiments to deliver mail. But if there is some it will be dropped off and then moved onward to the units as their couriers move between their headquarters. So eventually a letter should get to him but there is no telling how long it would take."

Sarah nodded and said, "Thank you."

They then moved on to the general's living quarters. It was a single room with a bed, a night stand, a dresser, a trunk, and a chair. Sarah looked around and thought, "They are going to pay me three dollars a month to keep these two rooms clean? This seems like it will be nothing more than I did at home."

She then said, "I can start now, what do you want me to do first?"

He told her, "The general is out at the moment, so now would be a good time to scrub the floors and get the rooms presentable for his return. After that, his laundry is in that bag in the corner. If you would then do that, I think it will be enough for the day. I will leave you to your work now. If you need me for anything, my office is right next door. Please check in with me before you leave in case there is something more that needs to be done. Thank you, Mrs. Hardy."

Sarah went back to the hut to get a bucket and soap to clean the floors. Then she stopped by the sutler's wagon to purchase a brush. She could hardly wait to tell Elizabeth about her luck, but she was not there. When Sarah started to pay the man, she mentioned that she just got her job with the general. The man asked, "This is for General Schuyler?" Sarah said it was, and he then told her there was no need for her to pay for it, he would put it on the general's bill and the army would pay for it. He told her any time she was doing the general's shopping to make sure the clerk knew it was for him and it would be taken care of. She thought, well, that is very convenient.

She quickly had the floors sparkling. At least, she thought they were sparkling. Next she tidied up the two rooms. In a couple of hours she was done. There was a community laundry consisting of several large vats filled with boiling water set up in the camp, at which several other women were doing men's laundry. There was a line to use the vats, and a sergeant seemed to be in charge of the area. She asked him who she needed to see to be able to use the vats.

The sergeant asked, "Whose laundry you got there, lady? This here area is for the officers' clothes to be washed."

When Sarah told him that she was there to wash General Schuyler's clothes he immediately went to one of the women and told her she needed to move over and wait until Sarah had finished doing the general's things. All the women turned and gave Sarah a "who do you think you are" look, but said nothing.

Sarah was quickly finding out that working for the general was a double edged sword. On one hand you did not need to wait for anything. On the other, you soon could feel the wrath of your jealous female counterparts.

She took the clothes back to the hut to dry, then pressed them using a flat stone that she had found and heated in the fireplace. Determined not to use the community laundry anymore, she would bring the clothes back to the hut and do them there. But she did not want to cause trouble with the other women.

Sarah took the ironed clothes back and hung them up in a closet in the general's bedroom. It was about five o'clock, she guessed, and she was done for the day. Before she left she went to see Major Cardin and asked if there was anything more needed for this day.

The major looked up from his desk and asked, in a tone that implied there was still plenty of day left, "Ah, Mrs. Hardy, done so soon?"

Sarah replied, slightly offended, "Well, Major, I scrubbed the floors and cleaned the rooms, and the general's laundry is washed and ironed and hung up in his closet. If there is something more you wish me to do I will certainly attend to it."

"No, no. That sounds like a fine day's work. I'm sure the general will be very pleased."

At that moment a distinguished looking older officer walked into the office. "What will the general be very pleased about, Major? There damn well isn't much about this fort or army that has pleased me since I arrived here. It would be very good to find out what I might be pleased about."

Sarah was surprised to see before her a rather sickly man. He was taller than the major and slender with long graying light brown hair. To Sarah he looked almost regal in his uniform.

The major stood up and came to attention. He said, "Oh, good afternoon, General. Let me introduce Mrs. Hardy. Her husband is with the 1st New York Regiment. I hired her this morning to be your housekeeper. We were just discussing her first day's work."

General Schuyler turned and noticed Sarah for the first time and bowed slightly. "I am very pleased to meet you, Mrs. Hardy."

Sarah curtsied and held out her hand and said demurely, "Hello, General, I am honored to have been selected to work for you. I hope my work meets with your approbation."

He took her hand and said, "Please forgive my language. I did not realize you were here. I'm afraid if you are going to spend much time around an army camp you will hear much worse before you're through though. Still we try to keep ourselves civil around the office. I am sure, as Major Cardin said, that I will be very pleased with your work. Lord knows it has to be better than we men can do."

Sarah realized that the conversation was ended and said to the major, "If that is all you have for me today, Major, I will be on my way and I will see you first thing in the morning. If there is anything you need me to do, General, please don't hesitate. Just keeping two rooms and your laundry clean doesn't seem like much to keep a woman busy. Good day, General, …Major." They said good afternoon and Sarah turned and left the building.

Seven

She could hardly contain herself to just walk until she reached the gate of the fort. Once she was outside she burst into a smile and began running to the hut. She had to tell someone about her day.

When she arrived at the hut Martha and Mary were already there. Their day had ended earlier and they were tending to getting something ready for supper.

Sarah could not contain herself. She did not even say hello. Instead she simply burst out, "You two will never guess who I am working for." Without waiting for them to respond she continued rather proudly, "I am General Schuyler's housekeeper."

The two women gasped and said how wonderful it was. With that Sarah went on to tell them about her day. As she was finishing her story she realized that she had ignored them and how their day went. She said, "I'm sorry, I was so excited I had to tell someone. I haven't even asked how your day went."

Martha started, "Well, the bakery certainly is not as exciting as working for the general, but I think it is going to be a good job. The army always needs bread. The work is not too hard, and come winter it will be warm. And besides, look at what we have brought to the table." She pulled a cloth off from two large loaves of bread.

Sarah realized that it had been weeks since she had tasted any real bread. She told them, "They are beautiful. Maybe the most beautiful things I have seen lately."

Just then Elizabeth came through the door. She said, "What is that I smell? Someone cooking supper? It smells wonderful."

Mary exclaimed, "Look what Martha and I have brought home to add to the table."

Elizabeth stared at the bread and whispered, "Ladies, I think this is the beginning of a wonderful family." At that they all laughed and sat down to eat. The bread was the best part of the meal.

Elizabeth told them about her job with the sutler, but wanted to hear all about the general. After Sarah had retold her story, Elizabeth said, "Dearie, you are the lucky one. General Schuyler was supposed to lead the force to Montreal but his sickness forced him to give up the idea and let General Montgomery led them. If he had gone you wouldn't be in your position."

"I did notice that he was a little sickly looking when I met him," Sarah said. "But how did you know about it and how he couldn't lead the troops?"

Elizabeth responded, "One of the reasons I wanted to work with the sutler is that there is nothing that they don't know about what is going on in the fort or with the army. They make it their business to know. They have to be ready to supply anything the commissary can't get and to know what it is before anyone else knows they need it."

After supper, Sarah and Elizabeth cleaned up the dishes. Then all four of them walked out to where a long trench had been dug for a latrine. They kept watch for each other while they attended to their needs. As they were walking back to their hut Mary commented, "I see there are some other women starting to move into some of the huts. Pretty soon we may have our own camp just for us women. We should try to meet some of them."

Elizabeth said, 'You are absolutely right, Mary. We do need to get together with those other women. We are going to have to build our own unit, and the more women we have in it the better off we will be."

Mary asked, "Do you think we are going to have to fight like the men, Elizabeth? Is that what you're saying?"

"No Mary. What I'm saying is this: There is a shortage of everything at this fort, and supplies don't come over that ragged road we traveled a few days ago very regular. So everything we get around here us women will have to compete with the men for. And the more women we have in the competition the more likely we will be successful in getting a share of what is needed. And one more thing I learned at the sutler's today: The barracks in the fort are very overcrowded. So it probably won't be long before someone in authority realizes these huts are being inhabited by us women. Don't be surprised if we don't get evicted sometime soon so's the men can move in."

"But where would we all go? What will we do?" Martha asked.

Elizabeth said, "I don't know right now. But it would be smart on our part to not get too comfortable in these huts and to keep an eye out for a likely new home."

The next day Martha and Mary went off to the bakery early and Sarah and Elizabeth collected fire wood and, like squirrels, any nuts, fruits or herbs they could find before they went off to their duties.

When Sarah got to work the major told her that the general was too sick to get out of bed this day and so she need only clean the office area. Once she had done that she knocked on the general's door and peeked in. He looked up and asked tiredly, "What is it, Mrs Hardy?"

Sarah said, "I'm sorry for disturbing you, Sir, but is there anything I can do to help you? Is there anything I can bring you to eat or drink that would make you feel better?"

He told her he did not want to impose upon her. But she said that she would fix him something and bring it by later.

She went to the commissary and asked for a chicken or some pieces of one. The man there looked at her as though she was crazy. "Why would I give you a chicken lady?" he asked.

Sarah thought for a second, and then decided to test the newfound authority that came with working for the general. She retorted, "Because,, Sir, I am Mrs. Hardy, the general's housekeeper, and the general is sick and I am going to make him some soup to get some food into him. Now, do I have to go get Major Cardin to come over here and order you to give me some chicken, or will you make it easy on both of us?"

With that the man sheepishly went and retrieved the carcass of a chicken that had been someone's meal already. Sarah could imagine whose. She said thank you and went off to see Elizabeth at the sutler's wagon. Sarah told her what she was doing and asked if she had anything that could go into the soup. Elizabeth went into the wagon and came back with some spices and an onion. Sarah told her to put it on the general's bill and went back to the hut to prepare the soup. When it was ready she saw that she had made plenty, so she left a goodly portion at the hut for them for supper.

She went back to the general's quarters and quietly went into his room. She woke him gently and asked if he might be able to get some soup down as it might make him feel better. He was surprised to see her there, but sat up and said that he would try some. Sarah found a bowl and poured some of the broth into it and brought it to him. Additionally, she had brought with her a small piece of the bread they had from the night before. At first he sipped slowly on the soup but soon was eating strongly. He also was able to eat the bread and keep it down.

When he was finished he thanked her and asked where she had gotten the ingredients to make the soup. She sheepishly confessed that she had had to use his name in vain to get the commissary to give her the chicken, but she thought that he needed it, and she hoped he wasn't angry.

He almost laughed, and said, "Mrs. Hardy, people use my name for many things around here. I'm glad someone used it to get something for me. Thank you." As she got up to leave he asked her, "Could you leave the rest of that pot with Major Cardin? I may want some more later this evening." She said, "Of course, Sir," and left.

When she got back to the hut it was still light. Since supper was ready, she, Martha, and Mary decided to take a walk around to introduce themselves to the other women who had started moving into the other huts. All agreed that they needed to band together to help each other.

It had only been a few days, but things seemed to be settling into a pattern. No one had heard anything from the men yet, but that was not unexpected, even by the women who were, of course, anxious.

Routine went on through September, except that the women now were being drafted to perform other duties within the camp for several hours each day. Sarah and Martha were assigned to a tailor shop where they were to make clothes to be sent to the army in Canada, while Elizabeth and Mary were assigned to making musket cartridges.

Although the weather in August had been hot, it was mostly fair. But during the first week of September tremendous storms battered the Northeast. A day after the storms had passed Sarah sat down and started a letter to John:

Sept 10, 1775

My Dearest John,

It has been a few weeks since you left and I have been busy getting settled here at Fort Ti. We have just gone through a few days of very strong storms. They have caused a great deal of damage here at the fort and everyone is just trying to put things back together today. They say that the storms are the remains of a hurricane that ravaged North Carolina and Virginia earlier in the week. I hope this letter finds you well and that these storms might pass you by.

I have been fortunate enough to get work housekeeping for General Schuyler. The work is not too hard and he seems to be a nice enough man.

I know he has a great deal on his mind as commander of the entire Northern Army. He is sickly a great deal of the time. I think it could be because he is constantly upset about the conditions here at the fort and of the roads that must be traversed to get supplies here and forwarded to you men in the field. It is only September but already we are in great need of many things and they don't seem to be coming in very fast. I do not know what life will be like when the weather turns cold and the snows begin. If the army can't get supplies here in good weather what will we do then?

We women have also been assigned to other tasks to help the army. I am working in the tailor shop making clothes. I hope that you will get some of them. Each piece I sew I think that you are the one I am making it for. I know it's silly but it makes me feel closer to you thinking that you might be wearing something I made.

We are living in one of the huts the men moved out of when you left for Canada. There are four of us living together. You know Martha? Tell Jeremiah that she is well. We have made friends with two other women, Elizabeth Hubbard, whose husband is a Sergeant in the 1st New York Artillery. Perhaps you might know him? And Mary Caldwell. Her husband is a young private with your company. We all get along pretty well but, of course, we all miss our dear husbands.

Enough about me. Please write to me if you get a chance and

let me know that you are well and safe. The hardest thing about being here is not knowing where you are or what is happening to you. There are large maps on the wall in the general's office and Major Cardin, his aide, has been kind enough to point out where he thinks you are. But that is not the same as hearing it from you personally. So, if you can, please write.

I will close for now. Please know I love you very much and miss you terribly.

Your Loving Wife,
Sarah

Sarah folded the letter and sealed it with wax from a candle. The next day when she went to work she gave it to Major Cardin and asked if he might put it with the courier to be delivered to John. He told her he would, but that it might take quite a while to get to him.

Later in the month, the day came that Elizabeth had foretold. A sergeant knocked on the door and when they answered he told them that he had been directed to inform them that they would have to find other accommodations, as all of the huts were to be confiscated for use in housing the army. They had three days in which to find other living facilities. Even though they had been expecting this news, they were incredulous. Who had given this order? Where were they supposed to go? The sergeant shrugged his shoulders and said that the colonel, the commandant of the fort, made the decision, and that he was the only one who could change the orders. As to where they were supposed to go, the sergeant had no idea as it was of no concern to him.

After the sergeant had left, Mary said, "Commandant? What is a commandant? I thought General Schuyler was in charge here."

Elizabeth then said, "General Schuyler is commander of the Northern Army. He has his headquarters here but does not have the time to run the fort and the army too. So there is a colonel who has been appointed as commandant of the fort. He is the commander of the fort and responsible for the troops stationed here." She turned to Sarah and continued, "Perhaps you could ask the general for help in this matter. I don't think he will countermand the Colonel's orders when it is the health of the soldiers that is in question. Regardless, we have to do something quickly to find a place that will get us through the winter. Sarah, you go over and at least ask the major what is going on and if there is something that can be done. They can't just throw us all out into the cold without some plan. In the meantime, there is a small hamlet a mile or so to the west of here, we will go over and see if there might be any living accommodations available there."

As Sarah entered Major Cardin's office she could tell that he was very busy, and she was almost sorry she had to bring her problems up to him. But he turned to her and said most agreeably, "Ah, Mrs. Hardy, is there something I can do for you? By the way, the general was most appreciative of the soup you made for him last week. It helped his disposition considerably, if nothing else."

Sarah nodded, then started, "Major, we have just been visited by a sergeant who told us that the commandant has ordered the women out of the huts so they can be used to house the soldiers. I know that we must take care of the men, Major, but where are we to go? What are we to do? We have just been through a hurricane, and if we had not been in those very huts many of us might have perished. The weather is not going to get better, and soon winter will be upon us. Is there anything that you or the general can do to help us in this matter?"

The major's attitude changed, and he replied, "I have heard of the Colonel's order, Mrs. Hardy, and I am afraid that there is precious little we can do to countermand it. The general is not inclined to interfere with the running of the fort if he can avoid it. Additionally, the men must be taken care of first. Currently they are living in overcrowded barracks, which are unhealthy at best. Something must be done to alleviate this condition. No one wants to see you women suffer, but what are we to do?" He looked at her with sympathy as he continued, "Look, the general has a meeting with the commandant this afternoon. I will tell him about the straights this action is placing you women in and ask him if he will bring the matter up with the Colonel. That is all I can do, and I do not promise anything will come of it. Come back to see me this evening and I will tell you what they decided."

Sarah thanked him, and as she walked back to the hut that had been her first home in this journey she sighed, "Oh, John, where are you? Why are you not here with me now? What am I—what are we—doing in this war?"

When she arrived back at the hut she found the others looking as forlorn as she felt. Elizabeth said they had visited the settlement, and it consisted of just a few huts which were not much better than what they had themselves. There was really no place for them to go there.

That evening, Sarah went back to see the major. He told her that there had been a small reprieve. First of all, the women would not have to move out immediately. They would be allowed to stay put until arrangements could be made to house those who wished to stay. For those that wanted to leave, the army would provide transportation back to Fort George or Albany as part of the regular supply runs. The general and the commandant hoped that most, if not all the women would avail themselves of this option, as they did not see things as being very pleasant here this winter and they could not guarantee the women anything. For those who chose to stay, the accommodations would be very Spartan indeed, at first consisting of tents until something more substantial could be built. He was sorry, but that was the best they could do.

Sarah thanked him and said she understood. But as she left the office she was stunned. What kind of choices were these? If she chose to stay they were going to be put up in tents! Tents were no shelter from the fierce weather that northern New York was noted for. If they had been in tents during the storms, who knew what would have happened to them. But if she chose to leave where would she go? How would she take care of herself? She thought of her parents and home. Maybe she should go back there. In a letter she received from her mother just before John and she had left Albany she learned that her father and brother too had joined the army and were off somewhere. Maybe she should go help her mother. "Yes," she thought, "maybe that is what I should do."

But before she had to make a decision, she needed to talk it over with the other women. She wanted to know what they thought. At least they had a small reprieve. They would not be evicted immediately. They had a little time in which to make their decisions.

The nights were colder now. And as they huddled near the fire the women discussed all their options. Sarah, Martha and Elizabeth all had someplace they could go to if they needed or wanted to. But Mary had no place. Both her and her husband's parents were dead. She was truly afraid of what was going to happen to her. If the others left, where was she to go?

Elizabeth was the first to make her decision. She had joined this war with her husband and she was staying. She would be here when he returned. The conditions weren't going to be great, but neither were they any better for Edward and the rest of the army in Canada. She did not try to convince any of the others to stay with her, but Mary breathed a sigh of relief. Now she could decide to stay and know she had someone she knew here with her.

Two decisions had been made. Now Sarah and Martha had to decide. Sarah knew that it would be better if she went back to her mother's. She knew she would be welcomed, and would dearly like to see her mother again. But something inside her said that John was her family now, and, as Elizabeth said, she needed to be here when he returned. After all, it would only be another couple of months. She could easily make it through whatever was to happen in that short of time. And there was something else. These women were also her family now. They were her sisters now, and she could not abandon them here. If they were staying, she was too. Martha was the last to decide and agreed her place was with the other three.

Most of the other women chose to take the army up on its offer to escort them back down the lake. Finally, there were just a dozen of them left. The tents were erected behind the area where the huts were located, and the women moved in. Their fire now was outside their tent and the four of them huddled together at night to keep warm. They welcomed the mornings so they could get to a warm place to work.

Within a few days the soldiers had taken over the huts, but there were still a few that were empty. Sarah and Elizabeth went directly to the commandant and asked if the women might move into those empty huts. After a couple of days of deliberation, he consented to give the women three huts. They were the oldest on the grounds, and in great need of repair, but they were better than the tents, and at least they had a fireplace. The women accepted them with gratitude, and quickly all of those who had stayed were crowded into them.

All the women joined together to perform the repairs on each of the huts. They all became some of the best scroungers in the fort. They found the things they needed to fix whatever needed fixing, and quickly learned not to ask permission to take it, because permission was almost always denied. What they didn't know how to do they quickly learned from a few helpful men who took some pity on them as they worked. Soon they were all almost cozy. All this had to be accomplished on their own time, as they still had jobs to attend to.

Eight

The first snow came in early November, and with it Sarah at last received a letter from John. She took the letter and went and found a secluded place to read it. She wanted to be alone with him, at least in her heart and mind. It was written on the back of her letter to him.

Oct. 25, 1775

My Dear Sarah,

I finally received your letter of September tenth about two weeks ago. I am sorry that I have not been able to answer you sooner but conditions have not permitted it.

We arrived at Fort St. Johns in the middle of September. Along the way we were engaged by a force and I am sad to say that many of our men acted most dastardly. Quite a few ran in the face of the enemy at the very first sounds of gun fire. But we recovered from that and beat off the ambush. We then proceeded on to Fort St. Johns. By the time we got here many of the men were sick and unable to perform their duties which has put a great strain on the rest of us. But after a nearly two month siege we are hopeful that we will succeed in taking the fort which is quite strongly defended.

The weather has been miserable. I reckon that it must be a part of that storm you wrote about. The trenches we have dug are filled with water and conditions get worse each day. I don't know where those clothes you're making back there are going but we sure haven't seen them. Ours are getting pretty ragged and with winter coming on I hope we get some warm clothes soon. We were short on all supplies until General Montgomery sent a force up North to Chambly. They were able to take the fort there without much trouble as I'm told it was not well defended. Our men brought back a great deal of food which has been most welcome. Additionally, they captured several cannon and ammunition which has enabled us to assert ourselves in the siege here. We are hopeful that the commander of this fort will finally surrender it to us soon.

I am glad to hear you have made some friends and that things are going well for you. I worry about you every day and your news has helped a lot to ease that worry. Jeremiah received a letter from Martha also and it said about the same as yours did. I did meet up with your friend Elizabeth's husband, Sergeant Hubbard. He seems like a good man and we are very grateful to have them and the extra guns that were captured at Chambly here with us now. Lord knows it's the artillery that will finally get these Redcoats to surrender here. I know Private Caldwell. He is in our company. He is one of the young ones and we try to keep a close eye on them as they have a tendency to get scared and run sometimes, although he has not. I think he will be a good soldier as time goes on.

Once we take this fort we will be on our way to Montreal. I hope success is quicker there than it has been here so far.

I am tolerably well given the weather and the conditions we are living under. At least I have not gotten sick yet and that is a blessing. I have lost a few pounds though. You may not recognize me when I get back. If they don't start feeding us better I'll be nothing but skin and bones.

I will close for now as I have to go on duty. Please continue to write whenever you can. We don't get mail often but a letter from you makes my days brighter.

Your Affectionate Husband,
John

Sarah read and reread the letter several times. It was so good to hear that he was well and had not been hurt. She wished there was something she could do to ease his suffering but knew that about all that was in her power was prayer. She said one of thanks at that moment and reminded herself to say one every day from now on for both their sakes. Additionally, she made a promise to herself to try and find a way to write to him each week.

Of course the news about the final taking of Fort St Johns had already reached General Schuyler and the fort before she received the letter. Each day as she went to clean the rooms she was given a friendly greeting by Major Cardin, which included a short update on where John might be. By the time she received the letter he was already well on his way to Montreal and the general expected to hear that the city had fallen any day now. The major seemed to enjoy showing Sarah on the map where the 1st New York were and how they were doing. Of course he did not divulge much beyond that little bit of information, but it was somehow reassuring to her to look at that map each day and kind of know where John might be.

Later in November she learned that Montreal had fallen to General Montgomery on November thirteenth without a fight. Sarah breathed a sigh of relief at hearing that, and said to the major, "Oh, how wonderful! That means that they will be coming home soon then."

Major Cardin looked at her curiously and said, "I'm sorry, Mrs. Hardy but I'm afraid you are misinformed. The men are now on their way to Quebec to assist Colonel Arnold in the taking of that city. That must be accomplished before they will be coming home."

So he still had to be in Canada until the end of the year. The news was not new, but somehow Sarah had made herself believe that all they had to do was take Montreal and then come home. Now they were going to have to continue the fight in Quebec. Sarah wondered to herself, "How long will this go on?"

On December fifth there was some excitement at the fort which she could write to John about. A very rotund man by the name of Colonel Knox had arrived at the fort with orders to take the cannon from the fort to Boston to help General Washington in the siege there. He and his men, along with men from the fort, dismounted all the cannon and loaded them onto sleds to get them to Lake George so they could be transported south. Although there had been snow, the weather was really quite mild for that time of year, so the lakes had not frozen over yet.

By this time Sarah had also taken over as the general's cook. Colonel Knox, of course, took his meals with the general so she had the opportunity to meet him. As she served the evening meal the two men discussed the war in general, and Boston and Canada in particular. Colonel Knox said that the siege of Boston was going well but these cannon were what were needed to push the British out of the city. Without these guns they were pretty much at a stalemate. That condition could not go on, as they knew that the British could ultimately get reinforcements in and things would change drastically. So he had to get the cannon to Boston most expeditiously so that the British must leave before any reinforcements could arrive. They discussed how the Colonel was going to get them down the lake and the difficulties he would face crossing the Hudson and getting the guns overland. Oddly, to Sarah, they were most worried about the fact that it had not been cold enough yet to freeze the water and ground, and that there was not enough snow for sleds to be pulled over. But Colonel Knox was both optimistic and determined that he would succeed in getting them to Boston.

The men went on talking as though she was not there. When General Schuyler began to talk about the battle for Quebec, Sarah's attention deepened. They had been eating at the table in the general's office, and as he spoke he got up and went to the maps. He showed the progress of General Montgomery's force and told about the taking of Montreal on November thirteenth.

Sarah already knew about that. She thought as she cleared the table as slowly as she could, “Get on with it. What is happening in Quebec?” What she was about to hear was not the news she was hoping for.

The general said that Colonel Arnold had arrived at the gates of Quebec on November thirteenth, but his original 1,100 man force had been reduced to only about 600 effectives. The march, disease, and desertion had depleted the rest. The general continued that Arnold had tried to get the city to surrender, and had for a short time blockaded it. But with only 600 men, and they not in the best condition, he moved them to Point Aux Trembles to await General Montgomery. According to General Schuyler, Montgomery had finally arrived with 300 men, some cannon he took from Montreal, and, maybe most importantly, winter clothing for the men.

Sarah wondered if John was a part of the 300 men who were with General Montgomery. But what she heard next gave her a great start. The general said, many of the enlistments were running out at the end of the month, and if Montgomery and Arnold were not able to convince many of the men to reenlist, all this effort might have been for naught.

Colonel Knox replied, “This is a problem we have throughout the army. We are constantly training a group of men only to have them leave in a few months and then train another group who will also leave. We must start calling for enlistments to be at least a year long, if not for the duration of this war. I hope General Montgomery is successful in getting many of these men to stay with him.”

Sarah almost dropped the dishes she had in her hands when

she heard the Colonel's words. Surely, she thought, John would not reenlist. He promised he would be back at the end of the year and he must keep his word. But something in the back of her mind told her that he might be one of the men to stay the course. Up until now she had not given it a thought. He never mentioned anything about reenlisting in his letters, so she had no reason to think about it. But now, after hearing Colonel Knox's words, she would not be able to get it out of her mind.

Sarah finished clearing the dishes and served the men coffee. But now she was almost in a daze as she thought about the Colonel's words and wondered what John was doing at this instant. Was he with them at Quebec or had he been one of the men to stay back at Montreal? More importantly, was he contemplating reenlisting? And if he was, what did it mean for her? How long was this to go on? The general looked at her and asked, "Mrs. Hardy, are you alright? You look a little pale. Is everything alright?"

She quickly snapped out of it and said, "Oh, I am sorry gentlemen. I guess I allowed my thoughts to wander to my husband as you were discussing the war. He is with General Montgomery in Canada right now, and your discussion just made me think of him."

Colonel Knox replied, "That is quite understandable, Mrs. Hardy. I hope nothing we said upset you."

Sarah said, "No, Colonel. I guess your conversation about Canada just made me think of John. I'm quite alright now. If you gentlemen do not need anything more I shall clean these dishes and be going."

General Schuyler said, "Of course. No, we are quite finished here. You may certainly go to your quarters. Thank you and have a good night, Mrs Hardy."

Colonel Knox said, "Yes, Thank you for this excellent meal, Mrs. Hardy. Good night."

Sarah said good night to them and went to wash up the dishes. She needed the time alone to think about what she had just heard. Try as she might, she could not bring herself to believe that John would not be coming home in a few weeks. Then she had another thought. Perhaps they would only need him until they had taken Quebec, and then he could be sent home. No, she knew that would not be the case. The more she thought, the more it became evident to her that John would not be coming home soon.

When she got back to the hut, she told the others what General Schuyler and Colonel Knox had said about the need for reenlistments. She said that she could not believe that John would do such a thing. After all, he told her he would be done in December.

At that Elizabeth took out a letter she had received from Edward. She said that she hoped she would not have to be the bearer of its news, but she thought she should share it now. In his letter, Edward told her that he had come to know both Jeremiah and John quite well. The discussion of their enlistments had come up several times over the course of the last month, and each of them believed they could not leave with the mission only half completed. They had all signed up for another year. They would be home just as soon as they had taken Quebec, and the war could not go on much longer after that, as the British would have to see that they could not win and negotiate for peace.

Silence filled the room. Sarah and Martha were, at the same time, both stunned and furious. How could John and Jeremiah do such a thing without consulting or at least telling them?

Mary had a frightened but knowing look on her face. She said, "Richard has a strong attachment to both Jeremiah and John, and if they have reenlisted he certainly would follow them without a second thought. From his letters, I think he loves them more than me." Sarah detected a sound of resentment in her voice, but said nothing.

Elizabeth looked around the room and said, "Well, ladies, what do we do now? The men have done made our decisions for us once again without even a by your leave. We can probably still take the army up on their offer to take us back down the lake. The weather isn't too bad and they are going to be moving those cannon in the next couple of days." "Or," she said with a kind of twinkle in her voice, "we can stay here 'til they come home, and after we ravage them with hugs and kisses, beat them to within an inch of their lives for being so inconsiderate and stupid. Which is it?"

They took a second, looked at each other, and then, in unison, shook their heads. Elizabeth had a way to take the edge off of almost any bad news. They knew there was nothing they could do to change what the men had done. And they also knew that they would stay for as long as it took. But Sarah was going to have her say to John, and sat down the next day and began writing a letter blistering him for not taking her into his confidence and at least discussing his reenlisting with her before he had done it. And even worse, she would tell him about the hurt she felt having to hear the news from Elizabeth instead of him. She knew she would not receive a reply from the letter before Christmas or even before the New Year, but she had to get her hurt and disappointment into words. But as she wrote she suddenly realized something. She wasn't crying. She was disappointed in John to be sure. But she wasn't upset. She did not know why. Maybe it was that somehow she had expected it. Or maybe she was starting to be a part of something she could still not define. Whatever it was, it caused her to choose her words differently as she wrote. She still let John know of her anger and disappointment but she softened it and finally she still ended with, "Your Loving Wife, Sarah."

Colonel Knox and his men left the fort on December ninth. Life settled back into a routine again and nothing much happened at the fort. The women had been making new stockings and warm clothes to send to the men as Christmas presents. They had finished everything and managed to get them sent with the courier in time to, hopefully, reach them by Christmas.

Sarah received a letter in the middle of the month, in which John told her he was indeed at Quebec. He also finally told her that he had reenlisted for another year. He was sorry that they could not have discussed it, but the time it took to send and receive letters just would not allow it. He went into great detail to explain the reasons behind it and to tell her that the war would surely be over before then and he would be discharged early anyway. The biggest reason was, of course, he could not leave the men he had gone through so much with, especially in this hour of great need. He could not leave with the job only half done. Sarah remembered Elizabeth saying that Edward would use those exact words when he told her that he had reenlisted.

Besides, now that they had combined forces with Colonel Arnold's, they surely would be victorious any day.

As usual, Sarah read the letter in private. But something was gone. He talked less about missing her and more about the army with each letter. She guessed she, like Mary, was a little jealous. She put the letter in her pocket and went back to work.

On Christmas day there was still bread that needed to be baked and the general still had to eat, so Sarah, Martha, and Mary went off to work as usual. Elizabeth remained home and prepared things to make the day as cheerful as possible.

At mid-afternoon the three women returned to the hut. Elizabeth had put up a few decorations and had even gone out and cut down a small pine tree and decorated it. When they looked at the tree they were amazed. Elizabeth said, "I hope none of you ladies are of a religious persuasion that don't like Christmas decorations. But I live with a great many Germans and they know how to celebrate a holiday. And to them and me, Christmas ain't Christmas without a decorated tree."

They had made each other small gifts to exchange, and they broke out food they had been saving from their rations. In addition to that food, Elizabeth managed to get a few things from the sutler's wagon, and as the general, in Sarah's estimation, could not possibly eat all that they gave her to cook for him, she managed to save some for their feast as well. To them it was a grand feast indeed. They had not eaten so well in some time. As they ate and chatted, the dismal world that surrounded them seemed to disappear for the moment. They all talked of memories of their favorite Christmas stories.

Elizabeth told about celebrating with Edward and her children and grandchildren.

Sarah talked about Christmas in her Mother's house. It was always warmer and brighter somehow at Christmas.

Martha told of Christmas with all the Germans in the Mohawk Valley in her youth. She said Elizabeth was right, the Germans really knew how to celebrate a holiday. After they married, she and Jeremiah usually had very quiet Christmases, as his family was much more reserved than hers. But they too were nice memories she cherished.

Mary sat quietly and listened. Then she told them once again how she was an orphan at a very young age and was brought up by an aunt and uncle in a very strict religious house. They did not celebrate holidays and thought the practice to be sinful. She said sadly, "I don't have much to contribute in the line of stories. As you might guess, as a child we didn't celebrate the holidays and this is my first Christmas since being married."

Elizabeth, trying to lighten the mood, said, "Well then, dearie, since this would be the first Christmas you'd be celebrating, let's make it your best Christmas. I have a little surprise for you ladies."

Martha replied, "Your tea isn't much of a surprise any more, Elizabeth. But it is always welcome."

"Why thank you very much dearie," Elizabeth responded. "But I have something even better. Have any of you women ever wondered why we are always excluded after supper when the men go off to their brandy and pipes?" They all nodded in agreement. "Me too. So a long time ago I sat down with Edward and discussed the issue. He brought out a bottle of Brandy and said, 'Woman, you think you want to try this? I guess it won't hurt nothing if you and me experiment a little together." He poured each of us a glass and we sat there and conversed over that drink for the better part of an hour. Well, the menfolk ain't here, but I have managed to procure a small sample of brandy from the sutler's store, and if you ladies are amenable to it I shall pour each of us a Christmas dram."

The other three looked at each other a little sheepishly, as though they were about to take part in some prohibited action that would surely damn them forever. Although they all had had glasses of wine and small amounts of hard cider, none of them had ever tasted brandy before. They did not know what to say.

Elizabeth said, "Come, come, ladies you are not about to commit a heinous crime. We are all grown women and we don't need anyone else's permission. Your menfolk do this all the time. Let us see what the enticement is." She poured each of them a small amount into their cup. She raised her cup and said, "To us, and all that we have accomplished these past few months together."

They all smiled at each other in their daring to take this step, touched cups and said, "To us." Then together they sipped the amber liquid. Mary quickly choked profusely as it burned its way down her throat. Sarah and Martha were little better in getting it down. Only Elizabeth drank it like she knew what to expect. They had only sipped a small amount of the contents of the cups. After that first sip they all put the cups down on the table and laughed once more. Martha said, "Elizabeth, I think I would prefer a cup of your tea. Men's taste buds must be nonexistent to like the taste of this stuff." Mary concurred.

Sarah thought the same thing, but something in her was rebellious this night, and she determined to finish the drink. Once it was down it warmed her in a way nothing else ever had. And the taste was not as bad as she first thought. Elizabeth poured herself and Sarah another drink and they sipped brandy as Martha and Mary drank tea.

Sarah opened the door to look out. She didn't know why. The brandy had warmed her. The night was bright and it was snowing ever so lightly. As she stared into the sky she said almost dreamily, "Look, it's snowing. I always love it when it snows on Christmas. It somehow makes things look right. I wonder where John is and what he is doing." The other women looked out the door with her. No one said anything more. Nothing more needed to be said.

The day had been a nice respite from the dreary life of the camp. But next morning they all were up and back at work as usual. The snow had continued all night, and by morning there were several inches on the ground. It was bright and clear and cold. Winter had arrived, and would be there for months to come. The routine continued into the New Year with no real news of what was going on in Quebec.

Nine

In January, as Sarah was cleaning the general's quarters, she overheard a report being given to him. The army had attacked Quebec in the early morning on New Year's Eve day and the attack had failed. General Montgomery had been killed and Colonel Arnold had a badly wounded leg. A Captain Morgan had taken over the attack until they were defeated. Captain Morgan and over 400 men had been taken captive. Then she heard, for the first, but certainly not for the last, time the frightening price of war: 60 men had been killed or wounded. They did not have the names as yet, but they would be in the next report. Arnold had reestablished his siege outside the walls of the city after the battle. He might yet be successful, someone said.

Sarah could listen no more. The officers were talking of numbers as though they did not represent human beings. One of those numbers could be John. She tried to think of something else, but all that went through her mind were questions. Was he dead or alive? Was he one of the prisoners? If so, what would happen to him? The torment was excruciating.

Sarah went off to find Elizabeth and tell her the news. Surely she would have a salve to help relieve this fear. But when she told Elizabeth what she had heard, she too was stricken with the same deep, dark fear of the unknown. Together they walked back to the hut and waited for Martha and Mary to return. Sarah told them about the battle and the numbers she had heard. The four of them sat silent for hours. None could eat anything, and that night they went to bed quietly, each with her own thoughts and fears roiling around inside her.

The days and the routine went on. Sarah performed her duties as if in a daze. Each evening with no news of their husbands the women ate sparingly in silence and almost immediately put themselves into bed where they could cry and pray in semi-privacy.

Then, a few days later, as she was cleaning, Major Cardin called her into his office. Sarah was almost afraid to go. She thought she knew what he was about to say, and although she needed to know, she did not want to hear it if it was the worst. She took a deep breath and went into his office and asked pensively, "Yes, Sir?"

Major Cardin looked at her with sympathy and said, "Mrs. Hardy, I know your husband was with General Montgomery in Quebec and that you have been worried about him since the attack. I have the casualty report, and I am happy to tell you that his name is not on it. He is still with Colonel Arnold, but from what we know he is all right. I hope this news helps you."

She looked at the major with tears in her eyes and could only whisper, "Thank you." She thought she was going to faint. The major pulled a chair over to her and she sat down. She was so relieved and happy she could not speak. But then she realized the news was not enough. She could not go back to the hut and tell the women that her husband was safe but she had no knowledge of theirs. Nor could she keep it within her. She had to explode with the joy she felt at this moment. Instead she regained her voice and said, "Major, I am very grateful to you for giving me this news. But I must ask another favor of you."

He asked, "Of course, what else can I do for you?"

"There are a dozen women here whose husbands are there. They too have been tormented by not knowing. I cannot go back to them knowing that my husband is safe and not be able to tell them what has happened to theirs. If I give you the names of the women, could you tell me what has become of their husbands? Someone must tell them before they go crazy with anxiety. If I must, I will be that one."

Major Cardin looked at her in amazement. He truly had not thought about who was going to notify the women. He had only thought of Sarah because he saw and talked to her every day. One statement she had said stuck in his mind; someone had to tell these women what had happened to their husbands. She pleadingly looked at him as he contemplated what to do. At last, he decided that it would probably be best for all concerned if a woman were to inform the other women of any bad news. So he told her, "I'm not sure if this is authorized, but I believe you are right. Please write down the names of the women you speak of and I will look up their husband's names on the casualty list and give their status to you. You can then tell each of them." He hesitated then asked, "Mrs. Hardy, are you sure you want to do this?"

Sarah nodded her head silently. The enormity of what she had just volunteered to do invaded her brain. She took a quill from him and quickly wrote down the women's names. As he searched the lists she silently said a prayer, "Please God, let them all be safe. If not, please give me the strength to do this mercifully."

As he found each husband's name he scratched down something next to a woman's name on Sarah's list. Finally, he completed the list. As he handed it to her he asked again, "Are you sure you want this duty, Mrs. Hardy? The army could send someone else to inform the women."

Sarah looked at him helplessly. She reached out and took the list from him and said, "No, Major, this is one thing we must do for ourselves. Whatever the news, it must be given with the sympathy of one who can feel what a woman feels. I'm afraid the man the army would send to do it might not be able to do that." She took a deep breath and took the list from him.

She went down the list quickly to find Martha, Elizabeth, and Mary's husbands' condition. All of them had made it through unscathed. Once again she sighed in relief. Then she looked at the other names. Of the other eight, one had been captured, one had been wounded, and—she stared at the piece of paper in disbelief—one had been killed. The rest were unharmed.

She looked up and asked if he could tell her anything more about where prisoners had been taken or what was being done to take care of the wounded.

He told her that he had no idea yet where the prisoners

would be taken, but in time, through negotiations, that information would become available. As for the wounded, the seriously wounded would be evacuated to a hospital in the rear. The slightly wounded would be treated there and sent back into the line. He did not know how seriously the one man had been wounded. He then looked at her and addressed the one question that had not been asked. "The dead will be buried in Canada," he said solemnly. "There is no other way."

Sarah sighed once more, thanked him again for his understanding, and left the office. As usual, her first thought was to find Elizabeth. She would know what to do and how to do it. When she found her she burst out with the news that Major Cardin had given her that Edward, Jeremiah, and Richard were all right.

Elizabeth said "Thank God." Then she saw that Sarah had much more on her mind.

Sarah showed her the list and asked, "How am I going to tell these women what has happened to their husbands?"

Elizabeth took Sarah in her arms and quietly said, "You are not going by yourself. We will tell Martha and Mary the good news about Jeremiah and Richard, then we all will go together." They went back to the hut and waited for Martha and Mary to return.

When they came in Sarah told them the good news about their husbands. Then she told them that she had volunteered to deliver the news, both good and bad, to the rest of the women. Martha looked from Sarah to Elizabeth and asked, "What is the bad news?"

Sarah told her about the casualty list, and that one husband had been killed while another was wounded and a third was taken prisoner.

Elizabeth then said, "Martha, we cannot let Sarah do this alone. We must go with her." Martha agreed immediately.

Mary was hesitant to respond, of which Sarah was instantly aware. She thought, "This girl is barely eighteen, and in a few short months she has experienced more of life than many ever will." She said to Mary, "Though you are certainly welcome to come I think you may serve a very useful purpose here, Mary. This is going to be a very painful visit for at least three women and they will need some nourishment later in the evening. If you would be so kind as to stay here and prepare some soup and coffee to take to them later I think they would appreciate it."

Mary looked relieved. "Of course, if you think that is best, I will be happy to do as you ask."

With that the three of them left and went next door to inform the women there about the news. As she opened the door to Sarah's knock the woman seeing the three of them said hesitantly, "Good evening ladies. What can we do for you?"

Sarah asked, "May we come in, Helen? We have some news from Quebec that we need to share with all of you."

Helen opened the door wide and the women stepped into the hut. The other residents of the hut were sitting at the table in the center of the room and looked up questioningly. Helen apologized for not having somewhere to sit. But Sarah said, "That's alright, we all have the same predicament."

Sarah told them how she came about having the status of the men, then she told Helen and two of the other women that their husbands were fine. When she came to the last women she said that she was sorry to have to inform her that her husband had been wounded. She did not know how severely or where he was at the moment. She then told her what the major had said about how the wounded would be handled. Sarah said that they hoped to have more information on the wounded and prisoners later, but that was all she had at the moment.

The woman burst into tears and her house mates rushed to her side to comfort her. In a few minutes she got control of herself and thanked Sarah for bringing the news. She said, "I thank God that he is alive. I have been at wit's end worrying about him. Now I know he is alive, but I worry about how he is being cared for. My trial will go on until I see him for myself." Then she began to sob again. One of the other women took Sarah, Martha, and Elizabeth outside and thanked them again for bringing the news. She said, "I know how difficult this visit must be for you. We will care for Jane and get her through this. Let's hope the doctors don't finish the job the British started."

Martha nodded and said, "If there is anything we can do, let us know. We are all in this together, and we must be strong for each other." The woman nodded and went back into the hut.

The last hut was the one that Sarah dreaded the most. As the woman opened the door she took a startled step back. Sarah asked if they might come in, and they were allowed. Here Sarah thought she needed to talk to the woman whose husband had died first. When she told her the news the woman sank away from everyone as her tears began to flow. She screamed, "No, no, no! It cannot be. There must be a mistake. They have got the name wrong. Something, anything. He cannot be dead." After a few minutes she asked no one in particular, "What will I do?

I have no one. I have no place to go. Lord help me, what will I do?"

Elizabeth and Martha tried to comfort the woman as Sarah took the other women outside and told them about their husbands. The one whose husband had been captured cried. Then she said, "I'm crying because he's alive, and finally at least I know it. It's been so hard. I still fear for his safety, but at least I know he is still alive. Thank you Sarah. Oh, my God, we have to get to Rebecca! What do we say? How can we help her?" With that they left Sarah and ran back into the house.

Martha and Elizabeth slowly walked out of the hut. As the three of them walked back to their hut they were all silent, each lost in her own thoughts. For no reason and without thinking they took each other's hands and squeezed them tight. Sarah wondered, "Did I do the right thing, asking to be the one to tell these women? Did I say things right? Did I cause more pain than I needed to? What if I'm the one who gets the bad news next? Who will bring it to me? Will I be strong when I hear it?" As she walked she could not feel the cold. She could not feel anything but the pain she felt for the women she had just talked to.

When they got back Mary had made some soup for them to eat. None of them were hungry, but they sat down and sipped at it just to be doing something so they would not have to speak. Finally, Sarah broke the silence. "I am worried that I should not have taken on this task, that I hurt the women more than I helped them. Did I do it for me or for them? Did they think that I was doing it just because John was not hurt and maybe I was gloating? Tell me, what should I have done?" She was almost in tears.

Elizabeth broke in, “Sarah, I watched you all evening. You were wonderful. You did exactly the right thing. And no one could have delivered the news you had to deliver any better. If the army had sent a male messenger, I assure you he would not have been as kind and gentle as you were. As for worrying about what someone might think now, don’t. You made a decision to do this. You carried it out as best you could and that is that. The Good Lord knows what you had to do was not easy and He also knows that you did it with only good intentions. Do not worry yourself about what others think afterwards.”

Martha agreed with Elizabeth. The she turned to her and said, “I was surprised that you did not say anything all evening, Elizabeth.”

Elizabeth gave a wry smile and good-naturedly asked, “Martha, are you trying to say I talk too much?”

Martha stuttered, “No, no... I... I...”

“That’s alright. Sometimes I most likely do. But this night there was no one who could say what needed sayin’ better’n Sarah. Anything I might have added would just have been me talking to hear myself talk. And nobody needed that tonight.”

Ten

Later in the month Sarah received a letter from John. He said that they had received the packages and thanked her profusely for the clothes. He said that many of the men were without any proper clothing for the winter they were going through, and the suffering was excruciating. He went on and told her he and Jeremiah and the company had been with General Montgomery on the Plains of Abraham when the general was killed. He had escaped without any major damage to himself, but there were casualties, as she probably knew by now. They were now with Colonel Arnold in a kind of siege. But with so few men he did not see how it could last for very long unless reinforcements arrived before the British were reinforced. They did expect some help to arrive any day now. Conditions were miserably cold and the snow was exceedingly great. It was a trial just to stay alive, let alone think of trying to take that walled city again. Finally, he told her that he loved her and missed her and could not wait to get back to see her, and signed it, "Your Affectionate Husband, John."

After she finished reading it she put the letter together with the others she was saving and stored them all away in a small box she had found. She sat and thought about the misery John was going through and felt sorry for him. Then she looked around and sighed to herself, thinking maybe he would hear her through the miles, "John, my love, things ain't much better here." She looked at the dress she was wearing. When she arrived in August it was almost new. Now it was a patchwork of mends. To keep warm she had layers of anything she could find that might have been discarded by the men to put on under it. Her cloak was still decent and helped against the cold and served as a second blanket at night. But her shoes had holes in the soles, which she fixed by putting leaves or paper, when she could find it, in them. The mends didn't last long, so she often walked around with her feet feeling the cold and wetness of the ground directly.

As the winter continued sickness invaded the fort. Many of the men were stricken with influenza. The women were drafted into working in the hospital as nurses. "Nurse" was a title they were given but there was really no nursing about it. They scrubbed the floors of the hospital and changed bed pans and cleaned up the men's vomit and excrement. They also helped feed and bathe those who could not help themselves.

At first Sarah balked at having to bathe the men. The sight of the naked men embarrassed her, and Martha too, she supposed. Sarah had seen her brothers naked and, of course, John, but she had never thought that she would be bathing complete strangers and tending to their personal needs in such a way. Elizabeth noticed their reluctance and once again came to the rescue. "Ladies, these men ain't got nothin you ain't seen before. And right now they need you to bathe them like they was little boys. Believe me, they ain't got the strength to be wondering 'bout what you are touching on them. All they are feeling is the coolness of that rag you are washing them with. So put away your prudish modesty and get to washing." Sarah looked at Martha and they both giggled at Elizabeth's practical crudeness. Soon the bathing too became routine.

There was little else they could do as there was no medicine. After a few days one man died. Then several more. Then more, until Sarah stopped counting.

One evening, upon returning to the hut from the hospital, they found Mary in bed writhing and sweating profusely. They knew immediately that she too had contracted the disease. They took turns trying to break her fever with rags cooled by water they got by melting snow. No one slept that first night, and they all feared that Mary would not make it through. They put their blankets over her and built the fire up to help keep her warm, for they knew that after the fever she would be shaking with the cold. No one wanted to leave her alone, but they all had to go to work. During the day each of them found time to sneak away and check in on her. She fitfully drifted in and out of sleep. Finally, after a few days Mary awoke. She was weak and unable to eat, but she seemed to be better. The sickness went on until one day she was able to get up on her own and get some food down. She looked like death. This lovely young girl had become emaciated from lack of food and was a disheveled mess. The women bathed her and washed her hair. After a few more days she was able to return to her duties at the bakery.

The outbreak ended almost as quickly as it had started. Finally, in mid-February the hospital was empty except for the usual injuries and sicknesses that attended an army camp. Sarah did not know how many had died. She did not want to know. Every day during the outbreak they buried one or two men, sometimes more. She was tormented by the helplessness she felt over the fact that nothing she did could have prevented it.

The women were relieved from nursing and returned to their normal jobs. Mary had fully recovered, and the women were grateful that none of the other women had taken ill. But the experience had taken a toll on all of them. They were all tired, and winter still had months to go before it ended.

In her letters to John, Sarah did not talk about the misery they were going through at the fort. He did not need any more worries to add to his burdens. She tried to be positive and say that things were fine. The letters, however, were getting shorter because she could not find it in her to continue to make up conditions that were not true. Better to say nothing than lie, she thought.

John's letters, too, became shorter and shorter, and they also became fewer and fewer. By the end of February she had received only one more letter, and that only a few lines.

One day something happened that caught Sarah by surprise. The woman whose husband had been killed in the battle had married another soldier at the fort. She had moved out of the huts and into his quarters. "How," Sarah wondered aloud, "could that be? Her husband died just two months ago. What kind of woman is this?"

Elizabeth explained, "She has no one. If she did not marry a soldier she would be sent away from the camp. You can only remain at the fort if you are related to a soldier. She has nowhere else to go. Don't look down on her, Sarah, she is trying to stay alive."

Sarah had never given that a thought before. This war got crueler at every turn. How many other women were in the same position as this poor woman? Did marriage really have anything to do with love? Or was it just a means of survival? She wondered what she would do if she ever got that terrible message about John.

In late March she received a letter from John that said that some reinforcements were starting to arrive and that they were hopeful to be able to force the city to capitulate soon. Later in the month they also got word from Boston that Colonel Knox had been successful in getting the cannon to General Washington, and that right after they had been put in place General Howe had abandoned the city. Everyone at the fort was elated. Spirits rose greatly. Finally, a victory. Now all they needed to hear was that the men in Canada would be equally successful after all their trials. Maybe there would be an end to this war.

April brought another new experience Sarah's way. One of the women in another hut was pregnant, and was about to deliver her baby. She had not given it any thought before, but counting back the months, Sarah could have easily been in the position of this woman at this moment. She had no idea what she would do with a baby had it happened to her.

The only woman among them who had actually had a child

was Elizabeth. She was elected to be the midwife. She asked Sarah to assist her. Although she had watched on the farm as animals gave birth, Sarah had never seen a child's birth before. Elizabeth told her not to worry, it was all natural and all she would have to do is follow instructions.

The day came and Elizabeth and Sarah went into the hut and all the other women were shooed out. All of the women from the three huts were there, pacing outside the little hut like expectant fathers. Sarah boiled some water to clean the table and pair of scissors. She washed down the table and she and Elizabeth assisted the woman to get on it. Sarah watched in amazement as Elizabeth calmly talked the woman through her screams and had her breathe and push at just the right moments.

Finally, the head of the baby popped out, followed by the rest of his body. Elizabeth cut the cord and cleared his airways. He burst out with a shout and a healthy cry. As Elizabeth cleaned off the baby, Sarah cleaned up the mother. Elizabeth placed him in a blanket that the women from the hut had made for him, then, she placed him in his mother's arms. Sarah thought about the miracle she had played a part in and how wonderful it was and, for the first time in a long time, she dreamed of the day when she would hold her own baby in her arms.

The days went on with no further word from Quebec. April brought spring, and a warming which finally started the snows melting, but with it came rain. Day upon day of rain turned the camp and the fort into a quagmire of mud. Just trudging from the hut to the fort to work half covered Sarah's dress with mud, and she worked through the day constantly damp. By the time work had ended she was almost dry, only to have to go through the same experience on the return trip. Finally one morning broke bright and sunny and warm. The women swept out all the straw from the floor. They took the straw out of the mattresses and hung out all the bedding to air. Mary and Martha went to the stables and got new straw for the mattresses and the floor while Sarah and Elizabeth got water ready to wash all their clothes.

When Martha and Mary returned, Elizabeth commanded, "Alright ladies, strip down. We are going to wash everything we own here." They started to protest but knew it would be of no use, so off came their clothes. They threw them in a pile and Elizabeth continued, "While I'm washing these clothes you ladies wash yourselves in that other bucket of water I got ready for you." She pointed to a second pot filled with hot water. The three of them stood there looking at each other in amazement. They had all found private moments during the winter to wash themselves as best they could, but never all together. Finally, Sarah said, "Well, I'm not going to miss this chance to get clean for a change." Soon the three of them were scrubbing each other's backs and washing each other's hair and playing and laughing like school girls. They looked at Elizabeth and then at each other, and all at once they grabbed her and poured water over her and scrubbed her too. She at first resisted, but quickly succumbed and laughed with the rest. They had to drip dry, but it didn't matter. For the first time in months they had an enjoyable moment, and were able to forget the drudgery of their lives. They put the clothes they were going to wear near the fireplace to dry quickly. The others would be dried outside once they got back into some clothes. As they waited for their clothes to dry Mary sheepishly said, "I hope no one comes to the door while we look like this." They all looked at each other once more and burst into laughter once again.

"Well, if anyone does I hope it's some good looking men. This poor ole body has not been gazed upon by a man since Edward left and it's starting to feel neglected," joked Elizabeth. They all were in a silly mood and playfully agreed.

Soon the warm sun dried out the mud and the days began to get longer. April turned to May and the vegetation started to bloom. The women started gardens behind the huts, and everyone took turns tending them. Sarah especially enjoyed her time in the garden. It reminded her of her youth and working beside her mother in the garden back home. She had not heard from her mother in several months, and worried that something might be wrong. There were a lot of Tories down there and Sarah worried, with her father and older brother both gone, whether her mother and siblings would be safe. But she knew there was nothing she could do to help if anything were wrong.

In May she heard from Major Cardin that the siege would soon be over. Not because the Americans were going to take the city, but because the British had given General Carlton reinforcements. They now outnumbered the Americans better than two to one. The men could not hold out against such odds. They would begin a retreat soon.

Sarah had conflicting feelings. On one hand, she felt elated. This would mean that John would soon be coming back. Maybe he might even be done with the army then. But on the other hand, she had a feeling of rage. Those men had been through so much. They had been told they would be reinforced so that they could take Quebec. Men had died. Not just those from the

New Year's Eve battle, but others before and since. Was it all for nothing? She did not understand what was going on. She felt this defeat personally, and she could not reconcile herself to it even in wanting to see John as badly as she did.

Once again she felt helpless. The army would do as it wanted, so she contented herself with thoughts of John's return.

The fort became a beehive of activity in preparation for the arrival of the men. Tents were erected in regimental formations and supplies were coming in. One day in June they were told that the men had reached Crown Point, only ten miles away. The men would be at the fort the next day.

Eleven

That night Sarah hardly slept at all. As she tossed she thought, "This certainly isn't improving my looks any." But the anticipation of seeing John again was too much and kept her awake. She wondered if the other women were having the same problem. She finally drifted into a light doze and was awake, up, and dressed at the first sign of dawn.

Sarah, and the rest of the women, spent the day primping. It had been nine months since they had seen their men. A woman from another hut had a mirror, and every woman wanted to use it to get herself ready.

When it was her turn to use the mirror Sarah hardly recognized the woman she was looking at. When she had arrived at Fort Ticonderoga in August she was a young, fresh-faced girl. But the woman she was looking at was worn and tired. How could she have aged so in such a short time? She started to feel sorry for herself, but then quickly told herself that there was nothing she was going to be able to do about it in the next few hours. She smiled at the thought of seeing John again, and the smile made her at least feel young again.

None of the women, and seemingly no one else either, knew exactly when the men would be arriving. But as the women went through their usual morning work there was an air of excitement throughout the fort and the camp. Finally, about noon, no one could stand it any longer, and everyone drifted down to the waterside to wait for the arrival of the boats.

As Sarah saw the first boat on the horizon her heart almost stopped. Then, one by one, more appeared. As they got closer to the shore she strained to see John. At first she could not make out any of the faces. They were all a blur. Slowly the boats came closer, but she could not find him on any of the decks. At last they docked, and men stepped off the boats. Many had to be carried.

What Sarah and the other women saw broke their hearts. One could hear the sound as they collectively caught their breaths at the first close sight of the men. Sarah grabbed Martha's hand and squeezed it painfully in disbelief. The men were all dressed in rags, and many had no shoes. They were filthy with dirt and lice, and covered with sores. A sickening stench came from the boats. Still, they were back, and Sarah only wanted to hug John.

But in typical army fashion, the men couldn't just be released. There had to be a formation. They left the boats, and those that could, formed up as units. Finally, she and Martha saw John and Jeremiah at the front of their company. Sarah could hardly recognize John. He looked emaciated. His face was gaunt and yellowish, and what clothes he had just hung on his skeletal body. She started to cry. Her tears were both for the condition that John was in as well as tears of joy at seeing him again at last. She wanted to run to him and throw her arms around him and hug him tighter than she had ever done before. The formation only took a few minutes, but it seemed like an eternity to Sarah. Finally, the soldiers were released. The wives who had been waiting rushed toward their husbands. The reunion was joyous for everyone.

The other men walked slowly off to the camp areas. There were no huzzahs. The only sound was of their feet shuffling along and a few murmurs as they talked to each other.

John and Sarah melted into each other's arms and she smothered him with kisses she had been saving all these months. The dirt, the smell, nothing mattered; he was back and he was safe, and that was all that mattered at that moment. There were words between them because there had to be. Through their kisses they mumbled to each other, "I've missed you so much," and, "I love you." But all that mattered was the feel of each other as they clung together.

At last John broke the embrace, stepped back and said, "Sarah, you are the most beautiful sight I have ever seen. I have dreamed of this moment a million times. Your beauty exceeds my wildest dreams."

Sarah blushed and said, "Oh, John, stop. I looked at myself in the mirror and I know I look terrible. But your return, I'm sure, has brightened my appearance." She did not comment on his looks.

John, however, did. "I can't imagine what you must be thinking as you look at me. I must look like a skeleton to you, and before I do anything I will have me a bath to wash this dirt and stink off me."

At that she looked at him and said with a smile and a little glint in her eye, "That would be very nice, dear. If you don't mind, let's find someplace private and I'll help you."

He looked around at the hundreds of men roaming throughout the camp and said, "Umm, finding a private place may take some doing. But I need to go see to the men getting settled into their tents first. It will only take a little while, and then we will find that place."

Sarah thought, "Oh no, not another army 'little while,' not today." But he took her hand and they walked to the area where his company's tents had been placed. He found Jeremiah and they drifted off alone toward the fort in a discussion, leaving Sarah and Martha standing there. Jeremiah turned and said, "While you're waiting, why don't you ladies go get your things. When we get back we'll show you which tents we'll be in."

The women looked at each other in amazement. Martha said with a little huff, "What, after all these months, could be more important than us?"

They looked at the tents all lined up in regimental formation, and for the first time the women realized that they would not be living together any more. They would be moving into the tents with their husbands and their mess mates. They would all have to move out of the hut they had shared these long months. Sarah no longer thought of it as a hut. To her it was now home, and for a moment she was sad to think that they would no longer be living in it. For better or worse, their lives would be changing again.

When they arrived at the hut Elizabeth was there. Mary had come, collected her things, and left with Richard already. Elizabeth said, "Well, dearies, how do your menfolk look after all this waitin'? I have to tell you Edward looks a little worse for wear. But I think I can fix that."

Sarah responded, "I would like to say John looks wonderful. But he's so thin, and he looks worn out. And they are all so dirty. It was heartbreaking to watch them come off those boats. But I think you're right, Elizabeth. There's nothing wrong with him that a good bath and some loving can't fix."

Martha added, "And the stench! Have you ever smelled anything like that? It'll take a week of scrubbing to get that off Jeremiah, and I'm not sure of it even then."

Elizabeth looked at her with a mischievous smile on her face and said, "Maybe so Martha, but I am sure that won't keep us from loving them up later today. That is, if we can ever get them in private and away from the army." Then her face changed and she asked, "I wonder what it is that was so important that all the officers and sergeants were off to meetings so quickly after landing?"

The thought passed without comment and Elizabeth looked around the hut. "We will have to figure out what to do with all this stuff we have collected. How will we divide it up? Looking at it all, it's not hard to understand now why the men left so much when they took off last August. It's amazing what you can collect in such a short time. We sure won't be able to move it all into the luxury accommodations we are about to share with our husbands and their friends."

Martha asked, "Do we really need to divvy it up now? Why

don't we just take what we will need for tonight and then come back tomorrow and arrange things when we are not so excited and anxious. No one will steal it tonight." Then added, "Will they?"

Sarah agreed and then went on, "I know it's not very lady-like, but I was wondering if we might not be able to arrange to use the hut to get some of that privacy you were talking about earlier. No one has told us we had to move out yet so I think the place is still ours until they do. Until then we should use it to our best advantage. Don't you agree?"

Elizabeth and Martha agreed. So they conspired to set a schedule where each of them would have the hut to themselves and their husbands. Martha then asked, "What about Mary? Shouldn't we include her in these plans?"

"Yes we should," said Elizabeth. "Let's put a time in for her and Richard and I will find her and let her know what we're doing."

They all collected a few things to take to their respective tents and went on their way.

When Sarah and Martha got back to the company area, John and Jeremiah were just returning from their meeting in the fort. They put their arms around the women and John said, "Ladies, we are yours for the rest of the day."

"And it's about time, too." said Sarah.

Martha and Jeremiah walked off to his tent and Sarah went with John to the tent they were to share with his mess mates. Sarah was glad to see that two of them were men who she had shared the tent with in August. William Johnson and Ben Gruber were going to share the tent once again. Sarah asked, "Where is Thomas? Why is he not with you also?"

The men looked at each other somberly and John explained, "Sarah, Thomas died from the typhoid up in Canada."

Sarah was shocked and ashamed. She had only had Major Cardin check the casualty list for men who were married to the women there. She did not know what to say. There was an uneasy moment that Ben relieved by saying, "We got a new mess mate though, Sarah. Let me introduce Joseph Reed, the newest member of this august group of sergeants. Sarah, Joseph. Joseph, Sarah."

Joseph step forward and said, "Pleased to meet you ma'am. John has told us so much about you, I almost feel like I know you already."

Sarah smiled and said, "It's a pleasure to meet you Joseph." Not knowing what else to say she followed with, "I only had the—ah… pleasure…of spending one night with William and Ben here. I hope we all get to spend a great deal more time together this time."

The men all laughed and said they hoped so too.

Then she looked at John and said, "I hope you gentlemen will excuse us but, John, I believe you said we have an appointment to make. Don't we?"

John actually blushed and stuttered, "Why … uh…yes …we do dear. Let's go."

The men all smirked in silence. Sarah knew what they were thinking. She didn't care. She just wanted John to herself. She led John off by the hand. She carried a package with her as they walked. She knew exactly where she was taking him.

As they headed down toward the lake, Sarah was at first

startled at what she saw. Hundreds of naked men were joyfully playing and washing in the lake. At first she tried to avoid looking at them but soon realized that there was no way to avoid it. The sight of them only raised her desire to see John in the same condition.

John, too, was a little embarrassed. He said, "I'm sorry you have to see that, Sarah. But the men really need to bathe."

She looked at him and smiled, "Don't be sorry dear. It's not the worst thing I've ever seen. And besides, you are right. They all dearly need a bath. But there is only one naked man I am interested in seeing today." She blushed as she said it. She never thought herself capable of being so forward. They looked at each other, she kissed him on the cheek and they hurried on.

Sarah took John to a spot she had found early in her stay at the fort. She had never shared it, not even with the other women. This was where she would come to read his letters or just to be alone with her thoughts and prayers. This was her place. Now it was going to be their place.

Where she stopped was a small clearing completely sheltered by the trees on three sides. In front of them was the lake. The lake was perfectly still and reflected like a mirror in the June sunshine. Across the lake the Green Mountains majestically rose, painted in multiple shades of green that could only be found there. Above them a hawk floated through the air, lazily catching the currents. The sounds of the camp were far off. It was just them, alone. Sarah was thinking, "I want this man so much. Is what I feel right now the sin of lust? If it is then I will gladly be a sinner and repent some other time."

Sarah looked up at John's gaunt face and touched it with one hand. Then she pulled his head down and kissed him deeply. When they parted she said, "I think you said you needed a bath. I brought you some soap." She undressed him then herself. She took him by the hand and walked him to the lake. The lake, as always, was icy cold, but it felt wonderful to Sarah and only made her feel more alive. They splashed each other playfully and laughed. She then took the soap from him and began to scrub the dirt from his body and the hurt from his soul. He closed his eyes as she washed all of him ever so slowly. Even the coldness of the water could not hide his desire for her. He took her hand and led her to the bank. They fell to the ground in each other's arms and unleashed pent up cravings that Sarah could never have imagined existed.

After, they lay together in the sun, not talking, just savoring what they had just experienced. For a few brief moments, there was no army and there was no war. Only the two of them together like they had never been before. Her thoughts about whether her feelings could be sinful came back. But she quickly repulsed them and said to herself with a smile, "No, nothing that feels this wonderful could be sinful. It can only be a gift from heaven. Thank you, God."

After a while they got up and went back into the water and washed each other again. When they were rinsed they walked out and Sarah went to the package she had carried with her. She handed it to John and said, "Welcome home, darling."

It was a new set of clothes she had made for him. Shirt, breeches, stockings, and waistcoat. He looked at her with pride and love and said, "Sarah, they're beautiful. I will be the best dressed sergeant in the regiment. Thank you." He hurriedly put them on.

As they dressed, she thought, "Soon this war has to be over and I will be able to go home and build a life together with this man."

He looked up and said, "They fit perfect Sarah. Thank you so much. I feel like a new man."

She chided him, "Is that all that made you feel like a new man?"

He smiled at her, took her hand, and they strolled back to camp. As they walked Sarah smiled and thought to herself, "Guess I won't be needing the privacy of the hut after all."

Twelve

When they got back to the tent, the men immediately noticed John had bathed and was dressed in his new clothes. They seemed not to notice Sarah as they razzed him unmercifully about them and about what he had been doing. She took it all in, and thought, "These men are really close. They're almost like a family of brothers."

Ben noticed John's eyes and said, "Oh, sorry, Sarah, forgot you was there. Did you make those clothes for John? They really are nice."

Sarah tried to look ladylike and properly offended, although she really wasn't. She then lightened the moment by responding, "Yes I did, Ben. Thank you. And by the way gentlemen, since we will all be sleeping in the same tent together, it wouldn't hurt you any to go down to the lake and introduce yourselves to soap and water also." Then she smiled and added, "However, I'm afraid you'll have to do it by yourselves, as I'll be busy cooking supper."

The men looked at each other and then everyone burst out laughing. Ben said, "Well, Sarah, I reckon we could use a little scrubbing at that. And with a lady's offer to cook supper in the mix, how could we refuse? But we ain't got no fancy duds to put on afterwards like John here. These will have to do."

Sarah looked at them and said, "John, why don't you go down to the lake with them and bring their clothes back up here and I'll wash them. There's no sense taking a bath and then putting dirty clothes back on."

Ben asked, "What'll we wear while you're washing our clothes?"

Sarah answered, "First of all, take a good long bath. And take blankets with you gentlemen. I'll be as quick as I can at getting those things clean."

The men went off to the lake and Sarah went back to the hut and picked up the laundry pot. When she got back John had returned with the clothes and had already got a fire started. She set the water to boil. While they were waiting for the water to boil, John said, "Thank you for this Sarah. The men really appreciate it." He paused and then continued, "You know, it's been a long time since any of us has had someone to fuss over us, and if we are a little rough it's just because we've been all men together for months with no women to keep us under control. I just want you to know they don't mean no harm, and I appreciate your kindness towards them. We'll all get better now we're back in civilization. But it may take a little doing."

Sarah looked at her poor emaciated husband and thought about the trials he and the others had been through. She said,

"John, the only thing I care about is that you—and they—are back and safe. We women have been in this army camp since last August. There isn't much we haven't seen or heard in that time. And I'm beyond getting embarrassed over men being rough in my presence. I know they will try to do right, and that is all I can ask. Now, let me get these clothes washed, or they will be back up here parading around in the altogether."

She finished washing the clothes, handed them to John and said, "They're still wet, but at least they're clean. Tell them to let them dry a little before they put them on. Supper will be a little while yet."

John went off and she began fixing supper. She knew this would be the first good meal the men had had in a long time, and she wanted it to be special. The women had been collecting herbs and vegetables for several weeks. The night before the men arrived Martha and Mary had brought several loaves of bread from the bakery also. While they were at the hut earlier, they divided up the vegetables and bread. Sarah had also confiscated some butter from the general's larder.

She made a stew with the rations and vegetables. In a little while the men came walking up to the tent. As they sat down to eat the stew, she handed out the fresh bread and butter. The men were overwhelmed, but too hungry to say anything. They devoured the meal as Sarah had never seen anyone eat before. When they were done there was nothing left. Sarah was so fascinated watching them eat that she failed to get any for herself. Only when they had finished did Joseph say, "Sarah, you didn't get any for yourself. We should be ashamed of ourselves. I'm very sorry we were so thoughtless. But honestly, that was maybe the best meal I have ever eaten."

Sarah looked at him and said, "Thank you, Joseph. Do not bother yourselves that I didn't get any. Just the satisfaction of watching you men eat like that was enough to satisfy me. Besides you know a cook never serves food she hasn't tasted beforehand. I got plenty in putting this meal together," she lied.

It was a warm June evening, and as Sarah cleaned up the dishes the men got comfortable in front of the fire and lit their pipes. When she was finished, Sarah sat and listened as the men talked about the campaign. They talked about the bravery of Montgomery and Arnold and of a captain from Virginia by the name of Morgan. They spoke of their disappointment in the failure of most of the Canadians to fight on their side. Some did, but most did not. They also brought up the deserters, and their hatred for them—even greater than they had for the Tories. They believed they should have been able to take Quebec, and if it hadn't been for General Montgomery getting killed and Arnold being so severely wounded they would have. They were bitter that reinforcements hadn't arrived in large enough numbers, or in time, to complete the mission.

Ben said bitterly, "I hear this fellow, Washington, has left Boston with his part of the army and is on his way down to defend New York City. I wonder if they'll have any problem getting reinforcements if they need them. Probably not. When you got the commander of the whole army I don't suppose you want for anything. What's he going to defend New York from? There ain't no British Army there, just a whole bunch of Tories. It shouldn't take mor'n a regiment or two to go down there and kill all those bastards." He looked at Sarah and sheepishly said,

"Sorry, Sarah, pardon my language." She nodded but did not say anything. He finished, "Then he could send the rest of the army up here where we're fighting a real war like he shouda done when we was at Quebec. If we had gotten reinforcements we would have taken that God damned place, and this war would be over."

William interjected, "Well, Ben, maybe we should send you down there to New York to be a strategic advisor to General Washington. I can't say I understand what's going on either, but I don't think I would want his job neither. It looks to me like he's caught between a rock and a hard place. That British army that left Boston last March didn't go back to England. So they got to go somewhere to fight. We already know what Carleton has up here and it don't include Howe's part of the army. General Howe has got some face to save after Boston, and I reckon New York is as good a place as any to do it."

Then John interjected. "Gentlemen, there ain't much use in our worrying about General Washington and those boys in New York. We got our own problems. And like Ben says, we probably won't get no help from down south to solve 'em. Carleton will be on his way down Lake Champlain with his whole army soon, if he's not already. They have to move their ships from the St. Lawrence over to the lake, and that will take some time, but he'll be coming this summer for sure. General Arnold says a man by the name of Schuyler, probably a relative of the general, is in charge of building new ships for us over at Skenesborough. When they are done we'll most likely try to head Carleton off further up North. So we'll probably become sailors in the near future, gentlemen."

Ben then added, "I don't know nothing about being a sailor, but I do know that this fort ain't ready for an attack by the Redcoats. I figure we will mor'n likely be put to work as engineers, rebuilding this fort and making it ready for an attack. It'll take a lotta work. This place is in terrible shape. Didn't they do nothing while we was gone, Sarah?"

Sarah was startled at the question. Of course, she had no idea what had been done. She thought that the men who were there had been doing some kind of building. But she really did not know. She said she thought they had been doing something over on Rattlesnake Mountain, across the lake. But she did not know what that was about either.

William said, "I think I agree with Ben, John. We ain't sailors. I think they will put us to work in building fortifications for this place and Crown Point. I think we have some time though. After all, we burnt everything of any use from Fort St. Johns to here. They will have to start from scratch if they are going to build a base, and like you said, it'll take a while for them to get their navy built and ready here on the lake. Let's hope, anyway."

John nodded and said, "Well, we'll find out bright and early tomorrow what the plans are. No use worrying about it tonight. In the meantime, I'm ready for a good night's sleep. Come on Sarah, let's go to bed."

As they prepared to bed down Sarah asked, "John, do you really think there is going to be a battle here? If there is what will they do with us women? Will they send us away?"

"Sarah, I'm sure we can't stop the British up north, so we have to prepare for a battle here. If we can delay Carleton long enough he may have to wait till spring. But he's coming. Sooner or later, he's coming. They need to get to the Hudson and we need to stop them. So there will be a battle at some point. Dear, I don't know what they will do about you women. Whatever it is, it won't be for a while yet."

Sarah tried to imagine what the future was going to be. But try as she might, she could not put it together. Morning finally came and Sarah saw the other women at the kitchen. While they cooked the breakfasts, Sarah told them what the men had been talking about the night before.

Elizabeth said that Edward and the men she was with had pretty much said the same thing. Jeremiah had not brought it up, but Martha said she would ask him about it.

Then Elizabeth said, "I don't know what this Army has in mind, but my mind is made up that I'm not going through another year with Edward gone away and me not knowing what's going on again. So whatever they plan to do they better plan on me being there too."

Elizabeth's words struck Sarah. She said, "You know, I've been thinking the same thing. If this war goes on, I will not be left behind again, either!" They broke up and went to feed the men.

After she had fed the men, Sarah went to General Schuyler's quarters to fix his breakfast. When she got there she was surprised to find two other men with him. He said, "Oh, good morning, Mrs. Hardy. These two gentlemen will be dining with me. Would you mind terribly preparing enough for the three of us? Where are my manners? Mrs. Hardy, let me introduce General Sullivan, as well as our newest general, General Arnold. They have just returned from Canada, as you know." They both shook her hand and said they were pleased to meet her.

General Sullivan appeared to be in his mid-thirties. He was a pleasant looking man with a receding hairline, but altogether rather nondescript as he stood next to Benedict Arnold.

Arnold on the other hand, although shorter than the other two men, was striking in appearance. His jet black hair, boldly glaring eyes and haughty demeanor seemed to command the entire room.

Sarah said, "Of course, General. That will be no problem. Will you gentlemen be here long? Should I plan on you for meals each day?"

General Schuyler said, "General Sullivan will be leaving tomorrow, but General Arnold will remain here for the foreseeable future. I would be pleased if you took your meals here, General. And Mrs. Hardy, would it be too much of an inconvenience to take care of General Arnold's quarters also while he is here?"

Sarah said, "No, Sir, it will not be any problem. I will be happy to look after the general's quarters."

Arnold said, "Thank you, General. It is most kind of you. And thank you, Mrs. Hardy, I truly appreciate your help."

Sarah prepared their breakfast and went about her business of cleaning the office and living spaces.

After the men had left the office, Sarah went back into Schuyler's office and looked at the maps. She found Skenesborough, where John said they were building ships. Then she looked northward down the lake and wondered where a ship battle might take place and what it would look like. And she wondered if it would be successful in keeping the British at bay.

Sarah didn't see John at all during the day. When they met at supper he told her that the Army would be put to work on getting Fort Ticonderoga, Crown Point, and Rattlesnake Mountain, now renamed Mount Independence, prepared for defense against the British.

Thirteen

The days were getting warmer. It wasn't like the summer before, when they had all lived together. Sarah, Martha, and Elizabeth made a point of finding each other each day and talking, but there was little time for the long discussions they used to have. Except for Martha working with her at the bakery, they did not see much of Mary.

Besides Mary, Martha worked with several other women in the bakery. She said that she was worried about one of the young women named Alice Waltham. Martha said she had become quite morose and quiet since the men had come back. As they were talking, Mary came running up. She was crying and yelling, "Martha, you gotta come quick! You gotta help! It's Alice, she is hurt bad!"

"Where is she, Mary? What has happened?" Martha asked.

Mary could hardly control herself. Through her sobbing she

said, “She’s down by the lake.” Then, as though it took all the strength she had, she blurted out words that brought terror to every woman in the camp, “She’s been raped.”

The women dropped everything and ran with Mary towards the lake. When they got there they found Alice lying on the ground. Her dress was torn and her face looked as if someone had beaten her. Martha ran to her and helped her to sit up. She cradled her in her arms and asked, “Oh, Alice, Alice what happened?”

Alice did not answer. She just sobbed as Martha held her close.

Martha became a woman that Sarah had never seen before. She immediately took charge and said, “Mary, you go get Alice’s husband, and bring him to my tent. You know where that is, don’t you?”

Mary, who was still crying, nodded that she did.

“Good, then go get him. Hurry. Ladies, please help me with Alice. Let’s get her covered up and take her over to my tent. We can take care of her there. Jeremiah will know what to do about finding whoever has done this.”

When they got to the tent Jeremiah and another officer were sitting in front. They stood as the women approached and Jeremiah asked, “Martha, what happened?”

Martha responded, “Sarah, you explain what happened to Jeremiah. Elizabeth, can you get some water please, and bring it in here?” She led Alice into the tent and closed the flap.

As Sarah was talking to the men, Elizabeth returned with the water and went into the tent. Sarah could hear soft voices coming from the tent. She was about to go in herself when Martha came out. "Jeremiah, you need to hear this. Then something has to be done about it."

The other officer excused himself, and Martha led Jeremiah and Sarah into the tent. Elizabeth was sitting on the cot next to Alice. She was holding her and rocking her gently.

Jeremiah sat down on the cot across from them and asked, "Alice, can you tell me what happened? Can you tell me who did this to you?"

Alice nodded and wiped tears off her face. She began, "I wanted to be alone, so I went down to the lake to wash up and do some thinking. I do that now and then. No one was there, and I was washing when a man grabbed me from behind. I started to yell for help but he hit me several times and covered my mouth. He was too strong for me to fight him off. I tried but I couldn't. He was on top of me, and..." She burst into tears. She couldn't go on.

Elizabeth took her in her arms once more and said, "There, there dearie, you're safe now. We'll take care of you."

Alice's husband arrived at that moment and entered the tent. He looked at Alice, then at Jeremiah, and said, "Oh, good evening, Sir. Alice, what has happened to you?"

Alice stopped crying and looked straight at him. Her eyes were burning with anger and hatred as she spat out, "Your drunken friend James Darby did this to me."

Darby was another private from Jeremiah's company. Everyone knew him as a drunk and a lout.

Alice's husband was stunned, and for a minute said nothing. His next words surprised Sarah. In a very stern voice he said, "Come on, Alice. I'll take you back to our tent."

Martha interrupted him and said with authority, "No! I think it will be better if she stays here tonight. Jeremiah, you and Phillip will have to find someplace else to sleep tonight. But right now you need to have this man Darby arrested. He cannot get away with this."

Jeremiah nodded and got up to leave. Just then John arrived, wondering what was going on. Jeremiah said, "Come on John, we got to go arrest a man." John looked confused. "I'll explain it to you on the way. Come on. Private Waltham you come with me too. I don't think there's much you can do here. The women will take care of Alice."

Sarah looked around the tent. Anger was burning within her. "I'm going with them," she said. "I have to see this man who did this terrible thing."

They stopped and picked up two guards on the way. When they reached Darby's tent he was there with a couple of other men. They all stood at attention as Jeremiah approached. He said, "Private Darby, you have been accused of raping a girl down by the lake this evening. What have you to say to that?"

Darby was clearly drunk and reeked of rum. He smugly looked around at the men with him and said, "I didn't rape that whore. She wanted it. She's just like all the other women here in this camp. The only reason they're here is because they're whores. Else they'd be at home like decent women." He looked directly into Sarah's eyes as he said it, smiled contemptuously and finished, "Ain't that right, honey?"

John started to punch the man but Jeremiah held him back. Jeremiah then said, "Private James Darby, you are under arrest for rape and drunkenness. Guards, take this man to the guard house and have him locked up."

Jeremiah sent Waltham back to his tent, then went to see the Colonel to tell him what had happened. The Colonel shook his head and said, "I've been waiting for this to happen. It was only a matter of time. Captain Quinlin, set up a Court Marshall."

The Court Marshall was convened. An officer was appointed to be prosecutor, and another to be the defense lawyer.

Sarah, Martha and Elizabeth were allowed to be there to support Alice. Her husband was there also. But to Sarah he seemed distant, as though this really wasn't about his wife being raped.

Since there were no witnesses, the trial did not take long.

Jeremiah was the first to take the stand. He stated how his wife had brought Alice to their tent and told him about what had happened, and that he had then gone to Darby's tent to confront him. He told them Darby was drunk and that he said that he had had sex with Alice.

The defense lawyer asked, "Captain Quinlin, did Private Darby say he raped Mrs. Waltham?"

"No. He said that she wanted to do it too."

"Did you ask any further questions?"

"No."

He was dismissed and Alice was called next. Her face was swollen from the beating she had taken, and her left eye was blackened and half shut. The prosecutor asked her to tell what had happened.

She told how she had gone down to the lake to wash up and was jumped upon by Darby, how he punched her and raped her. She was very emotional, and nearly broke down in tears several times as she retold the story.

The Defense lawyer asked, "Mrs. Waltham, do you know the rules against fraternizing and having sexual intercourse with men other than your husband?"

Alice answered, "Yes."

Then he asked, "Why were you down by the lake alone, Mrs. Waltham?"

"I just wanted to wash up, and I wanted some time by myself, just to think."

"Isn't it also a rule, Mrs. Waltham that women are not to be out of the camp without someone to escort them?"

She answered, "Yes." But her voice seemed to be asking a question at the same time.

Sarah wondered what that could possibly have to do with anything.

The defense lawyer then said, "So you intentionally broke the rule about not being out of the camp alone to go down to the lake. And then you exposed yourself. What did you think was going to happen, Mrs. Waltham? You are in a camp full of men. Were you looking for someone to have sex with?"

Alice burst into tears, "No!" She cried. "I just wanted to be alone and to wash up. He raped me!"

Sarah and the other women gasped in disbelief. How could this man look at Alice and not realize that she had been raped? How could he do this to her?

Alice was dismissed and James Darby took the stand. He was as smug as he had been the day before.

When asked to recount what had happened he said, "Well, I was down by the lake getting some water for the tent. I saw this woman." He pointed at Alice. "Well, she had her top down and was washing, like she said. Then she looked at me and started flirtin'. She didn't even try to cover herself up. So I walked over to her and she stood up. I asked her what she was doing. She still didn't cover herself up. She asked me if I wanted her. And said I could have her for two dollars. Well, I ain't payin' for no whore. So I took hold of her and kissed her on the mouth. She didn't fight much. Then we went to the ground and she started to fight a little. So I mighta smacked her a couple of times and she quieted right down and enjoyed it just like I did. I didn't have to rape her. She asked for it. She wanted me to. She's just like all the rest of these camp followin' women here. They're all just looking for it."

Alice stood up and screamed, "No, that's not true! He raped me!"

The judge banged the gavel several times and demanded that Alice sit down and be quiet.

Martha put her arms around Alice and tried to calm her down, but she continued to sob and shake violently.

The two lawyers made final arguments to the officers of the court and the members left the room to confer. In less than half an hour they returned.

The Judge asked, "Members of the jury, have you reached a verdict?"

The senior officer stood and said, "Yes, Judge, we have."

"What is your verdict?"

"We find the accused, Private James Darby, guilty as charged of drunkenness." He then looked around sheepishly as though he was trying to find a place to hide. What came out next stunned the women. "We find the accused, Private James Darby, not guilty of rape, but guilty of having sexual intercourse with a woman, not his wife."

Alice screamed "No!" once again and she and the other women all stood in unison.

The Judge banged the gavel and demanded that order be restored.

He then ordered the prisoner to stand and said, "Private Darby, having been found guilty of drunkenness I sentence you to sixty lashes. Having been found guilty of the crime of having sexual intercourse with a woman not your wife, I sentence you to an additional forty lashes. This punishment will be carried out by the Provost Marshal on separate occasions so as not to incapacitate the soldier or keep him from his duties for an extended time."

He then stunned everyone in the court room. He said, "Mrs. Alice Waltham, you will now stand. The act of having sex outside your marriage is a violation of military regulations and has caused a breakdown in the good order of this command. You are hereby ordered to be expelled from this camp and delivered to Fort George as soon as possible. From there you will be escorted back to Albany at the earliest convenience of the commander of that post. Until you are transported to Fort George you will be confined to a separate tent, and shall have no interaction with men of this post other than your husband."

He then added, "And to the other women living within the jurisdiction of this command. Let this serve as a warning that this type of action will not be tolerated. You are to follow military regulations or you will be expelled from this camp."

Turning to the Provost Marshall he said, "You shall post

the regulations regarding the actions of females attached to this command in a conspicuous place. Additionally, you shall call a formation of all women presently attached to this command and read those regulations to them. Now put both prisoners under guard and carry out the sentences."

The women were speechless. They were crushed. They could not believe what had just happened. A man clearly guilty of rape was given more punishment for being drunk than for the rape. And worse, Alice, and indirectly they too, were made responsible for this man's beastly behavior. They surrounded Alice and each hugged her tightly. She had stopped crying but was visibly shaken. She looked past the women toward her husband. He turned his back and walked out of the court room without a word.

Two guards came and took Alice away. There was a convoy that was going to Fort George with some sick men that left a few days later. On the morning Alice left the women went to see her off. Her husband did not come to see her. Alice was in a daze. Nothing they said to her seemed to move her. She just walked away without saying another word.

The sentence for Darby was carried out as ordered, and all the men and women attached to the company were ordered to be present on each occasion. It appeared to Sarah that the man who was carrying out the lashing did not put much into it. It was as if he really didn't want to do it. Darby was soon completely recovered, and was back to being his same disgusting self.

But life for the women had changed. It was subtle, but they felt it deeply. They no longer had the freedom of the camp that they had enjoyed before the rape happened. Many of the men were no longer cordial beyond what was absolutely necessary.

They went out of their way to let the women know that they blamed Alice for what had happened and that they also blamed the women who remained.

Even Sarah's relationship with John suffered. Not that he agreed with the decision of the Court Marshall—in fact, he agreed that Darby should have been convicted of rape and sentenced to death. But he tried to convince Sarah that she needed to move on. It only made her even angrier. Soon they stopped talking about. But it was never far from Sarah's consciousness. She began carrying a knife with her at all times. She told herself, "If one of these bastards tries that with me, he won't live to get army justice. I will mete out my own."

Fourteen

Life began to return to normal. Work was well under way with the construction on the fort and Mount Independence, and soon ships started to come over from Skenesborough. General Arnold took command of the job of fitting them out with cannon and the material they would need to be effective in a sea battle on the lake. John and his men were diverted from any fort construction to the mission of preparing the ships.

The women were again drafted, this time to help make what they were told were, gabions and fascines. They were told that hundreds of these items would be needed. A gabion was a basket about three feet tall and three feet wide. It was open on both ends. It could be filled with rocks and dirt and many of them could be put together to make strong walls and fortifications. Fascines were rough bundles of brushwood tied together. They were to be interlaced with the gabions to make the fortifications stronger. A couple of men instructed the women on how to make them.

A work crew had already collected piles of the brushwood so the women could start right away on making the fascines. Another work crew was working on skinning trees into long strips to be used in weaving the gabions. All the women, along with men who were not working on other projects, worked on making these items several hours a day.

The summer stretched on. Between the heat and the constant annoyance of the biting flies, mosquitos, and other swarming bugs the work was very difficult. But it continued unabated.

In mid-July they learned that the Congress in Philadelphia had passed a Declaration of Independence telling the world that the colonies would no longer be ruled by the King of England. None at the fort knew exactly what it meant or what to make of it. They were all anxious to hear exactly what this declaration said.

Finally, on the twenty-seventh of July, formations of all personnel at the fort were held for the purpose of having the Declaration of Independence read aloud to everyone. John's unit fell into their formation and the women stood in a small group behind them as Jeremiah read the document to the company.

It started out by saying that Americans held certain truths to be self-evident; that all men were created equal and endowed by their creator with the unalienable rights of life, liberty, and the pursuit of happiness. It then went on to outline all the things that the King and Parliament had done to subvert those rights of Americans. Finally, it said that because there was no solution to the problems which existed between the colonies and England, that the thirteen colonies now declared themselves to be "free and independent states."

At first there was a stunned silence, but quickly a great roar of huzzahs filled the air. Men were shaking each other's hands and hugging one another. Sarah could hear the men saying, "It's about time. Fifteen months already we have been fighting this war. And only now do those people in Congress have the nerve to declare independence. What do they think we have been doing out here? What have they been doing? Not doing anything for us that's for sure. Now maybe we will get some help from France or Spain."

The almost universal opinion was that this declaration was the right thing to do. It wouldn't mean a thing if the British won the war, but it was needed to make people finally decide which side they were on.

Sarah listened, and for the first time something started to click in her mind about what the ultimate goal of this war was. There were many things the declaration didn't say, but at least she could now see that there were many reasons that went far beyond the taxation issue. Why these things couldn't be sorted out without war she still did not understand, but as she listened she knew there could be no going back now.

That evening at supper she asked John and the other men what they thought of the Declaration, and what they thought it meant. Ben, of course, chimed in first. He said, "It certainly has taken them long enough. They should have done this a year ago, when they appointed General Washington as commander in chief and created this army. When they did that it as much as told the King, if we win we won't be part of his kingdom no more. This declaration just kinda formalizes what was done but not said a year ago. And, as for me, it says we won't stop fighting until we are out of the king's control or we die trying. Whether we want it or not boys, those enlistments of ours just became for the duration of this here war, 'cause we can't go no where's 'til it's over."

John then said, "I think we all agree with you on that, Ben. But the declaration has to be more than just telling the king we don't want to be part of his kingdom anymore. I guess he has already figured that out. But what does it mean for us? What if this war ends tomorrow? How will we be governed? Will we have one country or will we have thirteen? I don't guess most of us have given much thought about those things. But now that Congress has formalized it we probably ought to be figuring out what this independence is going to look like. How is it going to make a difference to you and me? Are we just trading in the King and Parliament for these men in Philadelphia? I don't know or trust them any better than I do Parliament—even the ones from New York. I've never talked to one of them, have any of you? How do we know what they are thinking while we are out here fighting for this independence they just declared? I know it says we were all created equal, but I don't think that General Schuyler, up there or this fellow Washington, or those men in Congress will ever really believe that John Hardy is their equal. No, I don't think this document says much to us. But like Ben says, we are going to have to fight it out to the end, and then we will see what we have won and hope to God that it's better'n what we have now."

Then they all started talking and arguing as only men can,

and Sarah went into the tent to think about what she had just heard. "They all have the same questions I have," she thought. "They don't have any better idea of what we are here for than I do. But they, and the men in Congress, are going to decide what is best for me, and I am supposed to accept it. It's the way things have always been, but if we are going to change, why can't we change that also? Why can't I have a say in how we will be governed?"

One other thing the men had said settled uneasily on her mind as she drifted off to sleep. They all, in one way or another, said that they were in this army till the end. They had already made up their minds that they were not getting out at the end of the year. This time she was going to confront John about it. Maybe her words wouldn't carry much weight in this decision and maybe they were going to stay with the army regardless of what she said. But she was going to as least have a say in it this time.

The next day she made a point of getting John alone so she could talk to him without the interruptions from the other men. She told him she had been thinking about what he and the other men had said the night before, and that she was concerned that each of them had talked as if their reenlistment for the duration of the war was already done. Had he reenlisted again without telling her?

John said, "No Sarah, we have not reenlisted. But this war is going to go on and it's likely that the army will need us to continue. We can't win if everyone keeps going home every few months. Someone has to stay and fight it out to the end. So don't be surprised if I do reenlist when the time comes."

"Why does it have to be you, John? Haven't you done your part? Haven't we done our part?" She was angry now. "I'm part of this too, you know. While you were in Canada I was down here working as hard as I can to help this cause. And I dare say I've worked a damn sight harder than some of the men the army left around here. Your decision to reenlist without so much as a by your leave is an insult to me. Instead of asking me to help in making a decision that will affect us both, you are telling me what we are going to do. I am part of that 'we' and I will at least have a say in this." She did not want it to, but her voice broke as she spoke.

John looked at her a little stunned. He said, "Sarah, I'm sorry you feel hurt. I never thought of it that way. These are decisions for men to make. You women don't understand the world of politics and the war and the army. How can you decide what is best?"

Sarah fired back, "John, I have listened to you and your friends often enough to know that I know at least as much as you and they do about what is going on. Since the very beginning you have been wrong on every point you have made about how long this will go on and how the British will simply quit once they see how determined we are. Without me you have made decisions on joining this army and staying in, leaving me to wonder what I am supposed to do. I know we have to win this war or we will lose everything. I want to be part of it and part of the decisions being made about how we are going to go on. If you are asking me to help fight for this independence, is it asking too much that I be able to participate in the decisions that are being made for me?"

John said, smiling condescendingly, "Who am I talking to? You are not the Sarah I married or left here last year. You are a different woman, and I don't think I know you." He then said softly, "No, Sarah, it's not asking too much. I am sorry for not including you in making decisions. I promise you I will talk to you before I make any decision to reenlist."

Sarah understood that the conversation was over. She realized she may have made a point which would cause John to at least talk to her before he decided. But she knew in his mind it would still be his decision to make. She had to be content with this small victory. But, she also now realized that from this moment on, this was her war. And, if everything she held dear was on the line over its outcome, she was going to play her part in making that outcome a victory.

Fifteen

One day while they were cooking breakfast Elizabeth said, "You know, ladies, along with making gabions and fascines, we have been making cartridges for the muskets now for quite a while. Have either of you ever shot a musket?"

Sarah and Martha looked at each other and then back at Elizabeth and shook their heads, "No." Sarah's voice had a lilt of humor in it as she asked, "Why do you ask, Elizabeth? Do you think they are going to draft us to do the fighting?"

Elizabeth sighed, "No, Sarah, I don't think that. But I have been giving this a lot of thought lately. If our newly minted sailors aren't able to defeat Carleton up north this summer, there is going to be a fight here. And one way or another, we are going to be in the middle of it. If our men lose then this place could be in a dire position, and we may have to defend ourselves. Look at this camp. Easily a third of the population in this fort is made up of Negroes and Indians. Now I don't have anything against them folks, but when the time comes they are going to take care of themselves and their own. I don't have much confidence in them sticking around to defend us if things get sticky here. We at least should be able to fire one of those things if the time comes that we need to. Besides, even if we don't have to fire them, we should know how to handle and load them just to be of service to the men in a battle. I don't know 'bout you two, but I don't plan on standing around looking pirty while there's a battle going on. Watta ya say dearies? Why don't we talk to the men and ask them for a little instruction on the care and use of muskets?"

Sarah and Martha were not exactly sure it was a good idea, but they said they would talk to their husbands about it.

That evening Sarah brought the subject up at supper. After Ben gave his expected harangue about the evils of putting guns in the hands of women, John said, "You know, Sarah, regardless of what our friend here has to say, that might not be such a bad idea. We're not just facing the British up here. I have some faith in them as being civilized about their fighting, and I don't believe they would intentionally shoot at women. But I wouldn't put it past those damn Hessians and murderous savages the Redcoats have working for them to kill anything that moves. It wouldn't hurt if you ladies learned how to use a gun. I'll talk to Jeremiah about it in the morning."

Ben huffed to no one in particular, "Fine thing when we have to arm our women to fight this war. If that damned Congress would send us the people we need we wouldn't be talking like this."

John offered Ben a drink of rum and said, "Now Ben, don't

take it personally. You know as well as the rest of us that the Congress is busy. They don't have time to worry about us out here in the wilderness while there are parties to attend to in Philadelphia." Everyone laughed, and the conversation turned to their training as sailors and when they would set sail to take on the British fleet that was also being built up north.

Next evening John told Sarah that he and Jeremiah agreed that it would be a good idea if the women learned to shoot. So they had gone to the Colonel and asked him about the idea. At first he was not too interested in it, but Jeremiah had convinced him that it would be a good idea.

The next evening, most of the women showed up for their first training session on firing a musket. Word had spread throughout the camp that the women were going to learn to shoot, and a large contingent of men showed up also. Most stood around joking and laughing about the uselessness of such a folly.

John, as the sergeant in charge of the activity, took command. He immediately shut the men up by stating very loudly that any man who did not have something to contribute to this training should either leave or keep their thoughts to themselves. The men fell silent.

Sarah was both startled and proud of how John looked and acted. She looked around and noticed that all of the men had stopped talking. Elizabeth looked at her, smiled, and winked. Though she didn't say anything Sarah imagined her saying, "You got a good one there, dearie." The thought made her even prouder.

Each woman had brought their husband's musket with them, and the men came as coaches to their wives. At first they were very excited about the idea of actually shooting. John soon dampened their excitement. They would not be given any ammunition until they had learned everything there was to know about the weapon and could disassemble, reassemble, and clean it. Each night for a week he drilled them on all the parts and pieces of the musket and had them take it apart and put it back together until they could do it without him speaking or anyone helping.

Each night after the training Sarah would take John's musket, clean it, and go over what she had learned. One night Ben, seeing an opportunity to not have to do it himself, said, "Hey Sarah, why don't you use my musket? You've got John's so clean he may not ever have to clean it again, and mine could use a good cleaning too." Sarah looked at John, who just shrugged. So she took Ben's musket apart, cleaned it meticulously, and put it back together again. All the men were duly impressed.

After John was satisfied that each woman could do it as well as Sarah, he told them it was time to learn to shoot. He told them that every step he was about to demonstrate had to be executed perfectly every time. No step could be eliminated or it could mean disaster. Two more days went by with the women dry firing the muskets.

Finally, the day came when they would actually shoot. The husbands who had been assisting John handed each woman a cartridge. They went through the process step by step. Bite down on the paper cartridge and tear it open with your teeth. Push the frissen forward and pour a small amount of powder into the flash pan. Push the frissen back into position to cover the flash pan. Hold the musket with the muzzle pointing up. Pour the rest of the powder into the barrel. Insert a lead ball and wadding into the barrel. Remove the ramrod from its storage pipe beneath the barrel and use it to push the wadding and the ball down the barrel. Replace the ramrod in the storage pipe. Raise the musket to a firing position, bracing the butt against the shoulder. Cock the hammer. Aim and fire.

Targets had been set up about twenty five yards in front of the women. As John went through the commands giggles could be heard coming from some of the women. Finally, he gave the command to fire. The muskets exploded and several of the women were knocked to the ground by the recoil. Not one of the targets was hit. One of the muskets had misfired. He stopped everything and began a new lesson on what to do when this happened.

They all shot several more rounds that evening, and by the end of the night most of the women had at least hit a target. Sarah was proud of herself for doing it on only the third try. She was excited and wanted to continue all night. But the training was over.

As they walked back to the tent John said to Sarah, "It's a good thing you don't have a mirror to look at yourself in."

Confused and a little hurt, Sarah asked why.

He laughed and used his thumb to wipe some of gun powder from her face and said, "I don't think you would like the powder you have on right now." She hugged him and laughed.

Sixteen

As the summer went on the women were once again drafted into being nurses as an epidemic of a fever hit the camp. Men were falling out by the score with the ailment, and the hospital was again full beyond capacity. Once again burials started to occur daily as men succumbed to the torturous malady. This time one of the women from another unit also came down with the fever. This was something Sarah had not expected. Up to then, for some reason, the women had been spared from any of the terrible maladies that had beset the men. But this woman's case changed that. Her name was Rachel Reynolds, and she had been with them since they first marched out of Albany. She was in her early twenties and married to a private. Sarah didn't know a lot about her, but she was one of them, and so she got special care.

They put her in a room by herself, and one of the women was

always with her. The care, however, wasn't enough. One night she went to sleep and never woke again. As the men died there was a detail to take them out and bury them with little or no funeral to speak of. Sarah realized that she had become immune to the men dying, and after the first couple of burials she had ceased paying attention to them.

This woman was the first member of their little band to die, however, and the women would not have her just unceremoniously put into the ground without a second thought. The women took care of preparing the body for burial. Sarah had been to funerals, but had never prepared a person for burial. They washed her and dressed her in the best dress they could find. Then they wrapped her in a shroud and the soldiers came and carried her to a grave. The women all walked behind, as did her husband, who seemed to be in a daze. Some of the women prayed, others sobbed quietly. The minister finally said a few words. "Lord, please receive these men and Rachel into your loving arms, and make their life with you a better one than they had here on earth. Help us all understand your intentions in taking them to your side at so young an age. And Lord, please watch over the rest of us as we fight through this, our terrible trial. Amen." Everyone quietly whispered, "Amen."

Then it was over. Everyone went back to work. Sarah said to Elizabeth, "Is this how it will be for us? Is this all there is at the end of one's life? This girl had done everything asked of her. She had hurt no one. Yet in the end a few people stood and watched her being placed in the ground, said a prayer, and then went back to work. There has to be more, somehow there has to be more. Oh, Elizabeth, this poor girl deserved more from life. She didn't deserve to die in this cesspool. She deserved to have a better resting place than that unmarked common grave. Is that what will become of us too?"

They walked a little way and Elizabeth answered, "Sarah, there are no answers that will satisfy you right now. You are a loving woman who feels for this girl, and that is a good thing. I hope you never lose that concern. Everyone needs to have someone care about what happens to them. But it is better to remember that Rachel, just like the men we bury here every day, came here and died for a reason. And let us hope that that reason will see us through this war and give us independence, or whatever the hell it is we are fighting for. We must do everything we can to make sure that Rachel and these men have not died in vain. Rachel is in God's hands now. We poor souls have to go on down here. And looking around, I'm not sure who is better off."

Sarah looked at Elizabeth's gentle face and it made her feel better. Sarah replied, "Of course, you're right Elizabeth. Thank you." They joined arms and walked back to the camp.

During the night someone placed a cross over the spot where they had buried Rachel. It simply had her name and the dates of her birth and death. But to Sarah, at least, it meant the world.

When they were not working in the hospital the women continued making gabions and fascines for the upgrades being made to the defense works.

Sarah and several other women were sent across the lake to Mount Independence to help with the work there. The men who were not helping with the ships were working on building a redoubt on top of the mountain.

The women cooked the meals for the men working on the

mountain. When not engaged in cooking, the women piled rocks into the gabions as the men filled them with dirt from their digging. The baskets were lined up and stacked, one upon another, until a wall was formed. As the wall of gabions was forming, the women weaved the gabions together with the fascines to give the wall strength. The work was strenuous, but Sarah enjoyed it. The mountain was a welcome change. It became a refuge from the monotony and grime of the fort and the stench of the hospital. The air was fresher and cleaner there. When she had a chance, Sarah would just sit and look out from the mountain top. She could see far down the lake, and pretended she could see John on his ship. She dreamed of the day when this war would all be over and she and John could finally settle down.

With all the work everyone was doing, time seemed to fly by. General Schuyler had gone back to Albany, and General Gates had taken over at the fort until he too left.

As Ben had predicted, the men spent most of their time fitting out the ships with sails, cannon, and supplies and learning how to become sailors. There just weren't enough real sailors in the wilderness to man all the ships they had built. So the soldiers were impressed onto the ships.

By mid-August General Arnold's armada was almost ready. He, and the ships that were ready, had already traveled north to position themselves to patrol the lake. John was on a ship called the *Congress*. So were Jeremiah and Edward. "At least," she thought, "they will be together to take care of each other."

Fortunately, General Arnold was an accomplished sea captain who had experience sailing ships to Europe and back during his civilian career. To Sarah, he seemed to be everywhere.

He oversaw the ships being built at Skenesborough, and fitting them out at Ticonderoga, and the training of the men. She continued to take care of his needs at the fort, and though he was a stern, and, at times, arrogant man, he was very good to her. Unlike the sickly Schuyler or the old granny looking Gates, she saw in Arnold what she thought a general should look and act like. Many generals had come through the fort over the past year, and most of them did not impress her with their military bearing. They acted like they deserved the rank because they were rich. But as she saw it, they did not inspire the confidence of the men like Arnold did. She was glad that John would serve under him and not one of the others.

From scuttle butt, a new term for rumor she had learned from the sailors, she knew that the British Navy too was nearly ready to start out. Sarah worried about the outcome of this coming battle. She had watched the men as they trained to become sailors, and wondered if they had learned enough to be proper fighting seamen. She listened to John and the men in the evenings as they discussed what was to come. Once they got through their bravado of invincibility, notes of doubt turned up in their voices.

One thing about the battle they were about to enter struck her as odd. During their conversations the men talked about how they didn't have to beat the British, just delay them long enough to make sure they couldn't attack Fort Ticonderoga and get to the Hudson this year. Sarah had thought that the army expected to win every battle. How could this attitude help them? How could they go off pretty sure they were not going to win? She remembered what the men looked like after Quebec. What would this battle bring?

One day, after the ships had left, Elizabeth came to her and exclaimed, "Get your things, dearie. You, me, and Martha are going to Crown Point."

"What are you talking about, Elizabeth? Why would we go to Crown Point? We have jobs here that we can't afford to lose. What are we going to do there? And besides, how would we get there?"

Elizabeth responded, "First of all, we are going because that is closer to where our men are. We all agreed that we weren't going to let them go off without us, didn't we? Besides, they are going to need some nurses there when the fighting gets going. As for your job, what job do you have now? Schuyler is in Albany and Gates is off politickin somewhere, and Arnold is out on the lake with the men. No one is going to miss you, and if they fire you I'll get you a job with the sutlers. They are always willing to have another woman around to do their slave labor."

Sarah thought and then asked, "And how are we going to get there?"

Elizabeth had arranged everything. "The sutlers are leaving to go up there tomorrow. Never can tell where you might make a sale, you know. They will have a military escort with them. We will go with them. Martha has agreed, so get your things ready dearie. We are leaving at first light in the morning."

Sarah's first thought was one of fear of heading to where there was sure to be trouble. But then she caught Elizabeth's enthusiasm and got excited about the adventure. Besides, how bad could it be? If there was to be a battle it was going to be out on the lake, not at the fort at Crown Point. She said, "Alright Elizabeth, I'll be ready. God knows we don't have much to get ready."

Sarah finished her chores for the day and then went to see Major Cardin. She told him what they were about to do and he said, "I don't recommend it, Mrs. Hardy. Things are going to be rough up there. But if you ladies are determined, I don't think anyone will try to stop you. And they will need nurses up there, that's for sure. Please be careful."

Sarah went to the tent that she was now the only occupant in and gathered her few clothes and the pots and pans she thought they might need for cooking the few rations she had left. The cooking utensils were heavy and she hoped that she would not have to carry them all the way to Crown Point. She would roll her blankets in the morning.

Next morning the three women met at the sutler's wagon and began the ten-mile trek through the woods to Crown Point. Sarah was very thankful that there was room on one of the wagons for their equipment. The road—what there was of it—was not more than a path. It was rutted and the wagons had to be pushed along much of it to aid the horses trying to pull them through. The women put their shoulders to the task along with the soldiers.

The greatest danger they feared along the way was an attack from the Indians who were patrolling the forests for the British. Everyone had heard the tales of what would happen if they had a run in with them. As they pushed through the wilderness Sarah thought, "I wish I had a musket." If the Indians did ambush them she would at least like to be able to defend herself. But nothing happened, and they arrived safely at Fort Crown Point just before dark.

The fort was built during the last war with the French. It

was, if possible, in even worse shape than Fort Ticonderoga. When they arrived the women found that there was no accommodation for them. They went and found an officer to ask where they might sleep. He was surprised to see them there and asked what their purpose in being there was. Sarah noted the disapproval in his voice and wondered what would happen now. Elizabeth, however, stood strong and told him, "We are nurses, and were sent up here to assist in any way we can. The commandant at Fort Ticonderoga believed we might be of some use to the surgeon. Now if you would be so kind as to show us where we might sleep it will be most appreciated."

The officer looked at her, shrugged, and said, "We don't have any tents for you, so you will have to build yourselves something. You can bed down behind that regiment over there." He pointed in the direction of a formation of tents. He offered no assistance other than that. Luckily Elizabeth had taken the tent she was sleeping in and had it stowed away in the sutler's wagon. With the help of one of the men who had marched with them, they put their tent up and, exhausted, they all went to sleep without anything to eat.

In the morning they were met outside their tent by the same officer from the evening before. He looked at the tent and asked, "Might I ask where you women came into possession of this tent? I told you we did not have one for you."

Not to be intimidated by this arrogant young officer, Elizabeth responded, "This woman," pointing to Sarah, "is General Arnold's personal housekeeper and cook. We are all nurses. He is aware of our coming here also. Knowing that the army would be hard pressed to provide us with one here, he authorized us to bring this tent along wherever we followed him." With that she pulled a piece of paper out of her pocket and showed it to him. The paper read, "This authorizes Mrs. Sarah Hardy and two other women of her choosing to transport and keep in their possession one tent for their use during their stay at Fort Crown Point." It was signed, "Benedict Arnold, Brigadier General."

In seeing the paper signed by General Arnold the officer became more civil. He handed the paper back to Elizabeth and said, "My apologies, ladies. If the general has authorized you to be here I am sure it is proper." He then called to a soldier and told him, "When these ladies are ready, see to it that they are escorted to the surgeon's marque." He looked at them again and said, "If there is anything I can do for you, please let me know."

Elizabeth said coldly, "Thank you. We will let you know." With that he left. Elizabeth asked the soldier where they might find him when they needed him and told him they would come and get him later.

When he had left, Sarah and Martha looked at each other and then to Elizabeth. Sarah asked, "Elizabeth, where did you get that order? General Arnold doesn't know we are here. And he certainly didn't authorize us to have a tent."

Elizabeth looked around as if she were about to tell a great secret and wanted to make sure no one could hear it. She whispered a rather loud whisper, "You know that and I know that, but that dolt of an officer don't. I knew when I borrowed this tent," she slyly emphasized the word borrowed, "that we might lose it to someone like him. And I figured the good general wouldn't want his personal cook to sleep out in the rain. So I created the order and signed it for him. I seen enough of his signature for supplies that I knew I could make a good enough copy that would pass by these folks who probably ain't never seen his signature. And it worked."

Martha said incredulously, "What if you get caught? We will all be in trouble. Then what will we do?"

Elizabeth answered, "Dearies, we ain't going to get caught. 'Sides, what are they gonna do, take our tent away? Make us go back to Ticonderoga? In the next few days we will endear ourselves to the surgeon, and then no one will think anything more about it. General Arnold is fighting a battle out on the lake. He won't be back here till it's over. And when he does get here he won't be worrying about that tent. Or us either, I suspect." She looked from one to the other as if to ask if there were any more questions, and when neither woman said anything, she finished, "Good. I am starving. Let's cook us up some breakfast and then take up that nice young man's offer to guide us to the surgeon. I'm anxious to get started at whatever it is we are going to be doing here."

Seventeen

The surgeon was an elderly local man. His name was Dr. Schmidt. He was tall and very slender, and though he was the doctor, he was not very clean in appearance. His sleeping quarters were in a marque in the rear of the headquarters. The marque also served as the place where he held sick call for the men and distributed medicine as needed. He was both surprised and grateful to see the women. He was not particularly interested in how they got there or why. He was just happy to know if they were really there to aid him. He and one surgeon's mate had been posted there in anticipation of casualties from the coming battle. He told them he wasn't very positive about what they could do as he had little medicine and, as they could see for themselves, the conditions were deplorable. But he would be grateful for their assistance just the same.

He took them to a building that had been set up as a makeshift hospital, all the while regaling them with tales of how difficult it was to get supplies of any sort to Crown Point. It seemed that hospitals such as this were considered, by some in authority, as wasteful. It was their belief that men who were so badly wounded that they could not be put back into action should be moved back to Fort George, where a general hospital had been set up. Those people obviously had never been in this part of the country, and had no idea how difficult it was to move wounded or sick men that far under the conditions they had to face.

As the women surveyed the wretched place that was designated as a hospital the doctor said, "Well, ladies, there you have it. Small here will help you find whatever you need. Anything you can do to help is appreciated."

A rather large man with dirty clothes and an apron took the pipe out of his mouth and said, "Howdy, ladies. What might you be doing here?"

Elizabeth told him they were there to help out, and asked where they might begin.

Small scratched his stubbly chin and said, "I don't rightly know. I guess you can start anywheres you've a mind to."

Sarah asked him how they should call him and he said, "Well, ma'am, we ain't too formal up here. My name is Jonathan Sewell but most folks just calls me Small, so that oughta do."

Elizabeth said, "How do you do, Small? I am Mrs. Hubbard, and these ladies are Mrs. Hardy and Mrs. Quinlin. Well, Small, it looks like this place could use a good cleaning. Why don't we start with that? Is there any vinegar or other cleaning supplies here?"

"Yes ma'am. Jes follow me and I'll show you ladies where they're at."

As they scrubbed the floor for what had to have been the first time it had ever been cleaned, they could not help but notice that the beds were filled with men with all sorts of maladies and diseases. Sarah whispered to Martha, "This place isn't a hospital, it's a living hell. If they put men wounded from the battle in here they won't have to worry about dying from their wounds, they'll die of whatever these men have."

With only a small break at noon to eat something, they worked all day on cleaning the place as best they could. It still looked miserable, but it looked a great deal better than it did when they arrived.

The next day they tackled a more formidable task: getting the men clean. They prepared a large vat of water behind the hospital and placed bars of soap with it. Then Elizabeth went into the building, rousted every man who was able to walk, and told them to get themselves outside and bathe. The men were stunned to see and hear this woman order them about. Several protested that they were too sick to go outside. Elizabeth then said to them in a very military voice, "Gentlemen, I am the head nurse here, and as of today this is my hospital. Anyone who does not go out and thoroughly wash themselves will be immediately discharged from this hospital and sent back to your unit. And starting today, as long as you are here you will bathe at least once a week. You may have noticed that we scrubbed the floors yesterday. While you are bathing the ladies here will wash your bedding. This will be the last time they will do either of those tasks. From now on, if I believe you are able, you will perform those duties as part of your military duties. Anyone who refuses will be sent back to their unit."

One of the men shouted back in challenge, "You can't order us about! You're just a woman, and you're here to do those things for us. Only the doc can send us back to our units."

At that point Small came into the room. Elizabeth turned to him and said, "Small, I have instructed the men to go out back and bathe. This gentleman seems to think that that is an affront to his dignity. Would you please encourage him to follow our instructions?"

Small looked very confused. Elizabeth pulled him aside and side. "Small, we are here doing your work. Now if you want us to continue doing it, get these men out back and force them to bathe."

With that Small grinned and said, "Yes ma'am, anything you say. It'll be my pleasure." He turned on the men and said, "Boys you got two seconds to start moving to that tub outside. After that I'm goin' to throw you out. And boys, I don't expect you'll give these ladies any more guff or you'll be answerin' to me. Now git." The men started to move, and he turned to Elizabeth, smiled and asked, "Anything else ma'am?"

Elizabeth responded, "No, that will be all for now. Thank you Small." He started to leave and Elizabeth gently suggested, "Oh, Small, it might not hurt you to use some of that soap and water too."

He shrunk just a little and said, "Yes'm." Then he went out back with the men.

Elizabeth went to the men who were too sick to comply with her orders and started bathing them herself. While she was doing that, Sarah and Martha pulled all of the bedding outside and dumped the old straw from them and washed the mattress covers. They looked like they had never been washed before. Sarah left Martha to finish the wash and returned to help Elizabeth with the other invalids.

Some of the men started to return, and one said, "Hey, where's our beds?"

Elizabeth told him that they were being cleaned also. Then she said, "There is no reason for you gentlemen to hang around in here. The beds won't be ready for a couple of hours. It is a beautiful day outside, I suggest you go out and take advantage of it—because if you stay in here you will be put to work." The men seemed to take the hint and quickly went back outside.

Elizabeth winked at Sarah and said, "I wouldn't be surprised to learn that several of these 'sick' men might not find it better to be back in their units rather than here before long."

They finally got all the bed covers cleaned, stuffed them with fresh straw, tightened the ropes, and remade the beds. Then they allowed the men back into the building. As they walked in, Elizabeth said, "Ladies, who are these gentlemen? They can't be the same dirty boys we sent out to wash this morning. They are all right nice looking men when they're all cleaned up." Then, addressing the men, she said, "Thank you for your cooperation today, gentlemen. I am sure you will find this place much nicer when both you and it are clean."

Sarah was once again amazed at how Elizabeth managed to control the situation. When they were alone she asked, "Elizabeth, what is this head nurse stuff? Who appointed you head nurse and gave you all this authority?"

Elizabeth gave her that smile of hers and said, “Why, Sarah? You wanna be the head nurse and order these men about?” Sarah bashfully shook her head.

Then Elizabeth continued, “Did you see that doctor? Or Small there? They don’t want anything to do with being in charge of anything or anybody. They just want to do what they do. I saw it right off. We don’t need nobody to tell us what our jobs are because they don’t know. We see what needs doin’ and we do it. These men are only used to having somebody tell them what to do. If nobody tells them to work, they don’t. So if we want to call ourselves head nurse or anything else they are not going to argue with us. If we run into a colonel or general who wants to think he’s in charge, we’ll simply say ‘yes, sir’ and continue to do what we do. Why, sometimes I can even trick Edward into believing I’m in charge.”

She continued, “And these boys here, why I’m old enough to be their mama. And they are mostly good boys who wouldn’t disobey or sass their mama. In fact, they wouldn’t say this, but many of them miss their mamas right now. So they’ll do as I say. Now you. To them you are a beautiful young girl about their age. If it weren’t for that ring you’re wearin’ and the fact that you call yourself Missis, and they don’t know exactly who you are Missis to, they would be fallin’ all over each other trying to show you how manly they are. Understand?”

At first Sarah felt a shiver run through her as she thought about what had happened to Alice. Then she nodded, looked at her admiringly and said, “Elizabeth, I don’t believe I will ever understand your mind, but you sure do bring excitement to this dreary world of ours.”

Once they got the hospital cleaned up, Elizabeth's prediction came true. Many of the malingerers found it better to be with their units than at the hospital under her reign. They did not see much of the doctor. He came by once or twice a day to check on the patients but did not stay long. Small was happy that the women were there, and was more than happy to assist them in any way they asked.

As order came to the previous chaos the women were able to give better care to the truly sick. Along with keeping the men and the place clean they fed the men who could not feed themselves. They cleaned and dressed wounds the men had gotten working. They would also write letters for men who couldn't write. Sometimes they just sat and talked to the men. It seemed to help the healing for the men in some way, and it broke up the work of the day for the women.

August turned to September, and with the autumn the trees of the Adirondacks and the Green Mountains turned brilliant colors. The days were pleasant, and at night the air turned a clean crisp cold.

Eighteen

Sarah and the other women took up residency in a single room in the hospital. The malingerers had all returned to their units in order to get away from Elizabeth, and the number of men actually still in the hospital was greatly reduced. Despite their efforts some men died.

In the hospital at this time there was also a young woman who had been there when they arrived. She was very sick with a fever. The women put her in a separate area of the hospital to give her some privacy and in hopes she would be able to pull through. But she also died. She was put to rest with the men, an unknown victim of this horrible war.

Sarah thought she had become immune to the dying, but seeing this girl being buried brought all the pain of watching the spectacle back. As she looked at the misery that surrounded them, she became very melancholy.

Elizabeth was, of course, very strong, and usually took charge of Small to have the bodies removed from the hospital and to arrange a burial detail. Sarah wondered how she could be so cool towards the deaths. She knew Elizabeth cared. It was just that she did not show great emotion, and Sarah could not see how she held it in.

Martha was also strong when death occurred. But her strength was different than Elizabeth's. She had an aura about her that brought calmness to the hospital whenever a death occurred. In her depression Sarah turned to Martha for solace. Martha seemed to understand, and without saying a word, she nursed Sarah through until she was back to normal.

Many of the patients had gotten better as the cool autumn air arrived. By the beginning of October there were actually beds empty in the hospital. With the women living in the hospital and the number of patients greatly reduced Dr. Schmidt and Small had even more reason to avoid visiting. There wasn't much the doctor could do anyway. There was such a shortage of medicine that all he could really prescribe for most of them was what the women were already doing for them. Sarah thought he looked almost despondent at his inability to do much for the men and that the reason he came so little was because it hurt him not to be able to help.

The night of October tenth it turned very cold and started to rain. It rained all night, and as dawn broke the rain turned to sleet being driven by a fierce wind. Sarah thought of John out on the lake in such weather. She remembered what the gundalows looked like. They were small boats that Sarah thought looked like fishing boats that had low flat decks built onto them for the guns. They provided little or no shelter for the men to take refuge in, and she worried about the men who were on them also. She wondered if they had met up with Carleton and the British fleet yet. And she wondered if they were alright.

As she crawled out of bed and looked out at the rain something inside her told her that there was a battle going on even in this horrible weather. It was as if she could see down the lake those forty miles and watch the battle as it raged. She felt she could hear the guns going off in all directions. But her vision was clouded with smoke. She could not see who was winning.

Elizabeth interrupted her thoughts. "Good morning, Sarah. How are you this morning?"

Sarah quickly turned and stared at Elizabeth for a moment as if she didn't know her. Then she said, "Oh, Elizabeth, you startled me. Good morning. I'm well, I guess." Then she turned back to look out to the lake and continued, "Elizabeth, do you believe that someone can know something is happening even though there is no possible way that they can?" Without waiting for an answer Sarah went on, "I've just been standing here looking at the lake and I am positive that I have been watching a sea battle going on. I could hear the guns exploding and men screaming. But I can't tell who is winning. I know it's not possible, but I just have this feeling that it is all happening this morning. And I think John has been hurt."

Elizabeth said, "Yes Sarah, I do believe that there are moments when some people can see or maybe feel things that the rest of us can't. Maybe the battle is going on this morning. But there is nothing we can do about it here. Between you and me, I think our job is harder than the men's. They at least are in the thick of it and don't have time to think about us too much. But all we can do is sit and wonder and pray a little. If the battle is on then it is all in God's hands. We will know soon enough what the result is. The best thing we can do is to keep busy and help these men here through their day. If we allow ourselves to wallow in our fears we will not help our men or ourselves and only drive ourselves crazy. Now let's get to work and think no more about this for a while."

As the day went on the weather got worse, and Sarah thought that it was not possible for a battle to be waged on day such as this. Elizabeth was right. Working and caring for the men did relieve some of her fears.

The next day the weather was still bad. But late in the day they got the first word that a battle had taken place the day before. A ship, the *Liberty*, that had not taken a part in the battle anchored, and the captain told those at Crown Point that the Americans did not fare well and were retreating as fast as they could. He did not know how many casualties there were, but most of the ships were either sunk or captured. This ship was soon followed by four more, the *Trumbull,* the *New York,* the *Enterprise,* and the *Revenge*. Sarah watched as these ships limped into Crown Point. They were clearly badly damaged from the battle. On the ships were many injured and dying men. John's ship, the *Congress*, was not among them, and no one knew anything about its fate.

Sarah's fears were now multiplied. The waiting was intolerable. She went through her duties mechanically, paying little attention to the men she was providing aid to. All the next day and the next she could not help but have a foreboding that John had been killed. Her thoughts jumped from asking God to save him to what she was going to do if he were dead. She looked at Elizabeth and Martha many times and realized they too were worried and needed comfort, just as she did. Jeremiah and Edward were with John. But comfort was not to be theirs. They tried to say things to give each other the strength not to break down while they waited without any word from the front.

Finally, on the third day the first remnants of the army began to stream out of the forest into Crown Point. The sight of them scared Sarah mightily. They looked like death itself. Many were seriously wounded, their clothes torn to bits.

Sarah looked for John but did not see him among the men who were coming in. She asked one man if this was all that was left of the army. He said, "No ma'am, there's plenty more comin' in behind us." So there was still a chance that John was safe and her nightmare would not come true.

Dr. Schmidt came out of the hospital and called to the women, "Come ladies, we must tend to these wounded men. I know you have menfolk out with the army but we must help these men now."

Sarah looked at him and knew he was right, but her legs just would not move. All she could do was stare at the men as they passed by her.

Elizabeth snapped her out of it and pushed her toward the men. "Come on Sarah, now is not the time to break down. John will be coming in soon. But right now we must help these men."

When Sarah got to the hospital Elizabeth told her, "Take these men and clean them up as best you can, then determine the extent of their wounds. The ones with serious wounds put into a bed, the rest, bandage up as best you can and send back to their units. The doctor will attend to the ones we put in the beds as soon as he can. Now hurry, there are too many of them to waste even one minute."

Sarah did as she was told. The first man had a musket ball in his leg. He was being half carried, half dragged by two other men who were only slightly wounded. One of the men said, "Take care of Billy here first ma'am, we can get by on our own." Sarah looked at the wounded man for a moment and thought to herself, "this is not a man; he is just a boy—maybe seventeen. What is he doing here?" It was the first time she realized how many boys were actually in this army. She saw them every day, but until now she did not realize that they would be wounded and killed without regard to their age. She wanted to cry, but she knew there wasn't time. Then she said, "Yes, put him right here on this bed." She started to clean the wound. She could see where the ball had gone in without hitting bone. The doctor came by and said, "Just dress that wound for the time being. We will take that ball out after we get rid of the more serious cases."

Sarah looked at the boy and wondered what the "more serious cases" could be. She soon found out. The doctor called her into a separate room where a man was laying on a table. The man's leg was half blown away. Sarah stared at the man and almost fainted. Dr. Schmidt said, "Sarah, you can't faint now, I need you, and more importantly this man needs you. Now Small is going to hold him down by the arms and this soldier is going to help. You must hold this strap of leather between his teeth. We are going to amputate this leg. We don't have any anesthetic, so he will fight until he passes out. The leather will keep him from biting his tongue off. But we must get this leg off before he bleeds to death."

She was not ready for what happened next. She put the leather strap between his teeth and the doctor brought out a saw and began sawing the man's leg off just above the wound. He left a large flap of skin and pulled it back from the wound. Once the leg was off, he tied off the blood vessels and used the flap to close the wound. All the while the man alternately chomped down on the strap as hard as he could or tried to screamed, until finally the shock of the amputation caused him to pass out.

Sarah nearly passed out herself several times. But as though he knew what was going through her mind, the doctor would say, "Stay with him Sarah. You can't pass out on him now, he needs you. Stay with him." Somehow she did it.

All she could think was "Get this done so I can get out of here." But when Small took the man away and she started to go the doctor said, "Sarah, you can't leave, we need you in here. There are many more men who will be coming through here." With that, Small and the soldier brought in another man whose arm they were going to amputate. It was as if Sarah was in a terrible dream she could not wake or escape from. Hours passed and man after man was brought in and the doctor kept sawing arms and legs as if he was sawing wood for the fire.

When the doctor was done with a patient, two men would take him out along with the severed limb. They would throw the severed limb into a pit behind the building that was quickly filling and place the man down on a blanket on the ground behind the hospital. All of the beds were full, and men were lying on the floor and on the ground outside.

The sounds of the hospital were maddening. There was the constant moaning and screaming of men. There was nothing to give them to help ease the pain. Worse was the mumbling and murmuring of those about to die. Sarah heard them even above the screams.

Finally, after she knew not how many amputations, the doctor told her to take a break and rest some, and to send one of the other women in to take her place. She hurried out of the operating room and found Elizabeth, who was bandaging the wounds of those who did not need the doctor's expertise. The air was cold and damp, but at least it was fresh. Sarah looked at the men lying on the cold ground and the pit where the limbs were being thrown. She could no longer control herself. She started to cry and throw up at the same time. How could this be happening? In her worst nightmares she never encountered the goriness of this day. It was beyond her ability to comprehend.

Elizabeth came to her, put her arm around her shoulder, and said gently, "We've seen a lot today, Sarah. It's been pretty hard at times, hasn't it? But maybe you helped save some of these men's lives. You have to keep that in your thoughts. If we weren't here, who would be here to tend to all these men?"

But to Sarah, it somehow didn't matter. She just wanted to find John and run away from this place. She didn't know where. Just somewhere other than here. All she could say was, "I know you're right Elizabeth. I'll get over it. Have you seen Edward, or John or Jeremiah?"

"No, I ain't seem 'em yet. And I'm going to take that as a good sign that they are alright until I find out otherwise. I advise you to do the same. It's the only way we will be able to stay sane."

Sarah nodded and looked out at the men still coming in from the forest. "Where is he? Why is he not here yet?" Then she saw Jeremiah. He was helping a man to walk in. The man was covered with blood. His clothes were nothing but blood soaked rags. Sarah saw Martha running toward Jeremiah and started toward him herself. Surely he would know where John was. As she approached she suddenly stopped. The man Jeremiah was carrying was John. She could not believe what she was looking at and no words came from her mouth. Embedded in his face and body were pieces of wood, some small, some larger.

Jeremiah said, "John is alright, Sarah. He was near where an explosion occurred and it splintered the wood of the ship and he caught quite a bit of it. It really looks worse than it is. Let's get him to the hospital so they can attend to him."

As they approached the hospital Sarah said, "No. Not in there. Let's take him to our room where I can attend to him. Martha, could you get some bandages and water so I can clean him up?"

Martha went to get the necessary articles.

Once he was on the bed Sarah began cutting his clothes off. She could see then that not only did the wood stick into his body, there was also cloth from his clothes in the punctures. Martha came back quickly and started to help Sarah gently pull the wood fragments and cloth from John's body. As Jeremiah had said, all the blood made it look a great deal worse than it actually was. They took everything out of him that they could find, then cleaned and dressed the wounds.

When they had finished, Martha stood up and ran to Jeremiah. She pulled him close to her and hugged and kissed him profusely. John had yet to say anything. Sarah just sat with him and held his hand. She could feel the life coming back into him even as he moaned in a semi-conscious state. She looked at Martha and Jeremiah and felt a pang of jealousy which she quickly rid herself of. She said, "You two don't need to stay here. I'll be fine, and so will John. Thank you, Jeremiah, for bringing him back to me."

Jeremiah said, "He's a good man, Sarah. He fought like a cornered lion out there. All of us did. I only hope that all this sacrifice has been worth it. We didn't win, but at least we let them know they are in for a fight when they finally get down here."

Martha asked, "Have you seen Edward? I know Elizabeth has to be as worried for him as we've been for you two."

"Oh, yes, I saw him right after we landed up north. He was very much alive, and not wounded as far as I could see. He should be showing up any time now. There weren't many behind us."

"Thank God, she will be so relieved," Martha responded. With that they walked away and Sarah was alone with John.

There wasn't much she could do for him. What she thought he probably needed the most was to sleep. When he woke up she would fix him something to eat. She stayed with him as long as she could before a soldier came to the door and said, "Pardon me ma'am, but the doc says he needs you. Can you come right away?"

She looked at John and then at the soldier. She didn't want to leave John alone, but now that he was back and relatively safe she knew that she had to go back into that room and help. She said, "Tell the doctor I'll be right there." Then she whispered in

John's ear, "You rest, dear. I'll not be far away. Just on the other side of the door."

She returned later with some clean clothes she was able to get from the quartermaster. When she entered the room John was trying to sit up. "John, what are you doing? Lay down before you get yourself bleeding again."

"I have to get up and see to our boys, Sarah."

"Your boys will do fine without you till tomorrow. Jeremiah has them under his wing. I believe they all must be back now. General Arnold came in a little earlier. Besides, wouldn't you look pretty rushing out of here naked as the day you was born? Jeremiah said he will send someone for you if you are needed."

He quickly looked under the blanket and asked how he got there. Sarah told him how Jeremiah had carried him in and how she and Martha dressed his wounds. "Your clothes were nothing but rags and didn't cover much, so I cut them off. Here are some new ones. But I would wait awhile to put them on to keep the blood from sticking to them. You can put them on in the morning. You can sleep here tonight. Martha and Elizabeth are staying with their husbands."

Finally, she knelt beside the bed, took his face gently in her hands, and kissed it lightly. She then said, "Oh, John, it has been terrible here. Since the men first started coming in I have been with the doctor in the surgery. I don't know what gave me the strength to stay there. He has been doing amputations of arms and legs all day. It is a most ghastly scene. I want to cry, but there is no time. I am so glad you are back. I want you to hold me in your arms and never let me go. I know you can't right now, but heal soon and then hold me."

"I will," he said as he drifted off to sleep.

The next morning, Sarah was wakened early by a rap on the door. She thought, "Oh, no, that doctor cannot be going to start this slaughter again so early in the morning." She whispered through the door, trying not to wake John, "Yes, what is it?"

A voice from the other side of the door said, "Captain says he needs Sergeant Hardy quick as possible ma'am. We are getting ready to head down to Fort Ti today."

John heard the conversation and was sitting up. He yelled through the door, "tell the Captain I will be right there. Sarah, where are those clothes you got for me?"

Sarah gave him the clothes, and while he dressed she wondered out loud, "What do you think he meant when he said you are moving down to Fort Ti, John?"

"Can't say, Sarah. But I'm going to find out soon enough." He kissed her and went out the door.

Nineteen

Sarah's day quickly became a whirl of activity. Once John had left she went into the hospital and was met by Dr. Schmidt and Small. The doctor said, "Oh, Sarah, I'm glad you have arrived. We have to get these patients ready to be transported to Fort Ti. Small and these soldiers," he pointed to a group of soldiers standing to his rear, "will carry those that cannot walk down to the ships. If you and the other ladies will make sure the other patients get down there also it will be a great help. Additionally, I will need some help to pack up all the medicines and medical equipment we can carry and get it down to the ships as well. I know there's not much. But what we have we need to save." With that he turned and left.

Sarah still did not know exactly what was happening, and was bewildered as to what to do first. Elizabeth and Martha arrived and she told them what the doctor had instructed her to do. Then she asked, "Do either of you know what is happening? All I know is that a soldier knocked on the door this morning and told John that he was needed to help get the soldiers ready to go down to Fort Ti. And when I got here a few minutes ago the doctor gave me the instructions I just told you about."

Martha then said, "Jeremiah came back to the tent this morning and said that General Arnold has ordered a complete evacuation of Crown Point. Every person and all equipment have to be moved today. He does not believe that this place can be defended from the British, and wants to get everyone back to Fort Ti to prepare a defense there."

Elizabeth said, "Well, ladies. it looks like our little sojourn here is over. We better get to work, or they might leave us here."

Sarah asked, "Elizabeth, I didn't get to see Edward yesterday, how is he? How did he make it through the battle?"

"Oh, he is fine, thank God. Just nearly exhausted, as are all the men. But I heard that John was hurt pretty bad. How is he?"

"He was near where a cannon ball hit and was struck with quite a bit of wood splinters. When Jeremiah and another man half carried him in yesterday he was covered in blood. I thought he was dying. But once Martha and I got him cleaned up and got the wood pieces out of him it did not appear as bad. And he got some rest last night. That probably helped him the most. He was much better this morning, and when that soldier came he was outta the room in a hurry. He looks like a porcupine threw its quills at him this morning, but I think he'll be fine."

"Well, thank God he's alright," Elizabeth said. "Now let's get these men down to the ships so we can get outta here also. Edward says they are marching back to the fort, and only the invalids will be going on the ships. I hope they put us on one of them also. We haven't had shoes since early summer, and I don't fancy walking ten miles in my bare feet today."

The weather was still cold and rainy and the ground was frozen in the morning and turned to mud as the day warmed up somewhat. Getting the men down to the ships was tedious as the footing was treacherous and the men had to lean on the women as they walked. In their weakened state most of the men placed a great deal of their weight on the women so that they were almost carrying many of them.

By mid-afternoon the men had all been taken down and were loaded on the ships. John stopped by the hospital to tell Sarah that he and Jeremiah and their company were taking off, and that he would see her in Fort Ti. He kissed her goodbye and ran off to join the march.

During the day the doctor told the women that they would be traveling by the ships also so that they could help with wounded. Each one of them would be on a different ship. There wasn't much anyone could do for the men except try to make them as comfortable as possible.

The early darkness of the northern Adirondacks had already set in by the time the ships departed. The last of the men, who were given the detail of setting fire to every building and everything at Crown Point, were doing their job well. Nothing was to be left for the British to use. As her ship slipped away and out onto the lake, Sarah could see the flames building higher and lighting up the sky with sparks that looked like a million shooting stars as they rose into the night and then fell into the lake. As she sat on deck watching the flames she wished that she might be nearer to them. The night was already cold and getting colder by the minute. She could use some of the fire's warmth just then. She also knew that the men too were very cold. There were not enough blankets for all of them. Everyone had to bear the cold as best he, or she, could. She knew it was not a long trip, only ten miles, but she worried about several of the men and whether they would make it or not.

Sarah felt very tired and wished she could sleep. But the drizzly, cold rain had soaked her completely, and she shivered from the cold. Additionally, the ship pitched and rolled as it tried to make its way through the rough waters. With each movement of the ship the men under her care moaned in agony. They too were drenched and freezing to add to the pain from their wounds. There was nothing she could do for them, and the sounds of their misery only added to her own.

The ships finally arrived at the fort hours later in the middle of the night. They were met at the shore by men from the fort and the men who had started out marching early that morning. John was there, and just seeing him helped to warm Sarah's heart, if not her body. As everyone hurriedly worked to get the wounded off the ships and to some shelter, John told her that they had made it even though they had had a brush with an Indian ambush along the way. A few more men were injured, but no one was lost.

At last everyone was disembarked and given shelter. All the supplies were unloaded and stored away. John took Sarah's hand and they silently walked through the freezing, rainy black night to the tent. Sarah thought she should be saying something, but none of her thoughts were about them. They were about all she had seen and been through since leaving Fort Ti months ago. She wanted to talk about it to John. But she thought that what he had been through over the past year must be even more horrible, and her problems trivial compared to what he had faced. Everything seemed trivial in the face of this war.

When they reached the tent Sarah was surprised to see John's old tent mates already there. Surprised, not because they didn't belong there but because she had forgotten about them. As she looked at them in the light of a single candle, she shed her thoughts, took a breath and said, "Why good evening gentlemen, it's very good to see you again."

They each said hello in a shy, embarrassed manner. A year ago they would have found an excuse to leave to give John and Sarah some privacy. But tonight they were not leaving the dryness of the tent and what little warmth they derived from their collective bodies for anyone else's privacy.

Sarah understood and said, "Gentlemen, it is indeed a miserable night out tonight, and I would not ask anyone to leave the luxury of this tent for me. However, I am going to get out of these soaking clothes, regardless of modesty. So have any of you something dry I might put on once I'm shed of these things?"

Ben, being the largest man there, reached for a shirt. "Here Sarah, this outta be large enough to cover all the important parts."

They all laughed a little and Sarah demurely said, "Thank you, Ben. I am sure it will be very adequate." At that Sarah felt a little bit of Elizabeth coming out in her. "Now I don't want any of you to have to go out into the cold rain for me and I have had my fill of it for the night also. So if you would all be so gallant as to close your eyes while I change into this lovely warm shirt, I would greatly appreciate it. And, if any of you feel the need to peek, I would ask that you remember that this has been a trying time and not judge by what you see tonight. I think John can attest to the fact that I can look better when I'm cleaned up a little."

The mood relaxed as they all laughed and promised not to peek. John added, "Don't worry dear, I'll keep my eye on them to make sure they don't peek. But I ain't promising not to peek myself."

Sarah, feeling rather risqué, responded, "You, my dear, may peek all you want." She took off her saturated clothing and quickly put on Ben's shirt. She thanked the men for their chivalry and placed her things in the rear of the tent so that they might dry by morning. With that John blew out the candle, and everyone wrapped up in their blanket and went to sleep.

Sarah snuggled as close to John as she could in order to get warm. As she drifted off to sleep she dreamed of the day he had returned from Canada and they had made love in the meadow by the lake. She wondered if they would ever feel that way again.

Twenty

In the morning Sarah waited until the men had all left the tent, then she took off Ben's shirt and started to dress. As she dressed she wondered if any of the men had chanced to take a peek. She giggled a little at the thought. Never in her life, except perhaps around her brothers, had she dared to be naked amidst a group of men. She knew she should have been embarrassed, but the thought actually gave her a little tingle of excitement. What would they have seen, she wondered? Then she looked at herself naked for the first time in she could not remember how long. The softness that was there when she began this journey was gone. It had been replaced by taut muscle and sinew. She thought, after all she had been through, that she still looked pretty good. And it pleased her to think that if it made the men feel good to have peeked, at least they shouldn't have been disappointed. She finished dressing, smiled, and left the tent.

The men were all waiting by the fire and looked at her as she came out. John said, "You certainly look happy this morning Sarah. What's given you such a bright smile on such a cloudy day?"

Sarah blushed to think that they might know what she had just been thinking about but responded, "Just having all of you back safe and sound has given me a lighter spirit this morning." As she said it she believed that in fact there was truth in that thought. She was happier this morning than she had been in weeks. And being once again in the tent and sleeping with the men last night had given her a warm comfort she had not known she had missed.

She picked up some cooking utensils and rations and went to the kitchen, where she met Elizabeth and Martha. They too were brighter this morning. Sarah noted this and Elizabeth put in, "Of course we're all happier this morning. Where else can a woman get the warmth of sleeping with four men and nobody thinks anything of it? I'm not saying I'd like to do it for the rest of my life now. But it sure is helpful on these cold nights."

Martha responded jokingly, "I'm jealous. I only got to sleep with two men."

"The perils of leadership, my dear. Just wait till that husband of yours gets promoted again. Then you will only have him to keep you warm, while no matter how many times John and Edward get promoted, Sarah and I will still have our male harem to keep us warm," Elizabeth mockingly chortled.

While they finished cooking breakfast the conversation turned to what they were going to do now that they were back. They had all left their previous jobs to go to Crown Point, and they wondered if they would be able to get them back.

Elizabeth put a good light on the subject. "Ladies, there is no need for us to worry about work around here. Have you taken a look at this fort this morning? There are more men here than when we left. Every able bodied person, including us, will be needed to help get this place ready to defend against Carleton if he chooses to attack us this year. No, there is going to be plenty for us to do. If we are lucky enough to get our old jobs back, so much the better. But mark my words, we won't be outta work long either way." With that they took breakfast back to their waiting men.

While they ate, the men talked about the battle they had just been through. Ben said, "Well, I hope whatever we did is enough to keep the bloody Lobsterbacks off for a while. I am not too keen on breaking our backs getting ready for battles that the generals know we are going to lose. Why did we build all those ships and go up there if we already knew we was goin' to lose? I heard General Arnold himself tell one of the ship Captains that our job was not to win the battle but to delay Carleton as long as we could, in hopes he might turn around and go back to Canada. John, you're the only real soldier amongst us, what do you think? After that whooping we just took do you think he's goin' to do that?"

John looked at him, then to the others, and replied, "I don't, Ben. But I know if we hadn't done something he would already be here and gone probably half way to Albany by now. Winter is going to set in pretty quick, and his supply lines are long and slow. So maybe he will think twice before starting a campaign this year. If he decides to wait for spring, we have bought ourselves some time to better prepare for it. If he does decide to attack us this year, which I think is what I would do if I were him, I don't think we can stop him. All we can do is slow him down, maybe, and hope for some relief from General Washington."

William then put in, "Uh, John, if what I heard in the camp last night is true, we ain't likely to be getting any relief from that quarter. The rumor is that General Washington's part of the army was roundly defeated and driven out of Long Island in August and is pretty much on the run too. If that's so, with him being beat down there and us getting beat up here, this here revolution ain't looking too good right now."

Everyone went silent. They all knew that the army's rumor mill was usually spot on as to the facts of things. It tended to exaggerate many of the details and left much to the imagination, but usually the basic facts of things were true. If it was true that Washington had been beaten then they were definitely on their own, and they knew they were no match for Carleton and his army.

"Well, boys, there isn't much we can do for or about General Washington and his situation. Whether he has been beaten or not, we still have a job to do here. It would be nice to get some relief from somewhere, but with it or without it we have to get ready for Carleton. Let's say we go to work," John finally sighed.

Sarah hadn't given the other parts of this war a second thought. She was so involved in what was going on in the Adirondacks that she believed the whole war was here, and it was to be won or lost here. She tried to put it all together in her mind, but it was too much to absorb so quickly. Instead she rather lightly changed the subject, "Gentlemen, I know this won't help beat the British, either here or down in New York City, but I am going to start out this return to our tent by washing my spare clothes. If any of you have anything that needs washing, if you give it to me I'll get it washed for you today. It isn't raining for a change, maybe it will dry."

The men looked at her and all realized that indeed, whatever happened, life needed to go on. Ben hugged her. "Sarah, you have a way of putting things into perspective. We ain't got much in the line of spare clothes anymore, but I for one will take you up on your offer. No matter what we gotta do, we might as well do it clean if we can."

He and the others went into the tent and came out with the few rags that made up their spare clothing and handed them to her.

John looked at her proudly and asked, "What else are you planning to do today Sarah? I know this little bit of washing isn't going to keep you busy for long. I know this isn't what I promised you when we got married, but I'm proud of you and all that you do for us and the cause. Thank you." He gently kissed her on the forehead and turned to leave.

Sarah looked after the four of them as they walked away. Ben couldn't resist a jab at John. "You call that a kiss, man? You got the only woman in the tent and that's the best kiss you can work up? You don't do better'n that I might have to take her away from you after this war is over." He punched John in the arm and they all laughed.

Sarah smiled at the good-natured camaraderie she just witnessed. They were all good men, and she realized that together they were becoming a family and she loved them all. John was right. She was happy this morning. It was still cold and damp, and life wasn't getting any easier, but she was glad to be back at the fort and to be with her men again.

When breakfast was done and the men had gone off to work, Sarah cleaned up the dishes and got the washing done. Then she set off to go find some work. Her first stop was at the headquarters. She was glad to see that although the commandant of the fort was now Colonel Wayne from Pennsylvania, Major Cardin was still the adjutant. She knocked at the open door and the major rose and came out from behind his desk and said, "Why, Mrs. Hardy, how very good to see you. I see you made it through the experiences up at Crown Point. I have heard that you and the other ladies were a great deal of help up there, and we all thank you for taking that initiative and for your assistance. Please come in. What can I do for you this morning?"

Sarah was surprised to hear that word of their efforts at Crown Point had reached the fort, but was grateful for the recognition. She replied, "Good morning, Major Cardin. It is good to be back and to see you again also. Thank you for those kind words. I'm not sure we knew what we were getting ourselves into when we left, but there was certainly enough to do up there to keep us busy. I hope it helped in some way." Then she came straight to the point of her visit. "The reason I stopped by this morning, Major, was to ask if you might be able to use me again."

The major looked a little sheepish as though he had bad news to tell her. "Well, Mrs. Hardy, I must be honest with you. As you probably know, Colonel Wayne is now the commandant. He is a marvelous soldier, but I'm afraid he is a little more, uh, rustic than General Schuyler. His needs are not quite as great as the general's were. So I am afraid that at the moment I can't use you here." He stopped, and she could tell he was giving it some thought. "But," he went on, "you just returned with General Arnold. You might go over to his quarters and ask if he may need someone to take care of his needs while he is here. I don't think he will be here very long—Generals don't seem to care much for the life up here—but it is a start."

With that he stood up and Sarah knew that the conversation was at an end. "Thank you, Major. I will inquire at the general's quarters. It is very good to see you again."

She turned to leave and as she reached the door the major said, "Oh, Mrs Hardy, I almost forgot, this letter arrived for you last week. I did not send it forward as I knew the units were coming back and it would probably get lost for weeks trailing behind you. I hope that is alright with you."

Sarah took the letter and saw that it was from her mother. She tried to remember when she had last heard from her, or written her for that matter. It must have been months ago. "Thank you, Major. It was most kind of you to hold this for me. I hope you have a nice day."

"And you too, Mrs. Hardy. And good luck."

Sarah looked at the envelope and then she looked around. She had to find a private place to read the letter. She left the fort and went back to the tent. Few people were in the regimental area at that hour of the morning. She sat on a stump in front of the dying fire and opened the envelope. The first words she read stunned her beyond belief:

Sept 10, 1776

My Dearest Sarah,

It is with a very sad heart that I write you today. I received a letter from your father this day and I must tell you that your brother Robert has been killed in action fighting with General Washington on Long Island. I know you share the grief I am feeling this day. Your father and James were with him when he died. Father says Robert was given as proper a burial as was possible at the time. I know we will never be able to bring him back and bury him in our land. It saddens me so to think of him alone amid strangers without a proper grave or to think that I will never be able to visit his grave and say a prayer over it for him.

As you may know, things are not going well for the army in New York. They have been soundly beaten at every step. They have been driven out of the city and Long Island by General Howe and his army and it is said they are retreating in an attempt to get away. The last I heard from your father, he and James were all right. But I worry, and pray constantly that they will return and this war will end soon.

Your sister and brother, Jane and Henry, and I are tending what is left of the farm. Marauding armies from both sides have taken just about everything we own, including your father's tools and all the animals and food. The local Tories are making life as miserable as possible. They have taken heart from the British victories and they have started burning out the homes of those who support independence. I fear that we may have to leave for a safer place soon, as I cannot help but believe we will soon be next. If so, I do not know what we will do. I guess we will try to get to your Aunt Sarah's place in German Flats on the Mohawk. But I understand they too have their problems with the Indians up there. I don't know what else to do, and at least your uncle is still there. He is part of the local militia and has not been called out yet to leave. According to your aunt, they are safe for now. I will write you and let you know whatever happens to us.

I have not heard from you in quite some time and worry about your and John's safety. Please write as soon as you can and let me know that you are safe. Please say a prayer for your brother's soul and for a quick end of this war.

God Bless You,
Mother

Tears streaming down her face, Sarah sat looking at the letter. This could not be true. With all she had seen it had never really occurred to her that this war would really take one of her own from her. Robert was her big brother. Growing up she had idolized him. He always seemed so big and strong. Next to her parents, he was her protector. He was the one she could tell her secrets to and know that he would keep them. He could make fun of her and she didn't mind. Now he was gone. She would never see him again. She stopped and started to say a prayer, as her mother asked. But the prayer wouldn't come. Instead, her thoughts were a diatribe against God. How could He let this war go on? How could He let her brother be killed in this senseless war? How could she now pray that God would take care of Robert when He didn't take care of him on that battlefield when Robert needed Him? How could He do this to her? She thought that she would never be able to believe and trust in God or pray to him again.

While she was deep in her despair, a soldier from John's company passed by. He noticed her crying and asked, "Mrs. Hardy, are you alright ma'am?"

Sarah stared blankly at the man. He was about the same age as Robert would be, and for a moment she thought it was Robert. She quickly came to her senses and responded, "Yes, thank you Private Henkel, I am—just some sad news is all." Then she asked, "Might you know where Sergeant Hardy is right now?'

"Yes ma'am, he's with the company working on the defenses."

"Could you please go ask him if he could come here? It is very important that I talk to him as soon as possible."

"Yes ma'am, I'll run right over there and tell him."

"Thank you," she mumbled.

She was still crying when John arrived. He ran to her and asked, "Sarah, what is wrong darling?"

She could not speak, but handed him the letter instead. When he began reading it he slowly sat on a stump next to her. He read the letter several times as though trying to put something to say together. All he could say as he took her in his arms was, "Sarah, I'm so sorry. I know you loved him most of all your siblings. I loved Robert too. It was him that taught me how to get along with your father when I first went to work in the blacksmith shop. He was a good man who knew how to work hard yet separate work from having fun when it was time. I will miss him greatly, and I know your sorrow must be immense. If there is anything I can do to relieve it, please tell me."

She looked at him with her swollen, red eyes. "No John, there is nothing you, or anybody, can do. Only time, I guess, will help." Then she cried, "Oh, John, when will this torment of a war be over? What terrible sins have we committed against God that he is punishing us so?"

John did not try to answer. He just held her tighter and rocked her in his arms. After a while she broke away and wiped her face again with her sleeve. She said, "Thank you for coming and holding me. I needed that. I know you are sad too, and that you must get back to work. I will be alright. I must write Mother now. Go ahead and go back to work. I will be fine." Then she held his strong hard hands in hers and added, "John, when you were off fighting I always wondered what it would be like if you —" she couldn't finish the sentence. "John, I could not bear losing you too. Please, always be careful."

He hugged her once more and said, "Sarah, my darling, I promise I will do everything in my power not to ever make you feel this way over me." They both smiled weakly, and he left.

She sat back down and absent-mindedly added some wood to the dying fire. She stared into the flames as the new wood caught fire. She tried to remember the farm and life as it used to be when they were all a big happy family. Although it was just a relatively short ride down the Hudson from where she sat, that home seemed a million miles away. She wondered if she should try to get down there and help out with the farm. But then she knew that there was little she could do even if she could get home. No, her place was here with John. But today, more than she could remember, she missed her mother and father and her brothers and sister.

Elizabeth walked up as Sarah dreamed of a home that would

never exist again. "John stopped by the sutler's and told me about your brother. I thought maybe I would just stop by and sit a while. Maybe talk if you would like. Say, how would you like a nice cup of tea? That always seems to help me when I'm feeling low. I just happen to have all the fixings here." She got some water into a pot and put it over the fire without waiting for an answer. They waited in silence for the water to boil. When it was hot Elizabeth filled two metal cups and put the tea ball in one and then the other. She handed one cup to Sarah and said, "Here you go, dearie. Now you drink this, and we'll just sit here and watch the fire together. If you feel like talking you just start right up. I've got nothing I'd rather do today than listen to you. And if you feel like crying, why that'll be alright too. Sometimes there nothing so soothing as a good cry."

They sat silently together for a long time sipping the tea. Finally, Sarah asked, "Elizabeth, what is today's date?"

"Why, I think it's about the fourteenth of October. Why do you ask?"

"I have to write my mother, and I want to put the date on the letter. You know, since we have been up here I don't ever think about what date it is or even what day it is sometimes. I know what season it is from how hot or cold it is. And most of the time I know what month it is. But it really doesn't matter much up here, does it?"

"You alright, Sarah?"

"Yes, I'm fine, Elizabeth. I was just wondering how long we've been here and how much longer we'll be here. I guess I'm thinking about a million crazy things in no particular order at this moment. Robert's death has me remembering things, and then this fire brings me back here and I'm just trying to sort things out in my mind. I know there is nothing I can do about Robert. And I know my place is here with John. But I can't help hating those Tories who are harassing my mother, and the British bastards who are instigating them. I wish I was a man and that I could take up a gun and personally kill all of those bastards. From now on, I will do everything I can to win this war on my terms. I will not rest until I am either dead or every one of them, British and Tory, is dead or driven from this land."

"Well," Elizabeth said, quite taken aback by Sarah's vehemence, "that is a side of you that I have never experienced. If I were one of those bastards I would not want to tangle with you."

"I am sorry Elizabeth. I didn't mean to explode like that. It is the British and the Tories I am angry at, not you."

"I know, dearie. And you needn't apologize to me. Who are you going to explode at if not at a friend? Besides, I agree with you. Let's make a pact. We'll create our own army of women and make this war our war and fight it on our terms. I don't know if you realize it or not, but you have already been fighting a pretty good war for the past year. You just didn't have a cause until now. I'm sorry that it took your brother's death to give you one. It's not our time yet to be pulling triggers, but believe me, everything we do that helps a soldier get back into the battle is adding to our ability to win this thing. I know it don't look like it right now, but I believe we will win this war. Somehow, some way, we will win. And us women will be a part of that victory. Just as much as any man who fights the battles."

Sarah looked at Elizabeth and could see that she was serious and really earnest about what she had just said. A little of Sarah's sadness left her. She was not as alone as she had felt earlier. She felt a little lightness reenter her heart and jokingly inquired, "And what shall we call this army of ours, General?"

Elizabeth smiled and said, "Maybe we best not give it a name. It'll be a secret army that neither side will know about. If we let it be known that we are helping, our men will find a way to take all the credit anyway, and the Redcoats will cry foul for the Americans using women and not fighting a proper war. We'll just secretly help the menfolk as they stumble along. We can't do no worse than they have done up to now. Well, if you are alright I'll take my tea ball and get back to work before they think I've quit again."

"Thank you Elizabeth. For the tea and for the shoulder." Sarah reached out and hugged Elizabeth tightly. "With you as our leader, ours will be a great army indeed. I'll walk with you as far as the gate. I need to see if Major Cardin will give me a couple of sheets of paper, a quill and some ink to write to my mother with. I haven't had any writing material for months."

The major gave Sarah the material she needed and offered his desk to her to write at. She had no idea how to begin, or what to say that would express her profound sense of loss. She started:

Oct 14, 1776

My Dearest Mother,

I received your latest letter finally today. I cannot tell you how the news of Robert's death saddens me. There are no words to express how very distraught I am today. I wish I could be there with you at this terrible time. I know it must be hard on you and Jane and Henry to be there without Father and James. Although I know that Robert is in heaven, I miss him and wish I could talk to him right now. He was always the one who knew me best and could make me laugh when I was sad. I will think of him always in that way and it will help me get through. I hope you too can have happy memories of him and keep him alive in your heart with thoughts of all the joy he brought to us all.

John and I are well. He was slightly injured in a naval battle that occurred last week on Lake Champlain near Valcour Island. He is fine though and was back at work the day after they returned. We are very sorry to hear that General Washington and the army down there are not doing well. As you probably know, our piece of the army was driven from Canada in June, and the naval battle was an attempt to keep the British from launching an attack on the Hudson this year. Although we were beaten, the men are hopeful that they were successful in that. We should know in a few days what the British General Carleton has decided. We must all keep up hope and do our best to defeat these Redcoats and the traitorous Tories who support them. I am sure we will win in the end. It is just so hard to be able to see that end through all the setbacks we have gone through.

I am very worried about you with the Tories being so active down there. Please take care, and if need be get to Aunt Sarah's sooner rather than later. We can always build another house but I could not bear it if anything happened to you.

I must close for now but will try to write more often in the future. We keep you constantly in our thoughts and love you all very much. Take care of yourself, and write when you know what you are going to do.

Your Loving Daughter,
Sarah

Sarah addressed the letter and gave it to Major Cardin to send out with other mail the next time a supply train came in. There was much that she wished she could have told her mother about the horrors she had already seen and of her fears for the coming battle. But that would only add to her mother's worries, and wouldn't help anything. She left the office and felt the cold rain that was once again starting to fall. She thought that the rain was a fitting end to this day. It was a day that had started out so light and airy but turned into the very dark cloud that she was walking through now. She walked back to the tent wishing that total darkness would fall soon so that she could go to sleep. Maybe sleep and a new morning would lift this misery from her.

Twenty-One

In the morning when Sarah awoke she was alone in the tent. The men had been very kind to her the evening before. They knew how sad she was and did everything they could try to make her feel better. John did the cooking and took the jokes for his failure in not being able to match Sarah's. Sarah went into the tent very early and they let her get to sleep. She sleepily felt them as they came into the tent, but did not stir again until this moment. Usually she was awake before them. For all her sadness she had slept sounder last night than she had in a very long time. Maybe it was exhaustion or maybe she just did not want to wake up and realize that yesterday was real and not just a dream. But she was awake now, and knew that it wasn't a dream and that she had to go out and face the world again today.

She heard the men talking outside the tent. They were discussing the war. John was saying, "...from what Sarah's mother's letter said, I guess that rumor about Washington getting beat up in New York must be true. If so it sure ain't looking good for us. We're getting pretty well beat up here ourselves. And with them losing down there, I wonder how we are going to hold together. If Carleton decides to attack soon we can't hold him off."

"What do ya suppose will happen to us if we lose this war, John?" William asked.

"Don't know. But it won't be good. That's certain."

She left the tent, and as she did the men all stood up. John said, "Good morning, Sarah. How are you feeling this morning?" The other men looked on expectantly.

Sarah looked from one to another of the men and finally said, "Good morning, gentlemen. I'm fine, John. I am going to be alright. I guess I needed that sleep. Thank you all for all the courtesy you have given me, and for giving me a moment to grieve. Now I think it's time to get back to normal. If I let you men go on like this you'll be serving me breakfast in bed next. Now go on with you and start acting normal. Yes, I'm sad about my brother, but we all must face what this war may bring. Robert died for something he believed in, and if we have to die in this war it is better that it be fighting for a cause. I know that must seem strange to you coming from me because I have always questioned what the cause we are fighting for is. But today I have my own cause, and it has somehow allowed me to accept Robert's death and vow to avenge it. Maybe there is no universal cause for why we fight. Maybe each of us has our own cause that we hope will be gained by victory. Whatever it is, I know we must go on, and may God help us." She caught herself. "Oh, my goodness, listen to me preach. Now go on, get outta here and go to work. I will be fine."

Ben laughed, "Why, Sarah, some of these officers should take lessons from you on how to inspire folks to fight. Best damned speech I've heard since we left Albany. And I know it has only been one day but I'm glad you're back. I was getting sick of John's cooking already."

They all agreed with Ben and started off to work. John held back and asked, "Are you really alright, Sarah? Is there anything I can do for you?"

"I'm fine, John, really. And if you want to do something for me, whip those Redcoats next time you meet 'em."

He reached down and kissed her on the forehead and left to join the others.

The day was colder than yesterday, and it looked like it was going to rain again. Sarah pulled her wrap around her tighter. She looked down at her bare feet and wondered where she was going to get a pair of shoes to see her through the winter. She had not been paid anything since she left for Crown Point, and John had not seen any pay in months. Besides, shoes were a difficult item to find even if you had money to buy them. She thought, "Well, I'm not alone. Most of the people here, men and women, are without proper shoes these days." She took a ragged shirt of John's and some left over canvas from a tent that was no longer useable, ripped them into strips, and wrapped her feet with them as she had seen some of the men do. "That will have to do," she said to herself.

She walked over to the fort and went to General Arnold's quarters. She rapped on the door, and to her surprise he actually answered it. He looked at her quizzically and said, "Yes?"

Sarah started, "Uh, good morning, General. I don't know if you remember me. My name is Sarah Hardy and while you were here last I had the honor of attending you."

His face seemed to brighten a little, "Yes, of course Mrs. Hardy. What can I do for you?"

"Well, Sir, I was wondering if you might need any help while you are here. I just came back from Crown Point also, and it seems the job I used to have when I was here before is no longer available."

"Please, Mrs. Hardy, step inside out of the cold. I do remember you. I did not know you were with the few women who were at Crown Point. Thank you for that. Now I do not intend to be here at Fort Ticonderoga very long. However, while I am here it so happens that I could use a woman to attend me. If you are available I would be happy to hire you. When would you be able to start?"

"Right away, Sir, today if you need me."

They went over what her duties would be: washing, cooking, cleaning. Sarah thanked him and he soon left.

While she was behind the quarters washing clothes there arose a great commotion within the fort. She went out front and saw most of the people heading out of the fort and going down to the pier. Sarah's curiosity forced her to follow them. She wondered what could possibly be so important that everyone, including the officers, were going down there. As she got closer to the shore she saw the largest ship she had ever seen coming straight for the dock. It was flying the British flag. The first thing that came into her mind was that they were about to be attacked. She asked a young officer, who was passing by, what was going on.

"Don't know ma'am. But that is one of General Carleton's ships coming in under a flag of truce. See the white flag? Maybe he has come to parley before he attacks. Or maybe he's going to surrender," the man laughed.

Men on the ship tossed lines to men on the dock and the ship was safely tied up. Once a gangplank was put in place a very smartly dressed officer came ashore and asked for the commanding officer. Colonel Wayne stepped forward and presented himself and asked what the purpose of this visit was.

Sarah maneuvered herself to the front of the crowd so as to hear what was being said.

The officer saluted. "Sir, I am Commander Smythe, Captain of this ship. I have the honor of presenting His Excellency, General Carleton's compliments. I have aboard one hundred and sixty seven prisoners who were captured during the scuffle a few days ago off Valcour Island. The general wishes to return them to you with his compliments. They are all well and safe and I assure you no great harm has befallen them while they have been in our care. May I allow them to disembark,, Sir?"

Colonel Wayne was not used to such formality, but he put his best formal look on, returned the salute, and said, "I'm Colonel Wayne, commandant of this fort. These are our boys, you say? Why of course, certainly. Let them off. And please thank General Carleton for this kind gesture."

The men started to come off the ship. They looked considerably better than the men who had come back from the battle a few days before. Their clothes did not seem as ragged, and they looked like they had been well fed while they were prisoners.

Their demeanor was very jovial, and many of them thanked the ship's crew members and officers as they disembarked.

Colonel Wayne turned to an officer standing near him and said, "Captain, put these men in a formation and march them to the fort." He then turned to the naval officer and asked with an expectant voice, "Is there anything else, Commander?"

The man replied, "The general would very much like to avoid any further unneeded bloodshed. He wondered if you care to discuss terms of cessation of these hostilities which would enable these men to get back to their homes before winter sets in."

Wayne pulled at his chin as if in thought. Then he smiled and said, "You may thank the general for his concern for our men. However, I am not in authority to discuss terms for cessation of hostilities. Our men will do their duty, as, I am sure, will yours. I am sorry I am not able to invite you in for a cup of tea but, you see, we don't use that substance any longer, and besides, I am sure you have seen quite enough of our fort from right here. Now, Sir, by your leave, my men will assist you as you depart. Once again, thank the general for his kindness to our men. May you have a safe journey, Sir." Wayne saluted the commander, who returned the salute, turned, and boarded his ship.

Everyone stared in amazement at what they had just witnessed. Sarah found John and asked him what he thought about what just happened.

"I don't know, Sarah. My guess is that they were just trying to feel us out and see as much as they could of our defenses so they could make plans for an attack. They don't want to feed and care for those prisoners. Their supply lines are too long to waste food on prisoners for very long. Bringing them back gives them a good excuse for coming here without any danger. I guess we will know in the next few days what Carleton's plans are."

Everyone went back to what they had been doing. The men who returned were marched back to the fort and each one of them was questioned in turn. Sarah asked John that evening what they were being questioned about.

"I suppose that Colonel Wayne and the general were trying to find out what the men might have seen while they were prisoners. Maybe they saw something that will give us some idea what Carleton is up to."

Ben observed, "Those boys sure seemed happy to have been prisoners. Carleton must have taken pretty good care of them. I talked to a couple of them and they couldn't say enough good things about the whole British Army, let alone Carleton. Sounded as if some of them might up and switch sides if they get the chance."

"Well, like I told Sarah this afternoon, we'll know soon enough what Carleton is going to do. He can't wait too much longer to attack or winter will set in on him. All we can do is sit and wait for now."

A few days later, all the men who had been prisoners of the British were sent back to Fort George. No one knew exactly why. They may have been sent back because they had been paroled and could not fight until exchanged for British prisoners of equal rank. But camp rumor had it that they were bad for morale of the rest of the men. Almost to a man they could not help but rave about how well they had been treated and about how well fed and provisioned the British were. According to them, when Carleton decided to attack he would take Fort Ti in a day. The commanders did not want them around to dishearten the rest of the men any worse than they already were.

The weather continued to get colder, and on October twenty-third, the first snow storm of the year hit. It came as a blizzard of snow and sleet. No one dared leave what little protection their shelters and tents provided against the cold and wind and snow. The storm lasted two days, then the sun came out. People slowly dug out, and began to build fires in an attempt to get warm. No rations had been handed out for several days due to the storm. Sarah and the men had subsisted on the few rations that they had not eaten. They were all gone after the first day. For the next two days they did not get anything to eat. Finally, the storm ended and the Quartermaster began issuing rations again.

As they collected their rations the Quartermaster Sergeant warned, "Go easy with these rations. There's no telling how long it will be before we get another supply train up here. And what with this storm and all, I can see us havin' to start cuttin' rations pretty soon."

When the snow stopped falling, the temperatures dropped dramatically. The women's clothes, as well as the men's, were worn out completely. It was a struggle for them to find something, anything to put on that would help keep them warm. Additionally, only about half of them had shoes or any kind of real protection for their feet. Some, just as Sarah had, tore up clothes that were beyond use and wrapped their feet in the strips, then covered them with canvas from worn out tents. Others just continued to walk around barefoot. No one was in any condition to fight if Carleton had decided to attack then.

About a week after the snow storm ended, a patrol, sent out

to keep their eye on the British and give early warning if they looked like they were headed toward the fort, came in with some very welcome news. It appeared that Carleton had called off any campaign for this year. The whole British Army was headed back to Canada.

Twenty-Two

Sarah could feel everyone's relief. The fort was safe from attack until spring. The feeling around the camp was one of jubilation. Yes, they had lost the Battle of Valcour Island. But they succeeded in keeping Carleton from taking Ticonderoga this year. To those at the fort it was as if they had thoroughly beaten the entire British Army. They had stood the test without breaking, and the morale boost it gave the army was enormous. More importantly, if they could hold the army together through the winter, they had time to prepare for next year's campaign.

The first thing that had to be done, however, was to get everyone out of the tents and into huts that would hold up to the winter. Luckily, after the first snow storm, the weather broke and the men were able to build a sort of village of huts much like those Sarah and the women had lived in the past year. Once they were built and occupied everyone was elated.

The elation did not last long, however. Soon after they moved into the new huts the winter pressed down upon the fort and its inhabitants. Just as the Quartermaster Sergeant had predicted, supply trains found it hard going to get through the snow over impassable roads to deliver supplies to the fort. They were soon on half rations, then they were halved again before the first sleds made their way into the fort in December with new supplies. Hunger became a way of life. Every scrap, every morsel of food was a feast not to be wasted.

As the winter grew colder the snow piled up, and as food became scarce the number of men there began to dwindle. John and the others talked every night about how many had simply left. Some of them were militiamen who had signed up for three or six months and their time was up. They had done what they thought was their duty and now it was time to go home to their families and take care of their other duties. Others just walked away in the night. Deserters! The word stuck in the men's throats and they spat it out with venomous sneers as they talked about those who would not stay the course. But as Sarah looked about the fort and the camp that surrounded it she thought, "who could really blame them?" They came to fight the British, but now they were being asked to subject themselves to misery with no end in sight and no likelihood of fighting anyone in the near future. John said that some would come back in the spring, but most they would never be seen again.

Work continued to be done to shore up the defenses of the fort and Mount Independence. But because of the weather, a lack of equipment and supplies, and the fact that the men were starving and without proper clothing, the work dragged on with little noticeable improvement.

General Arnold left soon after General Carleton went back to Canada, and Sarah found herself working in the hospital again. Although a General Hospital, capable of providing more complete care, had been set up at Fort George, there was no way to get the seriously sick or wounded there during these frigid winter months. So they remained at Fort Ti.

The hospital was now being run by a Dr. Potts. Sarah believed he was a great improvement on Dr. Schmidt, who had been at Crown Point. Potts was active and could always be found either at the hospital or doing something to try to improve the lives of the men.

Sarah enjoyed working for Dr. Potts, and began to learn a great deal from him. Instead of simply being a scrub woman, cleaning the hospital daily with vinegar, tending to the cleaning of beds and cleaning up after the men, the doctor took her on as a proper nurse and taught her how to prepare medicines and what to do for the men. She was quickly attending to those cases which did not require the doctor's personal attention.

The winter and lack of proper food was devastating to everyone, but seemed to hit the men worse than the women. Nearly all of the men were beset with the flux, dysentery, fevers, or a deep cough which caused them to spit up blood. Additionally, men would come in with wounds they received chopping down trees or in building the fortifications.

A remedy for some of the diseases was a potion called blue mass. It was a concoction of mercury, licorice, hollyhock, glycerin, and honey. Dr. Potts taught Sarah how to prepare the medicine and she also oversaw its administration to the patients.

Wounds would be cleaned with vinegar and water and stitched up. Usually a poultice would then be applied to draw out infection. Sarah and other women made these up in advance using herbs, barks, and other ingredients that would draw out infection and help the wounds heal. Once applied the women would tend to them each day by wetting the poultices and checking to see that the wounds did not discolor or begin to smell bad. If wounds became too infected it could mean amputation of limbs or even death.

Regardless of the care given in the hospital, men died each day. Sarah had almost become immune to the horror of finding men dead in the morning and seeing them carried out for burial. But it still caused her to wonder if the sacrifices being made here would ever be rewarded with victory in this war.

For some reason one thing caused her more anguish than all the others. Every day men would be carried in whose feet had been frozen so badly that they had turned black. The men would try to keep on working after they had been frost bitten until their feet finally were totally frozen. They reached a point where they could no longer walk. In these cases the only thing that could be done was amputation. The men would cry both in pain and fear of losing their ability to walk. Some would hide their feet from their fellow soldiers in order not to be taken to the hospital. They would die in their huts. The ones who survived the amputation would be sent home once the weather broke.

Sarah did not know why these men's condition brought her more grief than the others. Perhaps it was just that she could not bring herself to become totally calloused to all the suffering that surrounded her. She had to have something that made her heart ache in order to feel that she was still human and still a woman.

The winter got colder and the snow continued to pile up. One day as she was walking to the hospital she noticed that the tree line surrounding the fort had moved back nearly half a mile. When she had arrived, a year before, there was a lush forest that butted right up against the fort and the surrounding camp. But now all those trees were gone. Instead, nothing but stumps were left. The fields of stumps looked like cemetery markers, solemn reminders of the sickness and death that surrounded her each day. She hurried on, trying to blot the picture from her mind. But each day from then on she had the same thought as she walked to and from her work.

Everyone tried to work on, but the real work of the camp was trying to find a way to keep warm and stay alive. Trees that had been felled for construction or to make abatis were used for fire wood. As men died they were buried naked. Their clothes were taken from them and distributed to the living. What at first seemed unthinkable soon became necessary and routine. It seemed to Sarah that in their isolation in these mountains they had been forgotten and abandoned by the rest of the nation they were trying to defend. Supplies dribbled in only sporadically, and hunger and freezing were all they knew. They had descended to a state of humanity that no one could have imagined only months before.

There was one thing that Sarah had become obsessed about: cleanliness. She took great pains to ensure that she washed herself every day, even in the frigid conditions they were living in. And she insisted John and the men in the tent cleaned themselves at least once a week.

As things in the fort deteriorated the soldiers in the camp seemed to become unwilling or unable to care for themselves. Working in the hospital every day, she had to clean the men who were brought in, most covered with lice and dirt. They smelled terrible and had to be cleaned before their wounds or sickness could even be tended to. No matter how much she tried, she could never clean herself enough or get the stench out of her nose. Part of that was because even the cold cleanness of winter could not eliminate the stench of the fort and camp.

Another trial they endured was the occurrence of Indian ambushes on patrols sent out of the fort to reconnoiter the surrounding area. While the British had returned to Canada, they left their Indian allies in place to harass the Americans. Patrols sent out were routinely attacked. Men were killed and scalped or taken prisoner. The stories of what happened to prisoners were gory and frightening to hear. Sarah prayed fruitlessly that John would not have to go out on patrol.

Working in the hospital, Sarah experienced firsthand the results of one of these attacks. A scouting patrol had been out and failed to return. John was assigned to lead a second patrol sent out to find the first. They found what was left of it. All but one had been killed. John's patrol brought in all the bodies and the lone wounded man. Several of the bodies had been mutilated. They had all been scalped, and organs were ripped from some of them. The man who lived had faked being dead. He had been shot, and the Indians had scalped him. He was still alive when they brought him in. He was covered in blood and his skull was visible. The sight was horrific. The man would be disfigured for life. But he was alive, and the doctor removed the bullet and sewed him up. Later Sarah listened as he told the story of the attack to the men around him in the hospital. It made her shake with revulsion.

The Indians had been with them from the beginning. But the attacks now seemed to be more prevalent and more vicious. On the evening they brought the wounded man in Sarah asked John and the others, "What has made them so vicious lately?"

John answered, "Well, Sarah, I think it is because the British have left them here alone without any interference from the army. If the army was still here I don't think it would be as bad."

Ben roared, "You're absolutely right about nobody controlling them, John. But those bastards, 'scuse my language Sarah, but those bastards are just naturally nasty and vicious. That's how they fight. They believe they can scare the enemy away by being so vicious. It don't matter whether the British are there or not. The Redcoats might have some control over the brutes, but given any chance at all they will act as horrible as they can. I think the bloody Lobsterbacks have turned them loose and told them they can do anything they want, in fact the nastier the better. Look what happened down at Sabbath Day Point a couple of weeks back. Same damn thing. They scalped and mutilated the whole party. The only reasons these bastards will take a prisoner is so's they can take him back and torture him to death real slow. God help us all if they get to us before the British Army."

"Maybe you're right, Ben," John uttered. "But I don't think they have any plans of attacking us here by themselves. They know they would be out-gunned, and that's not the way they fight. No, they're just here to harass us through the winter 'till Carleton gets back. The British Army ain't gonna let the Indians have any of the glory in defeating us. I don't think they trust the Indians any mor'n we do."

"Well, gentlemen," Sarah responded, "thank you for the enlightenment. From what I heard none of you have any better idea about why these savages act the way they do than I."

Ben laughed and answered back, "Sarah, you have been with us too long now. You are starting to sound like a soldier. And you're starting to bring up subjects just to rile us up, just like we do. You better watch her, John. Before you know it she'll be wantin' to go on patrol."

Sarah looked at Ben feigning offence, "No Benjamin, I will not be wanting to go out on patrol. I am perfectly content to let the men, such as yourself, go out and protect us fragile, weak females from the heathen savages hiding in the woods. But as far as being around you too long, I could not agree more. The sooner this war is over and I can be rid of you scoundrels as bedmates the better, I say."

Twenty-Three

The long freezing winter dragged on. But there were bright moments even during these dreary winter months. The few women left at the fort met twice a week in the evening in a warm room in the fort to mend clothes, darn stockings, and knit. The idea had been Elizabeth's. "After all," she reasoned to Sarah and Martha, "we all have these chores to do anyway. Why should we do them in cold, cramped huts all by ourselves? I love Edward, and my boy, Robert, and the men, but let's face it, they are not very good conversationalists, nor do they have any good gossip to share."

Sarah and Elizabeth had not seen Mary, except in passing, for months. She showed up at the first meeting no longer a shy country girl but a mature young woman. Where once she was reticent it was evident she was now confident and a leader of the small group she belonged to.

Two of the women had children whom they brought with them. There was a boy and a girl both about one. They both had been born at Fort Ti. Because mothers had to work as well as the men, children found themselves with many mothers. Everyone had a hand in helping to raise them. And everyone thought of them as one of their own. They, like everyone in the camp, had on makeshift clothes and could have used a good scrubbing, but they charmed all the women. It wasn't much of a life for a child, but they never wanted for mothering as all of the women adored them.

One evening, Sarah cautiously shared her thoughts about the tree stumps reminding her of a cemetery and wondered if anyone else had similar thoughts. She was surprised when one woman said, "You know, Sarah, I had the exact same thought many times. God how I wish this war would end. The death and misery is too much to bear at times. And my husband doesn't want me to talk about our problems around the men. He thinks all I do is complain. The only time I see him is when the other men are around, so I try not to bring up any of these things."

Soon others shared feelings they had about the war and their part in it. They told about their worries for their husbands and themselves and their feelings of isolation as well. Although Sarah still had her moments of depression over these things it helped her to know that she was not alone. And the camaraderie developed at the gatherings seemed to help all of them meet the trials they faced each day.

In early December the mood of the people at the fort changed. Christmas season was in the air and everyone seemed to have a brighter attitude, even if things were still very bleak.

The women's group was especially jovial. They now called themselves "The Women's Regiment." Sarah had told the women of her and Elizabeth's discussion of a few weeks earlier and everyone thought it captured their thoughts also. Unlike the men's regiments, which were made up of men all from one state, the women were from the entire "Army of the United States." No one state or area had precedence over another. Where the men's regiments were filled with rivalry and distrust between regiments, the women were united in their cause. They only wanted to take care of the men in this army and to help bring this war to an end. Whatever they had to do or suffer to accomplish these two aims they would do.

One evening, Elizabeth opined, "I don't think Christmas will be as elegant this year as we had last year. Although the men were gone, I think we celebrated Christmas very nicely indeed. The menfolk probably have not given a Christmas celebration a first, let alone a second, thought. I think it is only right that we take command of this situation and plan something for this army. I'm tired of the gloominess of this place. Let's brighten things up a bit. What do you all think?"

One of the women retorted, "But, Elizabeth, there are thousands of men here. What can we possibly do for them all?"

"Look ladies, this does not have to be hard. These men have been living a miserable life since last year in Canada. It's time that someone did something nice for them. We can't change where we are, but there must be something we can do to lighten the mood around here a little, and it would be nice if we did something to bring a little Christmas spirit around here at the same time. Now we only have a few weeks, so I am looking for ideas, ladies."

Sarah chuckled, "Don't fight it ladies, the commander of this regiment has made a decision and I think the best thing we can do is follow along and do as she commands."

Conversations and suggestions went on excitedly. They all agreed to meet each night until they had gotten everything arranged.

Sarah went back to the tent that evening excited and with lightness in her heart that she had not felt since she had learned of her brother's death. The men were all in the tent as she entered. They had the same dour look on them as always. But she was going to raise their spirits whether they wanted it or not. She exclaimed, "Gentlemen, the women of this army just had the most wonderful idea for Christmas, and you are going to take part in it!"

They all looked at her without expression until Ben said, "Oh, no, what are you women going to do now?"

John condescendingly said, "Alright Sarah, what have you got planned for us?"

She ignored the tone in their voices and went on, "We are going to put some Christmas spirit into this camp if it kills you. Elizabeth, Martha and I are going to see the commandant tomorrow and get him to agree to let us do something. What I'll need you men for I am not sure right now. But when I am, I expect your full cooperation." She looked each one of them in the eye and finished, "That means all of you."

The men all silently looked at each other when her support came from an unexpected voice. Ben said softly, "Sarah, I think you have a damn good idea. We need a little cheer around here, and anything you gals can do to bring some in, I'm in favor of. Whatever you've got planned, count on me for some help."

As if the others were all just waiting for someone else to be the first to admit it was a good idea, they all agreed and told her they would help.

Sarah smiled affectionately at each of them, "Thank you boys. I knew I could depend on you. Now I have a busy day ahead of me tomorrow so I'm going to bed. Good night." She crawled under her covers and listened to the men as they tried to quietly talk about the idea she had just proposed. She smiled contentedly as she drifted off to sleep because she thought they sounded almost as excited as the women had, though she knew they would never admit it.

The next day the three women went to the Colonel Wayne's office. He stood as they entered the office and said, "Good morning, ladies. This is a pleasant surprise. What can I do for you?" He sat back in his chair and listened as Elizabeth explained what they proposed to do.

He sat quietly for moment thinking. Then he smiled and said, "Ladies, you have made my day. Most men come in here to complain. They do not have any solutions, only problems. You have come in here with a wonderful idea. You may count on me for my fullest support." He shouted, "Major, come in here please."

Major Cardin quickly came in and Wayne said, "Major, these women have a wonderful idea to raise morale around this fort by putting some Christmas spirit into it. They are working directly for me on this project and I don't want anyone interfering with them. Put out today that whatever they need to make this happen is to be provided. I expect the officers of this command to fully support their efforts, and any man asked to help is to give his fullest cooperation. Secondly, tell the Quartermaster that I don't care what he has to do but that I expect each man to get a full ration of meat, bread, and rum on Christmas day. That is all."

He looked back to the women, "Is there anything else I can do for you today ladies?

They were stunned by his enthusiasm and Elizabeth stumbled, "No, Sir. You have given us just what we need to get started."

"Good. Now I want you ladies to come back here once a week and let me know how and what you are doing. I mean it. Friday morning you be here with your complete plan and let me know if anyone is not cooperating. By God, these men will have a Christmas no matter how miserable it is in this camp. Thank you once again."

They left the commandant's office both excited and bewildered. They had gone in only to get his approval and now they were working for and reporting directly to him. Elizabeth expressed what Sarah was thinking. "Well, that was exciting. I didn't realize he would be so wholehearted in his support. We better do a good job now, ladies. We are working for the man himself."

The women quickly dove into their planning and just as quickly ran into road blocks. They went to each regimental commander and asked for their input on what should be done. That gave the women their first inkling of what troubles they might be facing. The commanders did not seem to think much of their ideas. They would not say no because Colonel Wayne had ordered them to cooperate, but neither did they have much in the line of positive input. Instead they only outlined problems that could be incurred.

First of all the women had to realize what a disparity existed within the states as to how Christmas should be observed. The men from New England were mostly Congregationalists, and held tightly to Puritanical beliefs that Christmas should not be celebrated but simply observed as the birthday of Christ, and that no other activities should be demonstrated. Men from the south, on the other hand, were mostly Anglican in their beliefs, and enthusiastically celebrated Christmas in their homes with singing and dancing and great feasts if possible. Men from the middle states leaned mostly with the southerners. They were Presbyterians, Lutherans, and a few Catholics. They too celebrated Christmas, but a little less exuberantly than the southerners. The many Germans among them also brought new ideas like Christmas trees and decorations into the planning, which were unheard of in most of the country.

Secondly, Christmas was in the middle of the week this year and any celebrations would interfere with operations at the fort. At each stop someone had another reason why the idea was just a waste of time.

The women's excitement soon turned to frustration. The commanders seemed to have little enthusiasm for what they wanted to do for the men. Friday came and they went to see Colonel Wayne. First, Martha laid out what they had planned to do.

"We know there is not much we can do for the men materially. So we thought that starting on Sunday the twenty-second we will start spreading out in twos and threes to visit each of the regiments and do the following: Sing a few hymns. Read a couple of verses from the New Testament on the birth of Christ. Just talk to the men about Christmas where they come from and how they maybe celebrated it. Finally we thought we would offer our services to write letters for any of the men who could not otherwise do it themselves."

Elizabeth interjected, "This last one we may need your help on, Sir. You know how scarce and valuable paper is and we don't have any. We were wondering if it is possible to get a supply of paper from somewhere to accomplish this. And a few good pencils would help too," she added sheepishly.

Here Martha hesitated and finally told him what they had run into with the commanders. She said, "Sir, it seems they do not want us to do anything. What do you think?"

Wayne sighed, "Ladies, welcome to my world. You have just experienced what I experience from these same men every day. Don't get me wrong. They are good men. But they only see problems. Solutions do not seem to be in their ken. And accepting solutions that they did not personally think of is not part of their nature. You did the right thing by going and talking to them. Now I want you to forget every negative thing you heard from them. Do not worry about how different parts of the country celebrate or do not celebrate Christmas unless it helps in your planning. I assure you that whatever you do for the men they will appreciate it in the spirit of the season, regardless of what those pompous commanders have to say."

He thought a second, and added only half-jokingly, "Oh, and by the way, after you have successfully completed your efforts they will be the first to take credit for them because they gave you such insightful input. I've heard your plan and I think it is a good one. Of course your visits will have to be in the evening. The men have work to do during the day. The major here will set up a schedule with the commanders to ensure the men will be there when you get there. Trust me, the commanders will be 'thrilled' to have you there. I do think you may want to start visiting the units on Friday the twentieth though, just to make sure you can get to them all. What do you think, Major?"

The Adjutant who had been sitting quietly in on the meeting said, "I think it's a wonderful plan, Sir. We might also declare a stand down for say, perhaps the twenty-fourth, to have the men clean out their living areas and replace the old straw with some new. It wouldn't hurt if we could get them to clean themselves that day too. Maybe have each unit set up a communal bath for the purpose. I know one of the projects the women are always working on is soap-making for their clothes-washing chores. Maybe we could prevail upon them to lend some to the troops on this occasion."

"Splendid idea, Major. Issue an order declaring the twenty-fourth to be a stand down day in which all the things you just mentioned are carried out. I know the new straw will be a problem for the Quartermaster, but tell him to find it somewhere. This place has become a cesspool. We will at least start out the New Year clean. Oh, and Major, see what we can do about providing some paper and pencils to the women for their project."

He then turned to the women and said, "Now ladies, get with the major here and set up your visits through him."

Twenty-Four

Finally, the night of the first visits arrived. Sarah had teamed with Mary, and the first unit they were visiting was their own 1st New York. Before she left the hut she told John and the men what was going to take place. She also warned them to be on their best behavior and help her through this. She was obviously very nervous.

John hugged her tight and said, "Don't worry, you will be fine. Thank you for doing this. You don't really know how much good you women will be doing this week. No one has given these men the compassion you are bringing tonight in a very long time. You will be wonderful." He kissed her and pushed her along, saying, "Now go get Mary and we'll see you there."

She went to the meeting room where all the women had congregated before lighting out. There was nervousness in the air. Sarah was glad she was not the only one who was unsure of herself. One woman suggested that before they left for their visits they should say a prayer. Everyone agreed and Elizabeth led them. "Dear Lord, give us the ability to lighten these men's load tonight. Bless each of these women as they spread the joy we all feel about the birth of Your Son. Bless the men of this army and help them achieve victory and independence for our country. In Your name we pray, oh, Lord. Amen."

Sarah and Mary approached the headquarters with the apprehension of not knowing what to expect. When they arrived the men were in formation. Sarah thought that a formation was not the proper way to carry out what they wanted to accomplish. She asked the Colonel if the men might be allowed to gather around the bonfire that had been set. He agreed and dismissed the men to gather around the ladies at the fire.

Once the men had settled down Sarah said nervously, "Good evening gentlemen. My name is Sarah Hardy and this is Mary Caldwell. I think you may know our husbands, Sergeant Hardy and Private Caldwell." With that the men hooted and yelled a bit.

"We would like to start out tonight by singing a couple of hymns we hope some of you might know. Please feel free to join in if you do." They started out with a couple of hymns from the Book of Commons that the Chaplain had loaned them. At first it was only them singing. But quickly a strong voice from the rear chimed in. Sarah looked up and saw Ben smiling at her and singing away. Soon several other men joined in. The mood of the men changed, and they joined in whenever there were words they could remember.

Next Sarah asked if there were any songs any of the men

might want to sing. After a moment, one private called out a song. Sarah said, "I don't know that song. Could you lead us in it?"

The men again razzed loudly. But the man began to sing and everyone went silent. A few more men knew the song and joined in.

Then Sarah opened the Bible and began reading from Luke 2:1-20, "In those days Caesar Augustus issued a decree..." As she read the men became very quiet. Sarah glanced up while she was reading and noticed that there were men with tears on their cheeks. All of them were silent and looked as though they were somewhere else.

When she was finished she said, "My mother always read that story to my brothers and sister and I every Christmas Eve. I think it is one of my favorites. I come from Newburgh, down the road a piece from here. Christmas was always a wonderful time for us. My mother would cook for days and we would have the best feast ever each Christmas Day. How 'bout you men? Anybody have any special memories they would want to share? "

One private began talking, "I come from the Mohawk Valley, and we're Germans. So we would have a Christmas tree and mother would decorate it on Christmas Eve after we kids went to bed. When we woke up we would always be surprised at how beautiful it was. We would all make little gifts for each other and give them out on Christmas morning too."

Mary followed, "I grew up in a very strict home that did not believe in celebrating Christmas. So being here with you is teaching me how other people honor the birth of Christ. Some of the things I like very much."

Others chimed in with stories of their youth and how their families spent Christmas. Soon it was time to leave. "Thank you gentlemen for coming out on this cold night and sharing a small part of your Christmas with us. I hope you enjoyed this as much as we have. Finally, if any of you would like one of us to help with writing a letter to someone, please stop us in the camp and let us know. If that woman can't do it, we get together every week and we will find someone who can. We will be happy to oblige you. Good night and Merry Christmas," Sarah finished.

As they were walking away the men all gave them a grand "huzzah." Sarah and Mary looked at each other and grinned with a sense of accomplishment.

John and Ben came up to them and John politely hugged Sarah. "That was terrific, ladies. You two were amazing. I think the men really enjoyed it. Where to next? Ben and I will accompany you to all of your visits, just to keep you safe."

Ben stepped up and asked, "Ladies, may I hug you too? I haven't felt this good in a long time." He didn't wait for permission, he just gave first Sarah then Mary giant bear hugs.

Mary turned red with embarrassment and Sarah laughed, "Thank you, Ben." She turned to John, "Now, John, that was a hug. You need to take lessons from Ben here. But Ben, please don't feel any happier as we go to the other regiments. You might crush us."

Each visit was the same. The men were at first reticent, then joined in and everyone seemed to enjoy it.

The women all came back to their meeting place and every one of them was as excited as Sarah and Mary. They talked about how much fun they had and how grateful the men seemed.

Martha had visited the fort's headquarters first. "I was so nervous, even Colonel Wayne was there. I wasn't sure how it would go. But once he started to sing with us everyone joined in."

They finished all the regiments on the twenty-fourth. When they returned to the meeting place Elizabeth had set up a small party just for them. "I have two batches of punch here, ladies. The good Colonel Wayne provided me with a small bottle of his personal reserve of some sort of liquor so the bowl on the right may be a bit stronger than the one on the left. I will leave it to you to decide which you wish to partake of. Now, if each of you will get yourself a cup, I would like to propose a toast."

She waited until everyone had a glass and then raised hers, "To the women of this army. You have made a difference in this fort and in this war. Congratulations on a job well done. Merry Christmas!"

The women all drank and said, "Hear, hear!" They broke up into small groups and everyone seemed to be talking excitedly at the same time.

Sarah, Martha, and Elizabeth went off into a corner to talk privately. Martha solemnly said, "Sarah, Elizabeth, I have something to share with you. I wasn't sure for some time but I am positive now. I am pregnant. You and Jeremiah are the only ones who know."

Elizabeth and Sarah were dumbfounded and could say nothing. Martha said, "Well, say something. I thought you might be happy for us."

They both grabbed her at the same time and hugged and kissed her repeatedly. Elizabeth finally said, "We are happy for you. We are ecstatic!"

Sarah cried, "Oh, Martha, how wonderful. We are going to have a baby. You know this baby has two built in aunts to help take care of him. Or maybe you will have a new addition to our women's army. Either way we are here for you. This opens up a whole new reason to meet. This baby will be the best dressed baby in this new country of ours."

Elizabeth asked, "Can we tell the rest of the ladies?"

Martha nodded.

"Ladies, ladies. May I have your attention please? Martha has just has just told us wonderful news. She and Jeremiah are going to have a baby. Isn't that wonderful?"

Everyone applauded and rushed to Martha to give their congratulations. The party broke up and only the three were left. Sarah said, "I have been waiting for everyone to leave. I wanted to give you both a small present. I know it isn't much, but here." She had knitted each of them a scarf and mittens.

Martha too had presents. She said, "Well, you'd think we planned this because I made us all hats."

Elizabeth put the gifts up against her face and said, "These are beautiful, and I for one am going to start wearing mine tonight on the way back. You both know I can't knit a lick. So I didn't make anything for you myself. But I do have a gift for each of you too." She then brought out two pairs of shoes. They were black men's shoes like thc ones soldiers wore, when they had shoes. They were well made of heavy materials and would last a long time if taken care of properly.

Sarah and Martha were stunned. Shoes were impossible to find, and even if some were available they were very expensive.

Sarah exclaimed, "Shoes! I haven't had proper shoes for a

year. I will cherish them. Thank you so much Elizabeth." She hugged her and gave her a kiss.

Martha looked at Elizabeth. "Elizabeth, thank you. These are the most wonderful gift I've ever received. But where did you get them, and how could you afford them?"

"I always told you two that working for the sutlers had its benefits. Let's just say they were very happy to get me back when we returned from Crown Point, and these were their way of saying so. Now I am going to put on my new duds and get back to my boys. Good night ladies and Merry Christmas. Tell your husbands Merry Christmas for me too. And once again Martha, congratulations." Sarah and Martha walked back to the huts together and marveled at their new shoes, which they would not put on because they didn't want to ruin them in the snow. When they got to Martha's hut they hugged and said good night and Sarah congratulated Martha once more.

Twenty-Five

Sarah was in a dream. The plans for the troops worked out better than they planned, she had new shoes and a new hat to keep her warm, and one of her best friends was going to have a baby.

The men were still up when she came in. John said, "Where you been? We were starting to worry about you. You know you shouldn't be wandering around this camp alone at night."

"Oh, thank you gentlemen for your concern. The women had a little party after we finished tonight and it got a little later than we all thought. But I wasn't alone. I was with Martha. Speaking of which, I have some wonderful news."

The men all shouted together, "Martha is pregnant!"

"How long have you men known that? She just told us a little while ago."

John stopped laughing long enough to say, "Jeremiah has

been worried about Martha being sick in the morning and he just couldn't figure out what was wrong with her. We do have a few fathers in this regiment who helped set him straight. So he confronted Martha and she told him a few days ago. We were sworn to secrecy. Sorry, Sarah, but you women aren't the only ones who can keep a secret."

Sarah pouted a little, then smiled and asked, "Isn't it wonderful news? Aren't you all happy for them?"

Everyone but William agreed they were very happy for Martha and Jeremiah.

William, who practically never had anything to say, very gloomily offered, "Don't get me wrong. I am happy for them if this is what they want. But I look around this hell hole and think it is no place for a woman to be pregnant and no place for a baby to be born. This place is nothing but a cesspool. There is sickness everywhere and practically no food to be had. It's going to take one hell of a lot of prayers to get both woman and child through this pregnancy here, I tell ya."

His words brought an uncomfortable silence to the tent. John was able to bring back a little positive thought to the issue. "Martha is one of the best loved women in this camp. I am sure the women will do everything they can to make sure she is taken proper care of. Don't you think so, Sarah?"

"Absolutely. This baby and its mother will get better care here than anywhere. After all they have a couple of dozen aunts and Lord knows how many uncles to look after them. I am sure they will be fine."

She put on a positive face, but William's words left an indelible mark on her thoughts. She knew he was right, and it worried her terribly. But she and Elizabeth would not let anything happen to Martha or her baby. Not if they could do anything about it.

"It's Christmas Eve. Let's be positive and think good thoughts for Jeremiah and Martha and their baby. And let's enjoy the spirit of the season. Look at the wonderful gifts I just received. Martha gave me this beautiful warm, hat and look at this," she pulled her new shoes out of the sack she always carried.

The men were as stunned as she had been. John asked, "Sarah, where did you get those? There aren't enough Continentals in the whole fort to afford those shoes. Who gave them to you?"

"Elizabeth gave both Martha and I a pair. She got them from the sutler she works for. I did not ask how much they cost her," she said sternly so as to stop any more conversation in that direction.

"Sarah, you better guard those shoes. There are men all over this camp who would steal them in a minute and try to stuff their feet into them no matter how small they are. Lucky for you there's nobody in this tent who could fit into them. You might have to fight to keep 'em," Ben laughed.

"I'll keep that in mind, Ben. But now I have presents for you." She opened her bag again and gave each man except John a pair of new stockings and a pair of mittens that had a trigger finger in them. She had made them over the weeks. "I hope they fit and that you men like them and enjoy them. Merry Christmas."

They all chimed in with thank yous and said how much they liked them.

John sat quietly looking at the men as they enjoyed their presents.

Sarah turned to him and said coquettishly, "Oh, John. I almost forgot. I made a little something for you too, dear." She pulled out a new shirt, stockings, mittens, and a stocking hat.

John's faced beamed with joy. "Sarah, they are beautiful." He looked at the ragged shirt he was wearing and said, "Thank you, darling, everything is beautiful."

The men thanked her again for their gifts and Ben had to get in one more word. "First off this calls for a small celebration," he said as he pulled his canteen from his knapsack. "Here, pass it 'round. I've been saving up my rations for a while and we ought to be able to celebrate on what's in here. Sarah, bearer of these beautiful gifts, you may be first."

John interjected, "Sarah, that is strong rum there. I don't think you will like it."

"Oh, I'll just take a little sip, just to be sociable, John. Thank you, Ben." She put the canteen to her lips and took a big slug of it without making a face then passed it to John, who was staring at her in disbelief.

"Whoa, I hope somebody else has saved up some rum too. If Sarah is gonna drink like that we are gonna need another canteen full. Good show, Sarah." Ben exclaimed.

She looked at John, who was still staring at her without saying a word, and said, "Are you alright, dear? Is something wrong?"

"No, nothing is wrong. Sarah, where did you learn to drink like that? I have never seen you drink anything before."

Sarah had never told him about the Christmas party the women had last year or that on occasion some of the women would "borrow" a little of their husband's rum rations and bring it to the knitting circle. Actually, Sarah thought she quite liked the taste now that she had gotten used to it. She asked innocently, "Isn't that the way you're supposed to do it? That's how I've seen you men drink it. I thought that was the way it was done."

John just shook his head.

Ben burst out, "Where did you get this woman John? I gotta get me one of those wives and I wanna get her in the same place. The woman can sew and drink too! You gotta be the luckiest man in this army, John." He then went on, "But Sarah, I think you give too much to your husband there. Don't get me wrong, Sarah. I love the new stockings and mittens you gave us. But John there always seems to one up us in the gift department. Now he's goin' to be the best dressed sergeant in the regiment. And there will be no livin' with him 'til that shirt has a few rips in it."

Everyone laughed and John chided, "Ben, ain't no woman would have you, let alone make a shirt for you. Lord knows we been trying to trade you to another group for a year now. Nobody wants ya. So we're stuck with ya."

After a couple more rounds of the canteen everyone quieted down.

Sarah and John went outside to be alone. It was an invigorating cold night. John took Sarah in his arms and kissed her lovingly. He said, "Sarah, thank you so much for the shirt and other things. And I am sure the boys appreciate what you did for them too."

She could tell that there was something on his mind besides saying thank you. He was very somber and quiet. Finally, she asked, "Is there something wrong dear? You don't seem yourself tonight."

"Sarah, I am very sorry that I don't have anything to give you for Christmas. I am sorry I brought you here and that you have to live like this in this miserable hell-hole. I wish there were something I could do to make it up to you. Since you got word from your mother about Robert I have been wondering if it might not be better for you to go down and be with her. I know things are tough for them also. But it has to be better than you have here. It's the only thing I can give you, Sarah. I want you to go."

"Now you listen to me, John Hardy, I am not going anywhere without you. We had this argument when you came home and said you joined this regiment. Well, I joined this regiment with you and I am going to stay right here and do my part. My brother died fighting for this cause and I am going to do everything I can to avenge that death and help us win this war. So you put any thoughts of me leaving out of your head. I love you and I love these men and I am staying." She had raised her voice and was nearly shouting by the time she finished.

Then she lowered her voice. "John, I can't leave. As miserable as this place is, it is all I have and all I know now. These men and women are the people I know, and I want to be with them no matter what. Yes, I would like to see my mother, but there is little I can do for her that isn't already being done by my sister and brother. And if they move up to the Mohawk Valley with my aunt, what then? No, John. This place isn't much, but it is what I know and I'm going to stick it out. As for you not having a gift for me, I don't want you to give it another thought. Tell me that you love me and that will be gift enough for me. Someday this war will be over and we will have plenty of time to worry over gift giving in our own home with our children. Until then the only gift I ask of you is for you to keep yourself alive and let me be here to help you. Alright?"

They hugged and the night no longer seemed too cold. He whispered, "Alright, Sarah. You win again. I should have known better. I do love you, and I won't bring the idea up again." They kissed once more and went inside.

Twenty-Six

With Christmas over life returned to normal for Sarah. The hospital was still overrun with soldiers who were too weak to fight off the diseases the camp spawned. The flux, typhoid, and cholera were rampant, and more men died each day.

The men continued to work on the defenses, but to Sarah's untrained eyes it did not look as though any great progress was being made.

Men were still leaving the fort every night, either deserting or leaving because their enlistment was up. One thing that Sarah noticed was that as the men were leaving there seemed to be more and more Negroes and Indians at the fort.

Sarah had never been around people of different races in such numbers before and she feared these new people would bring harm to her and the fort. One evening, she asked the men about them.

John said, "Most of the darkies are slaves. Some are on loan from their Patriot masters. Others are run away from their Tory masters. I heard Congress, or somebody, told the Tory slaves they'd be freed if they ran away and fought with our side. So we got 'em. The British have done the same thing with the slaves who belong to people on our side."

Ben vehemently spat, "What a stupid idea. Everybody knows they ain't smart enough or capable enough to do any real work. And we damn sure ain't gonna give them no muskets. No tellin' who they'd shoot first, the Redcoats or us. And what are we goin' to do with a bunch of freed blackies running around after this war? Where they gonna live? What are they gonna do for a living? They ain't gonna be livin' nowheres near me, I'll tell ya. They're just gonna be anvils hanging 'round our necks to take care of. I say leave 'em where they are. Let the Tories keep 'em, and when we run the Tories out of this new country they can take their slaves with 'em. And how 'bout the ones who ain't runaway Tory slaves? Where'd they come from, and what are we supposed to do with them?"

William chided, "Ben, your sense of humanity is just overwhelming. These people are human beings too. They didn't join up to become slaves. They were captured and sold into it. They want to be free as much as you do, maybe more. We all talk about this war as a means of becoming free from the British. But we were never slaves, and even if we lose this war those that live through it won't become slaves. England already has laws that abolished slavery. And when we win this war one of the first things those idiots in Congress should do is abolish it too."

John added, "Well, William, I don't care much one way or t'other about slavery myself. This here is the first place I actually ever ran into any slaves. But what kind of plan is it to free the ones who belonged to the Tories and not free the ones who belong to the Patriots? To my way of thinking, that's just a plan for disaster. If I was one of the Patriot slaves I would start a revolt and fight to get free too. And besides, Ben's got some points. What are we going to do with them after the war if they become free? Are you gonna have them live next to you? I say it was the British who started slavery here, and when the war is over we should make them take all the Negroes away from here. Take 'em back to Africa or take 'em to England and let them be free there. I don't care where they take 'em, but we don't need or want them here. "

William continued, "But John, many of these people are not slaves at all. There is a whole regiment of free black soldiers from Rhode Island here. They are as free as you and I. They have families, and farms and businesses back home. If they are fighting for the same thing we are, why should they be expelled? And if these slaves help us win the war, why should they not benefit from it too?"

Sarah looked around at the men and could tell that things were getting out of hand. She had a hard time understanding how these men she thought she knew and who she thought so much of could hold such differing views. She said, "Gentlemen, I am sorry I brought the subject up. I don't see that there is anything any of you are going to do about the Negroes one way or the other, so there's no sense getting all worked up over it."

For the first time she realized that before tonight her thoughts about the Negroes were probably closer to Ben's and John's than to William's. But the things William had said caused her to think differently about these poor people who had things even harder than they all did, if that were possible. She had not heard about the regiment from Rhode Island. She wondered what life was like in a place where the races lived together freely. How could it work? Would this new country find a way to let all people coexist freely? Was she fighting this war to let everyone be free, or just the white people? She had not thought about that question until William spoke up tonight. Now it bothered her because in her heart she did not know the answer.

She almost feared what bringing up the subject of the Indians would result in, but they fascinated her and she wanted to hear what the men thought.

When the Indians came, the women and children quickly set up thatched houses at the outer edge of the camp. The houses looked like baskets that had been overturned to Sarah. She noticed that they had fires inside them and could see the smoke coming out of a hole they left in the roof. The only thing she knew about Indians was what people said about them, and none of it was good. All Indians were considered savages, and to Sarah they looked like savages, especially the men. Their skin was a reddish brown color and many of them had tattoos painted on their faces. Most of the time they all had what Sarah assumed was war paint on their faces. Their heads were shaved except for a small piece of hair. Some of them had woven a feather into the hair, while others wore a cap with several feathers attached to it. They were dressed in leather breeches and wore a breech cloth over them. Their shirts too were made of leather. In the cold they wrapped themselves in colorful blankets or animal skins to keep warm. They seemed to Sarah to be the epitome of all the terrible things she had heard about Indians. Their presence frightened her greatly. The men did not work on the defenses, and to Sarah's mind didn't seem to do much of anything except walk around looking ferocious.

The women were less intimidating looking. They had long black hair and were dressed in dresses made of leather and wore a leather tunic over their dresses. Sarah especially noticed the moccasins they wore on their feet. They looked very comfortable and were decorated with beads of many colors. She looked at herself and the ragged clothes she was wearing and thought, "These women look a lot warmer than I feel. Why have we not learned from them?"

One thing she noticed was that all the work around the village was done by either the women or children. She thought that strange as she thought that men were supposed to do the hard labor.

She asked John and the men, "What do you know about these Indians? What tribe are they from? Why are they here? And can they be trusted not to cut our throats and scalp us in the night? Their men frighten me with the way they look."

John answered, "I don't know what tribe they are. They are one of the Iroquois tribes, I think. Most of them have sided with the British. But I guess a couple of tribes have joined up with us. The men are used as guides for patrols or they go out scouting to bring back intelligence on where the enemy is. Come spring I guess they will go farther north and keep an eye out for the British Army coming back from Canada."

"They are all red savages to me. I can't tell one from another and I don't trust them one bit. They ain't on nobody's side 'cept their own. And they will turn on us or desert us without so much as a by your leave. They give me the shivers too, Sarah," Ben heatedly bellowed.

"How do you tell what tribe they are from? Like Ben said, they all look alike to me," Sarah asked to nobody in particular.

William said, "The tribes are as different as we white folk are. We have English, German, French, Dutch, and others. How do we, or more importantly other people, tell us apart? By the way we talk and the way we dress. We all have different customs we practice. So do they. And if any of us cared to take the time to study them a little we could tell them apart just as easily as we differentiate ourselves. These people are from the Stockbridge Tribe, from Massachusetts, and they have taken a great risk to join our side. Most of the tribes have sided with the British. So they are on their own here."

"Maybe all that is true, William," Ben cut in, "and maybe you got the time and desire to study 'em, but I ain't turning my back on no Indians no matter whose side they claim to be on!"

Although the points William tried to make made sense to her, Sarah still could not get the fearsomeness of the men's looks from her mind. But each day she would look over to the Indian encampment and just watch the women and children go through their daily routines. William's words came back to her each day and she began to realize these women were doing the same thing she was doing. They spoke a different language and dressed differently, but they performed the same chores as she did every day.

One day while she and Elizabeth were talking at the cooking

fire she asked, "Elizabeth, have you ever met an Indian? I mean actually talked with one?"

"Can't say that I have, Sarah. Why do you ask?"

"I don't know. I've just been watching them over there and wondered if any of the women spoke English. They look like they are pretty much doing the same things we do. I thought I might go over there and try to talk to one of them. But I'm scared to go alone and Lord knows neither John nor the men would go with me. They would be upset if they even thought I was thinking about such an idea."

"You know, Sarah, that's not a bad idea. It would only be neighborly, now that you mention it. Why don't we give it a try? I don't think they would murder and scalp us here. Who knows, one or two of them might be thinking the same thing. Let's go over there this morning before we lose our nerve."

Sarah and Elizabeth held hands as they walked towards the Indian camp. Sarah could feel the excitement and fear in Elizabeth's hand, and could barely contain her own. As they neared one of the huts a squaw approached them. She appeared to have an air of authority and looked very stern to Sarah. But, to Sarah's surprise, she also looked very beautiful. There was no sign of fear on her face, only a calm serenity. Sarah wondered if the woman could see the fear that was in her heart at that moment. The woman did not say a word as they met. She simply looked from Sarah to Elizabeth with a questioning glance.

Sarah stuttered, "Good morning. We wondered if any of you might speak English."

The squaw looked at them for a moment and finally said, "We have lived among the white people for many years. I can speak your language. What do you wish?"

Sarah breathed a sigh of relief and smiled nervously. At least they found someone who they could talk to. That was a start. "My name is Sarah and this is Elizabeth. We have been watching you from our camp and we thought we should come and welcome you to the fort."

The woman continued to look at them silently for a moment then said, "You are welcome here also. Come sit by the fire and warm yourselves." She led then into the long house where a fire was burning in the middle of the very large room. The smoke from the fire went up through a hole in the ceiling, and although it was still smoky it was warm and dry. Other women were in the house working, and there were several small children there playing. There were pallets for beds, and each bed had what looked like warm animal skins on it that served as blankets. There was no other furniture. Stumps placed around the fire served as chairs.

Sarah and Elizabeth sat down and the woman said, "My name is Taima. But I also have a white man's name, and it is Elizabeth, just like yours." She pointed to Elizabeth, who smiled and replied, "Really, how do you come to have an English name?"

"We are of the Stockbridge Tribe. We come from Massachusetts. Taima is the name given to me by the tribe at my birth. It means 'one born in a thunder storm.' A white man's minister has lived among us a very long time. He brought the white man's religion to us and I was baptized by him and given the name Elizabeth."

"How do you prefer to be called, Taima or Elizabeth?" Sarah asked.

"Within the tribe I am called Taima. But amongst the white people I am Elizabeth. You may call me either."

Elizabeth laughed and said, "Then to avoid the confusion of having two Elizabeths we will call you Taima, if you don't mind."

Taima smiled a beautiful smile and replied, "That is very good."

Sarah asked, "Does everyone in your tribe speak English?"

"Most of my people can speak some English. Many of the men will not try because they do not want to become English. They fear that speaking the language will cause them to become too much like the English."

Sarah hesitantly asked, "Taima, I do not wish to be rude, but why are you here? Why did your tribe decide to fight with us?"

"You may know that we were part of the Iroquois Nation. But long ago we were not. We lived on our own. But too many wars and sicknesses have made us weak. The Oneida tribe of the Iroquois Nation adopted us as their own. Once the seven tribes lived together in peace. We met over a great fire that was never allowed to go out, and we solved our differences there by talking. During the white man's war we all fought on the side of the English. I believe you who call yourselves Americans did also. We were all very good allies then. Now you Americans and the English are fighting. Both of you have asked us to raise our tomahawks on your side. Most of the Iroquois tribes have decided to fight with the English. They promise much and have much more to pay for warriors. But we have seen the English before and although they promise much, they do not keep their promises for long."

She went on, "We did not want to go to war for either side,

but as our brothers joined with the English we were forced to decide. We do not deceive ourselves that we will be better off no matter which white men win. But we know you who call yourselves Americans will still be here when the war is over and the Redcoats will go back to their home across the water. When the war is over it is still you Americans we will have to live with. We hope by joining you in your war with the English that you will win and you will remember what we have done for you and that we will be able to live peacefully together in the future."

Taima's eyes turned sad and she finished, "We have done this knowing that we have made our brothers our enemies too. The great fire has gone out and the Iroquois Nation is no longer. Each tribe is on its own now, and I fear that old wars between us will someday return."

The three women sat silent for a short time, then Elizabeth said quietly, "Taima we thank you and your tribe for helping us. And we thank you for talking to us today, but we must go. We have work that must be done. We would like to talk to you more. Perhaps next time you could come visit us."

Taima's eyes were sad. "My people are not welcome in your camp. We are your allies and will fight on your side, but your men do not trust us and do not want us near them. Our men too are wary of the white men and do not trust them either. Many will wonder why there are white women in our camp today. We may become friends, you and I, but we will never change the hearts of our men. No, if you wish to talk you must come here. In your camp the men are in charge and they would not want me there. Here the women are chiefs and we decide who may come into our camp and our homes. You are both always welcome to come back."

During this time Sarah also met a black person for the first time. The young woman came into the hospital one morning looking afraid and lost. She looked as though she was searching for someone. Sarah looked around, then went over to her and asked, "Yes, can I help you, miss?"

The woman was startled and took a step back. She said, "The man said I was to work here."

Sarah didn't know what to say. "What is your name?"

"My name is Virginia, but everyone just calls me Ginny."

"Well, alright then, Ginny, my name is Sarah. I am pleased to meet you. We can always use extra hands around here." Sarah extended her hand to Ginny. Ginny looked at her quizzically, but then clasped Sarah's hand.

"We are in the process of cleaning the hospital at this moment. But first let me introduce you to a couple of the women who also work here." She took Ginny to meet two other women and was surprised at the coldness in their voices as she introduced Ginny to them.

"We're cleaning the floors with vinegar and water today. Want to help?" Sarah asked.

Ginny just shrugged and followed along as Sarah took her to the end of the room, where there was a pail and a couple of brushes. Sarah knelt down and started to scrub the floor. She looked up at Ginny, who was simply staring at her.

"Is there something the matter, Ginny?"

"No, no missus. But you work here too? Ain't you in charge?"

Sarah laughed, "No Ginny I am not in charge. In this hospital the doctors are in charge. Everyone else works."

Ginny knelt down, took the other brush, and started scrubbing.

Sarah started a conversation, "Please forgive me Ginny, but I have never met a black woman before. May I ask, are you a slave?"

Ginny looked at her coldly. "I was a slave for the Johnson family over in the Mohawk Valley. Mr. Johnson is a very important man with the Indians in those parts. He is also a very big Tory. The people in the valley hate him very much and caused him to take his family and slaves to Canada. I heard that if you are a slave that belongs to a Tory, the army will make you a free person if you join up to work for them. So I ran away the night before the Johnsons went to Canada and found an army unit that was coming here. They let me come along. So here I am. I don't know if I'm a slave or free. I hope this war will make me free."

Sarah rose up on her knees and said, "Ginny, I hope so too. I don't understand slavery and can't see how it is allowed. The English already have laws against it and we should too. When we win this war I hope we do away with it entirely and that all of your people are freed. And please call me Sarah. We don't stand on no formalities around here. Do you have any family, Ginny?"

"No. Not that I know of. Mr. Johnson bought me down south. I was separated from my family when I was very young and have never heard of them since."

"Oh, I am so sorry, Ginny. I cannot imagine what it must be like. Well, as of right now you are free. Can't guarantee anything down the road, but for what it's worth around here you are free."

From that moment Ginny stayed close to Sarah whenever possible. They talked every day and became very close. Sarah introduced her to Martha and Elizabeth, who also took her under their wings. But her reception with most of the other women was not as cordial. Sarah could tell that, just like the men, these women thought of this woman as only good for being a slave. They began to avoid Sarah as well as Ginny.

One morning at the kitchen Sarah philosophically asked, "Elizabeth, why do you think we are fighting this war? After listening to Taima I think that Congress is where our great fire is. And right now the states are the tribes of this nation. But once the war is over, will our great fire go out as the Iroquois' did? Will we be any better at ruling than the King and Parliament? Will you and I be part of one nation or citizens of separate nations? Will we one day find ourselves fighting each other? And what about the Negroes and the Indians? They are here and a part of this land. When I listen to the men—and some of the women—talk, it sounds as if these people are not even considered as people and don't need to be planned for. Our men definitely do not plan on them ever becoming citizens. So what is to become of them?"

Elizabeth responded, "Sarah, you think too much, and you are becoming too smart for your own good. First of all, you and I are only women. In our society we have practically no say in what is going to happen right now. We can only influence our own men, not the entire bunch of them who think they will rule whatever kind of nation or nations this war results in. We have to take one step at a time. And right now the first step is to win this war. So everything we do must be aimed at that goal. If we are successful in winning, then we women can start fighting our next battles. Then we can start working to make these idiot men realize that the war was not fought for them alone. We can start the battle to make them realize that what Mr. Jefferson said in that declaration wasn't just for men but for mankind. And that everyone has the God given right to 'life, liberty and the pursuit of happiness.'"

Then she laughed, "But that ain't gonna happen today, dearie. So don't let all this thinkin' you been doing get in the way of what we have to accomplish first. Let's win the war, then we'll convert our female army into something that will change the world!"

Twenty-Seven

Sarah took Elizabeth's advice to heart and dedicated herself to her work in the hospital. As the winter wore on things got progressively worse. Supplies for the hospital were almost non-existent, and there was barely enough food in the fort for half rations.

Finally, at the end of January 1777 they received some good news along with a supply train that finally made it through to them. In the official packet for the commandant came word that General Washington and the army in New Jersey were able to defeat the Hessians in an attack on Trenton on Christmas day, and followed that victory up by defeating a British unit at Princeton on the third of January.

Although they all were elated about their turning Carleton back in October, it had been so long since there had been anything like a real victory for the Americans that they were beginning to doubt their ability to win the war. They all knew Washington and his men were in the same dire straits they were, and to hear that he had attacked both the Germans and the British and won twice in a week was news that raised their spirits immensely.

The news reinvigorated everyone in the fort. Work on the defenses seemed to go smoother. The men were anxiously awaiting spring and another chance to have it out with the British. This time they were sure they would be able to defeat them.

Additionally, a pamphlet by Thomas Paine arrived. Every unit held a formation at which it was read aloud. It began: "*THESE are the times that try men's souls. The summer soldier and the sunshine patriot will, in this crisis, shrink from the service of their country; but he that stands by it now, deserves the love and thanks of man and woman....*"

As Sarah listened to Jeremiah read the rest of the pamphlet she could not help but feel that someone had finally been able to put into words what this war was about. She was filled with admiration for the man who had written it. She understood that their suffering would not be for naught. But more importantly she could feel that the men were inspired also. They were proud of themselves as the ones who had stayed the course when others left to go home.

She could not wait for evening, when she could talk to John and the others about what Paine had written. When she finally got back to the hut the men were already there and they were jabbering like a bunch of women.

Ben was saying, "I don't know much about General Washington but, after all they have been through down there, if he is able to get those men to attack in the dead of winter and beat the Hessians and the Redcoats I guess he must be a pretty good general. And he's got some good fighting generals with him too. Green and Putnam and Sterling all have good reputations. And that man Knox, who came up here to get the guns last year, is a good man too."

John added, "We've got a good man here also. They should promote Colonel Wayne to general. He is a fighting man just like Arnold. We haven't seen a general around here in months. Schuyler is down in Albany and Gates is off politicking with Congress. I ain't sure either one of them is fit to lead an army. There's goin' to be a major battle up here come spring. If they want us to win it they better get a good general up here to lead the fight. And they better start recruiting some soldiers. Between the ones who've left and those that are sick we are in no condition to take on Carleton."

"What did you men think of the pamphlet Jeremiah read today?" Sarah asked. "It was the first time I heard anyone put this war in such plain terms. I thought it was inspiring."

"Yeah Sarah, I think so too," William put in. "He certainly captured the essence of the Tories. And he put it plain that this war isn't going to get any easier from here on out for us or our enemies. But we will win it because we are the ones with something to lose. There are Tories fighting for the other side but only a relative few of them. Most of them are waiting for the Redcoats to save them from us. We are our own army, and we'll win because we aren't asking anybody to save us. We could use some help from the French maybe. But it's our war and it will be our victory in the end."

"You hit the nail on the head, William," Ben said. "We are going to win this war. No matter how long it takes. As long as we can hold this army together we will win in the end. The British over in England are going to rue the day they sent their army here to enslave us. It's been going on for nearly two years already and they haven't been able to beat us yet. I tell you, I was pretty worried when the army down there lost New York. But even then the Redcoats with all their Hessians couldn't catch Washington, and he was able to get away with most of the army. And with every battle I think we are learning how to fight 'em better. We don't have to win every battle. We just have to make their winning too costly for them to want to continue."

John put in, "I think you're right, Ben. But we need a real victory to get any other nations to recognize us or to lend us a hand. Let's hope by spring new recruits and some of the soldiers who left for the winter are up here, and maybe we can get that victory right here at Fort Ti."

It was the first time Sarah had heard any of them say anything good about General Washington or the army down south. And it was the first time since the men returned from the defeat at Quebec that she heard them speak so enthusiastically about winning this war. Conditions at the fort were still miserable but Thomas Paine had put it all in perspective. The suffering would be rewarded with victory in the end. She was now sure of it.

New recruits started to arrive in early April. The snows were melting and days getting longer. There was one incident that put a damper on everyone's spirits though. A group of recruits had been ambushed by a notorious Tory named McKay and a group of Indians. They killed and scalped several of the men and captured twenty one others. Colonel Wayne sent out a party, who intercepted them on their trip north, but McKay got away. The incident marked what all knew to be the beginning of the new campaign.

In late April the ground was finally soft enough to do some farming. Doctor Potts led the women in establishing several gardens to grow herbs for medicines and some vegetables to improve the nutrition of the army. Sarah loved being outdoors in the gardens. Once again she was reminded of her youth when she helped her mother in their garden. It was good to get dirt on her hands planting the seeds, and she couldn't wait to see the harvest.

They also got good news late in the month. Colonel Wayne was promoted to general on the twenty-first. Everyone was happy for him and thought it was long overdue. He was a Pennsylvania man, but it didn't matter. He was one of them. He fought with them in Quebec and in the rear guard action at Three Rivers. The men said he fought like a madman.

In spite of their husbands' consternation and warnings, Sarah and Elizabeth continued to visit Taima periodically. For Sarah each visit was a new learning experience. They met several other women, and she looked forward to the visits. She was finding that although these people were different than anyone she had ever met they were good people who just wanted to be left to their lands to live in peace. Seeing how their cultures were different was fascinating, but the more she learned, the more she realized they were only different in how they lived, not what they lived for. These Indian women were just like her. They just wanted what was best for their families, just like she did. They worked hard to give their families all they could, just like she did. Taima and the other women also shared their knowledge of many of the crafts they were so expert in with Sarah and Elizabeth.

In May a scouting party returned with news that General Burgoyne had arrived in Canada with a great number of reinforcements and he, not Carlton, would lead the campaign that spring.

John was offering his view of what they just heard as Sarah came into the hut that evening. "Well, if they have sent all those reinforcements they must have something big planned for this spring. But it's already May and we haven't seen hide nor hair of 'em yet. Except for their Indian friends they haven't even tried to get out of Canada yet, so far as we know. No matter. With all the new recruits we been getting from New England we'll be ready for them. Mark my words."

"And the defenses are looking good both here and over there on Mount Independence," Ben added. "I don't see why we haven't done much on that mountain behind us though. If it was me in charge I would've put more into that mountain than Independence. But I guess one's as good as the other."

"I hear they're sending us a new major general soon," William added. "His name is St. Clair or Sinclair or something like that. Some of the men say they knew him from last year. He was in Canada and down at Fort Edward after the retreat. Never heard of him myself, but that don't mean too much. I don't socialize in generals' circles much. I just hope he is a fighting general like Wayne or Arnold."

"Me too," added John. "I am sick of just sitting here building defenses. I feel like a prisoner or a slave the way we been working. I joined this army to fight, and since October all we been doing is starving, freezing, and building. I know we have to wait for the Redcoats to come down here before we get another chance at them, but I'm ready now."

"Can't be long now," Ben said. "It's already May, and the summer goes by fast up here. So if this Burgoyne fellow doesn't want to face the same fate as Carleton did last year, he'll have to come soon. Like William said though, I hope this fella St. Clair is ready to fight because everyone here is. I don't usually have much good to say about those New England lads. Can't say I like 'em much. But these new recruits they sent seem ready for a fight too. If we can keep 'em around long enough, that is," he added sarcastically.

John ended the conversation with, "Well, boys, we'll just have to wait and see how things come out. It's Burgoyne and St. Clair who will be calling the shots this summer, and neither of 'em is here yet. But I tell ya, I'm a little worried. With one army in Canada and another in New York City, the Redcoats—if they have a wit of sense—could squeeze us pretty good. If Burgoyne comes down here and Howe decides to go up the Hudson with the idea of meeting in Albany, both us and Washington's folks are gonna have one hell of a fight on our hands this summer."

When General St. Clair finally arrived in June he was not what the men expected. With Colonel Baldwin, the fort's engineer, leading the tour, the general inspected the work on the defenses that the men had been working so hard on. He immediately said the fort could not be defended and had everything moved to Mount Independence. The men could not understand or believe what was happening. It was as if the general had already given up the fort.

Sarah and the other women worked to get a new hospital set up on Mount Independence. The huts were abandoned and everyone moved back into the tents which were put up over there also.

News soon started coming in from many points. Two prisoners were taken and interrogated. According to fort rumor, they said that Burgoyne already had troops at St. Johns. According to these prisoners Burgoyne had a force that numbered near ten thousand, and many were already headed up the east side of the lake to get between Mount Independence and Skenesborough. And there was word that a British ship had been sighted near Crown Point. With this news the men were once again enthused. It didn't matter to them how many men Burgoyne had. There would be a fight, and this time they were sure they would win.

Word finally came that Burgoyne's armada had set sail from the Northern end of the lake. More frightening, however, was an edict he had disseminated that stated that anyone who surrendered to him and pledged allegiance to the crown would be welcomed and not abused. But he would turn his Indian allies loose on anyone who remained a rebel or supported them in any way. These Indians would have free reign to perpetrate any savagery they wished on anyone who did not fully comply.

This last news sent a shiver up Sarah's spine. What kind of man could this Burgoyne be to unleash the horror the Indians could inflict upon them, let alone upon the innocent populace? But rather than causing a panic, the news only reinforced everyone's belief that he had to be stopped. She felt safe at the fort, but she feared for those poor people who lived away from it.

One morning shortly after that news Sarah looked over at the Indians' camp as she walked to work. She was startled to see that it was abandoned. They had move out entirely during the night. She could only wonder where they had gone and why.

Twenty-Eight

At seven o'clock on the morning of June thirtieth, Sarah and everyone at the fort heard a shot come from one of the command's guard boats. It announced the sighting of the lead elements of Burgoyne's force. Everyone ran to get a first glimpse of what was happening. The women stood silently, holding each other's hands tightly. They stared north down the lake as if mesmerized. At first they saw nothing. But it wasn't long before they could see the ships advancing towards the fort. There were so many they seemed to fill the lake. The ships were still quite far down the lake and Sarah could see them put into the shore and begin unloading. All the waiting was over. Whatever was going to happen would begin now, she thought.

Almost immediately the fort became a beehive of activity. The men were all running and shouting their boasts of how they would show the Lobsterbacks what they were made of now. Everyone had something to do. All the supplies had to be brought inside the lines to secure them. Units formed up to get their instructions and picket assignments. It was as if a great festival was about to start. All the suffering, all the misery was gone. At last what they all had been waiting for had arrived

Sarah's heart quickened with anticipation. She wondered aloud, "Is this what the men feel like before they go into battle? My heart is pounding but I don't feel scared."

Many of the men left the hospital on their own to retrieve their muskets and get back to their units. They had come here to fight, and they were not going to miss it lying in a bed.

Things calmed down later in the day when everyone realized that it would take a couple of days for the British to land and organize all the troops and their supplies. There was sporadic firing that could be heard coming from the picket lines as Burgoyne's Indians tested the defenses. A couple of casualties were brought in, but they were not badly hurt and were treated and went back to their units. Throughout that night and all the next day and night Sarah could hear the terrifying noises coming from the Indian camps that were already close to the fort. Her feeling of exhilaration was changing to one of fear. Over the next couple of days she would take a break periodically and go look at the spectacle that was forming in front of them. Thousands of soldiers kept coming off those ships.

Mount Hope was due north of the fort. It was a place where Colonel Baldwin had built sawmills to process wood for his many projects. The Americans had established a picket line there. About mid-morning on the second of July, Sarah heard a smattering of gunfire and the incessant war cries from the Indians who had been

Map of the Northern Theater

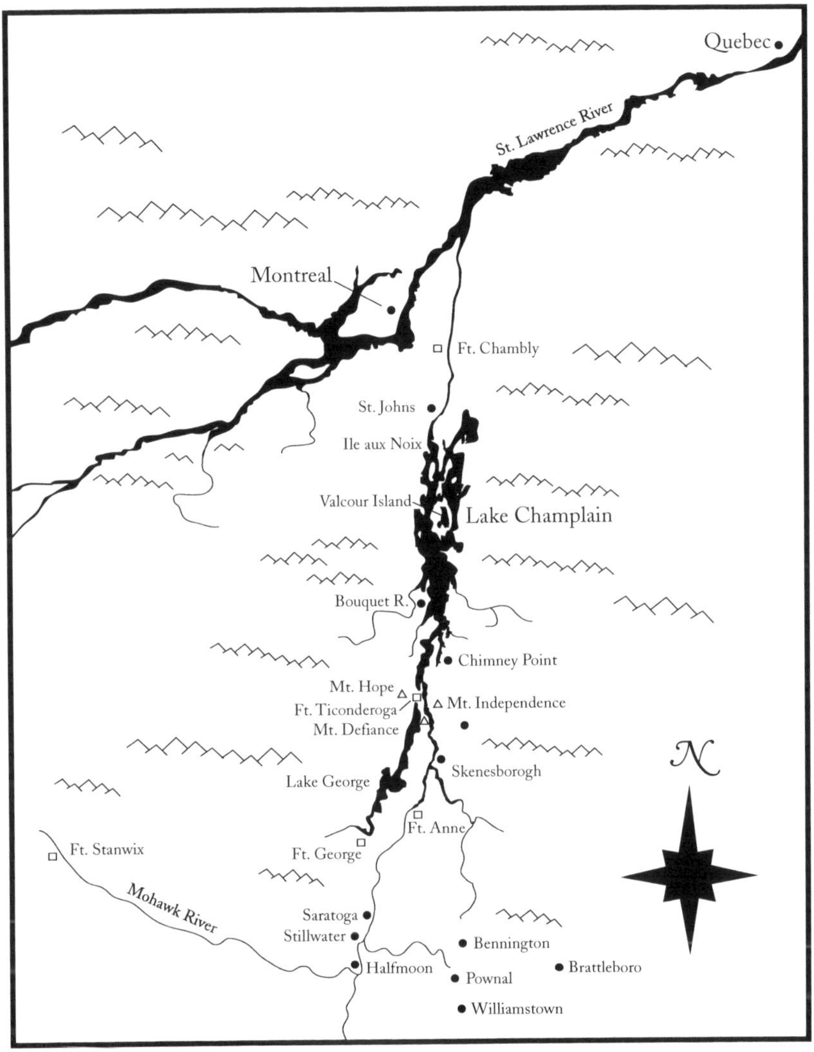

harassing the location for two days. She and Elizabeth raced to a spot where they could see what was happening. Several large billows of smoke could be seen coming from the area. They could also make out the men who had been at Mount Hope racing to get to what were called the French lines, trenches that had been built by the French during the last war to hold off the British when this place was called Fort Carillon. There were more musket shots, but nobody seemed to be hit and all the men seemed to have made it to the French lines.

Things quieted down after that. The fires on Mount Hope burned throughout the day, destroying all that the men had built there over the last year. The thick choking smoke drifted toward the fort, and for a while obscured the view of anything from the fort.

Around one o'clock Sarah once again heard musket fire, and the Indian screams seemed much louder. Once again she ran to a place where she could see. The Indians were attacking the French lines. There were about fifty men there defending them. For the first time Sarah witnessed an actual fire fight as the battle raged on for most of the hot sultry afternoon. She would go back to her duties in the hospital but would keep returning to stare in awe at what she was witnessing. Her legs seemed frozen in place. She could not take her eyes away from the sight. The Indians seemed crazed as they charged the lines over and over, their terrifying screams getting louder with each attack. More frightening than the Indians' war hoops were the screams and cries she heard coming from the men who were hit. She could almost feel the burning pain they must be feeling as the ball ripped through their bodies. She wanted to do something to help but she could only stare at the spectacle before her.

Sarah had not noticed John come up behind her as she watched. "Frightening sight, isn't it Sarah?"

Startled, she jumped and turned as she heard him. She threw her arms around him as tight as she could, wanting to hide inside him. "Oh, John, it's so terrible. Why isn't anyone doing anything to help those men?"

"There's a force forming up right now to go and relieve them. It's only a minor skirmish though. There doesn't seem to be any Redcoats involved, just Indians. From the sounds of 'em they're probably drunk and just couldn't wait no longer to get blood on their tomahawks."

She couldn't believe that he was so calm about what was going on in front of them. "John, a minor skirmish? Doesn't what is going on out there bother you? Don't you want to go help those men?"

"I'm sorry, Sarah, that was not what I meant. There are a couple of things you will need to learn if you are going to be involved in this fighting war. The first is, no battle is small to the men who are in it. To the people fighting in it, it is as large and important as any battle ever fought. So I should not have referred to what is going on out there as a minor skirmish.

"Second, up 'til now you have been in the rear. You haven't had to see or hear men getting shot or blown to pieces. The first few times it nauseates and infuriates you and you want to kill everything and everyone on the other side all by yourself. But sooner or later you get used to it, sort of. Then you realize that the only way this, or any, army can win is through discipline.

"You've heard us complain about the militias. Well, this is what we have been talking about. For most of them, their first response is to charge headlong into the battle. They're going to win it single handedly. But as soon as they face a disciplined, coordinated effort they run. Not because they are cowards, but because they suddenly realize they can't win the battle alone and they don't have the discipline to trust the men fighting next to them.

"Those men out there are doing just fine because they are remaining disciplined. We are sending out a force to aid them and they know it. As you look at the battle in front of you you're probably thinking the savages are winning because they are attacking wildly and making a great deal of noise. But noise don't win battles. Discipline does. So even if I wanted to go out there on my own, I know that it wouldn't help.

"There will be plenty of fighting before we're done and I'll have to do my share. You and I both have jobs to do, and right now mine is to wait for orders about what they want me to do. In a very short time yours is going to be to help those men who are getting shot up out there. You can't go out there and help them. All you can do is wait for them to be brought back to you so you can patch 'em up. Understand?"

"Oh, John, I'm scared and angry and I don't know what is going to happen. I'm so glad to see you and hold you. I love you, John. Please know that."

"I love you too, Sarah," he said as he held her tight. "I don't know what's going to happen either. And to tell you the truth, I'm scared too." He held her at arm's length and smiled. "But we just can't let fear get in the way of what we have to do. So buck up my dear. We will win this war, and you women will be able to say you helped."

"When will I see you again, John? It helps to see you and know you are safe."

"I don't know, dear. Everything is kind of confused right now. We are on standby alert and just waiting for someone to tell us what they want us to do. But I'll come by as often as I can to see you. Now, I think you may want to get back to the hospital. It sounds like this tussle is about over and you are going to have some work to do, no doubt. I'll come see you when I can."

They kissed and Sarah said, "Thank you, John. Talking to you has really helped."

Sarah went back to the hospital where she was met by Elizabeth. "What's going on out there? We could hear all the raucous. Those savages must be going crazy for all the noise they're making."

"It's hard to see for all the smoke. But the Indians keep attacking the French line. I spoke with John and he said the men are doing fine. But you can't help but hear the screams and cries of those that have been hit in those attacks. It sounds like it's pretty much over for now. They'll be bringing in the wounded soon, I think."

"You all right, Sarah? You look in a daze, dearie. Why don't you sit down here for a minute?"

"No, I'll be fine Elizabeth. It's just that I've never seen anything like that before. It was like watching a play, but it was real. They weren't play acting. They were real people getting shot and killed and wounded. And the screams weren't play acting either, they were real too. I just need a moment to get my mind straight. I'll be fine."

"Well, if you're all right, it looks like we'll be needing your help. They're bringing the first of them in now. Why don't you work with the doctor over there evaluating them?"

When they brought the casualties in, seven were dead. About a dozen were seriously wounded, and another dozen or so had minor wounds. The doctor told Sarah to take care of the men with minor wounds and send them back to their units. She finished that task quickly. Several men just walked off without any care at all.

Once she was finished she went to the room where a doctor was performing an amputation. She did not know why, but being able to take care of this man now seemed to ease her mind. When she was watching the battle she was frustrated because there was nothing she could do to help. But helping with this amputation took her mind off the battle, and all she thought about was what she needed to do next. She could almost ignore the blood and gore of the operation and focus on helping to keep the man still while the doctor performed the surgery.

Sarah was everywhere, doing anything she could to help and stay busy. Time flew by without her even noticing it. Sometime after dark they were finished. All the men had been taken care of. Now other women would take over and nurse the men through the night. She was done for the day. She wondered where John was.

Martha and Elizabeth met her at the door. Elizabeth said, "You keep working like you did today and you'll be in one of them beds, dearie. This was only a small engagement. Wait 'til the real thing happens. You try to tend to them all then and you'll be of no use to nobody. You got to slow down, dearie, before you wear yourself out."

"I'm sorry. It's just that watching that fight out there today lit a fire in me that I couldn't put out. I wanted to be a soldier and go out and help those men. I wanted to kill every Indian in these forests singlehandedly. I have never felt such rage before. I had to do something to burn it off. I'll get better. I promise."

Sarah looked at Martha, who was now beginning her eighth month. She asked, "How are you feeling tonight, Martha? You aren't doing too much here in the hospital are you? You shouldn't even be here. You should be somewhere resting."

"I'm alright Sarah, thank you for asking. As for rest, where is there a place to rest in this fort? No, I can wrap bandages and do the little things that need doing here. I'm just a little tired is all. Let's get outside and get some air." The three of them walked into the warm summer night.

As they strolled they could hear the men talking about the day's battle. They all sounded excited about the way the men in the trenches had held off the savages. It was about nine o'clock and just turning dark. All of a sudden a series of cannons exploded and lit up the night. Sarah grabbed a soldier's arm and asked excitedly, "What's going on? What's the cannon fire for? Are we under attack?"

The man laughed and said, "Naw lady. General St. Clair was so excited about how the men fought today he has ordered a *feu de joie.* Usually everybody fires off a round with their rifles and muskets but he decided to do it with thirteen cannons tonight in honor of the thirteen states."

Elizabeth asked, "What did you call it?"

"A *feu de joie.* It's French. Means fire of joy, they tell me. Armies do it when they have won a battle. So I guess the general thinks we won one today. Have a nice evening, ladies."

They walked along casually talking about the week's events until Martha stopped quickly and bent over in pain. She cried, "Elizabeth, you've been through this—is it supposed to hurt so badly? It's not time yet."

Elizabeth took her arm and helped her back up. "Is this the first time you've felt the pain?"

"No, I felt it a couple of times the last few days. Do you think it's time?"

"I don't know, dearie. But let's get you back to the hospital and have a doctor take a look. Sarah, hurry, go get Jeremiah and bring him to the hospital quickly."

As she ran, Sarah could hear Martha moan as she and Elizabeth walked back to the hospital. Sarah was running as fast as she could, all the while praying that Jeremiah would be there and that Martha was alright. When she reached the tent she yelled, "Jeremiah, are you in there?"

A lieutenant was there and said, "Jeremiah is not here, ma'am. Is there anything I can do for you?"

"Where is he? It is urgent that I speak to him. His wife is in the hospital."

"He's with the Colonel, ma'am. They're in the middle of a meeting."

Sarah left without another word. She ran to the Colonel's marque. The flap was open and she could see the men sitting at a table talking. She burst in and said, "Excuse me, Sir, but this is an emergency. Jeremiah, Elizabeth has just taken Martha to the hospital. She is in a great deal of pain."

The men were silent and all looked to the Colonel. He stood and said, "Well, go, son. We can handle this meeting without you."

As Jeremiah and Sarah ran towards the hospital he asked, "Is she having the baby? She's just starting her eighth month. Isn't this too early?"

Sarah answered, "I don't know Jeremiah. We were walking and she just bent over in pain."

They finally reached the hospital and both of them burst through the doors. Elizabeth was holding Martha's hand and the doctor stood and looked at Jeremiah. He quietly said, "Captain, I am sorry. The baby was stillborn. Your wife is weak but I think she will make it through. I am truly sorry."

Sarah burst into tears and rushed to Martha's side and took her other hand. She could think of no words to console her. She just held her hand as tight as she could.

Jeremiah was stunned. All he could say was, "No, no, this can't be true." He looked at the doctor, then to a nurse who was holding something wrapped in a blanket. Tears streamed down his face as the truth sunk in. He walked over to Martha, and Elizabeth stood and moved away. He knelt down beside her and kissed her face. Their tears mingled together but neither of them said a word.

Elizabeth took Sarah by the arm and they left Martha and Jeremiah alone.

Sarah cried, "Oh, Elizabeth, how can this be happening? What more can God put us through? The men I can understand. They are fighting a war. Their wounds and deaths are terrible. But this. How could He take Martha's baby?"

Sarah's words became bitter and her sorrow turned to anger. "That child was not fighting this war. He had done nothing to injure anyone in this world. Maybe we, all of us, have displeased God enough to make him put us through this war. But not this baby."

Elizabeth took Sarah in her arms, “I know, dearie. It’s gonna be alright. We’ll all stick together and get through this and anything else this God we all pray so hard to has a mind to throw at us.”

Sarah wiped the tears from her face and said with a weak voice, “I know you’re right, Elizabeth. I just needed to vent all the frustrations I have felt over the past few days. I will be alright. Elizabeth, I love you and Martha more than my own family. We are closer than sisters. You two are my family now.” She reached out and hugged Elizabeth tightly.

The next morning, after the usual burial of the men who had died over night, Jeremiah, Sarah, John, Elizabeth, Edward and their son gathered with Reverend Allen and held a private funeral for the dead baby. Martha and Jeremiah had given him the name James. It was a name they had picked for a son months before. He was laid to rest in the same mass grave as the soldiers who had just been buried. Like them, there was no marker or anything to note who he was or even that he was there.

The scene broke Sarah’s heart and she cried uncontrollably. John put his arm around her and held her tight. She recovered some and quietly whimpered until the service was over.

Jeremiah had spent the night with Martha and looked like he had not slept at all. He was stoic during the very brief service and he walked alone back to the hospital. There was nothing more to say or do. The rest of the group broke up quietly and went their separate ways back to wherever their duty called.

Twenty-Nine

The next few days were relatively quiet. There was cannon fire going off sporadically in both directions, but it seemed to Sarah that whoever was aiming the guns must have been inept, because though they made a lot of noise, nothing ever seemed to get hit.

Martha rested for a couple of days and Sarah and Elizabeth doted on her constantly. Jeremiah came by several times each day to look in on her. After two days she finally said, "Thank you ladies for all the attention, but I will be alright. Take care of the men. They need you more than I do. In fact, I want to get up and go outside. This place is very depressing."

Sarah said, "Are you sure you are alright, Martha? It has only been two days, and you should get as much rest as you can."

But Elizabeth interrupted, "No Sarah, Martha is right. The best thing for you, Martha, is to get up out of that bed and go out and sit in the sun for a while. It will brighten your spirits better than anything we can do in here. Just don't try doing any work, or we will tie you down to this bed."

Martha promised she would be good. Sarah and Elizabeth helped her out of the bed and walked her outside. As she sat down she said, "Thank you both for everything you have done for me. I don't know if I could make it through without you two. Jeremiah is not very good at this. He tries hard but it is so awkward for him. Can we just talk for a minute?"

"Sure, dearie. What do you want to talk about?" Elizabeth asked as she and Sarah sat down on either side of her.

"For two days I have been laying there thinking about my baby. Wondering what I did wrong. Could I have done it better? Was it my fault? I don't know the answers. But more importantly it's what I feel right now that bothers me. I'm sad and hurt that I lost James. But a part of me says that maybe this is the best thing for him. What kind of life could I give him here or wherever we go from here? I don't want to put my children through the misery we have been living for the past year." She started to cry and both women put their arms around her. "Is there something wrong with me? How should I feel right now? Beyond sad, I am almost glad he is with God now instead of here. What is wrong with me?"

Elizabeth looked into her eyes and said, "Martha, there is nothing wrong with you. The feelings you are having are those every woman who ever lost a baby has felt. I too lost a baby when I was young. Once the sadness begins to wear off, the feelings of guilt that it was your fault stay with you longest. But Martha, it was not your fault. You did everything you could to keep that baby well. But look at this place," she waved her hand around. "A baby has maybe one chance in ten to make it through the pregnancy. And, if he is born, probably even less of a chance to survive a year in conditions like this. You didn't create these conditions, and what happened to James is not your fault. We have to believe that God, in his wisdom, has a plan and part of it was to take him and keep him safe from all this. Martha, you are a healthy woman and you will have more babies, I promise you. And they will be born in a better place than this. I'm sorry, I didn't mean to preach. But you—we—must go on from here. Sarah and I share your pain and we will be by your side when you need us. Just know and believe that you—we all—will get through this."

Martha wiped her eyes. "Thank you, Elizabeth. Thank you both for being here with me."

"Dearie, we are here for you. As Sarah said last night, we are sisters. And we will help each other through whatever comes our way." She patted Martha on the arm and said lightly, "Now you just sit here and enjoy the warm sun while Sister Sarah here and I get back to work."

Late in the afternoon of July sixth, Sarah saw all the generals heading towards General St. Clair's office. About an hour later they all came out. Each of them had a very serious look about them. At about five the camp came alive with a great deal of activity, but no one seemed to know what was about to happen.

Shortly after nine o'clock she found John and the other men at the tent and asked what was going on.

John said, "I don't know, Sarah. We just got told to draw extra rations for five days, draw extra ammunition, and get ready to move. Since the Redcoats put cannon on top of Mount Defiance yesterday, this place is not very safe. Maybe we are going over there to drive them off."

Ben however had different thoughts. "We ain't gonna do no fighting, John. We're gonna run. We been up here for a year waiting to get at the Redcoats again. And this bastard St. Clair shows up here and in two weeks decides we gotta run. I tell you John, this cause of ours is doomed if we can't get some leaders who are willing to fight. Those idiots in Congress keep promoting men like Washington and St. Clair and Granny Gates. None of 'em wants to fight. Why don't they give men like Wayne and Arnold a chance? We might lose but at least they will fight. You mark my words, John, we'll be running tonight."

John looked at Sarah and then at Ben. "You may be right, Ben. I don't know. What I do know is those guns on Mount Defiance will blow this place to hell in a very short time. And it don't take no genius to look out there and count the thousands of soldiers Burgoyne is going to throw at us in a day or two. That and the Hessians headed our way make this place about useless. So whether we are going to fight or retreat doesn't matter much right now. What matters now is that we follow orders and get ready to face whatever comes next. Now quit your bitching and let's get to work. Sarah, we don't know what is going on either. You best get back to the hospital and see what is going on over there. Maybe they have a better idea."

She stepped to him and kissed him on the cheek. "Alright John, but you'll let me know when you know something?" she asked anxiously.

"Yeah, just as soon as we know what the hell is going on, I'll let you know," he answered morosely.

Little did they know it would be more than a week before they saw or heard from each other again. A week of hell and anguish Sarah would never forget.

When Sarah got back to the hospital she found the place very quiet compared to the rest of the fort. She found Elizabeth and asked, "Have you got any idea what's going on? I was just talking to John. The men are breaking everything down and taking it down to the docks. They have drawn five days rations and ammunition. He thinks they might be going to attack the British at Mount Defiance, since they put cannon up there. But Ben thinks we're getting ready for a retreat."

"Don't know, Sarah. Something definitely is going on. But no one has told us anything. We are waiting for the doctor to come in. He's in charge of here, maybe he can shed some light on what we are supposed to be doing. I'll tell you one thing though. Wherever they're moving to, if someone has the bright idea of leaving us and the wounded behind for the British to tend to they better come up with a better one, because where this army goes I go."

Sarah looked around and asked, "Where's Martha? Is she alright?"

"Oh, she's fine. I figure sometime soon somebody's going to be coming through that door shouting for us to get everything ready to move, so I told her to start packing up the bandages and such. There isn't much in the way of medical supplies left, so getting this place ready to move shouldn't take too long. They better send us some soldiers to help carry some of these wounded and sick men out of here though. We won't be able to do it ourselves."

At dark the American cannons began to fire. They seemed to be firing at intervals, first from the left side, then from the right. The firing continued into the night.

Just before midnight the doctor came hurrying in, just as Elizabeth had predicted. "The general just told me that we are evacuating the wounded tonight. We must get everything packed and taken down to the ships at the dock. There will be some soldiers here in a few minutes to help move those who can't make it on their own. If you women will take charge of getting the rest of the men down to the ships, I will go down and see to things at the dock."

Elizabeth asked, "You said we were evacuating, does that mean they are just evacuating the wounded?"

"No. From what I have been told, most of the army is going to retreat overland to Fort George. We are taking the wounded and sick on the ships with the army's supplies. With any luck we will be in Skenesborough tomorrow and then march over to Fort George the next day. The army will meet us there."

The sick and wounded that could walk were sent down to the dock to board the ships. Soldiers soon arrived to carry those that could not make it on their own. Martha and most of the other women went with them.

Elizabeth, Sarah, and a couple of sergeants were the last to leave. Before they left Sarah checked in on four men who they were leaving behind. It broke Sarah's heart that they had to leave these men, but they were too sick to be taken with them. She knew that their best chance of survival would be with a British doctor who might have the medicines they needed. She also knew that they would probably die before morning in any case. But it still hurt her to have to leave anyone alone and suffering.

They checked everything one last time and started the walk down to the dock. On the way down, Sarah said, "I hope we have time to see our husbands before we depart. I want to say a proper goodbye to John. We just casually parted up at the tent a while ago. I didn't even tell him I love him or kiss him goodbye."

"I know what you mean, Sarah. I haven't seen Edward or Robert since breakfast. This is not the way to part. I pray that we have not seen them for the last time, but I think it's going to be quite a while before we see them again. All we can do is silently send them our love and tell them we love them in our hearts, and then hope that they feel it too."

Everything at the water's edge was in confusion. Men were showing up every minute with all their personal belongings as well as all the material that was required to be moved. Even to Sarah it was evident that there were not nearly enough boats and ships to carry all the material that was accumulating on the shore. There were five galleys being loaded, as well as many bateaus. The doctor was also there. He assigned the women to different ships to oversee the care of the invalids on them.

When he assigned Martha to a ship, Elizabeth spoke up, "Doctor, Martha here has just had a miscarriage and is not able to take on these duties. I think it would be better if you assigned her to the same ship with me. I will make sure that she is taken care of, and that everything that needs to get done is handled."

The doctor shrugged and switched Martha and another woman.

As Sarah listened to the orders being given it struck her that the politeness and gentler treatment the women used to get when they first arrived over a year ago was no longer there. Then they were always politely asked to do whatever it was the army needed doing. But now they were issued orders just as if they were an actual part of this army.

It was about three o'clock in the morning when the ships were finally loaded and the long procession of ships and bateaus started out on the thirty mile trek towards Skenesborough. It was a beautiful night, warm and not too humid. Cool air coming across the lake was a welcome relief to the heat and sweat of the earlier part of the evening. Lake Champlain was perfectly still and smooth, its glass-like appearance broken only by the oars from the boats. The early morning quiet had not yet been broken by the waking of the birds and insects. The darkness hid the squalor of the war that pervaded this idyllic setting.

But suddenly the dark night exploded with light. As she looked back she saw an enormous fire light up the top of Mount Independence. She could clearly see the men scurrying around preparing for their departure. Surely the British could see it also, she thought. While they had been preparing to leave, it was an order emphasized over and over that no one could have any light whatsoever, lest they give away to the British what they were doing. She wondered what the fire could mean.

The sun slowly came up over the mountains and the day promised to be clear and the sailing smooth. The air on the ships was almost festive. The sullenness that pervaded the fort's attitude earlier in the evening seemed to be gone. Sarah could only wonder what was happening with John and the other men who were making this trip on foot. Had they gotten away without causing suspicion in the British and Hessian lines? How long was it going to be before they would arrive? Then it struck her. Where were they going to arrive? They had just abandoned Fort Ti, the fortress of the north. Where were they going now, and if they couldn't do it from Fort Ti, how would they hold off the British at one of these lesser forts? Sarah put it from her mind. Surely these generals knew what they were doing and had a plan. She drifted back to sleep with that thought.

When she awoke the sun was high and it was a beautiful but very hot day. They seemed to be drifting along at an almost leisurely pace. She started talking to a Captain from one of the units on the ship. Their conversation finally got around to the speed they were traveling at. Sarah said, "Don't you think we're going awfully slow? Last night it seemed that we could not get under way fast enough. Now it feels like we are out for a morning sightseeing tour."

The Captain laughed, "Don't worry, ma'am. The commander of this expedition, Colonel Long, knows exactly what he's doing. It'll take the Redcoats days to break through the bridge and all the obstacles Colonel Baldwin has built. No ma'am, there's no danger. We'll be on our way to Albany before they can even get out on the lake in pursuit of us."

Thirty

The armada arrived at the landing spot on the east side of the lake near Skenesborough about midafternoon. The sick and wounded, as well as all the supplies and baggage, would have to be taken off the ships and bateaus and placed on the shore. The bateaus had to be portaged up a steep incline past a waterfall to a stream named Wood Creek. Then the invalids, supplies and baggage would also have to be carried up over the waterfall and reloaded onto the bateaus before this little army could advance.

When Sarah got off the ship she immediately went searching for Elizabeth and Martha. She found them disembarking from their ship. "How was your cruise?" she asked good-naturedly.

"Well, dearie, they certainly took their own sweet time getting here. And a bunch of the men got hold of some liquor somewhere and drank the night and half the day away before they passed out. You probably heard them singing, if that's what they call it. They sure won't be worth a tinker's damn helping move anything this afternoon," Elizabeth sputtered.

"Yes, we could hear them alright. But things were pretty quiet and restful on our ship. How are you feeling, Martha?"

"Oh, I'm fine, Sarah. I guess all the noise didn't bother me as much as it did Elizabeth. Maybe I was just too tired to even hear it."

"Well, I'm glad someone got some rest on this trip," Elizabeth snapped. "Let's go find the doctor and find out what he wants us to do about these men."

They found him organizing men to assist taking the wounded up the hill. Elizabeth asked, "What is it you would like us to do, Doctor?"

"Oh, ladies, how very good to see you. If you would round up the rest of the women and get your baggage and as much of the medical supplies as you can carry and get them up over the waterfall it would be most helpful. I've talked to Colonel Long and he wants us to move the sick and wounded men away from here as soon as possible. No telling how far the British Army is behind us. There should be some bateaus up there soon. When they get there, would you please organize loading the men and our supplies into those boats and get them moving on?"

It was very hot and the insects were swarming around the sweating bodies in droves. The women got their few meager things and the medical supplies and started the climb. It quickly became very steep and slippery. They struggled up, grabbing small branches or shrubs to gain their balance and aid them in getting up the hill.

At the top of the hill stood Fort Anne. It consisted of a small fort and a block house. There was a company of soldiers stationed there.

They were not very long into this portaging when the afternoon stillness was exploded by the sounds of cannon going off and the crashing of cannon balls into the trees around them. Sarah looked out into the lake. What she saw took her breath away. A fleet of British warships was standing just off shore. All of them had cannons blazing. They quickly destroyed three of the American galleys, which sat burning at the water's edge. Soon the other two had struck their colors and surrendered. The large war ships could not get into the narrow passage but were unloading soldiers onto boats and they were rowing towards the shore.

Sarah wondered where the smug Captain who told her it would take days for this fleet to get away out of the lake was.

The guns continued to pummel the landing point and the entire hill. Men began to run into the trees to get away. Most of the sick and wounded had already been loaded into the boats and were on their way to Fort Edward, thirteen miles to the southeast. There were two more boats to be loaded. Sarah, Elizabeth, and Ginny were the only women left. Sarah told the other two to take the next boat and she would go with the last one. But Ginny said, "No Sarah, I will stay and go with you."

There was no time to argue. Sarah and Ginny helped push Elizabeth's boat off and began helping to load the final one when a mortar round exploded right over the bateau. Sarah was yards away from the bateau helping a soldier. Ginny was standing in it, helping other men.

For a moment Sarah was in shock from the explosion. It had knocked her down but did not seriously hurt her. The impact caused wood splinters, water and mud to erupt and pour over her and anyone near the boat. Then she looked down at herself and realized that she was covered with mud. Mixed in with the mud were blood and pieces of Ginny and the men who had been in the boat. She looked at what remained of the boat. The men who had not been killed were in agony, screaming and struggling to get themselves out of the water, while the dead were just floating there. Sarah waded into the water. It had turned a reddish brown color as the blood mixed with the mud to make an eerie concoction. The mud in the creek bed sucked at her shoes as she tried to reach Ginny. She was still standing knee deep in the bloody, muddy water pulling at Ginny when one of the soldiers pulled her arm, "Come on, ma'am. We gotta get outta here. The Redcoats are coming up that hill and will be here soon."

"But we can't leave her or these men. They'll be captured, or worse," Sarah cried.

"Ma'am, she's dead and so are most of these men. I'm sorry for them too, but if we stay here we will be captured or worse also. There is nothing we can do for them right now. With luck the soldiers coming up that hill won't be in a heat of battle yet and will simply capture them that's alive and take them to a doctor for treatment. Now if you're coming, start running." Several of the soldiers who had been helping started running into the forest.

Sarah looked at Ginny in her arms and then at the men laying at the edge of the creek and the ones still trying to get out of the water. She did not know what to do. The man who had been talking to her finally grabbed her arm and shouted over the din of cannon and musket fire, "Come on ma'am, we gotta go now."

She let Ginny go and said softly, "If there is a God in heaven, you are free now, Ginny."

With the man's help she pulled herself from the water. As she did the mud sucked her shoes off her feet. She stopped for a moment and took one last look at Ginny, then she followed the man into the trees, running as fast as she could. As she ran she could hear the buzzing of musket balls as they whizzed overheard. After what seemed to her a mile run, but was probably only a couple hundred yards, Sarah fell into a ditch. It had six inches of water in it. She was drenched from head to toe with mud and muck. It took a moment for her to get her bearings and realize that there was a man in the ditch with her. She turned to ask him what to do next when she saw that he had been hit in the head by a musket ball. The ball had entered the back of his head, gone through, and blew away most of his face, which was now just a mass of blood and brains. She turned and vomited at the sight. She tried to stand so she could run again but her legs wouldn't move.

At that moment another man fell into the ditch with her. She was afraid to look to see if he was alive or dead. "You alright, lady?" It was the man who had pulled her along out of the creek. Sarah nodded. "You know how to use a musket, ma'am?"

Sarah looked at him and nodded once again, too stunned to speak. He pulled the musket from the dead man and wrestled his cartridge box off him. "Here, it looks like it's already got one in it ready to fire. Just aim and shoot at anything with a red coat on."

She was numb. She was lying next to a man whose face was blown off and this man was ignoring it and telling her to start killing others. She couldn't think. She was paralyzed.

The man slapped her across the face and held her face in his hands. He stared into her eyes until she seemed to respond. Then he yelled, "Listen, lady, that man is dead and we will be too if we don't start fighting back. You don't want to shoot, you can at least start loading it so I can shoot faster. But you gotta do sumpin'."

Sarah shook her head and finally came back to her senses. She looked at the man and said, "No, I can shoot it."

She checked the musket just as John had taught them months ago. It was loaded and ready to fire. She rolled over onto her stomach and looked to her front. Men in red uniforms were charging at them.

The man next to her yelled, "Fire, damn it, fire."

She put the musket to her shoulder just as John had said. She aimed at a man who was running towards them screaming something. She held the gun tight and pulled the trigger. She heard the gun explode and felt the kick hard against her shoulder.

It was as if everything was going in slow motion. She thought she could see the ball heading straight at the man. Suddenly he yanked back as though he were tethered and had just run headlong to its end. She saw the ball rip into the man's coat and the blood spurt from the hole.

The man just stopped and fell forward. As he went down his eyes met Sarah's. They looked at her quizzically. But she could discern no emotion or pain from them. At that moment she thought of her brother and was glad she was here right now.

The soldier next to her shouted, "Good shot, keep it up."

Sarah's mind was blank. But she mechanically went through the steps she had learned to reload the musket. She did not know how many times she fired or how many men she had hit.

As she kept loading and firing she suddenly felt a splash of warm liquid spray onto her face and hands. She turned to see a gaping hole in the side of the man's head. For a reason she could not fathom she ignored it and kept right on firing.

The first moment she came back to reality was when two British soldiers stood over her with bayonets pointed directly at her. She lay on her back still clutching the musket, in the middle of reloading. She stopped and looked at the two men. One of the men was about to run her through when an officer came from behind them and shouted, "Stop."

The blade was inches away from her chest when it ceased coming forward. She took a deep breath and only then did she wonder what was going to happen to her next. The officer came up and reached a hand down to her. Sarah hesitated, then reached up for his hand to let him pull her out of the ditch.

He said mockingly to her, "Your army must be in rather bad straights, madam, when they have to have their women do their fighting for them as they run away into the forest."

"Thank you for saving my life, Captain," Sarah said politely. Then she glared at him with hatred in her eyes. "You will find that our army is made up of men and women all fighting to rid ourselves from the likes of scum like you and your fiendish Hessian friends. I'm your prisoner now. But in the end your entire army will rue the day you invaded our country."

"Quite so, madam. I have rued the day I ever stepped foot in this God-forsaken stink hole of a country, as you say. And once we have taught you rebels about loyalty to His Majesty we will be only too happy to leave."

"If you are waiting for us to learn loyalty to him then you have condemned yourselves to this place for the rest of your days. For no matter how many of us you kill, there will be an ever growing number coming along behind them."

"Well, we shall see about that. Won't we? Private, escort," He looked at her and said, "I'm sorry, madam, I didn't catch your name."

"Mrs. Sarah Hardy," she said defiantly.

"Yes, quite. Escort Mrs. Hardy to the rear please private. And make sure nothing happens to her along the way," he added as if in warning.

"I hope the rest of your evening is more pleasant than most of your day seems to have been. And just for the record, Mrs Hardy, I do admire your courage."

The soldier pushed her with the butt of his musket and said, "All right lady, move out." They climbed a hill, and at the top a type of pen had been set up where she saw a small group of men from the ships gathered together under guard.

The private pushed her past the men and took her to a major who was sitting at a field table issuing instructions to other soldiers. When he was through talking to the soldiers he looked at her. He looked her up and down.

It was then that Sarah looked at herself. She had lost the shoes Elizabeth had given her. She remembered sinking into the mud in the creek and her shoes being pulled off her feet. So she was barefoot and covered from head to toe with mud and blood. She could only imagine what this smartly dressed British officer could be thinking about her.

"What have we here, Private?"

"Sir, this woman was caught in a fire fight about a mile down the hill. She had two men with her but they was dead. The Captain told me to bring her back here."

"Was she actively engaged in the shooting or were the men just trying to protect her?"

"No, Sir. She was fighting and shooting at least as good as the men. I almost run her through with my bayonet until the Captain stopped me."

"Thank you, private. That is all. You may leave."

The major looked at Sarah once again. "May I ask your name, madam?"

"Mrs. Sarah Hardy," she answered curtly.

"Well, Mrs. Hardy, from the looks of you, you've had quite an exhausting day. We're not used to taking female prisoners of war. We will see to getting you some water to clean up with, and then we'll have to figure out what we are going to do with you. For the moment you may stay here behind the tent. I don't want to place you in amongst the male prisoners. But I will need your word that you will not try to escape."

Sarah was suddenly very tired. She just wanted to sit down and drink some water. She shook her head and said, "Yes, Major, I give you my word that I will not try to escape. May I have some water to drink?"

"Good. Private, go get Mrs. Hardy a canteen of water, and bring a pail of water and some soap, if you can find any, for her to wash herself with. Now, Mrs. Hardy, if you would please go behind this tent. I'm afraid the accommodations are rather primitive, but I'm sure we can find you a chair or something to sit on."

Sarah walked slowly behind the tent. There were two men there to guard her. One of them pointed to a large log and said, "Have a seat, ma'am."

The private brought the water back and Sarah took the canteen and gulped the water down until she thought she would drown. She had not realized how thirsty she actually had been. It was just cool enough to slide down her throat and start to cool her insides. She looked at the men and then at the pail of water and bar of soap the private had given her. They looked embarrassed and one of them said, "Of course, ma'am. We'll just turn our backs and give you some privacy."

Sarah smiled at them and said, "Thank you very much, gentlemen." They looked to be about her age, though for some reason she felt a great deal older than them. She thought they looked and acted like, under other circumstances, they might be friends of her brothers. "How did they end up in this mess of a war?" she wondered.

As she started to wash herself she lifted her skirt up so that she could get the mud from her legs. The young men were both trying to peek, but would quickly turn back when they thought she would catch them. She smiled to herself. She ignored them and finished washing. She straightened herself up and lightly teased, "It's all right now gentlemen. You can turn round and guard me again."

The guards treated her with a great deal of respect. One of

them asked, "How'd you end up fightin' against us, ma'am? No disrespect, but we heard what you did out there and I know it took a lot of courage. Now we got a lot of women followin' along behind this army too, but I hain't never seen one of 'em pick up a musket and get into the battle with us."

She thought for a minute about the Captain who had captured her and his arrogance. These young men were not like that. So she answered, "I must admit I do not make a habit of joining into fire fights. I am no hero. Until today I have only fired a musket at targets. Never at a person. However, the situation was that I was trying to help sick and wounded men get away in a bateau when everything erupted around us. Things escalated, and suddenly there I was in a ditch with two men. One of them was dead, so it seemed as though I should help the other as best I could. And now I am your prisoner."

"Well, Mrs. Hardy, we will try to rectify that once things settle down a little." The major had silently come around the tent and had apparently been listening to her as she talked. The men snapped to attention. "Stand at ease, men. I have talked to the general about you and he has instructed me to send you over to your army under a flag of truce once we figure out where your army is. Seems they have disbursed to all points of the compass and we are having a devil of a time locating anything that even vaguely resembles a headquarters to which we might release you. In a day or two I am sure we will have you back with what's left of your people. Until then we will do our best to make your stay with us as comfortable as possible."

He continued, "Mrs. Hardy, I have been instructed to give you your unconditional parole. While you are with us we will not place a guard on you. You are free to go if you wish, although I would suggest that you stay with us until we can properly exchange you. You will be restricted as to where you may wander about the camp but other than that you may go as you please. Do you understand?"

Sarah nodded, "Yes, Major, I understand. I feel quite confident that our men are regrouping right now and will rescue us before you have a chance to exchange me. But I will abide by your limitations and am very grateful to you for your considerations."

"Very good then." He gave a smug smile and continued, "I guess we shall see about what your army will or will not do soon. Won't we Mrs. Hardy?" His face turned almost kind, "When was the last time you had something to eat?"

"Sometime yesterday," Sarah said, trying to think exactly when it was and what she had.

"Well, then. Private, go get Mrs. Hardy some food, and after she has eaten take her to a tent for the night."

The private came back with her dinner, hardtack and boiled pork. She realized that she was ravenous. She wolfed the food down so quickly that it almost made her sick. The privates took her to a tent where she was to sleep. They gave her two blankets and she went inside. She looked around and suddenly realized that she would be all alone this night. She tried to remember when the last time was that she had slept alone. "What a luxury," she thought, "an entire tent to myself." She put one blanket on the ground, laid down on it, and covered herself with the other. "They won't have to guard me too closely tonight," she thought as, exhausted, she quickly went to sleep.

Thirty-One

The next morning, Sarah awoke to the familiar sounds of an army camp coming alive. It took her a second or two to realize that she was not back at Fort Ti with John and the men. She was a prisoner in a British camp. She rose and started out of the tent but was met by a private who had brought her some breakfast. "Thank you. This is very good of you. Am I confined to this tent? Is that why you brought me breakfast in bed?"

"Er, oh no, ma'am. The major said you was not to be molested and had pretty much free run of the place. He just thought, 'cus it was raining so, you might like something to eat without having to get soaking wet. I hope I didn't offend you, ma'am."

"No private, you have not offended me. Thank you very much. It was most kind. Please thank the major also. By the way, what was all that shooting I heard last night?"

"Oh, some of the rebels tried to attack this position. But we of the 9th Regiment held them off. Our commander, Colonel Hill, has sent for General Philips to bring up reinforcements. There should be a couple thousand men coming in today sometime, and they'll probably bring some of those Indians along too. No offence, ma'am but, they always puts a scare into them rebels."

"Well, thank you once again private. I'm sure you have duties to attend to." She closed the flap of the tent and sat down and quickly began to eat her breakfast. She said to herself, "These Redcoats certainly eat a lot better than we do." There were eggs and bacon and real bread on her plate. She hadn't seen any of them for a long time, and she savored every morsel. When she had finished, it occurred to her that everything she just ate was fresh. She realized that it had to have come from local farmers from around the lake. She wondered if they were Tories who gave or sold it to the British or Patriots from whom the food was simply stolen. And if they were Patriots, were their farms destroyed too?

She put those thoughts out of her mind. She could not deal with those things now. Instead she concentrated on what to do next. The major said she had free run of the place and could even leave if she chose. She knew she wouldn't even have any idea of which way to go if she did leave, so she quickly put that out of her mind also. But as she thought about the information the private had given her about the reinforcements coming she wondered what other information she might be able to pick up if she went out and wandered around the camp.

She opened the flap of the tent. It was raining torrentially. She pulled a blanket over her and ran out into the rain. She bumped into the major as she ran. "Is there someplace you wish to go on such a terrible morning, Mrs. Hardy?"

"Uh. Oh, Major, well if you must know, I am in need of a privy. Might there be somewhere I might have some privacy for a few moments?"

"Well, I can't guarantee how much privacy you'll find around an army camp, but I might suggest you try in those trees over there." He pointed off behind the camp. "Did you enjoy your breakfast?"

"Thank you. Yes, I did very much. Excuse me, Major, I shall try and find that private spot you suggested."

"Of course madam. It might be a good idea if you stay in your tent as much as possible today. It looks like it is going to continue raining like this all day. I doubt that your rescuers will be out in such weather. We fairly ran them off last night."

Sarah walked into the trees. She found she really did need to use the privy but she also took the time to look over the camp for the first time. She thought that if she did make it back to the Americans, any information she might be able to gather could be of use.

She saw where the other prisoners were. They were still in the penned up area. They must have spent the night there without shelter. She could see that all of them were drenched.

As she scanned the area she noticed that a great many of the British soldiers had pulled back up onto the hill. And the perimeter was much closer than it was yesterday. Additionally, there were soldiers all around that perimeter keeping watch. She thought that little skirmish last night must have had some effect. Finally, she saw a most interesting sight. At the rear of the camp a group of women had set up their area. It was the first time she had seen any enemy women, and she tried to imagine what their life was like compared to hers. She resolved that if the rain stopped she would venture over there and talk to a few of them later in the day.

She walked back to her tent trying to observe anything that might be of interest. However, given how hard it was raining there was little else she could see that might be helpful.

About midmorning Sarah heard shots being fired out on the perimeter. She quickly ran to the flap of the tent and peered out. Men were scurrying with their muskets to get in line on the perimeter. The intensity of the fight soon increased to a point that the entire area was covered in smoke from the muskets.

Sarah ran to the pen where the male prisoners were being held. They were all lying down on the ground to protect themselves from the musket balls whizzing overhead. She dove to the ground also and landed between two men. "Well, good morning, ma'am. What brings you here? Out for a morning stroll, were you?" one of them asked.

Her face was inches from his. His face was filthy and as he smiled at her she could see his teeth were rotten and his breath smelled horribly.

"I was captured yesterday moving the sick and wounded onto the creek. I figured that since you are all Americans here it would be the best place to be if our army is able to rescue us."

"Well, welcome to our humble accommodations ma'am. You just pull up some ground here and make yourself comfortable while our boys show these Lobsterbacks what real forest fightin' is all about. Not much for us to do here but watch the excitement unfold."

The rain continued to fall and the fighting became even more intense. Sarah could see the British soldiers pulling back ever tighter inside the perimeter. Soon she could see the American soldiers closing in on them. They reached the pen where Sarah and the other prisoners were. The men guarding the pen withdrew with the other Redcoats. An American officer came up to her and inquired, "You one of ours, ma'am?"

"Yes, I was captured yesterday at the creek."

He turned to the two men she had fallen between and said, "Alright, you two men take this woman to the rear. The rest of you find a musket and join this party."

Sarah and the two men moved as quickly as they could through several hundred yards of forest when they ran into Colonel Long and his staff. The fight was still being bitterly contested and he was shouting directing men to close in and surround what was left of the British force.

He stopped for an instant and looked at Sarah. "Mrs. Hardy, isn't it madam?"

Sarah nodded as she ducked to the sound of a musket ball going over head.

"Yes, I heard that you had not made it out of the creek. We were afraid that you had been killed. I'm very glad to see you well. Keep moving to the rear, there is a doctor back there somewhere if you need him."

He turned and shouted some new orders at someone.

They found the doctor a few hundred yards from where they were. He asked if she needed any attention. She told him no, but that she had some experience nursing and if she could be of any help she would lend a hand.

"Wonderful, madam. I never turn down a helping hand when I can get one. Not too busy yet, but from the sounds of things we will be soon. How do you happen to be here right now?"

"I was one of the women helping to move the invalids yesterday when I was captured at the creek along with a group of men."

Soon wounded men were being brought back to be treated. One of the wounded was Colonel Van Rensselaer, the commander of the same New York militia unit that John had belonged to before he joined the Continental Line. He had been shot in the hip. Sarah helped as the doctor tended to his wound. For some reason she felt proud that a New York unit was there. Often during the long winter she felt bad about how few New Yorkers were with them at Ticonderoga.

The fight had been going on for a couple of hours when, just as suddenly as it had begun, the noise of the battle seemed to stop. The Americans were returning back through the woods and did not seem to have anyone chasing them. Orders were given for everyone to head back to Fort Anne. Sarah joined with Colonel Long's staff and marched back to the fort. Along the way she had the opportunity to speak with the Colonel. "I don't know if this is anything important Colonel, but I was talking to a private this morning and he told me that the unit you were just fighting is the 9th Regiment and it is commanded by a Colonel Hill. The private also said the Colonel had sent word to General Philips about their situation and asked for support. He said the general was expected to arrive today with a couple thousand reinforcements and some Indians."

Colonel Long looked at her with some surprise and said, "Thank you, Mrs. Hardy, I wish I could get my soldiers to give a report as well as you just did. That is very important information and it concurs with other reports I have had. If you ever want a job as a spy come see me."

Sarah tentatively asked, "Colonel, how is this retreat going? Have you heard anything from the men who were marching overland?" For the first time in two days she worried about John and how he was.

"Well, Mrs. Hardy, things are not going exactly as we planned them. But that is to be expected. We've pretty much got things under control now. Your husband with those marching with General St. Clair?"

"Yes, Sir, he is."

"You know, Mrs. Hardy, that is a mighty arduous trip they're making and it will take a few days to get through the wilderness out there. We haven't heard anything from them yet, but that too is to be expected. In a couple of days we should hear from them. I shouldn't worry about them too much, Mrs. Hardy. I am sure they're doing fine."

It made her feel better to hear him say it, even though she was becoming soldier enough to know that if the Redcoats were able to catch up with the ships so easily they probably were right on the heels of the other force also.

Sarah made the rest of the march to Fort Anne in silence. The other women and their charges had already been evacuated to Fort Edward. They were not at Fort Anne very long before the officers in charge made the decision to abandon the fort and also make for Fort Edward.

There was no road to speak of, simply a narrow paths through the dense forest. The insects were ravenous as they swarmed around the defenseless trekkers and feasted on their bodies.

Sarah's bare feet throbbed with every step, and they soon began to bleed. At a stop she tore strips of cloth from her clothes and wrapped them around her feet. She wished she had some canvas tent pieces or other strong material to fortify her new "shoes," but she would have to make do with what she had.

Thirty-Two

They reached Fort Edward the next day. Sarah stumbled along at the rear of the column. She was the only woman with them. Everyone at the fort turned out to stare as they dragged through the gate. Off to the left Sarah saw a group of women all huddled together. She tried to focus on them to see if she recognized anyone. Martha came running toward her. She hugged Sarah and said, "Oh, thank God, Sarah! You're alright! We've been so worried about you."

Sarah was exhausted. She almost collapsed in Martha's arms. Words would not come to her. She looked into Martha's face and then around at the other women.

Then she heard Elizabeth's voice. "Come on, dearie, let's get you someplace to rest. You look like you've had a bad couple of days."

They led her to an area where the women's tents had been

set up. "Here, you're gonna bunk in here with Martha and me." As Sarah sat down in the tent, Elizabeth gently said, "We never doubted you were going to come back to us, so we saved you a spot. We got a space all set up for you." Then Elizabeth seemed to realize that Ginny wasn't with Sarah. She solemnly asked, "Where's Ginny, Sarah? What happened to her?"

Sarah stared at them and then burst into tears. It was the first time she had thought of Ginny since the soldier dragged her away. "She's dead," Sarah cried. "We were to loading some men into a bateau and a mortar round exploded. I tried to save her, but she and the men were dead."

Elizabeth wrapped her arms around Sarah, "Now, now, dearie. Don't talk about it anymore. Lie down and rest. We will get you cleaned up and get you some clean clothes. You'll feel better after you have rested."

She looked out the flap of the tent to where several women had gathered. She saw them but she felt so alone. She thought of her parents and her brothers and sister. She had not heard from them in months. Were they safe? She wanted to hug her mother right now.

Elizabeth was the closest thing she had to a mother right then, and she clutched her tighter and cried like she had never cried before in her life. Her whole body shook with emotion she could no longer hold in.

Elizabeth held her tight and cooed, "That's it, dearie. Let it all out. We're here with you now. Everything will be all right. Just let it out."

When Sarah awoke, she was alone in the tent. She didn't remember it, but the women must have bathed her, and she had on a clean dress. She struggled to get up and slowly stepped outside the tent.

Sarah sheepishly walked over to the fire where several women, including Martha and Elizabeth, were sitting, talking. All of the women looked up at her. No one spoke, seeming to wait for someone else to break the silence.

Finally, Elizabeth stood and asked, "Sarah dear, how are you feeling? You look much better. Here, pull up a stump and sit by the fire. If it's not obvious, we were just talking about you."

"I feel much better. Thank you all for everything you did for me this afternoon."

"This afternoon? Dearie you slept all through the night and all of today. We was beginning to worry about you. Are you hungry? We still have some food left from our supper. The food—what there is of it—ain't any better here than at Fort Ti. But it's something."

"No, I'm not hungry, thank you. Oh, my goodness. I must have been much tireder than I thought to have slept so long."

Sarah looked around at the women and asked hesitantly, "Has anyone heard from the men?"

Martha replied quietly, "Word is that they were in a pretty big battle up at Hubbardton. They say there were quite a few casualties and some men were taken captive. But we don't have any word on who they were yet. It appears though that most of the command got away and are headed for Manchester somewhere east of here. When they get there we should hear more."

Elizabeth added, "Our real problem, and theirs, is how far behind the Redcoats are. Seems like we been fairly whipped the last few days, and if Burgoyne's got any sense he'll be pushing us as hard as he can."

Sarah retorted, "Whipped? I don't think we got whipped at Fort Anne. We were surprised, yes. But, once they got organized, I think Colonel Long and Colonel Van Rensselear were pushing the British back pretty good there, and would have completely defeated them if we had not run out of powder."

"Oh, it's we now, is it?" Elizabeth joked. "We heard about your exploits from one of the men that was near you. Guess you think you're a regular soldier now, eh? Still willing to be part of our women's army, Private Hardy?"

Sarah blushed and was grateful it was dark so the others couldn't tell. "I honestly don't know what came over me. This soldier pushed a musket into my hand and shouted at me to start shooting. I looked out and there was a Redcoat coming at us, so I pulled the trigger. I don't know what happened after that until I was captured. All I was thinking about was that these bastards killed my brother and Ginny and the others. I wanted to kill every one of them. When I was finally taken prisoner, the men on both sides of me were dead and I was covered in mud and blood. I can't imagine how I must have looked to the men who took me prisoner, or to you for that matter. You must have thought I looked like a demon from hell."

The women looked at her in awe. One of them barked, "You actually killed some of them? You fought alongside the men? Oh, how I envy you. What I wouldn't give to kill a few of them myself."

"I don't know if I killed anyone. I know I hit at least one and maybe more. But I don't know if I killed them. As for fighting alongside the men, I suppose I did. But let me assure you it was not because I planned it, nor would I recommend it. The experience has given me a whole new appreciation for what our men are doing."

Another asked, "So what were the Redcoats like? How did they treat you?"

"Actually they were quite considerate. They treated me with more respect than I thought they would. They gave me my own tent to sleep in and they fed me pretty well. I talked to several of them and, you know, on a personal level they were even quite nice. A couple of privates reminded me of my brothers and their friends. I noticed a group of camp followers with them, just like us. If I hadn't been rescued I was intending to go over and talk with them. I wonder what it's like for them."

Sarah stared into the fire and said, "We're all almost in walking distance of getting home if we had to. But they are thousands of miles and an ocean away from home. We're fighting for our homes. But what are they fighting for? Do they hate us? I never thought about them until I saw them in the camp. I don't think I hate them. What must be going through their minds tonight as they sit in front of their fires?"

A man came walking up to the fire and the women looked at him questioningly. Sarah finally recognized him and stood up. "Colonel Long, good evening, Sir."

"Good evening, Mrs. Hardy. And to you ladies," he bowed. "I heard you were feeling poorly Mrs. Hardy, and I just stopped over to see how you were doing."

"Oh, thank you for your concern, Sir. I'm fine now. The ladies have taken good care of me."

"That is very good to hear. You ladies make sure you keep

Mrs. Hardy, and yourselves, well. This army does not know what it has in you. And we can't afford to lose a one of you."

He continued, "By the way, Mrs. Hardy, I passed your bit of intelligence on to General Schuyler when he got here today and it seems it confirms what he has received from other sources. It appears that Colonel Hill has indeed been reinforced by General Philips, and your estimate of the numbers was almost spot on. The general asked me to thank you for the service you have provided. Well done, madam."

He looked at the women and said, "I suggest you ladies get plenty of rest. We will be moving out sooner or later. This retreat is far from finished, I'm afraid. Good evening ladies."

As he walked away all the women turned and looked at Sarah. "Well, soldier, is there anything else you were doing while you were out there just being one of the boys?" Elizabeth quipped.

Sarah blushed again. "I just told him what I saw and heard while I was in the British camp. That's all. I didn't think it mattered much at the time."

"Don't apologize, dearie. We are all very proud of you and your exploits. As a matter of fact, most of us probably wish it was us who got left behind and had your experiences. Think of the stories you'll have for your grandchildren when they get bored with Grandpa John's stories."

Most of the women nodded in agreement. Then Elizabeth said, "Well, like the Colonel said, I need my beauty rest. I think I will go to bed." Everyone but Martha said goodnight.

Martha looked into Sarah's eyes and asked, "Are you really alright, Sarah? I can't imagine what you have just been through. I am not one of those who wishes she could have been in—uh—

your shoes." They both looked at her shoeless feet and smiled. "Maybe I'm just a coward at heart, but I have no desire to carry a musket and fight like a man. I don't know how you did it."

"To tell you the truth Martha, I don't know either. I had no control over myself. Something in me snapped as I held Ginny in my arms, and whatever it was just took over my mind and body. I don't have much desire to ever feel like that again. But how are you feeling?"

"I'm as good as can be expected. I've got Doctor Elizabeth doting over me, so I'm feeling a great deal better. It still hurts some when I think about it. But I try not to, and it's been pretty easy to keep busy these past few days. I worry more about Jeremiah than I do anything else right now. It's maddening not to know what is going on out there. I feel like I would like to steal a horse and ride over to Manchester myself, just to find out how he is."

Sarah nodded in agreement. "I know what you mean. Not knowing is the most disturbing part of this whole debacle. We weren't given any choice in the matter. We were just ordered to go with the hospital on the boats. But I tell you, when I saw those women with the British Army I said to myself 'that is where I belong, with John and the men marching overland.' Why not? If those women can do it so can we. Our men are in need of nurses just as much as the British are. Next time Martha, if I can, I'm marching with the troops."

Martha teased, "Sarah, you get more like Elizabeth every day. It wouldn't surprise me to one day find you out in the front of this army giving orders. Well, I think I'll retire too. Coming?"

"No, not right now. I had a pretty good rest already. I just want to sit here by the fire and enjoy the quiet for a while. I'll be in after a while."

Sarah sat watching the fire. She threw another log on and watched the sparks fly up into the sky and mingle with the stars. She pulled the blanket she had over her shoulder tighter around her. She wanted to share what she was feeling with someone. But who could understand her thoughts? She wished John were there. Surely he would understand. He would be able to make sense of all that was going through her mind this night.

She sobbed silently. She now understood why the men drank so much when they came back in from a battle. She wished she had some rum right then to help kill the pain and fill the emptiness she felt. She lay down and drifted off to sleep in front of the fire. She woke just before dawn. Heavy dew had saturated the blanket and her clothes and had given her a chill. She rose, stoked the coals of the fire, and added some wood to help her warm up and dry out before the other women got up.

Thirty-Three

Soon after she awoke, Sarah was startled by the reality of war. The horror of Burgoyne's Indians had descended upon them. Frightening screams filled the forest all around them. These sounds were soon added to by those of musket fire from the pickets, engaging the Indians. Then Sarah heard new, different screams as soldiers were mutilated in attack after attack by the fiends.

The women came running out of the tents. Everyone wondering what was going on. A soldier ran up to them and shouted, "Ladies, the general says for you to go get to the center of the fort and report to the doctors so's you can help set up a field hospital. We're under attack from the redskins."

Sarah and the other women did as they were told. The doctors, their enlisted aides, and the women set up a makeshift field hospital. Men began to stumble or be carried back in from the skirmishes that raged around them. Some of the wounds were from musket balls, but most were from tomahawks, diabolical war clubs and knives wielded as the Indians charged into the soldiers. A couple of the men had been scalped alive.

Sarah's thoughts quickly went from fear and horror to the work at hand. Many of the women, and indeed some of the men, cowered behind trees or rocks for protection. But she and Elizabeth waded into the work of nursing the wounded. The activity seemed to calm her and give her strength. She could hear the battles going on around her but they sounded as though they were off in the distance. The gore of the wounds no longer upset her. They were now just a part of her work. There was no time for feelings as some of the men died. There was only time for saving the living.

Men also started to come in from the work details that had been sent out to place obstacles in the Redcoat's way. They too had been attacked by the savages.

Through all this however, there were no British soldiers, only the Indians.

The morning sun was bright and the day promised to be terribly hot. Sweat soon saturated Sarah's clothes and ran off her as if it had been raining, and it made the dirt stick to her as mud.

In the afternoon a torrential rain began and the attacks ceased. Late in the day there finally came a chance to eat. Rations were very meager. But Sarah realized she was starving and ate the meal ravenously. It was the only meal they were to get that day.

When darkness fell it was not easy to sleep as throughout the night she could hear the terrible noises of the Indians screeching in the forests all around them.

Finally, only the sounds of the swarming insects could be heard and Sarah drifted off.

The morning sun arose once again, bright and hot. Sarah saw a passing officer and asked, "What's going on? Where are the Indians?"

He answered, "Good morning, ma'am. Well, as best as we can make out they must have got tired of attacking a fortified position and went off to attack the settlers instead. They don't much like getting into fights like they had yesterday. Feel sorry for any farmers out there, but I'm glad they're not attacking here again today."

Elizabeth came up at that moment and asked, "Have we heard anything from the men who went overland?"

"Well, ma'am, the last we heard, General St. Clair is supposed to be on his way here from Castle Town with the Continentals. Don't know where they are exactly."

"Do you have any idea about casualties?" Sarah asked.

"No, ma'am, haven't heard anything yet. I must be on my way. Good morning, ladies."

Later that day, General St. Clair and the Continentals arrived at Fort Edward. Sarah, Martha, and Elizabeth huddled together at the hospital watching for signs of the men. Just as at Crown Point, it seemed like they were last to arrive. Martha saw Jeremiah first followed by John. Edward and Robert were with the artillery, so they were even further to the rear of the column.

John looked tired and drawn as Sarah approached him, but he smiled when he saw her and they held each other very tight. Sarah whispered, "Oh, John, I am so glad to see you. I have been so worried about you."

John's mood immediately changed. He became dark and somber as he pushed her away and said in disgust, "You needn't have worried about us. All we have been doing is running since we left Fort Ti. Colonel Warner and the Vermont boys had a rear guard fight with the Hessians at Hubbardton but we didn't get any of that. We were running to Castle Town. And from Castle Town we came here. I don't know what St. Clair is thinking, but we ain't fired a single shot at the British in over a week. I don't know when he plans on fighting, but at this rate we will be fighting them in Albany before we stop running."

Sarah heard Ben's booming voice behind her, "John, we ain't been doing nothing since Valcour Island 'cept digging ditches and building defenses at that God-forsaken fort. And the first time the Redcoats show their faces we hightail it and run. We would've been better off just leaving last year like the rest of those boys. We'd of saved ourselves a lot of misery, that's for sure. If they weren't goin' to fight, why did they have us do all that work?"

"I don't know, Ben," John sighed. "Maybe somebody's got a plan. But it sure don't seem to be Schuyler or St. Clair. Let's go see where they're putting the unit and get them settled in."

Sarah walked at John's side. She wanted to talk to him and tell him about what had happened to her. But she decided to wait until a better time. John quickly became engaged in working with the men to set up their camp. Sarah quietly walked away, back to the hospital.

Things were different at Fort Edward than they were at Fort Ti. The women were all camped together in one spot while the men were with their units. So it was the next day before Sarah had a chance to speak with John. There seemed to be stiffness between them, as though they were strangers.

John was angry, distant and cold. Sarah did not know how to begin telling him of her experiences of the past few days. There was so much to talk about, yet they were silent.

John finally broke the silence. "I heard what you did at Skenesborough, Sarah. I don't know whether to be proud of you for your bravery or angry with you for your foolishness."

"Oh, John, I hope you will be proud of me. But don't think I did anything out of bravery or because I wanted to. I would much rather have gotten away with the rest. But there were men who needed help, and Ginny and I were all that were left to aid them. We were almost ready to escape when a mortar round killed Ginny and some of the men. Cannons were going off and muskets were firing all about us. A soldier grabbed me by the arm and we ran."

Now she was crying.

"We both fell into a ditch. There was already a man there. He was dead. I was so scared I did not know what was happening. The soldier gave me the other man's musket and told me to start shooting. I remembered what you had taught me and just began shooting and loading and shooting. I think I killed at least one man. Oh, John, it was awful. Then the soldier next to me was killed and I was captured. They led me away to the British camp. I didn't know what was happening around me. I was in a daze."

She stopped crying, wiped her eyes with her sleeve, and continued, "A British officer was kind to me and treated me respectfully. He said that they would send me back when they had a chance. But next morning when I heard the fighting begin I ran to where the male prisoners were. I was overjoyed to see our men routing the British."

John look at her and his coldness disappeared. He took her in his arms and hugged her close. "Sarah, I am proud of you. I'm proud of you for all you have done, for all your sacrifices."

Then he lightly said, "But I hope you don't think you need to pick up a musket and join the ranks now. I want you to promise me that you will be more careful in the future to not let yourself get into another scrape like that again. We need you—I need you—to stay alive and keep helping us win with your skills as a nurse."

Sarah kissed him gently. "I promise that I will not try to become a soldier. One experience like that is enough for me."

Then John became dark and moody again. He said, "Well, at least someone in this family has had an opportunity to fight. I can't see when I will get that chance. All we keep doing is running. I fear that we are losing, Sarah. I feel like we are going to keep running until there is nowhere else to run. Then these generals will just give up and surrender us all. And all of this will have been for nothing. We have to stop and fight soon or Burgoyne will be in Albany before we know it."

The next few days were spent at Fort Edward. Very little happened. Sarah threw herself into working with the wounded. She and John would meet at the end of the day and talk for a few minutes. But the rest of the time she worked. Food was scarce, but she did not feel very hungry and ate very little.

No one understood why the British had not caught up to

them and attacked. Sappers were sent out daily to destroy everything between Skenesborough and Fort Edward and to chop down trees across Wood Creek and to put as many obstructions as possible across any path that General Burgoyne might use to move his troops through the dense forest.

At last the army began to move again. The march was torturous. The days were mixed with intense heat followed by torrential downpours. The paths were a quagmire of mud and movement was very slow. At the end of that first day they arrived at Fort Miller.

Fort Miller, like Fort Anne, hardly deserved the name "fort." It had been built for the French and Indian War and was left to deteriorate after. But it provided them with a resting place for the night. The rain stopped by the time they had reached the fort. Still, everyone was soaking wet, and there would be no tents set up to sleep under. The woods around them were still filled with Indians who had been following them, so no one ventured out to get wood to start fires. Although the night was hot and humid, Sarah shivered with cold.

No one had eaten since a quick breakfast before setting out in the morning. Dinner was to be a piece of hardtack and some salted pork.

The women had, as usual, marched at the rear of the formation, so Sarah had not seen John all day. Once they had set up camp for the night John found Sarah sitting together with the other women. Elizabeth and Martha had wrapped her up in a blanket, but she was still shivering. John looked at her and then asked Elizabeth, "What's the matter? Is she alright?"

Elizabeth answered, "Well, John, she's come down with a

case of camp fever. She is alternating between shivering and burning up with fever. All we can do is keep her warm and hope we can get her to where ever it is we are going so we can get her some shelter."

He sat down next to Sarah and put his arm around her. She looked at him but her eyes were blank. She looked terrible. Her skin was ashen, and around her eyes were great dark circles of fatigue. As he held her, he could feel her tremble under the blanket.

"Sarah. Dear, is there anything I can do for you?"

She closed her eyes and just shook her head.

"John," Elizabeth said, "she's tough. She's gonna be fine. We'll make up a bed up for her and take care of her tonight. Tomorrow we'll get her on a wagon."

"Thank you Elizabeth. You may have to fight to get her on a wagon. You know the edict they put out about no women allowed in the wagons. But if you have any problems come and get me. I may not have used my musket much lately, but I will gladly shoot the first son of a bitch who gets in your way getting her a ride."

"Don't worry, John we'll get her on one of the wagons. And we'll take care of her along the way. She's gonna be fine."

The next morning Sarah was still feverish and very weak. Elizabeth and Martha half carried her to where the wagons were being loaded with the sick and infirmed. Elizabeth found Small in charge of loading one of the wagons. She went up to him and said, "Small, Mrs. Hardy is very sick and needs to ride in one of the wagons today. Now where do you want us to put her?"

Small looked around as if he was about to tell her a secret.

He said, "Ma'am, you know we ain't supposed to have no women in the wagons. I could get in trouble if I let Mrs. Hardy on."

Elizabeth eyes burned directly into his eyes. He tried to avert them but all he could do is lower his head. Elizabeth said in a strong voice, "Small, you know this woman. She has been working day and night helping keep these men alive for more than a year. She has worked side by side with you. Why, she has done more for this army than most of the derelicts you got on these wagons have even thought about doing. She even has fought more than most of them. Now she is very sick, and orders or no orders, she is going to ride on one of these wagons. Now you can help me find her a spot or I will personally go up there and throw one of those men off. Now what's it gonna be, Small?"

Once again he furtively turned his head left and right to see if anyone was looking. "Alright, Mrs. Edwards, we'll put her in this here wagon. But don't go telling folks about it. I could get inta trouble for this."

"Thank you, Small. I commend you for your bravery," Elizabeth said mockingly. "You just walk along next to some other wagon. We'll walk next to this one," she pointed to Martha and herself. "If there is any trouble I will take care of it."

Small nodded and said, "Yes ma'am. Thank you ma'am."

Just then John walked up. "Good morning, Elizabeth, Martha. How is Sarah? Is there any problem here?" he asked while looking sternly at Small.

"No, no problem John. Small here was just about to help us get Sarah into this wagon. But now that you're here you can help. Tell you the truth John, she's about the same as last night. Still freezin' then sweatin'. But she doesn't seem to be getting worse. I think she will pull through fine. Although I am not looking forward to this march today. It is already hot, and if it's like yesterday it won't be good for any of us, let alone Sarah." She looked over to Small and said, "Alright Small, thank you for your help. We'll take care of Mrs. Hardy. You can go."

Small scurried off, looking as though he was glad to get away from Elizabeth.

John went to Sarah and gave her a hug. "How you feeling, dear? Do you feel any better?"

Sarah nodded and said weakly, "Yes, I think so."

"Well, Elizabeth has gotten you a ride in this wagon. Here, let me help you up." He lifted her into his arms and carried her to the wagon. Then, trying to put a little levity into the moment, he asked jokingly, "You ain't playing a trick just so's you don't have to walk, are ya?"

Sarah tried to smile and shook her head.

He kissed her on the forehead. She was still burning up. "You rest as best as you can," he said as he and two men in the wagon lifted her in and laid her on the floor. John turned to Elizabeth and said, "We're just a little ways up ahead. If you need me send someone up and I'll get right back here." He looked worried as he added, "Take care of her, Elizabeth. I need her."

"Don't worry, John. We'll take care of her. We all need her."

The army once again started moving and the sun burned down on them, making the heat unbearable until mid-afternoon when the rain came once again in a downpour so thick one could hardly see a few feet in front.

They were now going south along the eastern side of the Hudson. Between the heat and rain the march was agonizingly slow, and the insects had no mercy either. They, as usual, defended their domain with a vengeance from these human intruders.

The army marched on. No notice or assistance was given to a sick woman who was just a camp follower. Each night they camped out in the open. As always, the women took care of their own. Elizabeth and Martha took turns watching over her. Sarah seemed to be barely hanging on to life. The women did all they could to shelter and comfort her, but she wavered in and out of consciousness for several days.

John looked in on her each morning and evening. As the days passed his concern became more and more grave. After several days he asked, "Elizabeth, is she going to make it? She doesn't seem to be getting any better. She looks so weak. What will we do if we lose her?"

"We're not going to lose her, John. She will pull through this. God won't let her die." Then her voice rose as she looked at Sarah and emphatically said, "I won't let her die."

That night Sarah's fever broke, and she was able to keep some liquid down. They were able to build fires, and Sarah slept calmly throughout the night for the first time in days.

In the morning John stopped by to look in on her. She still looked tired and weak but she was clearly getting better. She was able to talk and said she was a little better.

John kissed her and said, "Well, you ride in the wagon again today. The weather is going to be about the same as it has been and there's no need of you being out in it. I'll try to stop by if we take a break in the march. Otherwise, I'll see you tonight. You take care of yourself."

"I will, dear. You too."

He turned to walk away when Elizabeth asked, "John, do you know where we're going? Is there any word on where the British are?"

"Elizabeth, I don't have any idea where we are going. I don't believe anyone else does either. That includes the generals leading us, as far as I can see. As for the British, word has it that they are still at Skenesborough waiting on supplies. Hopefully, when they do start after us, all the work that has been done to put obstacles in their way will keep them occupied long enough to let us get somewhere where we can put up a fight. To tell you the truth, Elizabeth, I'm not sure the generals on either side want to fight. Ours keep us running away and theirs are just sittin' in Skenesborough. I don't know what they're waiting for, but I guess I'm glad they are. See you all tonight." He shook his head and walked off.

That morning they crossed the river. The army marched on and stopped for the night. Next morning Sarah awoke feeling better than she had in a week. She was able to eat some solid food and she tried to walk as they marched towards Stillwater. But, although she felt better, she was still too weak. She climbed back into the wagon and rode the rest of the way.

That evening they reached a spot just south of Stillwater where the Mohawk River flowed into the Hudson. As the women gathered around a fire Sarah thought about the day they had all started out so many months before. So much had happened in those months. What lay ahead?

Thirty-Four

It was August seventeenth. It was hard for Sarah to believe that it had been a month and a half since they had fled Fort Ti. She had missed over a week while she was sick and had so much to catch up on. John came by. He greeted the women and sat down next to Sarah at the fire. The other women drifted off as if they had something else to do.

John said, "Good evening, Sarah. How ya feeling? You scared us to death."

"I'm feeling much better, dear. I'm sorry I've been so much trouble."

John stopped her, "You have not been too much trouble. We have all been very worried about you. It is so good to see you feeling better."

Sarah wanted to know what had been happening with the army since she had taken sick.

"Funny you should ask, my dear. First of all, we have finally stopped retreating. That alone has greatly raised the spirits of many a man in this army." John's demeanor cheered up as he continued.

"Secondly, we heard today that we have a victory to be happy for. General Stark and the New Hampshire men defeated a Hessian force over in Bennington yesterday. That is certainly something to be proud of. I only wish we could have been there to help in the victory. Regardless, it's a goodly force taken away from Burgoyne, who by the way, the scouts say is having the devil's own time getting through all the obstacles we laid in front of him and is having a tough time getting supplies."

He went on, "Another bit of news is that General Schuyler and General St. Clair have both been relieved and General Gates will be taking over this army again as soon as he gets here from Philadelphia. General Schuyler is still in Albany but General St. Clair has already left for Philadelphia to defend himself in Congress."

Sarah asked, "What's he defending himself against? Did he do something wrong?"

"Well, from what we hear, the New England folks and some in Congress are furious with him and Schuyler for not putting up a fight at Fort Ti. They both sure got some explaining to do."

"What do you and the rest of the men think, John? Should we have stayed and fought there?"

"Sarah, this retreating has been hard on everyone. For weeks now we were sure that Schuyler and St. Clair were wrong and that we should have stayed and fought. Some even thought they were cowards, or worse, traitors. But after being here a couple of days and having a chance to think on it some, I think a lot of us are beginning to believe that they might have known what they were doing. We certainly would have lost if the whole army had stayed there. We were nearly surrounded when we left. Another day or two and the Redcoats and Hessians might have put us all in a bag and cinched it up. So I guess they saved the army to fight another day. Since we've been here, the spirit of the men seems to be getting better. The hope is that when Gates gets here he has a plan to go after Burgoyne and his army. Right now we are digging in, so it looks like we might make a stand here."

He reached into his pocket and said, "Oh, I almost forgot. A letter from your mother arrived. How any mail ever finds anyone up here I will never know. We haven't stood still long enough for mail to catch up to us. I think you may be the only one to get any mail in weeks."

"A letter? Oh, John, let me have it, please. I haven't heard from Mother in months." He handed her the letter and she hurriedly tore it open.

The letter read:

Aug 10, 1777

My Dearest Sarah,

Once again I write to you with some bad news. Your uncle has been killed and your father was wounded a few days ago at a battle near Oriskany. Father is back home with us, and we believe he will recover but is very poorly right now. Of course, we are all very saddened by your uncle's death, and your aunt is most distraught. It is good, I suppose, that we are here with her during this sad time.

After Robert's death, Father was released from the army and came home. Things became very difficult with the Tories right after that and we decided to go live with your aunt over in German Flats. The whole family is here now. Right after we got here your father joined the local militia, led by a German by the name of Herkimer.

Soon after that the trouble with the local Tories and the Indians started to get very bad. We have been very lucky so far as your aunt's place has not been hit yet. But we stay on guard at all times, as we never know what to expect from day to day.

A couple of weeks ago we heard that a force led by a Redcoat named St. Leger was headed this way from Lake Ontario. The force was made up of British soldiers, Johnson's Tories, and Indians led by Joseph Brandt. The stories we heard were blood curdling. Well, they reached Fort Stanwix, I guess they call it Fort Schuyler now, where there are a bunch of Continental soldiers. We heard down here that St. Leger was putting on a siege of the fort and allowing the Indians to run wild throughout the area, killing innocent civilians as well as anyone who might be a soldier.

General Herkimer called out the militia and your father and uncle left with them. They were marching towards the fort when they were ambushed by a group of Indians. Your father says it was a very bloody battle mostly fought hand to hand. He was wounded when he was hit across the shoulder with a tomahawk. We thank God that he is back with us now and safe. After the battle the Indians returned to outside the fort, and as of right now the siege is still going on. We are all hopeful that a relief force they say is coming up the Mohawk will be able to drive them all off.

Dear Sarah, I am sorry to only have bad news when I write, but I'm afraid there is not much of any other kind during these trying times.

I have not heard from you in a long time. If you can, please write soon and let us know what is happening with you and John. We heard that Fort Ticonderoga was taken by the British and that the Northern Army was in retreat. We are very worried for your safety and pray that you are alright. Give our love to John. We love you and think of you always.

Love,

Mother

Sarah looked up from the letter and sighed. She handed it to John and said, "Here, you read it too. Then let's talk some more."

For some reason she felt guilty about not being very upset over what she had just read. She loved her father and wanted to be more concerned about his having been wounded. But he was going to be alright. Her real concerns were with this army and what was going to happen to it.

As she mulled over these feelings, Elizabeth and Martha came over and asked to join them.

"Oh, please do," Sarah said. "John was just telling me about what has been going on in the world since I was sleeping away this march. He's reading a letter from my mother. Bad news, I'm afraid. She says my uncle was killed and Father was wounded in a battle up there."

"I am sorry to hear it, Sarah. Will your father be alright?" Martha asked.

"Mother says she thinks he will be. You know it's strange, the family all moved to German Flats to get away from the violence the Tories were carrying out down in Newburgh, and they walk into this now. They are just up the Mohawk here a little ways. We are so very close, but it might as well be a million miles."

"Well, that explains a few things. I'm sorry about your uncle, Sarah, but I'm glad your father will be alright," John said as finished reading.

"This St. Leger must be part of Burgoyne's strategy. If he is successful in coming down the Mohawk to right here where we are and can join up with Burgoyne that will be devastating. I heard that General Arnold is leading the force your mother talks about heading up to relieve Fort Schuyler from this siege. Let's hope he is successful. We've got to do something about these damned Tories and Indians. They are out of control, raiding and plundering everything and everybody. The Indians don't care which side the settlers are on. If anyone is in their path they will be killed, scalped, and God only knows what else."

Elizabeth then said, "I heard a rumor that they even murdered and scalped a young girl who was the fiancé of an American in the British Army. Have you heard about that, John?"

"Yeah, her name was Jane McCrea. She was living with an aunt and they were taken prisoner by Burgoyne's Indians. Both the girl and her aunt were killed and scalped. When they got back to Burgoyne's lines they wanted their bounties for the scalps. The girl's fiancé recognized her hair and was devastated.

Burgoyne apparently tried to do something to punish the culprits but the tribes would have none of it. Nobody is going to control those brutes. Nothing happened. That can't have made the Tories he's supposed to be protecting feel very safe. If he can't even protect the women who belong to his own army, how is he going to protect others living there?"

Sarah said, "That sure doesn't make me feel any better for my family. Everything west of here is mostly wilderness. Who will protect them against the likes of Brandt, who is one of the worst?"

"Well," John replied, "let's hope that Arnold and his force are successful in driving St. Leger and his savages back to Canada. That will be a start."

Thirty-Five

Two days later General Gates arrived. Even before his arrival, General Washington sent Continental units from his army north to join those already there. And the states were sending militia units as well. The camp was swelling with new soldiers daily.

There seemed to be an excitement and enthusiasm about the camp that hadn't been felt in months. Everyone was sure that now they were going to get their chance to fight the battle that had been taken from them at Ticonderoga.

Within a few days the order to march was given again. This time, however, it was to march north, not south. There was no grumbling. They were going after Burgoyne and his army.

When they reached Stillwater the men began re-digging and reinforcing battlements that had been started when the army was there previously. But a couple of days later they were marching north again to a place called Bemis Heights.

Work began in earnest here. Soon the men had built a veritable fortress with revetments, breastworks, and artillery batteries fully emplaced. The women too joined in. Once again they were put to work making gabions and fascines or carrying food and water to the men as they worked and contributing in any other way they could.

General Gates' Headquarters was at the top of the hill. The units were set up all around it. The women and the hospital were set up back behind the military units. Sarah and Martha went to work in the hospital, and Elizabeth went off to help Edward and Robert with the artillery.

By August twenty-fifth the camps were well set up. That evening Sarah went over to John's tent. She hadn't seen him since they arrived. When she got there the men were eating and seemed to be in a very good mood. As she approached they stood and Ben shouted, "Sarah, where have you been? John has been forcing us to eat his cooking, and I assure you it needs your touch." The others, including John, laughed and agreed with Ben.

John went to her and kissed on the cheek and said, "Hello dear, I'm sorry I haven't been down to see you sooner but this is the first we've had any time off since we got here. How are you feeling, Sarah? You look tired. They haven't been workin' you too much at that hospital, have they? You don't need to be getting sick again."

Sarah took a seat by the fire. She looked at the men with a smile. It was good to be back with the men, she thought. She missed them, and she missed the conversations. "Oh, I'm fine,

John. Just a little rough around the edges maybe. Good evening, gentlemen. You all look like you are enjoying yourselves. What were you talking about when I came up? I don't want to interrupt. I want to hear everything you know about what's going on."

John began, "For starters, Sarah, we got word today that General Arnold, and some men General Washington sent up, have driven St. Leger out of the Mohawk Valley; they have the British and their Troy and Indian friends headed back to Canada. It looks like St. Leger and his force was supposed to be a part of Burgoyne's strategy to box us in. I suppose a third leg of that plan is to have Howe come up from New York and they all meet in Albany. Well, nobody knows what Howe is doing, but at least one leg of that plan is eliminated. And Burgoyne isn't moving too fast through those woods on the other side of the river. Maybe Schuyler and St. Clair weren't as dumb and cowardly as we were quick to make them out about leaving Fort Ti.

"I know you're worried about your family over there in German Flats. We don't have any information about the settlers, but with the Indians gone now things should improve for them."

He looked at Sarah and continued, "From what the messenger was saying, your father and those boys from German Flats got themselves into a hell of fight. It was with Indians and some Tories. The Redcoats were at Fort Schuyler putting on a siege. They say that German General, Herkimer, was wounded in the battle but, cool as a cucumber, had himself pulled up against a tree, lit his pipe and directed the battle sitting there. It was hand to hand, man against man." John's voice rose and he became animated. Sarah could tell he wished he had been part of it.

"Anyway," John continued, "they drove the Indians off finally. Too bad though, the messenger said that General Herkimer died of his wounds the other day. I'm sorry to see any fighting general get killed. Lord knows we got enough who don't seem to want to."

Ben thoughtfully entered the conversation. "Ya know, sometimes I wonder about this war and whether we're right. But every now and then we hear about folks like them up the Mohawk there. This Herkimer don't even speak English, they say. Yet he up and forms a militia and goes off to fight a battle that maybe ain't even his. And those folks all join up and follow him. It makes you realize how different we are than the British. Americans ain't just British. We got people from almost everywhere living here. And a lot of them don't even speak English yet. But they are fighting just the same. Those folks back in London don't understand that yet. They think we are all just English subjects like we were a hundred years ago. When I get to thinking like that, I know we are right and we're going to win this thing."

Sarah put in, "You know, Ben, I have the same thoughts sometimes. Since Ginny died back at Skenesborough I keep asking myself, what was she fighting for? Did she believe we were going to let her and her people be free if we win this war? And then I ask myself, are we? What is this independence we all keep saying we're fighting for?"

No one said anything. They all stared into the fire deep in their own thoughts. Sarah then changed the subject, "Have you men heard anything about where Burgoyne is? Are we going to be moving north again?"

John looked at the other men and then once again spoke.

"According to the scouts, they're slowly making their way down the other side of the river. But they are running short on supplies and the going is very rough, thanks to all our hard work of placing obstacles they ain't used to dealing with in their way." The men all chuckled. Sarah thought it was good to see them all with such high spirits again.

"They're going to have to cross over to this side pretty soon. The only good road to Albany is right over there next to the river. And unless they want to continue to fight their way down through the Grants, they gotta come here. They got scouts and our traitors too, so they know we're here. Their purpose is to destroy us, and to do that they have to get over here. So one day soon they'll be crossing. We got good high ground, so I reckon we will be fighting here."

Sarah asked solemnly, "Can we beat them, John?"

"We have to beat them Sarah," John said. "We're all that stands between here and General Washington's backside. And he's got Howe to deal with in front of him. If we lose here, this war will be about over. Burgoyne and Howe will squeeze that army down south till there ain't nothin left to fight with. No, I'm sure we're gonna make our stand here and we are gonna win."

The men all cheered, "Huzzah, huzzah!"

"Do you think if we beat them here the war will be over?" Sarah asked.

Ben said, "If these Redcoats got any sense it should be. Washington and those New England boys drove them out of Boston in seventy five, and if they lose here they gotta start thinking they can't win this war."

William then spoke, "That might be a proper thought for

a soldier Ben. But soldiers aren't running this war for them any more than they are for us. The politicians in Parliament make all the decisions about this war for England, and they aren't about to let a single defeat change their mind. Not when they have so much invested in this war already. Anyone who seriously thinks a battle here will end the war isn't thinking clearly. General Washington was soundly defeated time and again and driven out of New York. General Howe, if he doesn't decide to come north, will undoubtedly try to take Philadelphia and will most probably do it. No, if we win here, and I believe we will, we'll leave some units up here to secure the north, but the rest of us will be marching south to join Washington. And this war will go on."

"You're probably right, William," John said. "Still, it's nice to think that we could end it all here. But even if we force the British out we still have the Tories to contend with. I know we got our share of Tories up here but they say there are more Tories than patriots down in the Deep South. You notice you ain't seen no overwhelming show of support in the way of troops coming from down there. We can count on Virginia for some, but the people down in the rest of those states must be enjoying life 'cause they sure ain't up here fightin'."

"Well, John," William added, "we can't spend too much time worrying about them now. We have a battle of our own to fight and win before we can do much about winning over the rest of these so called 'united states'."

Sarah stood and said, "Gentlemen, I miss listening to all of you each night. Thank you for letting me back in for the evening. It has been most informative and enjoyable. But I better head back to the women's camp before they think I have been captured by Indians or something."

They all stood and Ben said, "Good evening Sarah, you come back anytime, preferably earlier so's you can cook instead of John." Then he hugged her and said, "You take care of yourself, Sarah. We all heard about your exploits and your getting sick. John ain't the only one who needs you, you know. We all need you to keep us on the straight and narrow. Be safe."

It was dark and Sarah hoped that no one could see that she was blushing. "Thank you, Ben. I'll do everything I can to keep safe. You gentlemen do the same. Good night all."

John said, "I'll walk you back, Sarah. You shouldn't be walking around alone in the dark."

"Why thank you my dear. Just like when we were courting." Then she said especially loud so the men could hear, "Maybe I'll let you steal a kiss or two in the dark also. Just like when we were courting."

The men heard her and all laughed. She could hear them joking among themselves about what else John might be able to steal, and she smiled as she thought about the same thing.

They had not made love since before they had all evacuated Fort Ti. The late August night had just a hint of fall in the air. The sky was filled with stars and a bright golden moon. As they came into a dark secluded place within some trees Sarah stopped and turned to John and kissed him passionately. She thought about how they had made love by the lake the night he had returned from Canada and how beautiful it had been. This was not quite as beautiful a scene. It lasted only a few minutes. When it was over they laid in the dark, not saying a word. Finally, John said, "I better be getting you back to camp or those women will be thinking something happened to you."

"Something did happen to me," she said teasingly.

John pulled her to her feet and said cheerfully, "Come on, you vixen, let's get going."

On August thirty-first, General Arnold and his force came into camp from their excursion up the Mohawk. The army was really ballooning now. Sarah did not know how many thousands of men were in the camp, but the numbers kept growing daily.

Most of the work at the hospital was routine, so Sarah enjoyed the opportunity to take food and water to John and the men working on the construction. She would linger with the men as long as she could before returning back down the hill, to the hospital. It amazed her to see so many men laboring as one to build what to her seemed a fortress.

John sat with her one noon and explained the entire layout to her. It was a glorious early fall day. The sun shone brightly but there was a cool breeze across the top of the hill making the temperature quite pleasant. Sarah stared out on the horizon to all sides and wondered what exactly she was looking at. As they sat there talking she could almost ignore the fact that there were so many people around them. She was fascinated by what John had to say.

They sat facing north. John said, "If you look far out to our right front, across the river there Sarah, that's where Burgoyne and his army are slogging through the forest right now. Sooner or later he has to cross, and the best place to do that is right out there a couple of miles. If he decides that he doesn't want to cross, the going will continue to be rough for him 'cause there's no good road to Albany over there. And besides, we have a pretty good size force on that side of the river too. But he'll cross. We're told that his supply lines have been pretty well cut off now and he has to live off the land. We didn't leave very much on that land as we retreated, so his men have got to be getting hungry."

He pointed to their right rear, "Over there is where Bennington is. That's where General Stark and the New Hampshire boys beat the Hessians up a couple of weeks ago. Now if you look right down there by the river you can see where Edward and Elizabeth have been building breastworks and emplacing some artillery across the road. And right down at the bottom of the hill are some more artillery batteries. Once Burgoyne gets here, that's the road he'll want to secure. And all around this hill you can see we have built a fort. It stretches from over here to our right all across the northern front and around to our left. I'd say we are in a pretty fine spot to take on the British and their Hessian friends from here."

"So you think, once he gets here, he'll charge us from out there?" Sarah asked pointing directly to the north. "Or will we charge him?"

"Well, Sarah, I don't know. But my guess is that we're building this fort for defensive reasons, and if Burgoyne wants to get down that road, he's going to have to make some kind of frontal assault. If that's so, I'll take my chances behind in this position. It is solid."

He kissed her on the cheek and said, "Well, I gotta get back to work. You have a good afternoon, dear."

Sarah looked down to where the artillery batteries were being built and wondered what Elizabeth was doing. She wished there was more that she could be doing and envied Elizabeth being with the men and actually working. She looked out across the span in front of her and to the northwest she saw some open fields within the almost impenetrable forest that surrounded them. They were farmers' fields, abandoned when the army arrived. It made her sad to see the unharvested crops still in the ground. "What a waste," she said to herself as she rose to go back down the hill.

As she walked back she could hear the noises of the workers all around the camp. She felt good about being there. She also felt good about the fact that John had taken time to explain things to her. It was the first time he had ever really done that, and it made her feel like she was getting to be a real part of this army now.

General Arnold had been in camp about two weeks when he and General Poor set up headquarters in a farm house in the northwest corner of the fort. The house belonged to a man and his wife by the name of Neilson. They gave it up to the army to use.

General Gates had divided the army into two arms. General Arnold was in command of the left side. Sarah knew she wanted to be closer to what was going to happen and that Arnold's headquarters was the place to be. On the day he moved into Neilson's house she boldly walked up the hill and told the guard at the door she wanted to talk to General Arnold.

The door was open and he came to the door. "What is it, Private?" he asked.

The soldier came to attention and said, "Sir, this woman says she wants to talk to you."

"Sorry to bother you, Sir. I hope you remember me. I'm Sarah

Hardy and I worked for you at Fort Ti," Sarah uttered quickly.

"Of course, Mrs Hardy. What can I do for you?"

"Well, Sir, I heard you and General Poor were moving into this house today and I was wondering if you needed anyone to help you to keep house and cook for you. If so, I would like to volunteer."

Arnold looked at her for a few seconds as he thought. Then he responded, "You know, Mrs. Hardy, there are a lot of people who don't care for me and would do anything not to work for me. I am not sure why you want to take care of two rather difficult men. Why do you want to?"

"Sir, right now I work at the hospital, and I know that working at the hospital is important. But if there is going to be a battle here, I want to see it and be as much of a part of it as I can be. I figure your headquarters is the best place to do that. As for others not caring to work for you, I can't explain that. My husband thinks you're the best general we have, and if he wants to fight with you, I do too."

Arnold gave a satisfied smile and said, "Why yes, as a matter of fact, we will need some help around here. I do remember you and your work, Mrs Hardy. You've got the job. I like people who are aggressive in getting what they want. When can you start?"

"Well, Sir, I've already told the doctors at the hospital that I was coming up here to work for you. So I guess I can start right now."

He laughed and said, "In that case come inside and let me introduce you to General Poor and show you our luxurious accommodations"

The next day, as she was working in the house, Sarah overheard the first reports that Burgoyne was crossing the river just a few miles north of them. For some reason the news gave her conflicting feelings. On one hand there was fear of what was to come. But more intense was an excitement she had never felt before. The idea that she was actually there as a major battle was about to unfold filled her with an exhilaration she could not explain.

For the next three days reports kept coming in on how many British and Hessian troops had crossed and how they were building fortifications just out of sight from where she stood. Finally, the entire force was across and began to fully spread out in the hills and ravines in front of the American bastion. Sarah wondered where the women who were with the enemy were and what they were doing as these two armies prepared to battle. She had seen them during the short while she was a captive, and wondered how their lives differed from hers.

Thirty-Six

In the early morning darkness of September nineteenth, Sarah climbed the hill from the rear of the camp, where her tent was located, to the top of Bemis Heights and General Arnold's headquarters. A thick fog hung over the area and she could barely see but a few feet in front of her. She wondered when it would burn off. The fog made the air cool and it felt refreshingly brisk. She knew that when the fog finally did burn away it would be another hot, sticky day.

She also wondered if this was to be the day of the great battle. The battlements and defensive positions had been completed several days before, and everyone in the camp was anxious for something to happen. The tension of waiting for the British to make the first move was becoming increasingly hard to bear. John and the other men were grumbling the night before about how they wished they were out on one of the scouting parties.

At least then they would be able to see the enemy and have some idea of what they were doing. But the waiting, knowing the enemy was just a few miles out in front of them yet not being able to see them, was the hardest part of the past few days.

Since General Gates had taken command things in the camps had become almost comfortable. The men had received new clothes and the rations were better than any of them had been in months. They did not seem to want for anything. Anything, that is, but a chance to fight.

As Sarah approached the farmhouse she heard men talking. She clearly heard General Arnold's voice above the others. She had heard this discussion going on for several days now. Every day he lectured Generals Poor, Learned, Dearborn, and Colonel Morgan about what General Gates was not doing that he should be doing. His voice would continue to rise, along with his anger, until he would storm out of the house and go over to General Gates' headquarters to argue his position, only to return disappointed and even angrier than when he left.

Sarah took a deep breath and sighed to herself, "And why did I want this job?"

She knocked on the door and clearly heard General Arnold's angry voice, "Come in." As she walked in four of the men turned and looked at her as if amazed to see her here amidst their strategy planning session. General Arnold, however, gave her a quick glance and said, "Oh, good morning, Mrs. Hardy. Glad you're here. Would you be so kind as to fix us some coffee and breakfast?" Without waiting for an answer he turned back to the map on the table and began once again haranguing the others.

"Now, Poor," he said, "I want you to put yourself in Burgoyne's shoes. You are out here," he pointed at the map, "a few miles from this very spot. You've got reports about the strength of this position. What would you do?"

"Benedict, we've all been over this many times. You know what all of us would do. We would move a force around behind those ravines and hills out there 'til they were in a position to attack us at our weakest point, which is right here on our left. The position we are here to defend. In addition, if he can take that open field out there he can place his cannon there and blast this place to pieces before he attacks."

"Exactly," Arnold replied. "And yet we sit here. We don't have any idea what they are doing. At this very moment they could be moving troops over there. At the very least we should have Morgan and his men out in those woods observing what is going on."

"General Arnold," General Learned said, "you're right. We all know you're right. You don't have to convince us. But we also know that General Gates believes he cannot be beaten if he stays behind these walls. He is not an offensive minded man like yourself, Benedict. But you have to convince him to let us out there so we can get into position to take on Burgoyne's forces before they can get set to attack."

Sarah was exhilarated to think that she was here listening to these men talk about the coming battle in such a way. She almost felt as though she were a part of the discussions. The entire house was no bigger than a large room. With the fireplace on one wall and a large table in the center of the room she was only a couple of feet from the men. Coffee and breakfast ready, she turned to the table and said, "Excuse me gentlemen, but may

I serve you now?"

The men stopped talking again, looking at her as though they had not realized she was in the room. Colonel Morgan answered for all of them, "Why Mrs. Hardy, that is the best suggestion I have heard all morning. Please do."

Sarah liked Colonel Morgan. He was different than the rest of the men at the table. First of all, being from Virginia, he was the only southerner in the group. His voice was softer than the others when he spoke to her. Where General Arnold had only one tone of voice—gruff—Morgan's voice could change from one as fierce as Arnold's to that of a kindly gentlemen in an instant. She had heard John and the others talk about Morgan and his men in admiring terms. They talked about how he had fought in Quebec and took command when Arnold was injured, even though he was not the senior man. They talked about how expert his men were in firing their rifles, and about their bravery and ferocity in battle, and how they always took on the hardest missions and worked alone outside of the regular infantry units.

She could tell by the look on his face that General Arnold was a little put out at the interruption. But he looked at her as though he were surrendering to a superior force and sighed, "Go ahead Sarah. Feed these ravenous men. There is nothing to be gained by our continuing this argument amongst ourselves. I am going over to General Gates' headquarters to see if I can talk some sense into the man."

She poured some coffee into a tin cup and brought it to him. "Here, take this with you, Sir. You may need it, and besides, you don't know what they'll serve you over there in the enemy's camp." When the men heard those words they all looked at each other warily. They knew Arnold's moods and waited for an explosion.

Instead, for the first time that morning Arnold smiled. "Thank you, Sarah. You're probably right. If I know General Gates his repast for me will probably be a large portion of humble pie." With that comment the men visibly relaxed and everyone laughed.

"Good luck, General," Sarah said as he walked towards the door.

He opened the door and looked out. It was lighter, but the fog was still very thick. "Well, one good thing, this fog is just as thick for them as it is for us. I don't think they can do much moving until it lifts some. Let's hope I can convince General Gates to let us move some people up into the woods by that farm out there. If they are going to try to come around to our left they'll have to pass by there. *Bon appetite,* gentlemen."

The men ate their breakfast and then went back to their units.

As she was cleaning up, Sarah's thoughts went back to her last exchange with Arnold. It struck her that for the first time since she had known him he called her by her first name and not Mrs. Hardy. He was usually very formal, and this small bit of familiarity in front of the other officers seemed quite out of place for him. She thought it was very nicc, and she liked it. But she also wondered what the other men might have thought of it. Certainly he meant nothing by it, she was sure. But army camps are always rampant with rumors started over the slightest comments or actions. She would talk to him about it at another time.

When he returned he had all four men with him and he was

in a very excited mood. Once again they all crowded around the table and Arnold began to speak. "Gentlemen, I believe today is the day. We have confirming reports that Burgoyne is about three miles from here and moving his forces as we speak. I have finally convinced General Gates that we need to get some people up here in and around these woods," he showed them on the map, "and to head off any movement of his forces in that direction. We must not let them take that farm on the hill.

"Morgan and Dearborn, General Gates has approved moving your units up here and to the left," he again pointed to the spot on the map, "to observe what is happening and engage any force that may attempt to come this way."

"Reports indicate that the Hessians are coming down the road by the river. Gates himself is in charge over there, and he will have to handle them. Burgoyne will probably send a force to his far right, into those woods, to see how far he can get. Morgan, Dearborn, you must stop that force. I believe his main force will come behind them and come straight down the middle."

He then looked to Generals Poor and Learned and said, "Gentlemen, I am certain that he is coming this way. I want you to have your troops ready to move out on a moment's notice. We must carry the fight to the enemy before he can get himself set to attack us. So at the first sign of a fight I will send you forward also. Are there any questions?" He looked around and looked each man in the eye. There were no questions. "Alright then, you know what to do. Morgan, Dearborn move out. The rest of you will be ready to move at a moment's notice."

Sarah stood in the corner observing in awe what was taking place in front of her. She had been in a fire fight, it is true, but it was a spontaneous action with no planning involved. The people she was with simply got caught by the advancing British force. Now there was going to be an actual battle between the two armies. She had just been in the room as General Arnold laid out the plans for his piece of the army, which John and she were a part of. It startled her how calm the officers were as they discussed the coming battle. She thought by the end of the day many men would be dead or severely wounded, yet they talked about the battle as though it were a game of movement of pieces on a map. She wondered what was going through their minds.

The meeting broke up and the officers went to their respective units. Sarah was left alone with General Arnold. She looked at him as he gazed fixedly at the map on the table. She could tell he was deep in thought. Was he questioning himself and the actions he had just ordered? How could a man be so sure he was right when so many lives were at stake?

Arnold looked up from the map and for the first time recognized she was standing there. "Well, Sarah, what do you think? Are we going to win today?"

Startled, Sarah responded, "Uh, uh, I certainly hope so, General. But I guess only God knows for sure. I don't think I'm the one to answer that question. Do you?"

"Truthfully, Sarah? No, I don't. Right at this moment not one of us on either side of this battle is in a position to answer that question. I suppose I should say it's all in God's hands now. But the truth is God doesn't care who wins this battle, or even this war. War is man's invention. We all pray to him and ask for his help, but God doesn't pick sides. He lets us fight it out amongst ourselves. There are good and bad men on both sides,

Sarah. And many of them will die today. God will sort out their souls after the battle, but He will not interfere. No, today will be decided by the men we have just sent out to fight."

Sarah was struck by a terrifying thought. Could it be possible that this man in front of her, whom she held in such high regard, did not care about what was about to happen? Did he really think it was just a game? "Excuse me, General, but don't you believe you're right? You couldn't send men out to die for something you don't believe in. Could you?"

"Oh, please don't misunderstand me, Sarah. I truly believe in our cause and I know we are right. If I could win this battle without losing a single man I would do it. But I know men will die here today. And I also know that the outcome of today's battle will depend on two things. First, whether we generals make the right decisions. And second, whether the men carry out those decisions to the utmost of their abilities. I believe we will win, or I would not have sent those men out there. But Sarah, never forget this, the man on the other side of those hills this morning believes just as fervently that he is right and is going to win. Do you understand?"

"I think so, General. But it all seems so cold and calculating. And, if you don't mind, I think I'll say a few prayers asking for God's help. Just in case you're wrong about Him."

Arnold laughed. "You know, Sarah, you are one of the few people in this camp brave enough to even suggest that I might be wrong about anything. Just on the outside chance I may be wrong, however, would you please put in a word for me too? Right now I better go see to our army. Wish us luck."

"Good luck, General, and God be with you." Sarah stood

there alone with her thoughts.

Soon she heard the first reports of sporadic musket fire. She ran outside to see what was happening, but all she could discern was that the shooting was coming from the area north of the house by that open field. It was exactly where General Arnold had predicted. Once again her faith in him rose. "He may be cold," she thought, "but he sure seems to know what he is doing."

Then for the first time that morning she thought about John. She was with him and the other men for a short while the night before, but the men were doing all the talking, or rather, grumbling, and she soon left. If Arnold sent out the rest of his force John would be with them. Between their work they had not seen much of each other. They had not had a quiet talk together, said they loved each other, or even kissed for days. She had at least told General Arnold good luck as he went out the door. Now John too was about to go into battle, and could possibly die without another word being spoken between them. Surprising herself, she was rather stoic about the possibility of his death. She thought, "John is a good soldier and will do his duty without help from me." But at the same time she vowed, if he lived through this battle, she would not let him to go off without a word again.

She stood on the hill trying to see what was happening. She heard the firing going on but she could see nothing. A couple of times she heard the sound of cannon going off. The anxiety she felt was overwhelming. After a half hour the shooting ceased. At that point she made her decision. She could not wait another minute. She grabbed a wooden bucket and filled it with water and began walking out towards where the shooting had been taking place.

All the fog had lifted by then and the sun was once again bright and hot. On her way out to the line she saw wounded men trying to hobble back to the rear. Other men were being helped or carried by comrades. She stopped to give them some water to drink and then kept moving closer to where men were huddled down, waiting for the next part of the battle to begin.

When she reached the point where she could see the field of battle she was stunned. The guns were quiet now, only an occasional shot could be heard. But out in front of her lay the dead and wounded of both sides. She could hear the screams and moans of the wounded begging for water or for someone to end it for them. But nobody could reach those men. They were in the middle of a no man's land where anyone who ventured out to aid them would become a casualty themselves. The heat of the day was becoming scorching. As she took in the sight before her Sarah had to stop to breathe in order to keep from vomiting.

Sarah could also hear the sounds of the enemy maneuvering men into place in the woods out in front of the line of men she was giving water to. She soon shed her bucket and carried as many of the men's canteens as she could back to a creek a few hundred yards behind the line. She filled them and carried them back to the men. She made this trip several times before she saw that other women had come out and were also doing the same thing.

The day was getting hotter with each minute. On one of her trips to the creek she saw the forces of General Poor coming out and forming up on the right of those of General Dearborn.

As she was filling some canteens at the creek a shadow covered her and she looked up to see Arnold on his horse. "What are you doing out here, Sarah?" he asked.

"Well, General, it's hot and the men need water, so I thought I would lend a hand and get it for them. Besides, I had to see what was happening out here. I couldn't just sit on that hill any longer listening to the battle and not know what was going on. Right now, though, it don't look like nothin' more is happening."

"Sarah, I'm sure the men appreciate what you're doing for them. This battle is far from over. Soon this place is going to explode. Now you take care of yourself and stay back from the line of fire. We're going to lose enough men today. I don't want to lose you too."

"I will, and you take care of yourself too. I don't want to have to find a new job." She didn't know why she felt so at ease that she could talk to him in that fashion. It just seemed natural.

Arnold looked at her fondly and shook his head. Then he rode off towards the front.

At that moment the air filled with cannon fire from the British lines. Soon the noise of battle was so great that Sarah became momentarily disoriented. Over the din of battle and through the clouds of smoke she could hear the buzz of musket balls flying over her head. As cannon balls crashed into the ground they threw dirt everywhere. Soon she was covered with dirt turned into mud from her sweat. The smoke from the guns filled the air and burned her throat and eyes. She struggled to see what was happening.

A doctor had set up a field location to take care of wounded being sent behind the lines, and she was quickly recruited to aid him. Wounded men came streaming in.

She worked feverishly. The noise of the battle seemed to be just background. But periodically Sarah would stop to look out to the front. Then the noise had meaning. She could see the fire ripping out of the cannon the British were firing and feel their resounding blasts. Musket fire from both sides filled the void between the cannon blasts. Somehow over it all she heard the screams of the men who were being hit by this unmerciful rain of lead.

She could only stand to look at the field for a quick moment. Smoke obscured most of her vision, but in those glimpses she could see men being torn apart. The battle seemed to wave in front of her. First one side would press forward, only to be driven back, and then they would push back again. Out on the field there were spots where hand to hand combat was taking place. Men bayoneting each other or using their muskets as clubs. Sarah stared at the sight in disbelief. The men seemed crazed, and she thought nothing but death could stop them.

At one point she observed that there were other women who were struggling to carry ammunition boxes up to the men from wagons which had been brought forward. These women were going right up to where the men were fighting to deliver the much needed ammunition.

Then, as she was observing the battle, she saw Arnold riding his horse up and down the line, waving his sword and shouting to the men. Through the smoke she thought he looked like a ghost riding across the front. She could not hear what he was saying, but she thought to herself, "How could I have questioned that man's resolve this morning?" She looked at him without fear

First Battle of Saratoga

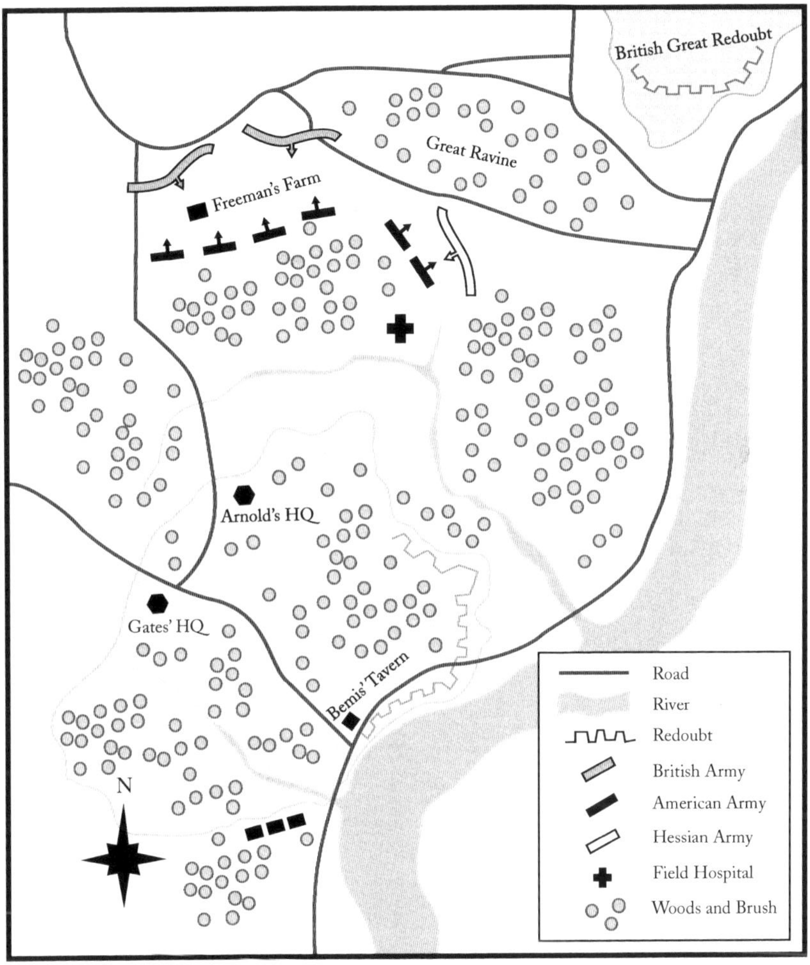

of his being killed. He seemed invincible to her.

At another time, as she was up near the front pulling a wounded man to the rear, she looked out over the line and saw an immaculately dressed British officer on horseback. He too was riding up and down his lines encouraging his men. Only later did she learn that he was General Burgoyne. She wondered what made these few special men so fearless that they would make targets of themselves in order to keep their men fighting. She also wondered how they lived with themselves knowing this carnage was taking place at their commands.

The battle raged on unmercifully until evening was setting in. At that point a force of Hessians attacked the Americans on their right flank. Although they had held their own up to this point, the Americans had to fall back as this new threat came onto the field. Finally, darkness came and the fighting ceased. But the sounds of the men still lying on the battlefield, moaning and screaming in agony with no one able to help them, broke Sarah's heart.

As the night wore on the temperatures dropped precipitously. All who had sweated without relief throughout the day were now shivering with the cold night of the Adirondacks. The torture could only have been doubled for those men lying out in the field and forest, Sarah thought.

In the last rays of daylight Sarah looked at herself. She was covered in sweat, dirt and caked on blood of she did not know how many men. And there were holes in her clothes where musket balls had passed through without her even noticing. She realized she was hungry. She had not eaten since breakfast. But she was too tired to try and find food. She could live until tomorrow without food but she could not stay awake a moment longer. Someone covered her with a blanket. As she dozed she dreamed she heard wolves howling and musket shots going off in the distance.

Thirty-Seven

Sarah awoke before dawn broke. Even in the darkness she could see that the day was going to be a repeat of the day before. Fog hung thick and close to the ground. She shivered in the morning cold and wrapped the blanket around her to try and get warm, but it was no use. The blanket and her clothes were saturated with the heavy dew. She noticed that there was a fire going already and a few men were around it talking. She wandered over to the fire and asked, "May I join you and warm up by the fire, gentlemen?"

One of the men stood up and said, "Oh, Mis' Hardy, of course. Please take my seat here next to the fire." Through the fog she thought she recognized the voice, but she couldn't make out who it was. As she stepped closer she saw that it was Small. She had not seen him in quite some time, and was surprised to see him this morning. She went to him, hugged him and said,

"Small, it is so good to see you. Where have you been? We've missed you at the hospital."

"Good morning, Mis' Hardy. It's good to see you too. Me? Oh, I been working down at the general hospital in Albany. They sent me up here a few days ago to help transport the wounded and sick back down there. I guess they knew there was a battle gonna take place. Looks like we're gonna be pretty busy. Where are your two friends? And what are you doing way up here on the front line? Here, have yourself a cup of coffee. You must be freezin'." He poured some coffee into a tin cup and handed it to her. "Sorry, ma'am, we ain't got no fixins for it, just black coffee."

"This is fine, Small." She held the cup in both hands, trying to warm them. She stepped closer to the fire to try and get her clothes dry and warm up. She looked into the fire and said, "How I got here is a long story. Let's just say that, just like at Crown Point, I wandered too far away from where I should have been. And once I got here a war broke out and men needed help. But it looks like you men have everything under control here now. I think I'll head back to the rear and see if I can be of use there."

Dawn was breaking and the day was getting lighter, but the fog remained very thick. She stared out towards the battlefield and wondered if there were any men still alive out there. The morning stillness was eerie. No sounds, not even those of animals or insects, disturbed the silence. She could not see the field because of the fog but imagined the carnage that must still be on the ground out there.

Then she turned to the men and asked, "Did any of you hear wolves howling last night? I thought I dreamed I heard them, but I'm not sure."

One of the men answered somberly, "You weren't dreamin', ma'am. There sure enough were wolves out there attacking the living as well as the dead. Some of the boys from both sides tried to scare 'em off by shooting into the night, but that didn't do much to help, I don't think. Sure is a scary quiet, ain't it ma'am? Well, if we ain't fighting again this morning maybe someone will set up a truce of some kind and let us go get the men that's still out there. I'm sure the Lobsterbacks want to get theirs as bad as we want to get ours."

Sarah shivered. Whether it was from the cold or the thought of those poor men still lying out on that field she couldn't say. She gave the cup back to Small. "Thank you for sharing your fire, gentlemen. I think I'll head back now. Take care of yourselves."

Small said, "It was good seein' ya again, Mis' Hardy. You take care of yourself too."

Sarah nodded and started walking back. Two years ago she had been a girl on a farm, and the thought of butchering an animal brought tears to her eyes. Now here she was amidst carnage she could not ever have imagined could happen, and not a tear would come. She wondered where Elizabeth was. She needed to talk to a friend.

Then she thought of John. Why she had not thought of him until now she did not know. She felt a pang of guilt for not thinking of him first. She picked up her step and went searching for the area where his unit was camped. She found him talking to several other men by a fire. When he saw her walk up he went directly to her, took her in his arms and hugged her tightly.

"Sarah, where have you been? I went back to the hospital and to your tent and no one had seen you. You're all damp; here, let me get you a dry blanket." He picked a blanket up and wrapped it around her. "Take a seat close by the fire."

She could not think of anything to say that would fit the moment. Finally, she replied, "I stayed down at the aid station here at the front. I fell asleep outside, and the dew was rather heavy last night. I'm alright though, just a little cold right now. I'll be fine once I warm up some. How are you, John? I worried about you all through the fight." This wasn't exactly true. She did think about him periodically during the day yesterday, but truthfully she had wrapped herself up so in her work that she had hardly given him a second thought until a few moments ago. She felt a pang of guilt.

"I'm fine dear," he told her. "We didn't get here 'til later in the fight, so we didn't see much of it until the Hessians came into it. They pushed us back but we held here when darkness fell."

"Do you think there will be more fighting today, John?"

"Well, I don't think yesterday settled too much. So I suppose that we'll be at it again after this fog lifts. It's a good thing General Arnold got us out here yesterday though. If we hadn't met them they would have flanked us for sure. As it is we fought 'em to a standstill and Gates hasn't seen any action yet. So his side is fully rested if need be. I sure wish he had used some of our artillery on them yesterday though. It would have helped, and maybe even pushed things in our direction. We took some terrible losses from their guns over there on the left, I'm told. Where were you during all the fighting, Sarah? Could you hear those cannons go off?"

She was glad the fog clouded his sight of her. She knew her

face would betray her as she lied to him once again. She could not tell him that she was at the front line in the thick of things. She could not tell him what she had witnessed. It would do no good and only worry him when he should be concentrating on fighting. "Oh, I heard them all right. But I was way back at the aid station and couldn't see much." She emphasized the "way back" in order to give him assurance that she was not in danger. She pulled the blanket tighter around her to hide the holes in her clothes and the blood of the men whom she had helped carry from the field.

She looked at him through the fog. His face and hands were still blackened from the powder of his musket and his clothes were dirty, but she was filled with a pride for him that she had never felt before.

Then she said, "John, I tracked you down this morning so I could tell you I love you and that I'm proud of you. Please take care of yourself. I do not want to lose you." She stood and went to him, hugged him and kissed him deeply.

The men standing around turned their backs a little and she could hear tittering as she released him. "Now I think I'll go see how General Arnold is and then go find Elizabeth and Martha. By the way, how is Jeremiah? How could I forget to ask?"

"Tell Martha he's fine. You know, Sarah, he's become a fine officer. The men love him and so do the senior officers. I wouldn't be surprised if he gets promoted soon."

"Well, when you're not taking care of yourself, you take care of him too. We don't want to lose either of you."

She was feeling better. Talking to John always made her feel better, and seeing him unhurt lifted her heart enormously. She even felt a little light-hearted. As she kissed him goodbye she turned to the men and said jokingly, "Now don't you boys pick on my Johnny just because his wife came out to kiss him." She winked at John and whispered, "I'll see you later, dear. Do take care."

The men laughed raucously and she knew they would razz him terribly when she left. She smiled at the thought. Once again she tried to sort out the emotions she was going through. She wondered what it is in us that we can find humor in something so trivial when all about us is destruction, death, and carnage?

John looked at her with pride and said, "You take care of yourself too. Stay back at the hospital, Sarah. You don't need to be up here, and I don't want you up this close. It's not safe."

Sarah responded dutifully, "Alright, dear. I will be careful too. I love you." But she knew that if there was fighting again today she would be back out here. There was something in her now that would not allow her to stay in the rear again.

The men had established their defensive position about a mile and a half from Bemis Heights, and as Sarah made her way back through the trees she noticed how they were in their full fall glory of reds and golds. She could not think of a time when the colors of the trees in fall had struck her so profoundly. Even through the fog they had a beauty she could not describe but could only feel.

She next stopped at Arnold's headquarters. She heard the men talking as she knocked on the door. Arnold shouted sharply, "Come in." As she entered he looked and said "Oh, it's you Sarah. I wasn't expecting you to come today."

Sarah responded, "I was just returning from the aid station

this morning and stopped by to see if there was anything you needed, General."

"Why thank you for thinking of us, but I think we can manage for a day or two. I heard that you put in a pretty full day yesterday and thought you would be over at the hospital today. They need you more than we do here."

Sarah was a little disappointed with his reception, but said, "Of course, Sir, if that is what you think is best. I will go over to the hospital right away. Uh, General, do you think there will be fighting again today?" she asked pensively.

"Well, Sarah, we were just discussing the same topic. Yesterday we put up a mighty fight until the Hessians came in on the right. If I were Burgoyne, I would be forming up to attack right now. But Burgoyne is not me, and maybe he will be a little hesitant to throw his army back into battle so quickly. I don't know. But I do know a couple of things. First, he is low on supplies. And second, we have cut off his ability to get any from up north. So he has to fight again sooner or later. Most importantly I know we will be ready for him whenever he decides to attack again. I don't suppose that answers your question, does it, Sarah? But it's all we have right now."

Sarah looked at him and said, "I guess it's as good an answer as I could expect. I'll listen for the shooting and find out then like everyone else I guess, Sir." The men all laughed. Then she said, "General Arnold, I saw you riding up and down the front yesterday. It was very brave of you and very dangerous too, I suppose. Don't you think maybe you ought not to be doing that? I would hate to see you get killed."

Colonel Morgan chimed in, "That advice, Mrs. Hardy, has

already been given by several other people in this room. I'm afraid the good general is not likely to accept it from you any better than he has from us. I'm afraid, madam, General Arnold must be General Arnold." There was an anxious laugh from the others in the room, including Arnold.

Arnold replied, "Well, Colonel Morgan, I am touched by your, and Mrs. Hardy's, concern for my wellbeing. And I will gladly start leading from the rear whenever you do."

Sarah knew it was time to leave. "I fear I have stepped into something I have no business in. So with your permission, gentlemen, I will excuse myself and head over to the hospital." They all bid her good day and she was off.

She didn't go to the hospital right away. Before she could go there she needed to find Elizabeth. She needed to talk to a woman. She needed to talk to a friend.

She found Elizabeth over on the far right side of the line by the river. She was bringing breakfast to the men working at one of the cannons there. Her husband and son were on that gun. When she saw Sarah she put down the buckets she was carrying and they ran to hug each other. Elizabeth uttered, "Sarah, I have been so worried about you. I went over to see Martha and no one had seen you. Where have you been? Are you alright?"

"I'm fine, Elizabeth. My clothes might be a little worse for wear." She stepped back to show Elizabeth the sorry state of her dress.

"My God, Sarah, what did you get into yesterday?"

"I was working in General Arnold's place when all the shooting started. I waited until it stopped and then I could wait no longer. I only went out to help bring water to the men. But just as I got to the front the whole place erupted again. I joined a doctor and his assistants in setting up an aid station near the front. Before long we were carrying men back from the line and we were swamped with wounded. We worked until it was too dark, then I just collapsed with a blanket under a tree."

She started to tremble, "Oh, Elizabeth, it was horrible. Yesterday I watched as men were blown to pieces and tended men who had lost arms and legs and had other serious wounds, yet through the whole day I did not shed a tear. Is this what happens to people in war? Do we just cease to feel? Is that how we get through this horror? Once we become like this do we ever get back to what we were? What is wrong with me? What kind of woman am I, Elizabeth?"

Elizabeth took her in her arms and held her tight. "There, there dearie, just calm down now. You're tired is all. Of course you blotted it outta your mind. You have to, or you'll go crazy. There is nothing wrong with you. You, and all of us, are faced with things we could never have imagined. A lot of women, and a lot of men too, have deserted these camps because they couldn't take what you've endured. You're still here facing the unimaginable. Sometimes the only way to cope with it is to force it outta your mind as best as you can, and to remember that you're helping these men. I know you want to save them all, but out here you can only do the best you can to help the living. The dead we have to trust to God's care."

Then she let Sarah go and, smiling, looked into her eyes. "Now come on with me and we'll help the men eat up these vittles. When was the last time you ate, anyway?"

The talk helped Sarah to feel better. She smiled back and

said, "You know, Elizabeth, now that you mention it, I haven't eaten since yesterday sometime. I'm starvin'."

After eating breakfast, Sarah started walking back to the hospital. Talking to Elizabeth had made her feel better. But her walk didn't take her straight back. Instead she found herself walking back to the front where the dead and wounded still lay waiting for someone to come and get them.

The fog was lifting and it was promising to be a bright, sunny and hot day. But there were no guns going off. Sarah knew the sight she was going to see would be horrible, but she was not ready for what she actually did see. The ground was covered with the bodies of men. It was soaked with their blood. At first she did not see anyone moving and thought to herself, "Thank God, at least they are at rest now and no longer in agony." But then she saw something moving amongst the bodies. At first she thought it must be the wolves come back for more. She stared out, trying to see through the gray morning fog, and she was startled to see that movement out there was not wolves but human beings. Several soldiers and women were going from body to body and stripping them of their clothes and valuables. She had heard that this kind of scavenging occurred but the sight of it in the gray early morning made her physically sick, and she leaned against a tree to steady herself. She could look no longer and turned and walked away.

As she walked back she tried to put the sight she had just seen out of her mind. She thought about how desperate those people must be that they needed to strip dead bodies for clothes. She hoped that the scavengers were doing it because of need and not greed, but her view of humanity at that moment was as low as it had ever been.

She tried to think of other things. She remembered what Arnold had said earlier about the possibility of fighting again today. He said if it were him he would be attacking again this morning. But to her mind, there weren't very many Arnold's in this war, so there probably wouldn't be any fighting today. Still, she wondered when it would start again.

Thirty-Eight

Sometime over the next couple of days the bodies were recovered from the battle site and burials were held. The officers were buried in separate marked graves and the enlisted men were buried in a mass grave with all the military honors the army could muster.

Over the next couple of weeks, the men occupied themselves reinforcing defensive positions. Additionally, they built a bridge made of boats across the river.

The British and Hessians seemed to be building their own defensive works at the same time. John told her about two redoubts they were building over by where the first battle had taken place. They too constructed a bridge formed by boats tied together.

Once again the tension of waiting for what was to come and not knowing when filled the camp. Scouting parties went out each night and returned in the morning with news of what the enemy was doing. These parties tested the enemy's defenses by entering into small skirmishes. Sarah could hear the sporadic shooting every night as she tried to sleep. John never told her when he was going out on one of these forays, so sleep was hard to come by as she worried that he might be involved. Each morning she arose and went to his tent to find him. If he was not there she sat in the tent until he returned before going on to work. The question on Sarah's mind, and those of the men was, "What are they waiting for?"

At the hospital they busied themselves evacuating the wounded back down the river to the general hospital in Albany. After the carnage at the front line during the battle, the hospital seemed almost clean. But in reality it was a miserable filthy place. The seriously wounded were housed in a converted barn.

In a few days Sarah quickly found she was no longer really needed at the hospital, so she went back to working at General Arnold's quarters.

The day after she returned to his quarters he burst into the house in a rage. General Poor and Colonel Morgan were there and he directed his fury at them. "Do you know what that son of a bitch has done?" he shouted. Without waiting he continued, "He wrote a letter to Congress extolling his great accomplishments in the battle. In the letter he barely mentions that we had anything to do whatsoever with the success of the day. Imagine, he who never took so much as a step outside these revetments giving himself all the credit for what we accomplished. I swear gentlemen, I do not know how much longer I will be able to serve under such a duplicitous man."

General Poor responded in a much quieter tone, "Well, General, I suppose in time we will be able to write our version of the day's events. Right now there's not much we can do. He is the commander. Did he happen to say anything about preparations for the next battle?"

"Bah," Arnold huffed, "The man's a moron. He hasn't a military thought in his head. He plans to sit behind these walls and wait on General Burgoyne to attack. He thinks we have delivered a death blow to the enemy and maybe they will just disappear. But Burgoyne and that Hessian general are tough soldiers, and they know their situation better than we do. They know they have to fight here, and they would like nothing better than to have us sit here and let them blow us to pieces with their guns. We stopped them the other day because we surprised them by going out to meet them. And if we are to beat them thoroughly we will have to do it again, only this time we must put this whole army into the fray. We have them outnumbered and the men are ready for the fight. The sooner the better."

Seemingly for the first time, Arnold recognized that Sarah was in the room. "Oh, Sarah, I didn't realize you were here. Please forgive my language."

Sarah said, "No apologies necessary, General. Sometimes we just have to get things off our chests in order to set them right. Besides, since I've been with this army I have become quite used to the—uh—colorful language of soldiers. And sometimes I have to use some of it myself."

As the days went on Arnold's mood became more and more foul. His anger with General Gates would reach almost uncontrollable lengths, and his drinking increased greatly. Each day he threatened to leave and go back down to Albany. And each day the other generals convinced him he was much too needed for him to leave.

The morning of October seventh dawned bright and warm, a perfect autumn day. After visiting with John, Sarah walked to work and thought that things had almost returned to normal. Any thought of battle was far from her mind as she enjoyed the warm air and the brightly colored trees that surrounded her.

As she was preparing breakfast a sergeant came in and gave General Arnold a report from the last night's scouting parties. He said that there was a great deal of movement within the enemy camp and that they believed the British were about to take some action this day. Then he finished by saying, "Oh, and General, there is a Hessian deserter that came in this morning and is over at General Gates' office. He says that General Burgoyne is going to attack today."

Arnold stood and asked, "Are you sure, Sergeant? He said they were going to attack today?"

The Sergeant nodded and said, "Yes, Sir. That's what he said. And everything we can figure from the scouts says so too."

"Very well. Thank you, Sergeant. That will be all."

As the sergeant left Arnold began to pace and talk to himself. "It's about time. The man must be getting low on supplies. He can't wait much longer. Winter will be setting in soon. The only way to come is the same way he did last month. I must get our side of the army out there. I must get over to General Gates' office. He must know that he has to get the army out there now! He can't wait here any longer!"

With that he walked out. A short while later he returned. He shouted, "That man is an idiot! He has all the information he needs sitting in front of him and still he won't move. But at least I have convinced him to send Morgan and Dearborn's forces out to the left to find out more of what Burgoyne is doing."

Sarah could see that he was excited now. He said, "No time for breakfast today. General Lincoln and I are riding out with Morgan and Dearborn to get a firsthand look at what is going on. When we get back maybe we will be able to talk some sense into that rock of a head of his." He thought for a moment and then he commented, almost lightly, "You know, Sarah, it's almost as if the man didn't trust me to tell him the truth. He'll believe a sergeant who comes in after a long hard night scouting. But he's sending General Lincoln along with me to make sure I don't exaggerate what I'm talking about. Hell of a way to run and army, isn't it, Sarah?"

She followed him out the door, and as he mounted his horse she thought how handsome he looked and how brave he was. She waved to him and whispered softly, "Good luck Benedict, and keep safe." As he and General Lincoln road off Sarah thought about what she was going to do this day. There was no doubt that there would be a battle, but what was she going to be doing? Should she stay here like John had told her or should go out and be part of it? Once again she looked about her at the beautiful scene the mountains made and noticed what a beautiful day it was. She needed to talk to Elizabeth.

She went back into the house and cleaned up a little, then she headed out to find Elizabeth. She found her on the other side of the hill with the men at one of the guns. "Sarah what brings you over this direction this morning? I heard there might be a battle today and I thought you might be getting into it."

Sarah chuckled nervously. "That's why I came by, Elizabeth. I am in a quandary. John has told me he does not want me out in the front again. But I just watched General Arnold ride off and I know I will be needed today. I can't sit back at the hospital and wait. It will drive me insane. What am I supposed to do?"

"Dearie, you know I can't tell you what you are supposed to do. As for me, I will be here with this gun," she pointed to the cannon the men were standing around, "and my husband and my son. Where they go, I will go. As for you, I think you know what you're going to do. You can't sit in the rear and wait, so you're going out there just like you did last time. You can't help yourself. Whatever is drawing you to the roar of the guns and the smoke and the screaming and carnage won't let you not be there. No Sarah, you're going out there today and so am I."

Sarah was stunned. "You're going out there today? Why? The last time they didn't even attack on this side."

Elizabeth looked at the gun where her husband and son were working and said, "The army will be using this gun today. The men are limbering her up to move her to wherever she'll be needed. Like I said, where those three go, I go."

Then she added rather sadly, "I don't know why, but we'll both be out there. Keep your head down and stay safe, dearie, and with God's help we'll see each other after it's over. God bless you, Sarah." Then she simply turned and walked away toward the gun and her family.

Sarah did not know what to do or say. For the second time in an hour another person she loved simply turned and left her. She looked at Elizabeth's back as she walked away and could only call, "Bless you too, Elizabeth. Keep safe."

Elizabeth did not look back. She only raised her hand in reply and kept on walking.

Sarah walked back to Arnold's quarters. Elizabeth was right. She was going to find her place out in the field. Now she had to find the courage to tell John. "Funny," she thought, "I don't have any fears about going into battle but I'm scared to death about what John will say and do when I tell him I'm going to do it."

She found him amongst several men who seemed to be getting ready to move out. As she approached he looked surprised to see her. He stopped what he was doing and came over to her and kissed her on the cheek. "Sarah, my dear, how are you this morning? Why aren't you working over at Arnold's place?"

"I think there's going to be a battle today, John. He and General Lincoln went out with Morgan's and Dearborn's troops to reconnoiter some movement they heard the British were making. I wanted to see you before anything happens and tell you I love you and to stay safe."

He took her in his arms and hugged her and said, "I love you too, Sarah." Then he said lightly, "As for keeping safe, I'll do my part, but it would be nice if you could tell the Redcoats and Hessians out there not to shoot my way. That would make the task much easier."

He looked her in the eye and said, "Sarah, I think this is the day we have been working so hard for these last two years. We're getting ready to move out too. From what we know, we have them outnumbered and we're better supplied. If Granny Gates doesn't mess this up we'll end this day victorious. Why he hasn't sent us out there already, I don't know. But we're going out there sooner or later, and I hope its sooner. You say Arnold and Lincoln are out there taking a look around? Well, maybe they will come back and convince him to hit the enemy with everything we've got and drive him into the lakes."

Then he looked sternly at her. "Now, Sarah, I want you to stay back here today. I don't want you up at the front again today. Do you understand me? It's not safe up there for you, Sarah. Now promise me you'll stay here."

Sarah spoke almost timidly. "That's another reason I came to see you John. I can't promise you I will stay back here." Her voice became stronger now. "If there is a battle up there today I am going to be there too. I'm on my way to see the doctor assigned to your regiment and volunteer to work with him."

John started to interrupt but she continued forcefully, "No John, we're not going to argue about this. Whether you or anyone else wants to admit it, I am part of this army and I am going where you go. If you're going to face danger, so am I. Men are going to be killed and hurt out there today and I can help them. I pray to God that it will not be you. But whatever happens I must—and will—be there. Please understand. I too will do my best to stay safe."

She surprised herself with how forceful she had been. John looked at her in defeat and said, "I guess I lost this battle two years ago when I let you convince me to come along then. I suppose you and Martha and Elizabeth have talked this over and they're going out there too."

"Well, Elizabeth is, but I think Martha will be back here at the main hospital. She is kind of a mainstay there now, and they need her the most. You're not mad at me, are you, John? I don't want us to go off today with any angry thoughts about each other. Please tell me you're not angry."

He hugged her and kissed her tenderly. "No Sarah, I'm not mad at you. I think you're crazy. But I am very proud of you for your courage and compassion. Please take care of yourself." He kissed her once more and finished, "Now go find that surgeon and see what you can do for him."

Sarah said, "Thank you darling, I love you."

She found the surgeon and made arrangements to move out with him at the appropriate time. He knew of her, and was very glad to have her volunteer. He said she would be most welcome and needed. Then she excused herself to go back to Arnold's quarters to let him know what she was doing.

It was now about noon. When she got to the quarters the general had not yet returned, so she busied herself to keep her mind off what might be coming later.

Suddenly Arnold burst through the door. He was in a black uncontrollable rage. He stormed about the cabin shouting obscenities at the top of his lungs. He did not care who heard him. From his rantings Sarah learned that General Gates had relieved him of command and placed General Lincoln in his place as the commander of the left side of the force. It seemed to her that Arnold had been placed under some kind of house arrest. He would not be part of any action on this day or maybe any other.

Sarah knew there was nothing she could say or do to console him, so she tried to make herself invisible in that tiny house. She quickly went outside and left him to fume alone. Sarah was shaken with this turn of events. "How could Gates be so stupid," she thought, "to relieve his best general at the beginning of a battle?" Surely this was a mistake and everything would be sorted out before the fighting began. She knew he did not care about what she would be doing this afternoon, and made her way to the regimental surgeon's area.

Once there she busied herself, along with the doctor's assistants and litter bearers, with packing bandages and medicines and making ready to move out on command. About mid-afternoon the order came to proceed. As they marched out to their position Sarah could hear that a battle had already started out in front of them. The firing at first was sporadic, but as they got closer she could hear it intensify.

She would take a peek out to the front every once in a while, but all she could really see was the smoke from the guns rising and covering the field. She heard explosions of the British cannons going off and the cracking of the trees as the balls crashed through them. "They must be the enemy's," she thought, "our's could not be here yet." She wondered for a moment where Elizabeth was and what she was doing.

The battle was raging now, and Sarah went out with the litter bearers to the front to help the wounded back to safety. The now-familiar smell of burnt gun powder filled her nose and throat. Through the smoke her first glimpse showed men of both sides writhing on the field amongst bodies of men who had already been killed. Over the shattering noise of the cannons and muskets she could hear the screams of men who had been wounded. She determined to save as many of them as she could.

She met a man who had been wounded in the leg. She quickly tied a tourniquet around his leg, took his arm over her shoulder, and dragged him back to the field hospital. The doctor looked briefly at the soldier's wound and said, "Looks like it went clean through. Doesn't appear that the ball hit any bone. Take him over to the sergeant, Mrs. Hardy. You and he can clean this man up and close that wound then send him back to the rear."

Sarah got a couple of soldiers to help her move the man, and in a few minutes she and the sergeant had done all they could do for him and she was off to the front again.

The fighting went on savagely. The deafening clamor continued, and the smoke from the guns choked her and made it hard to breathe. She thought she could tell the difference between the enemy's cannons and those of the American's, which had now been brought up. Whether it was because of the direction they were shooting or the wind she did not know. But she was sure she could feel that Elizabeth was out here somewhere and it was her gun she was hearing.

There was no way for her to know who was winning the battle. To her it all looked like utter chaos. But as she observed the men on the line and the charges being made it seemed to her that the Americans must be winning. Then out of nowhere a man riding a gray horse came charging from the rear, passing right by her, and up to the front. He startled her so that she barely recognized General Arnold. She could not make out what he was shouting, but he waved his sword and commanded the men to follow him towards a redoubt on the other side of the field. He and the men crashed into first one, then a second, larger redoubt further into the enemy's lines.

All she could do was stop and stare. Her heart was filled with pride for the bravery of the man. Then it struck her that he quite possibly could be killed taking this rash action. As she watched in awe and fear she suddenly realized that not only was Arnold out there, but that John was one of the men that followed him. Once again her heart stopped. The two men she cared most about in this world might be killed before her very eyes. Yet she could not turn away. She was absorbed in the battle. She had to see what was happening. She moved forward, right up to the very edge of the battle area.

Second Battle of Saratoga

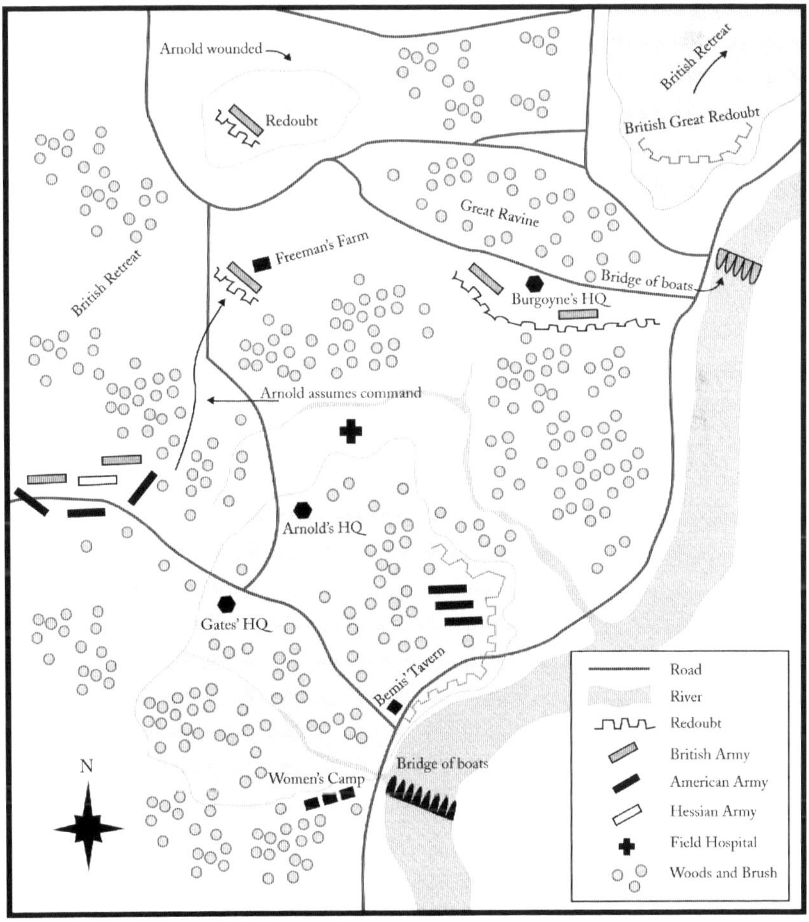

She could no longer see them. They had gone too far off into the smoke of the battle. The shattering noise of the guns and the men shouting orders and the screaming of the wounded were maddening, but it all seemed to be somewhere in the background as she strained to see what was happening out in front of her.

Her trance was interrupted by a voice. Someone touched her on the shoulder and said, "Ma'am can you help Johnny? He's been hit and is hurt bad."

Sarah jumped at his touch. She looked, in disbelief, at a young boy barely into his teens, dressed in ragged clothes of a farm hand and carrying a musket. "Huh? What?" She forced her mind back to the work at hand. All she really heard was that Johnny had been hit and was hurt bad. Her mind was not fully reengaged, and she could only equate the name to her John. She was filled with fear.

"My friend Johnny, Ma'am. He's been hit and is hurt real bad. Can you help him? He's right over here."

Sarah took a few steps with the boy and knelt down beside another boy of about sixteen or seventeen who had been shot in the stomach. She felt guilty but was relieved it was not her John. She knew the boy had very little chance to survive, but she couldn't bring herself to say so to his friend. There was nothing she could do for the wounded soldier, but she thought at least she could get this other boy away from this front.

"Son," she said, "You carry your friend back to the field hospital. You stay with him there. They'll do what they can for him."

Her mind was now back on her work. She spent the rest of the afternoon and evening working like she had never worked before. She had no idea of how many wounded men had come through their little hospital. Then there was a great commotion as some men brought in one man that everyone seemed to be concerned about. He was being carried in on a blanket made into a stretcher. She looked down and saw that it was Arnold.

His leg was badly wounded, but he was ornery as ever. Sarah went to his side and asked, "General Arnold, what happened?"

He looked at her a little quizzically then as he recognized her he said, "They shot me in the leg, then they shot my horse out from under me and he fell on my leg and broke it. Same damn leg as got hurt in Quebec. Where's that damn doctor?"

"Right here, Sir," the doctor said as he came up behind them. "Let's take a look at that leg. Yes, looks like we'll have to amputate it, General."

"Like hell you will. No one is going to amputate my leg. Now get me back on a horse."

The doctor looked at Sarah with a "what are we to do?" look, then said "Men, take the general straight back to the hospital. They will be able to take better care of you there, Sir, and will get that leg set properly."

Arnold shouted, "There is a battle going on out there doctor, and I need to get back to it. You fix me up here and have someone get me a horse."

"Well, General," the doctor replied, "from what I hear it sounds like the battle is about over. You'll have to trust the other Generals to clean up the rest of those Redcoats and Hessians for ya. You've done about all you can for today."

For the first time Sarah realized that the shooting had been reduced to sporadic firings, and she could hear "Huzzahs" being shouted up and down the line. Could it be true? Had they beaten the British at last? She looked around her and everyone seemed to be wondering the same thing. No one could believe it was true.

She looked admiringly at the general who had made it all possible and smiled, “I told you, you could get hurt running around out in front of the soldiers, General. Now you’ll have to take some orders from the likes of me for a while.” She squeezed his hand and said, “You were magnificent today, Sir. Now relax and let the doctors take care of you.”

He looked back at her sadly and silently nodded. The men raised the litter and started carrying him back to the hospital.

Sarah could hear the murmurs around her. “Who is this woman? Nobody talks to General Arnold like that. He would shoot any man who spoke to him like that.” She knew there would be camp rumors, but she didn’t care. She was proud of him and happy that he was safe.

Her mind then turned to John. Where was he? Was he safe also? There was nothing she could do but wait. She said a quick prayer for his safe return and then poured herself back into the work of getting the wounded back to the rear. With each soldier that came through that was not John, she breathed a sigh of relief. Once again she worked far into the night. As the men set up defensive positions for the night she wondered where John was.

There was no way to move all the wounded back to the rear during the night and they were forced to try and sleep on the cold ground until morning.

Sometime before dawn, as she was tending to some of the men, John appeared. He called her name gently.

At first she did not see him. She only heard him call her name. She was filled with foreboding. What was he doing here? How bad had he been hurt? She turned and saw him standing behind her. Through the firelight he appeared ghostly and was almost unrecognizable. As she focused her eyes she saw his clothes were in rags and his face was black with gunpowder and dirt, and it was filled with grief. But he did not look like he was wounded. She ran to him and hugged him. "Oh, John, are you alright? Have you been hurt? I saw your regiment charge with General Arnold and I have been worried about you ever since. He came through here a while ago. His leg was pretty badly hurt, but I think he'll be alright." She was talking incomprehensively while she held him.

John took her by the shoulders and said, "I'm fine Sarah. Let's get away from these folks. I have something I have to tell you." They walked a few yards away and stopped by a large tree. He took her hands in his and said, "Sarah, I don't know how to tell you this, and I am so sorry to be the one to have to tell you. Elizabeth was killed in action yesterday."

John's words struck her like a great blow to the stomach. She could not breathe. She collapsed against the tree. John took her and eased her gently to the ground. Her mind was racing. This could not be true. She had just talked to Elizabeth. She couldn't be dead. They had too much more to do together. How was she going to go on without the woman who gave her strength?

Tears welled up in Sarah's eyes and rolled down her cheeks. But she stifled them and would not cry. She looked at herself in her filthy blood-drenched dress, at the carnage around her, and then at John. She was filled only with rage and anger. She was angry at John for bringing her the news and for bringing her into this war in the first place. She was angry with the army because she knew they would not even acknowledge Elizabeth had even been there, let alone died a hero. She was angry with the British for bringing all this upon them and for killing Elizabeth. She was angry with Elizabeth for caring too much and doing too much and for being out there. Mostly she was angry with herself for not being the one who had died.

John sat beside her and took her in his arms and gently rocked her. No words were spoken. After a while he got up and went over to a doctor and spoke for a few seconds. When he came back he reached down and pulled her up by her arms and said, "Come on Sarah, you have done enough here. Let's get you back to the rear where you can get some rest."

She did not argue or fight with him. The two of them just started walking quietly.

Thirty-Nine

The victory had been complete. During the night the enemy could be heard moving out of their encampment. They were retreating.

The euphoria in the American camp was overwhelming. They had been driven out of Canada. They wallowed in shame as they retreated in the face of Burgoyne's army. Now after two long, hard years they had finally won. Burgoyne was the one on the run now, and they would catch him or drive him all the way back to Canada.

Sarah found little joy in the victory, however. Elizabeth was buried in a common grave with Edward and Robert and the rest of the enlisted men. John would not allow Sarah to go see it. He told her the sight of the bodies after the scavengers had stripped them was horrendous. Instead he said, "Sarah, remember her as she was. Seeing what's left of her body will not help you heal. It will only hurt you more."

Sarah knew he was right. All she could think about was the last time she and Elizabeth had talked. Thinking back on that conversation, Sarah wondered now if Elizabeth had had a premonition of her death. The things she had said and the way they said goodbye made Sarah believe that she had.

Sarah desponded in her tent for several days. She did not eat. She hardly spoke to anyone, not even to John or Martha. The loss of Elizabeth was hers alone, and she could not share it with others.

John told her how it had happened. Elizabeth had been carrying powder bags up to the gun her husband and son were working at when a mortar shell from the enemy exploded among them. All of them along had been killed. The bomb must have hit them directly, for when they found the bodies, they were in pieces. They could only tell a woman had been there by her clothing. Her name was not even mentioned among the casualties. The only evidence given in the report of the battle of her death was a note that two women had also been killed.

Sarah only knew the other woman casually, but was sure that someone was hurting for the loss of her just as she was hurting for the loss of Elizabeth. They deserved more recognition of their contributions than an off handed comment that "two women had also been killed."

After several days Sarah came out of her tent. She had had a dream. Elizabeth came to her and told her she could not mourn any longer. She and her husband and son were fine. They had no regrets. They had fought for a cause and had helped win the battle. Their dying was part of the price that had to be paid if the

Americans were going to ever gain their liberty. Elizabeth told her, "Sarah, you must go on and finish what we started."

Sarah went and found Martha first. She told her about her dream and Martha smiled sadly. Sarah realized at that moment that Martha too had lost a cherished friend, and the two of them hugged each other and Martha cried deeply into Sarah's breast. They held each other close for a very long time, not saying a word. Finally, Martha sniffed and wiped her tears and her nose with her apron and said, "Sarah, when this is done here I'm going to go up the Mohawk and visit with my folks. I need some time away from all this death and butchery. I need to see my family again before it's me that gets blown to pieces. Do you think I'm a coward? Do you think I'm running away? Am I being selfish?"

Sarah answered, "No Martha, you are not a coward. Our friend Elizabeth once reminded me that many others have run from the trials that we have been through together. But we have stuck it out and now we have helped win an important victory. You are not being selfish either. You have earned the right to do just exactly what you want to do. And if going to see your family is it, then by God you go do it, and to hell with what anyone else thinks, dearie."

As she spoke the word "dearie" she realized that Elizabeth was still with them. Sarah and Martha gave each other knowing looks.

Sarah said, "I'm going over to see if there is anything I can find to send to Elizabeth's daughter. I think I need to write her a letter and let her know how heroically her family died. I don't trust this damn army to do it in any compassionate way, nor do I know if I can find the words. But I think it's important that she know that her mother was loved and will be truly missed by us as well as her. And if there is something of Elizabeth's that I can send her that might help also. Do you want to come?"

Martha looked at Sarah through bloodshot eyes, and with tears running down her cheeks she said, "No, Sarah. I can't. Thank you for being so brave. But I just can't. It hurts too much."

When Sarah got to the tent where the army was holding the casualties things there was a sergeant standing outside of it. She said, "Good morning. I'm Sarah Hardy and I was a friend of Mrs. Hubbard. I wonder if I might see the Hubbards' things. I am writing a letter to her daughter and want to send along anything that might help her heal from the pain."

The sergeant looked at her indifferently. He said, "Well, ma'am, it's over there in the corner, what's left of it. Mostly been picked over already by other folks. All the good stuff's already gone. But you're welcome to take whatever's left."

Sarah could barely contain her rage. The thought that Elizabeth's things had been gone through by the scavengers of this camp who preyed on the dead made her physically sick. And that this oaf had the temerity to think that she was one of them also filled her with hatred for him. She wanted to scream profanities at him, but took a deep breath and tried to think how Elizabeth would handle this lout.

Then she said in a calm voice with all the sarcasm she could muster, "Thank you very much, Sergeant, for caring so much for your friends. I hope when it is you someone will be just as kind and considerate of your belongings."

The sarcasm was lost on him, she knew. He looked at her quizzically, shrugged, and said, "Take whatever you want ma'am.

I gotta be off." Then he walked away.

Sarah looked through the small pile of things that were left. All of Edward's army things were gone, as were the cooking utensils and blankets. All that was left was a dress and some other small clothes belonging to Elizabeth and a small box wrapped up inside the dress. Somehow the scavengers had failed to find the box, or it too would certainly have been taken. Sarah unwrapped the box and slowly opened it. The first thing she saw was Elizabeth's tea ball. She took it in her hand and her eyes misted over as she clutched it to her breast and said to herself, "Oh, Elizabeth, where are you? I need you so much. How will I get through this war without you?"

While she knelt there she could almost hear Elizabeth's voice gently saying, "You're gonna be fine, dearie. Just do what ya gotta do and don't let any of these menfolk push you around. We love 'em, but they ain't too bright sometimes."

It lightened her heart as she thought about Elizabeth's way of saying things and getting things done.

In addition to the tea ball there was a small bag filled with the remnants of Elizabeth's "genuine contraband tea." Somehow the bag had always remained filled over the past two years. None of the women could figure out how she always had tea, and none of them thought it prudent to ask.

The bag felt heavy to Sarah. She felt some hard objects inside of it. She opened the bag and carefully poured out its contents. What fell out were several shillings and Elizabeth's wedding band.

It had been months since the men had been paid, and then it was only in almost worthless Continental paper money. But the women who worked for the officers quite often received some pay in real coin. She herself had a few shillings she had received wrapped up and kept in a pocket she kept hidden under her skirt.

Sarah looked at the ring and sadly thought, "This is all that's left of two people's lives together." Then she thought, "No, Elizabeth would say that the ring was not what was important. She left a daughter and grandchildren. They are what is important. The ring is only a reminder."

Sarah carefully put everything back in the bag and went to see Martha again to show her what she had found. As they looked upon the meager belongings Sarah said, "I must find a way to get the money and ring to Rebecca without it being stolen along the way. I'll talk to John. He'll know what to do."

She was quiet for a moment, then asked, "Martha, would it be wrong if I kept the tea ball?"

"What? Why on earth would you want to keep the tea ball?"

Sarah wistfully said, "Remember at Fort Ti when she first brought it out and made tea for us? There is something about the tea ball that reminds me of her independence and her spirit. Nobody was going to keep her from having tea if she wanted it, even if she had to break somebody's rules or laws to have it. That's how I want to remember her, and this ball will help me do it."

"But," she said, "I don't want to be considered one of those scavengers who rob the dead out on the battlefields. If you think I should, I will pack it up with her other things and send it along to Rebecca too."

Now it was Martha's turn to comfort Sarah. "You and I know

you are not a scavenger. Elizabeth would want you to have it. You have earned a right to something of hers, and if her daughter is anything like her mother she would want you to have it too. I do think you should let Rebecca know you have it and offer to send it to her if she wants it. But if she does not I have one request of you. Don't put it away and let it be forgotten. Use it on special occasions like Elizabeth did, and when you do, remember her and us and our little women's army."

"Thank you, Martha. I will. Right now I will go find a way to get these other things to Rebecca, and write her a letter telling her how much we loved her mother and how precious her memory will always be to us. You know, I was having a hard time trying to think of what to say in that letter about Elizabeth's death. But I will write about her life instead. That's what Elizabeth would tell us to do."

They hugged and Sarah went off to see General Arnold before he was evacuated to Albany. She knocked on the door to his quarters and gently opened it. When he saw her he sat up and said, "Sarah, how good of you to come by. I was afraid you had deserted."

"No, Sir. I didn't desert. But I've had a few bad days. Sorry for not being here."

"Nonsense, woman. I heard about your friend, and I am sorry for you and I understand your grief. Besides, I have had more people fawning over me the last couple of days than I can stand. I'll be glad to get back to Albany where I'll probably get court-martialed for disobeying Gates' orders. But, other than sad, how are you, Sarah?"

"I'll be fine, General," she said without conviction. "After we have this battle all cleaned up I was thinking I might go up the Mohawk to German Flats to visit my parents for a while. I expect that might cheer me up some. I haven't seen them for a few years. My father was with General Washington on Long Island and with General Herkimer at the Battle of Oriskany before you got up there to save the day."

"Oh, I don't know how much I saved the day for them, Sarah," he chuckled. "Those Palentine men and the men at Fort Schuyler did pretty well without us. All we had to do was chase St. Leger off after they had done all the hard fighting."

He smiled at her. "Taking a short vacation from all this luxury are you? I guess I'll be taking one too," he patted his leg. "Don't know if this thing will ever be the same. It's the same damn leg that got it up in Canada. Maybe someone is trying to tell me something."

"Well, General," Sarah said mockingly, "Colonel Morgan and I tried to tell you about what could happen running around like that out in front of the troops. You just wouldn't listen."

"Well, madam," he injected, feigning indignant, "if they ever let me get back to generaling again I probably won't take your advice then either. As for Morgan, I say again, when he starts leading from the rear I'll think about it. But when I think about such things I am reminded of Gates, and that alone would keep me from doing it."

"Anyway, General, whatever happens, you will always be the hero of this campaign. You alone led this army through the battles here to victory."

"I am very glad you think so, Sarah. But," he continued bitterly, "I'm afraid the hero of this campaign will be General

Gates. Because, you see my dear, he is the one who will write the history of this campaign. So in the end he will singlehandedly be the one who saved this army that, in his opinion, Schuyler and St. Clair almost lost. And he alone will be the one who won the battles that were fought here. I, just like you, Sarah, will not even be a footnote to that history. If I am remembered at all, it will be because, as he will write it, Gates had the good sense to relieve me of command and replace me with General Lincoln."

"I can't believe that's true. There were too many of us here to see what really happened. We will always tell the true story of what happened here."

Arnold let the subject drop and said, "I guess we better say goodbye, Sarah. They should be coming to get me soon and take me to my fate in Albany and beyond. It has been a pleasure knowing you and thank you for everything you have done for me." He put his hand out to shake hers.

Sarah looked at his hand, then into his face, and with a glimmer in her eye she reached down and kissed him on the cheek. Then she said, "Thank you, General, for everything you have allowed me to be part of. I'll not say goodbye, but until we meet again, God speed." She left the house not knowing if she would ever see him again but truly thankful for having known him.

Burgoyne's army was on the run now. Scouts reported he was moving very slowly and was only about eight miles north. General Gates had sent a force to follow and another across the river to cut off any escape in that direction. Most of the men were ultimately moved forward to crush the enemy if he did not surrender. John's unit was one of those that went out.

At the hospital the business of sending the wounded down

to Albany continued. Sarah worked alongside Martha each day, and the work seemed to help relieve the pain of thinking about Elizabeth. But the nights were very lonely, and she could not sleep. She often went to the hospital to lend a hand. Even though she was not really needed, the work helped her get through.

One day, about two weeks after the battle, Sarah received a letter from her mother. It was the first one she had received in months. She was anxious to read it. Before opening it, however, she thought about what was going on in her life. After hearing that Martha was planning on going to visit her family, she wishfully too had given it consideration. She had even told General Arnold that she planned to go. But she was unsure.

She didn't know what was going to happen to John and his unit, or if he was going to be discharged. Or if he was offered a discharge, if he would take it. She thought that he had done his share over these past two years and had earned a discharge. Most of the members of the militias were being sent home. But a rumor had been going around the camp that the British had sent a force up the Hudson to try and take Albany. Gates had already sent some of the army south in response. If this was true then John, as a continental soldier, would be heading down there too, most likely.

Additionally, although the victory here was a great one, they had heard that General Washington had lost two more battles in the past month to General Howe. That brought the realization that the rest of the British Army was still in America and would have to be beaten before this war could end. This part of the Continental Army would probably have to join up with Washington to help out. She knew that John would have to be a part of that. If he had to go south with the army, could she leave for she knew not how long just to see her family?

She sighed deeply with no answers to her own questions. As she opened the letter she noticed that it was dated September seventh. So much had happened since then. The world had changed so much. Before she started to read she closed her eyes and said a small prayer. "Oh, please, Mother, have some good news to help me through all this. Please don't tell me of any more tragedy. I cannot bear it."

Sept 7, 1777

My Dear Sarah,

I pray this letter reaches you and that you and John are safe and well. We have all survived the battle that took place here, although many of the local people are suffering from the losses they suffered at the hands of the Indians at Oriskany. When we moved here from Newburgh we thought that we would be getting away from the Tories that were running around there. But there has been little respite from them and their savage allies since we have been here. We are hoping that now that St. Leger has returned to Canada and the British are no longer here to support them the attacks will stop. But this is truly the edge of the frontier and we can expect more attacks from the Indians until we can finally drive them away completely. Your father believes that because the British are no longer here to support them they will stop soon and head back to Canada before winter sets in.

Other than that we are all doing as well as can be expected.

Everyone is healthy. We don't know when we will be able to get back to Newburgh, or what to expect when we do. We hope that maybe when spring comes things will be settled in our favor and we will be able to go home. Until then we must make the most of what we have and give thanks to God and our family that we have a place at all.

We understand that there might be a deciding battle at your location soon. We pray that our side will be successful and that you will be safe throughout. Please take care if you are near it.

Write when you get a chance. We dearly want to hear from you and know you are alright. Give our love to John and know that we love you and pray for both of you every night.

Affectionately,
Mother

Although it was good to hear from her mother and the letter did not contain any real bad news, neither did it contain the good news Sarah thought she was looking for. It did not help her make up her mind about whether or not she was going to go with Martha to see her family.

Forty

After most of the army had gone north to surround Burgoyne, a woman was escorted into camp and to the hospital. Sarah and Martha were on duty in the hospital. One of the patients they had been attending to since the night of the last battle was a British major by the name of Acland. He had been shot through both legs. The woman who had arrived was his wife. The escort officer introduced her, "Ladies, it is my honor to introduce Lady Harriet Acland. She is, of course, Major Acland's wife. Lady Acland, these women have been attending to your husband. They are Mrs. Martha Quinlin and Mrs. Sarah Hardy. They are the wives of two of our soldiers. I will leave you in their capable hands. If there is anything else I can do for you, please let them know. They know how to reach me, and I am sure will be glad to help you."

Lady Acland said, "Thank you, Lieutenant. I truly do appreciate all your help in getting me to my husband." Although it was hard to tell at that moment, Sarah noted that she was a pretty woman probably a little older than herself. She was dressed in what had obviously once been a very expensive dress that had been ruined by the hardships of the retreat she had just gone through and the terrible storms of the past couple of nights. She was also obviously very pregnant which added to her look of weariness.

She did not appear to be fearful in any manner and Sarah thought, "Oh no, now we are going to have to put up with some haughty ladyship and all her demands." Nor did Lady Acland travel alone. She had a maidservant and a man with her that Sarah later found out was the major's valet.

There was a quiet pause in the conversation as the officer left. Sarah and Martha looked at each other as if to say, "What are we supposed to do with this woman?" Neither of them had ever been in the company of royalty of any kind. They had no idea of how they were supposed to act. But Sarah was determined that she was not going to put on any airs for this woman. After all, she was just a camp follower like herself, and technically a prisoner besides.

Sarah broke the silence, saying, "Well, uh Lady Acland—is that how you wish to be addressed? Let me take you to your husband. I am sure he will be surprised and happy to see you and uh, other friendly faces." She looked at the two servants.

Lady Acland looked at Sarah rather sternly, and Sarah thought, "Here it comes, she's about to tell me how important she is back in England." But instead her countenance softened and she said, "First, let me thank you, Mrs. Hardy and Mrs.

Quinlin, for taking care of my husband. Secondly, I plan to stay here with him as long as he is here and to attend to him myself as much as possible. So we will be in each other's company during that time. I would like that to be as comfortable as possible. So, if you don't mind, please just address me as Mrs. Acland. That is the title I am most proud of, and under the situation I believe it is the best one for all of us."

She hesitated, then went on. "I know our husbands belong to different armies and have been fighting each other relentlessly for a long time now. We women have followed them and do what we can to help them do their duties. But for my husband, and thus for me, this war is over. Your army has won this battle and whatever becomes of us will be decided by your leaders. But there is no reason the time we have to spend in each other's company should not be civilized. I do not know what will happen to us next. At this moment I just want to see my husband and do what I can for him." She looked at her stomach and put a hand on it, smiled, and said, "I would like him to be able to see his third child."

"Of course, Mrs. Acland, let us show you to him," Sarah responded, much more relaxed.

Sarah was touched by the way Major Acland responded to the appearance of his wife. He smiled through the pain and said, "Harriet, my dear, you should not have come. It must have been very dangerous. How are you, my love? How are you being treated?"

"I am fine, John. Everyone has been most hospitable and," she leaned in and whispered rather loudly, "besides, things are considerably better here than a little further up north right now.

The question is, how are you? I am quite put out with you, you know. You promised me you wouldn't go and get yourself shot, and here you are shot twice."

"I am quite sorry about that, dear. But it seems I am not quite as quick as I used to be in getting out of the way of stray bullets. And from the looks of things I won't be getting any quicker," he finished, looking down to his covered legs.

Lady Acland, the major, and their servants turned and looked at Sarah and Martha, who had not moved. Sarah realized they were staring, and with a start said, "Well, if you don't need us we'll just move on to other patients. If you need anything, Mrs. Acland, just let us know."

That night while Sarah was working she noticed that Mrs. Acland was still there, sitting up in a straight back chair by her husband's bed. He was asleep and she was nodding off and re-awakening with a start as her head dropped. Sarah went to her, tapped her on the shoulder gently and said, "Mrs. Acland, you really should get some rest. Your husband seems to be sleeping peacefully, and in your condition a little sleep could be quite helpful for the two of you," she looked at the other woman's protruding stomach and then into her eyes gently.

Mrs. Acland smiled and said, "Yes, you are probably quite right Mrs. Hardy. I guess we could use some sleep. But I feel more comfortable here next to him. There isn't much I can do for him, I know. But I want to be here just in case he needs me. Do you understand what I'm trying to say, Mrs. Hardy?"

Sarah felt a pang of sympathy for her—a woman of title and wealth, sitting in the squalor of an American barn posing as a hospital. Now she was just a very tired pregnant woman worried about her wounded husband.

Here they were, two women from totally different worlds sitting together in the middle of the night in the midst of a war, watching over the wounded husband of one of them. "Yes Mrs. Acland, I think I can understand. As I work here in this hospital I live in fear every day that someone will bring my husband in. And each day I say a prayer of thanksgiving when they do not," Sarah finally responded.

"Mrs. Acland," Sarah asked, "if it is not too impertinent, what made you come to this war? I mean, you are woman of title and I assume great means. You had no need to come here. When my husband, John, joined the army we had nothing. I, and for that matter most of the women here in camp, had no place to go, and so I was forced in a way to follow our army wherever it led. But you could have stayed in England. What made you come?"

Lady Acland looked at Sarah and asked, "Do you have any children, Mrs. Hardy?"

"No madam I do not," Sarah replied a little defensively. And she wondered what that had to do with her question.

"As I said, this is my third child," she patted her stomach. "We have two more back in England. The decision to come to America and be with my husband was the hardest decision I ever made in my life. My two children are home with my parents, and I miss them terribly. I assure you, Mrs. Hardy, that everyone in my family tried to persuade me not to come. Even the major here tried to convince me."

As an aside she asked, "Did you know he is not just a soldier? He is a Member of Parliament also. I don't suppose that will give you any reason to treat him better than others though, will it? I really had no idea what this war was all about. I suppose, being a woman, as my husband and father had said many times, I could not understand the politics involved. Neither could I understand how the Americans could be unhappy being subjects of the British Crown, nor how they could think they could rule themselves without the King and Parliament."

She sighed. "Anyway, I had been with my husband before during wars on the continent, and thought I knew what to expect. And I thought I knew better than anyone what was best for me and for my family. Sitting here tonight I cannot honestly say what brought me here though, Mrs. Hardy. Was it stubbornness, pride, an idea of great adventure in the wild America? I had listened to my husband tell how easy this war was going to be. Why, he said that once the Rebels see the might of the British Army they would come crawling back into the King's fold in a hurry. 'We'll be home before spring,' he kept saying. So I convinced myself that it would only be for a few months and that it might be a lark to see what all the fuss was about. I truly believed that no band of Rebels could stand up to our army. The danger could only be slight, and after a few months I would be home again. So I left my children and came. Never in my wildest dreams could I have imagined the magnitude of the wilderness here or the depravity of some of the fighting, especially by the natives on both sides. Most importantly, I never imagined the earnestness with which you Americans would fight and defend your ideas. I tell you madam, I never imagined the hatred your people have for us or the will with which your men fight on."

Sarah looked up to the ceiling and chortled a quick laugh. Lady Acland gave her a hurt looked and asked, "Did I say something funny, Mrs. Hardy?"

Sarah recovered and said, "No, Mrs. Acland. As you were speaking, I was just thinking about how I got here. Except for the circumstances of our existence we have exactly the same story. I can hear my husband and father saying the same things to me about my inability to understand the meaning of this war. The boasting words, 'When the British see us in battle and know we mean business they will turn tail and run, and this war will be over by Christmas,' still ring in my ears. Well, several Christmases have come and gone and another is coming up, and it still is not over. No offense, Mrs. Acland, but I hope the results of this battle will convince your husband and the rest of Parliament and our Congress to find a way to end this war. Truthfully, I'm still not sure what it is all about. Nor do I have any idea what any of us will have left when it finally does end. All I know is that as long as it goes on I will have to follow my husband and this army until the menfolk decide to end it," she sighed.

They both fell silent, each in her own thoughts. Then Sarah said, "Thank you for talking to me, Mrs. Acland. I wonder if there will ever be a day when we women will be in a position of authority or will be allowed to fight as soldiers. And, if there is, will we be any better at it than the men have been? Now you really do need to get into a bed and sleep some. I will take care of your husband till morning. I hear that they will be evacuating you and him down to Albany tomorrow. There is a better hospital there and they will be able to do more for him. The trip, however, might be a little rough on you, and it would be best if you got some rest beforehand."

"Yes, I suppose you are right, Mrs. Hardy. Thank you for

watching over him. I think I will take a short nap. It will help make tomorrow's journey easier, I am sure."

As Lady Acland left Sarah looked at her back. She was bent over slightly, and Sarah thought how sad and tired she looked. "No matter what happens with her husband," Sarah thought, "she has something to go back to. What will become of me if anything ever happens to John?" She quickly put those thoughts out of her mind and returned to tending to the men.

Next morning they came and got Major Acland, Lady Acland and their servants. Sarah walked down to the river's edge with Mrs. Acland. As they were loading onto a boat Sarah said, "I wish you the best, Lady Acland. Thank you for talking with me last night." Then she said lightly, "I'll always remember the time I talked to a real person of title. I hope you will remember me."

"I will, Mrs. Hardy. And thank you for being so kind and for caring for my husband and me. Take care, and pray this war will end soon. Goodbye."

Sarah did not know why, but she reached out and hugged her as she said, "Goodbye." She watched the boat sail down the river until it was out of sight. She wondered what the Acland's fate would be.

Forty-One

Somehow Sarah had to force herself to write the letter to Elizabeth's daughter. She had been agonizing over it for days. She had secured some paper and a pen and ink, but the words just would not come to her. How was she supposed to tell this woman of the death of her family? This day, however, she was determined to get it done. She knew that Elizabeth would not want her to continue to wallow in her self-pity. She thought about Elizabeth and how she might write the letter if things were reversed. Finally, she was as ready as she would ever be.

Oct 13, 1777

Dear Rebecca,

My name is Sarah Hardy. My husband and I have been serving together with your mother, father, and brother since the beginning of this terrible war.

It is with much sorrow and regret that I must write to tell you of their deaths.

On October seventh, our army met the British forces in a second battle here at Bemis Heights near Saratoga, New York. Your father and brother were manning one of the cannons and your mother was helping to bring ammunition to them. During the battle their gun position was struck by enemy cannon fire and they were killed instantly. Your mother, father and brother were all together when they died. I hope it lightens your burden somewhat to know that they died in a cause they all very much believed in. And in knowing that they will have been very great contributors to the independence they fought so hard for. As your mother reminded me many times, we will achieve it.

Your mother was a source of strength to us all, and especially to me. She never failed to help us through our bad times, explaining that this cause we are fighting for is right and just. As hectic and busy as we were, she always found time to fix us a cup of her special tea and sit for a while for a soothing conversation and hug when it was needed.

I will never forget your mother. She will be in my heart and mind forever. She spoke often of you and her beautiful grandchildren. She prayed each day for your safety and happiness. Your mother, father and brother are buried together in a peaceful place on a hill overlooking the Hudson. They are together on the land they defended and won for this new country of ours. I know they are in heaven and watching over you and your family, and all of us also.

I am sending you a box of things that belonged to her. I hope this will bring some peace to you. Your Mother had her own special tea ball that she used on special occasions. I respectfully ask that you let me keep it. When I hold it in my hands I can feel your mother's hand in mine. However, if this is a family heirloom and you want it for your children, I will, of course, send it to you.

Please know that my prayers and thoughts are with you. Although we have never met, I feel I know you through your mother's words and I am,

Affectionately Yours,
Sarah Hardy

Sarah prepared the package and the letter and sent it with a militia soldier from the area where Elizabeth's daughter lived. His enlistment was up and he was returning home. That was really the only mail system that worked during this time. All she could do was hope that he would take the time to deliver it.

The next day John returned with a detail from Saratoga, where the army had surrounded the British and Hessians. He was very excited to tell her of the situation up there, but he also had some very sad news.

"Sarah," he began excitedly, "I don't know where to begin. We have them cornered. It is only a matter of hours, or at the most a couple of days 'til they will have to surrender! Can you imagine it? We have beaten them. After all the misery we've been through, we have beaten them." He hugged her, swung her around and they both laughed in joy.

Sarah was as happy as John, but when he put her down a

nagging thought brought her back down to earth. "Oh, John, how can you be sure? I have heard so many times the bragging of this army only to find out that it was only bragging with nothing behind it. Are you sure? Is it over?"

"Yes Sarah, I am sure. Burgoyne has sent an officer over the line to begin negotiations for the surrender. There are only formalities now. There is nowhere for him to go. We have cut off all his paths to retreat. We have part of the army on its way to retake Fort Ti. Once they hear of this defeat up there they will have to retreat to Canada or be captured also. Burgoyne must surrender or perish."

Sarah looked at him and drew pride from the pride she saw beaming on his face. She began to fire questions at him. "John, how does an army surrender? I mean is there a ceremony? Does everyone on the losing side put their hands up? What happens next? What do you do with all the prisoners?" Then finally, as if the question hit her for the first time she asked, "What will they do with the ladies that are with that army?"

"You know, Sarah, I don't know. I've never been in on a victory like this before. I am sure there will be some sort of ceremony for the generals to make things official. But I don't know about any of the rest. You know," he said with some pride, "you have been as much a part of this victory as anyone. We're headed back out in the morning. Why don't you come with us and we'll learn together how it feels to be on the winning side."

"Oh, John, may I really? I do really want to be a part of whatever it is that is going to happen. I want to be able to tell our children that we were both there when America won its independence."

"Well, dear, at least you'll be able to tell them we were here at the victory at Saratoga. But as to the rest, I'm afraid that is a long way off. We have won here but things are not going so well down in Pennsylvania."

"Whatever do you mean, John? Surely the British won't continue fighting after losing an entire army up here. Will they?"

"Sarah, Washington is being beaten and driven back through New Jersey and Pennsylvania. The British have taken Philadelphia and our Congress has fled the city. He has lost several battles in the last month. In one, at a place called Paoli Tavern, it is said General Wayne's men were massacred by the Hessians. It also appears that General Clinton, who is in New York, has sent a force up the Hudson, which is causing a great deal of trouble for the folks there. General Gates has already started sending troops down river to provide support to Albany. When we are done here we will probably have to head that way too."

Sarah thought for a minute, the joy gone from her heart. Then she asked cautiously, "John, haven't you done enough? Haven't we done enough? Isn't it time for someone else to start fighting for this cause? John, you, no we, deserve a discharge and a chance to go home and start living again. We deserve a life that too many are living without giving up a damn thing," she finished bitterly.

John swallowed hard. He said nothing for a moment. Then he replied, "Sarah, you are right. You have given more than any woman should have to. Hell, you have given more than most men in this nation of ours. You deserve for it to be over. But if it ends now, all we have done is to have thousands of people die to get back to exactly where we were when we started. The British will never agree to our independence unless they are completely beaten. Their pride, let alone the money they have put into this war and the money they will lose if they lose us as colonies, won't let them. And, if they win, you and I will have no place to go where we will be allowed to live. The Tories will hunt us down and make sure of that."

He hesitated, then said, "You know, dear, Martha is going up the Mohawk to live with her parents when we are done here. Maybe you should think about doing that too. I don't see an early end to this war any more. There is no, 'We'll beat 'em by Christmas,' anymore. I don't know how many Christmases it will be before we have won and sometimes I even have doubts if we will ever win. This victory gives us great hope, but there is still a long way to go. I believe in the next couple of weeks this place," he waved his hand and looked around, "will be abandoned, and we will be on our way to support Washington somewhere. Then we will go to some God-forsaken place to spend another winter in misery. I have signed up for the duration of this war, come what may. You didn't, and you shouldn't have to go through another wretched winter. Yes, I think you should go with Martha and on to see your folks. It will be better for you."

Sarah closed her eyes, thought hard, and breathed a sigh of relief. Then she hugged him tightly and said into his chest, "Thank you, John. You have helped me make up my mind. Ever since Martha told me she was going I have pondered about whether I should go too. I would truly love to see my family.

But you and the men and women of this army are my family now. I will not leave you or this army until this war is over."

He started to say something but she put a finger to his lips. "Not another word, John Hardy. I didn't get a vote on you signing up for the duration, my dear. You don't get a vote on this decision any more than you did in '75 when I signed up to follow you." She thought about Lady Acland and Elizabeth and finished, "Don't you worry about me, dearie. You just keep yourself alive and win this damn war."

Early next morning Sarah was ready long before the men. She was reinvigorated and wanted to get to Saratoga and see what was happening. They took a bateau and the eight miles up to Saratoga went smoothly. The weather had turned very cold, and it rained off and on throughout the day, but Sarah did not seem to mind it.

October 17, 1777 was one Sarah knew she would never forget. The morning was cold, dark and damp. The ever present fog hung over them as usual. The men had been called out early and sent to the far side of a creek that led down to the Hudson. Sarah and the women who were there stood behind the men trying to get a look at these people they had been fighting so long. They waited all morning long, wondering what was going to happen next.

Sometime after noon Sarah saw a tall stately looking British officer riding in front of an entourage of other officers. Given that he was dressed in a fabulously adorned scarlet uniform while the others appeared to still have on the clothes they had been in for days Sarah surmised that it must be General Burgoyne himself. She remembered him from the battlefield.

She wondered where he could possibly have gotten such an impeccable uniform under the conditions both sides had been in for more than a month. He and the others rode on past. Still later the long lines of men marched out to a field to ground their weapons. Some smashed the stocks before they laid them down.

On their side of the creek the Americans stood almost in awe at the sight of this once powerful army marching out in defeat. No one spoke, but Sarah could hear above the fife and drums of the British the sounds of American fifers playing "Yankee Doodle." This song that had been devised in ridicule by some British soldier during the last war had become almost an anthem for this American Army.

Once that ceremony had finished the British and Hessian soldiers were marched across the creek and down a road that led to the river. The Americans lined both sides of the road. Sarah looked at the men who were now prisoners of war. Although their uniforms were torn and ragged from the weeks of fighting they were still impressive, and both the British and the Hessians looked like armies should, Sarah thought.

She then looked at the Americans lined up on either side of the road. There were few real uniforms. Some officers had one on that they created for themselves. But the men were mostly dressed in the plain clothes they brought from home. Many, just like her, had no shoes. And the clothes they had on were mostly filthy rags. She marveled with pride that this bedraggled mass had suffered through so much and had still been able to defeat some of the best soldiers the British and Hessians had to send against them.

The march went on hour after hour, into the early evening. Finally, dragging up the rear appeared several hundred women and children. Many looked as though they were on their last legs. Their clothes too were rags, and they looked like they had not eaten in days. Sarah's heart broke as she watched one woman carry a crying child while a second scrambled to keep up next to her. The women looked like they were carrying everything they owned on their backs, pots and pans and all the other things they needed to survive and to maintain some semblance of a family. To Sarah it looked as though they were carrying the weight of the entire war on their backs as they staggered along.

Where there was ceremony and honor in the surrender of the armies, these women seemed to be totally unseen and unnoticed, almost as though they did not even exist. Looking on these women, Sarah realized it was like looking into a mirror. "Do I look as bad as these women do?" she asked herself silently, knowing without answering that of course she did. The joy of the victory at that moment seemed to diminish within her. "There but for the grace of God go I. What will be their fate? What will be my fate if ever I am in that position?" She wished she could stop the march and sit down with a few of these women and just talk about each other's plights. But she knew their story. It was the same as hers. And she knew that no matter what hardships they had to endure, they would go on. They had to go on. They had no choice.

She forced herself to stop thinking in that manner. This was a victory celebration, and she should not dampen it with thought of the miserable plight of the women on both sides.

Just then a carriage carrying a woman and two children rode by. "That must be another aristocrat like Lady Acland," Sarah thought.

Once again Sarah wondered what it was it that drew a woman born to aristocracy to subject herself to this deprivation when she could have so easily stayed home in the comfort of her mansion. Although she had the privilege of riding in a carriage, the woman did not look much better off than the other women. Her dress, Sarah could easily see, was once of the finest quality. And her demeanor was that of a proud woman. There was no hint of defeat in her. Regardless of the situation she had the look of a woman who was ever in charge of her destiny. "Well," Sarah mused, "at least one woman will get a ride to wherever it is she is going today. The rest of us will just have to keep walking."

The next few days became a mass of hectic confusion for everyone. The army was dissolving in front of Sarah's eyes. The militias were being discharged and going back to their farms, their homes, and their families. Part of the Continental Army was assigned to guard and escort the enemy prisoners to Albany.

John and Jeremiah and their unit were heading south to try to stop the British, who had ventured up the Hudson in the past few weeks and were wreaking havoc on communities south of Albany. When that was finished they were to march on and join up with Washington's force somewhere in Pennsylvania. Sarah would be following them in a couple of days with the rest of the camp followers who were still there.

After helping to evacuate the rest of the wounded back to

Albany, Sarah and Martha had little to do. They could have ridden with the wounded on the boats taking them south, but they chose to walk instead. They attached themselves to a company that was heading south and began retracing the steps they first made together with Elizabeth two and a half years before, and had made several times since. Strangely, they didn't talk a great deal. They didn't talk of all the adventures they had together or of the misery they had endured together. It was as though they knew what was in each other's heart and just didn't have the strength to put it into words. They stopped at Stillwater for the night, and the next day they reached Half Moon.

This was where Martha would turn and follow the King's Road that runs along the north side of the Mohawk towards her home and family up river. They went off by themselves and just sat for a while holding each other's hands. Sarah finally broke the silence. "I am going to miss you, Martha. I know this is the best thing for you and I wish you the very best. But I wish you were staying with us. I'll be all alone, and I don't how I will get along without you."

"Sarah, leaving you is breaking my heart too. I don't know what I'll find at my parents place. But I cannot do this anymore. Maybe once my heart is healed from losing Elizabeth I will be able to come back. But right now I cannot go on."

Then softly she said, "Sarah, I am going to tell you something that only Jeremiah knows. I am pregnant again."

Sarah leaped to her and hugged her as tight as she could and said, "Oh, Martha, how wonderful. I am so happy for you. But why have you have kept it a secret?"

"Because the last time everyone got so excited, and in the end..." she didn't finish the sentence. "I'm going home to have this baby because I want this baby to live. I want it to grow up in something that resembles a home. Can you understand, Sarah? Can you forgive me for abandoning you to face this war alone?"

"You're not abandoning me, dearie. You will never be more than a thought away, just as Elizabeth is never more than a thought away. No, you go home and have this baby and you take good care of it because when this is all over I am coming to see you and I want to see a plump happy child and a happy mother doting on him or her. Oh, Martha, this is so exciting. You have made my day. I may have to tread south with these boys but my heart will be with you. Can you do me one favor? I have written a letter to my mother explaining that I will not be coming to German Flats but going on with the army. When you have the time could you go visit them and give her the letter? I know she would enjoy seeing you so much. I have told her all about you and Elizabeth."

She gave the letter to Martha and Martha said, "Of course I'll deliver it. I'll be happy to. I want to meet your family too."

Martha was going with a company that was headed for Fort Schuyler. A soldier from the company came up and shyly said, "Mrs. Quinlin? Excuse me ma'am, but we are about to take off. The sergeant says if you want to come along you better come now."

She looked at the soldier and then to Sarah; there was nothing left to say. Tears misted up in Martha's eyes and they hugged one last time. Sarah whispered, "I love you Martha

Quinlin. You take good care of yourself and of that baby. I'll not say good bye, but just go with God until we see each other again."

Martha was crying and could not say anything as they parted. She joined the soldiers and headed west up the Mohawk River to her family.

Sarah watched as Martha walked away. The wind picked up and suddenly it seemed very cold. She wrapped her shawl more tightly around her and joined the army once again. She was headed south down the Hudson. She had no idea how long it would take or what to expect when they finally got to some place called Valley Forge, Pennsylvania.

The End

About the Author

Mr. Reardon was born and raised in Herkimer, New York amid the beautiful Mohawk Valley. He spent forty-four years serving with the United States military as soldier and civilian. He is a graduate of American Technological University and the U.S. Air Force War College. He and his wife Cindi have a daughter, two sons, and four grandchildren. He is retired and lives with his wife in Williamsburg, Virginia. This is his first novel, but he is a contributing poet to the anthology, *Distant Horizons, As Seen by Williamsburg Poets.*